BETWEEN
EARTH *and* SKY

D0182009

Books by Amanda Skenandore

BETWEEN EARTH AND SKY

THE UNDERTAKER'S ASSISTANT

THE SECOND LIFE OF MIRIELLE WEST

Published by Kensington Publishing Corp.

BETWEEN EARTH *and* SKY

AMANDA SKENANDORE

KENSINGTON BOOKS
www.kensingtonbooks.com

To the extent that the image or images on the cover of this book depict a person or persons, such person or persons are merely models, and are not intended to portray any character or characters featured in the book.

This book is a work of fiction. Names, characters, places, and incidents either are products of the author's imagination or are used fictitiously. Any resemblance to actual persons, living or dead, events, or locales is entirely coincidental.

KENSINGTON BOOKS are published by

Kensington Publishing Corp.
119 West 40th Street
New York, NY 10018

Copyright © 2018 by Amanda Skenandore

All rights reserved. No part of this book may be reproduced in any form or by any means without the prior written consent of the Publisher, excepting brief quotes used in reviews.

All Kensington titles, imprints, and distributed lines are available at special quantity discounts for bulk purchases for sales promotion, premiums, fundraising, educational, or institutional use.

Special book excerpts or customized printings can also be created to fit specific needs. For details, write or phone the office of the Kensington Sales Manager: Kensington Publishing Corp., 119 West 40th Street, New York, NY 10018. Attn. Sales Department. Phone: 1-800-221-2647.

Kensington and the K logo Reg. U.S. Pat. & TM Off.

eISBN-13: 978-1-4967-1367-4
eISBN-10: 1-4967-1367-2
First Kensington Electronic Edition: May 2018

ISBN-13: 978-1-4967-1366-7
ISBN-10: 1-4967-1366-4
First Kensington Trade Paperback Printing: May 2018

10 9 8 7 6 5 4 3

Printed in the United States of America

For my parents, Colleen and Gary,
whose love and altruism are my guiding star.

And for Steven
always.
Kunolúhkwa

CHAPTER 1

Philadelphia, 1906

Her past arrived that morning on page ten, tucked between a cross-hatched cartoon of striking trolley workers and an advertisement for derby hats.

INDIAN MAN FACES GALLOWS FOR
MURDER OF FEDERAL AGENT

Alma held the newsprint up to the light and read the article twice, three times, as if the words might change upon closer inspection.

That name. She knew it as well as her own. Her lips moved around the syllables—yet familiar after all these years. The accompanying sound died in her mouth.

His face coalesced in her mind: broad cheekbones, tall forehead, coppery skin. His clever eyes once again met her own. But he was just a boy then, a youth when they'd parted. What of the man he'd become?

She drew in an overdue breath and shook her head. No, she could not picture him a killer. The journalist must have gotten it wrong. That sort of thing happened all the time. Had the paper used his real name—his Indian name—the name she'd breathed a million times, then she would know for sure.

Surely the other dailies had run the story, too, and with more detail. A different name, a different man. And if not? If it was him, what would knowing bring save more heartache?

She pushed away the paper and groped for her teacup. It slipped from her fingers and shattered atop its saucer. Hot tea bled into the tablecloth.

"You all right, Mrs. Mitchell? Heard a noise clear from—Your tea!" The maid scurried in and threw a towel over the shattered porcelain.

The clock sounded in the foyer, each chime beating in Alma's ear. She had a ladies' auxiliary meeting to sit through at nine. Later the Civic Club and a few laughterless games of euchre. Busyness, after all, was the best tonic for regret.

She stood, but her knees wavered. Her feet refused to move. More of that first day came back to her: wagon dust and smoke, cornbread and fire. The leather doll. She must know if it was him. "Edie, did we get the *Record* and the *Inquirer* this morning?"

"Your dress, ma'am. The tea's done spilt onto the lovely batiste. Best get it off before the stain sets."

She waved the maid off. "Never mind that. The papers?"

"I'll fetch 'em, ma'am. Along with some vinegar for that stain. But sit down, won't you? Your face has the air of the grave."

CHAPTER 2

Wisconsin, 1881

For the sixteenth time that day—she knew, for she'd counted—Alma searched the horizon. She wobbled atop her toes and craned her neck that she might see beyond the bend where the road disappeared into the forest. Empty.

She rocked back onto her heels and squeezed her eyes shut, listening for the pounding of hooves or cry of wagon wheels. A bird cawed from above. Leaves chattered. Pans clanked from the kitchen at the back of the schoolhouse. But nothing of her father, the wagons, and the Indians he promised to bring.

After another searching glance, she spun around and skipped toward the schoolhouse to see how far the hands on the grandfather clock had moved since last she'd checked.

"Alma!"

Not the sound she'd hoped to hear.

"Yes, Mama?"

"What did I tell you about running? Now you've gone and rumpled your dress."

Running and skipping were not the same thing, but the sharp look in her mother's eyes told her it was best to mind her tongue.

"Keep to your best behavior now," her mother said as she fussed over Alma's dress. "These children will look to you as an example."

"Yes, Mama."

"But don't be overly familiar either." She straightened the pearl brooch at Alma's collar. "They're Indians, after all."

Indians. Her mother spoke like it was a disease. Surely not. Her father wouldn't bring them here if that were so. Surely they could still be friends without Alma falling sick to whatever it was her mother feared.

Galloping horse hooves enlivened the quiet as a pair of wagons rounded the bend into view. Their iron-rimmed wheels ground over the gravel trail. Dust swirled amid the trees. She bounced on her heels and clapped her hands, willing the sweat-slickened horses to press their gait.

At last the wagons arrived, stopping in the boxy shadow of the great schoolhouse. Her father jumped down. Alma abandoned her mother and ran . . . er . . . skipped to his side. He picked her up and kissed her, his bushy mustache tickling her cheek. "Here they are, kitten, your new classmates."

Thirty-seven black-haired children huddled in the wagon beds. She counted each one twice, just to be sure. A smile readied on her face. She waited for her new friends to look her way, but they kept their heads down and gazes lowered, their knees drawn tight against their chests, as if the day were cold and cloudy, not sunny and fair.

Her father set her down and opened the back gates.

None of the Indians moved.

When he touched the shoulder of the nearest child, the boy shrank back as if stung.

"Come now, no one here will hurt you," her father said.

Why didn't they climb down? It couldn't be comfortable crowded in like that, nothing but scratchy hay to sit upon. Couldn't they smell the sweet cornbread Mrs. Simms had just finished baking? Alma looked beyond them at the schoolhouse. The freshly painted trim gleamed white and three stories' worth of windows sparkled with sunlight. Surely, they hadn't such grand buildings on their reservations.

Finally, a boy seated near the edge raised his head. Alma guessed him to be only a year or two older than she was. Loose strands of hair danced about his round face, catching the light with their glossy sheen. He pushed them behind his ears and glanced around the yard. She followed his gaze from the clapboard outbuildings, to the nearby picnic spread, to the lawn and surrounding forest. Then his dark brown eyes fixed on her.

Alma forgot her smile. His stare reminded her of the fox she'd seen sniffing at the edge of the yard two days before. Intelligent. Cautious. Just as curious about her as she was of him.

The boy scooted across the wagon bed and dangled his legs over the edge. For the count of several seconds he sat there, undecided, his leather-clad feet swaying high above the grass.

Jump down, Alma breathed.

At last he did.

One by one the other children followed. The school's new teacher, Miss Wells, shepherded them toward the picnic table. Alma moved to join them, but her mother grabbed her hand. Despite the dusting of rouge she'd seen her apply that morning, her mother's face was in want of color. She stared at the new arrivals with the same pinched expression she brandished at stray dogs and street-side beggars.

"You said they would be clean and affable," she said to Alma's father.

"Wagon dust, Cora. They've only just arrived."

"Humph. Not a very impressive lot."

"Give them time."

"A millennium would not be long enough."

"We're their salvation." Her father's voice hummed with excitement. "Here they shall be reborn, civilized and good."

Alma kept her face lowered, tickling a dandelion with the toe of her boot. She knew better than to interrupt her parents' conversation but wished dearly they'd hurry up.

Her mother gestured around the yard. "Indians or not, how are we to raise a genteel young lady in this wildness?"

"Come now, La Crosse is only a few miles away."

"Provincial. Hardly fit to be called a city."

Her father squatted down. "What do you think, kitten?"

Alma glanced at the children corralled before the picnic table. "They're awfully funny looking."

"That's just on the outside. Inside they have the same potential as you or I."

"Really?"

"Yes," her father said at the same time her mother shook her head *no*.

Alma looked over again. It would be so nice to finally have friends her own age. "Let's keep them, Papa. Can we?"

Her father rose and took her hand. He offered his other to her mother. She didn't take it, but strode nonetheless beside them to join the others.

Standing before the picnic table, her father cleared his throat. "Almighty God, Creator and Preserver of the white man and the red man alike, we call upon Thee to bless the founding of this school and the children within its fold. Banish the wickedness from their souls and guide them toward lives of industry and righteousness. . . ."

As her father's gentle voice grew louder, full-throated like that of a ringmaster, Alma peeked at the new arrivals. A few children prayed as they should, hands clasped and heads downturned. The others wandered their gaze around the yard or stared wide-eyed at her father, whose outstretched arms had begun to vibrate along with the timbre of his voice.

Their skin was not really red, but varying shades of brown and copper. Many wore their hair long in braids or ribbon-wrapped ponytails that snaked down their backs.

The Indians she'd seen in her father's color-plate books were strange and fearsome: feathers splayed about their heads, bright bobbles adorning their chests, paint smudged across their cheeks. These children bore little resemblance to those drawings. Most wore pants and dresses similar to those good Christians wore. But whereas Alma's clothes had lace and ruffles, their outfits were ornamented with beads and brocade of astounding color—blues like the sky and the river, reds and yellows like the newly changed leaves. One boy had what looked like horse teeth sewed to his shirt. They jiggled as he shifted from one foot to the other. She reached out to touch one, to see if it were truly a tooth, but dropped her hand at her mother's sharp *ahem*.

". . . Finally, O Lord, bless this food before us. May it nourish our bodies as Thy word nourishes our souls. Hear these our prayers, we beseech Thee, in Christ's name. Amen."

Mrs. Simms bustled from the kitchen at the back of the schoolhouse. Smears of grease and crusts of dried food blotched her apron.

She distributed tin plates to the children and motioned with pride to the buffet. They hesitated, but once the first descended upon the food, the rest did likewise, clumping around the table despite the cook's efforts to form them into a line.

One boy with only a narrow patch of hair on the back of his head picked up a chunk of cornbread and brought it to his nose. After several sniffs, he bit off a small corner, then frowned and returned it to the tray. Another child dished out potato salad with his bare hand. A piece of fried chicken was passed and examined by several children before a small girl finally claimed it for her plate. Alma couldn't help but laugh. Didn't they have picnics where they came from?

A whistle cry cut short her giggles. The children froze.

"Halt!" her father cried, blowing his whistle again. "Order, children. Order."

He bustled among Indians, arranging them in a straight line. Alma skipped to the front and took a plate. "I'll show them, Papa."

She dished out small portions of each food, even the mushy-looking green beans—she was, after all, to set an example—and sat down on the unshorn grass a few paces off, carefully tucking her skirt around her.

The next boy in line was a head shorter than Alma. He wore a gray shirt and dark blue pants gartered at the knee. His hair hung loose down to his shoulders, and a nest-like cap of feathers topped his head.

When he turned with his plate of food, Alma grinned up at him and motioned to the grass beside her. He circled wide, plopping down cross-legged several yards away. The other children parted around her in similar fashion, spreading out in small clusters across the lawn. Few would meet her eye. None returned her smile.

Why didn't they want to sit with her? Did she have chicken grease on her face or smell of rotten egg? They were the ones who were strange, after all. She cast aside her half-eaten lunch while the Indians—after a great deal of picking and sniffing—devoured their food and returned for seconds.

After the picnic, a man arrived with a small satchel. A scowl lurked beneath his neatly trimmed mustache. He followed her father to a nearby chair and side table. With one eye still on the Indians, he reached into his satchel and withdrew several metal tools.

"Line up," her father said, and again blew his whistle.

The Indians looked at one another, then back at her father. No one moved.

He sighed and walked among the children, picking out several from the group and molding them into a line. Miss Wells took charge of the others, arranging them single file and marching them around toward the back of the house. The first group, led by her father, moved toward the man and his silver tools.

Alma scrambled to her feet and watched her father maneuver the first child into the chair. The bearded man picked up a pair of long scissors. Sunlight glinted off the tapering blades. He grabbed hold of the girl's long braids and, with two fluid snips, severed the black plaits from her head. The girl cried out and dived to the ground, scrambling toward her hair.

Alma gasped. Why would they cut away the girl's beautiful hair? Then she looked closer at her clothes—threadbare trousers and a button-down shirt. Not a girl. A boy.

Her father pulled the boy back into the chair and, with the help of the surly groundskeeper, Mr. Simms, held him in place while the barber combed and trimmed. All the while, the boy twisted and hollered.

Alma couldn't move. She knew a haircut didn't hurt, but the boy grimaced and fought as if it did. "Stop, you're—"

"Alma!" Her mother's voice cut across her own. "Come here this minute."

She tore her eyes from the boy and hurried to the edge of the schoolhouse, where her mother stood.

"They're stealing that boy's hair."

"You don't see good little white boys with long hair, do you?"

Alma glanced back toward the shining scissors. "But they're hurting him."

"Of course they're not. They're helping him. Less beast, more boy."

It didn't look like they were helping him. Her fingers found their way into her mouth and she gnawed at the soft skin around her nails.

"Stop that." Her mother slapped her hand. "Now come on."

At the back of the house, the Indian girls huddled near three large basins filled with sudsy water. A large bonfire crackled at the edge of the yard. The falling sun hung just above the treetops, the color of a blood orange in the smoky air.

Miss Wells waded among the children, her sleeves rolled and a starched pinafore draped over her gown. She bent and pried off one of the girls' dress and leggings. The girl neither fought nor aided, but stood stock-still with the look of one too frightened to cry.

With puckered lips, Alma's mother tugged at the dress of another. The cook then prodded the naked Indians into the tin basins.

Alma watched, her frown deepening. "Why must they bathe outside?"

"Pestilence, my dear. Must you ask so many questions? Come, we need your help." Her mother held out the girl's clothes at arm's length. "There's an apron for you there by the steps. Put it on and collect these rags."

Pestilence? Alma didn't know the meaning, but her mother spoke as if the word itself tasted foul. She grabbed the apron and collected the clothes, examining each garment for some sign of this awful pestilence. When her arms were full, her mother nodded toward the bonfire.

"Burn them?" Alma looked down at the heap of bright cloth in her arms. "But they're so—"

"Filthy. Fleas, lice, who knows what else."

Though much of the fabric was patched and frayed, Alma saw only a few stains and smudges of dirt. Still, the thought of bugs crawling up her arms made her shiver, and she hurried the clothes across the yard.

At the fire's edge, she hesitated. Tall flames rose above her head. Heat bit at her cheeks. Was it fair to burn their colorful clothes? But then, they were getting new clothes, pretty black dresses to match her own; ones without holes, tatters, or pestilence. She cast the bundle of cotton and leather atop the logs and watched it singe and blacken. The smoke finally chased her away, but only after the shape and color of everything was lost.

When she returned, her mother was bent beside a young girl whose two front teeth were only halfway in, the very same as Alma's. The Indian wore a blouse, calf-length skirt, and leggings, all cut from black broadcloth. Embroidered flowers wound across the fabric. In her arms, she clutched a small doll.

She looked from the doll to the girl's face. Brown eyes stared back, wide like a spooked pony's. Alma had imagined these children would be as excited as she about coming to the new school. But this—the whistle, the haircuts, the burning of their clothes? Would they still want to be her friends afterward?

Her mother yanked the Indian's blouse up and over her head and then pulled at the ties of her skirt. The girl's copper skin turned to goose flesh in the cool evening air. Her cheeks bloomed pink. She covered herself with her arms, clutching the doll in the crook of her elbow.

When Alma's mother reached for the doll, the Indian cowered back. With a huff, her mother pried it from her arms, ripping the seam along the doll's shoulder as she jerked it away. The girl cried and clawed after her treasure, as her mother tossed it to Alma.

"The doll, too?" Alma asked.

A withering look sent her shuffling toward the flames. Behind her, the girl continued to wail. When Alma reached the bonfire, she hesitated again. Singed silk ribbons fluttered among the embers. The charred remnants of a beaded moccasin glinted in the waning sunlight.

She looked over her shoulder. The girl stood naked, hugging her arms around her chest. Mrs. Simms unbound the girl's braid and doused her head with kerosene. Even at a distance, Alma could smell it. Her nose wrinkled and her arms tightened around the heap of clothes. But she could not look away.

Tears pooled in the Indian's eyes as a fine-toothed comb raked through her ebony hair. Her head arched back with each pass and the skin at her temples pulled taut. Once her hair lay smooth, the cook led her to one of the basins and heaved her in. She coughed and shivered when her head surfaced above the soapy water. Alma's throat grew tight.

After the bath, Mrs. Simms dried and dressed the girl—stockings, white chemise and drawers, black dress and boots—just like Alma.

But even though she was outfitted in new clothes, tears continued to run down the Indian's cheeks.

Alma looked at the doll. Soft fuzz, like the tips of lakeside cattails, spilled from the tear in its seam. Its leather body and cloth dress were well worn. By now the logs at the edge of the flames smoldered red. A cold breeze ruffed the back of Alma's skirt, while the front ballooned with heat. Her heart lurched. After a backward glance at her mother, she hid the doll beneath the waistband of her apron before tossing everything else into the fire.

CHAPTER 3

Wisconsin, 1881

Alma's eyes wandered from her slate to the bank of windows lining the classroom wall. Outside, the Indians plodded across the yard in jumbled rows. A whistle sounded, followed by the groundskeeper's gravelly voice.

"Don't you Injuns know what a line is? Left foot forward, now. Stay in formation for criminy's sake!"

Alma choked back a giggle. She wasn't allowed to march. Only the wild and indolent need suffer such discipline. Or so her mother had said when Alma tried to join the Indians in the yard.

Another pipe from the whistle. "That ain't yer left!"

Her father's soft voice cut in. "That's enough drilling for this morning, Mr. Simms. It's their first day. Come inside, children. Time for lessons."

A thrill raced through Alma's body. Finally. She faced forward and sat up extra straight. President Arthur's beady eyes stared down at her from a large portrait above the blackboard, his plump face somber, feathery whiskers hanging from his jowls. Smaller paintings of Washington and Lincoln flanked him on either side. Red, white, and blue ribbons festooned the tops of all four walls like the scalloped hem of a ball gown.

Beneath the ribbons and austere portraits, Miss Wells stood at the blackboard, writing out a list of names—boys' names in one column, girls' in the other. She was much taller than Alma's mother, thin and angular, as if God had drawn her form with squares and rectangles instead of soft ovals. Her script marched across the ebony surface, each letter perfectly formed, her bony fingers choking the chalk. Alma expected the stick to snap in two at any moment.

"Excuse me, Miss Wells. Don't the Indians already have names?" The teacher did not turn around. "None fit to utter. Now back to your work, dear."

Alma glanced at her slate—blank save for the first few lines Miss Wells had tasked her to copy. Unlike the teacher's, her own lettering strayed and bunched, loose at the beginning and cramped near the edge.

Great sins require great repentance.

Do unto others as you would—

At the sound of footfalls in the adjacent hallway, she abandoned her lettering and looked toward the open doorway. Her toes wiggled inside her newly polished boots. A dour old governess had seen to her instruction back in Philadelphia, but never in a *real* classroom, never with *real* friends and classmates seated beside her.

Her father strode into the room. The Indian children shuffled in behind him, their haphazard line unraveling as they entered. His proud smile, the same one he'd sported yesterday, held despite the disorder. "I give them unto your care, Miss Wells." He beamed a moment longer, winked in Alma's direction, and then turned from the room.

"All right, children, take your seats," Miss Wells said. "Young men on this side; ladies over here."

The children stared blankly. Unruffled, the teacher steered the first few students to desks and the others followed. Their steps were clumsy, slow, as if burdened by their shiny new boots.

Alma scooted toward the far edge of her double-wide desk and grinned up at the approaching girls. They avoided her gaze, just as they had yesterday at the picnic, last night in the dormitory, and this morning in the dining hall, squeezing in three to a desk to avoid sitting beside her.

After all thirty-seven children had settled, the bench still loomed empty beside her. Begrudgingly, she returned to her lesson book, the water in her eyes blurring the text.

From the front of the room, Miss Wells addressed the class. She wore the same air of pride, of purpose, as Alma's father. But unlike his, her voice was flat. "Good morning, students. Welcome to Stover School for Indians, your home for the coming years. Thanks to the beneficence of the United States Government, you have the opportunity to fully immerse yourselves in civilized culture and to wash away the sins of your former existence."

Alma peeked at the other children as Miss Wells spoke. They didn't look sinful. Most hung their heads, stealing sideways glances around the room. The girl directly in front of Alma pulled at the collar of her dress. Across the aisle, another squirmed in her seat and swung her legs beneath the desk. Many of the boys tugged and fingered their newly cropped hair. None gave any indication that they understood the school-ma'am's lecture. But the teacher continued undeterred.

"We shall begin today by choosing Christian names." Her thin lips parted in what Alma supposed was a smile, baring white, cock-eyed teeth. She gestured toward the blackboard with a ruler and then pointed the instrument at a girl in the front row. "You first. Come to the board and select a name."

The girl shrank down in her seat until her nose was level with the desk. Miss Wells paid no mind. She grabbed the girl's arm and led her to the blackboard.

Even from the back row, Alma could see the girl trembling. She gaped up at the blackboard, but made no motion toward the names. Several moments passed, each one adding weight to the silence. Finally, Miss Wells grasped the girl's hand and uncoiled her index finger. Like a puppeteer, she guided the small finger toward the first name on the board.

"Mary. Good choice."

The girl scurried back to her seat. Miss Wells followed, pulling a spool of thread and needle from her dress pocket. With a few quick stitches, she sewed the name *Mary* onto the back of the girl's dress.

Alma frowned and cocked her head. Was this to help the other students learn the girl's new name? But they couldn't yet read. Papa had told her so. Maybe it was just for her, so she could learn her new friends' names faster. Tomorrow she'd sew *Alma* on the back of her dress with her neatest stitching. That way, when the Indians did learn to read, they'd know her name right away.

After returning to her desk and jotting something in her ledger, Miss Wells pointed her ruler at the next pupil.

Alma watched the second girl rise. Her glossy hair lay coiled in a braid at the nape of her neck. The fabric at the front of her dress bunched in several places from misaligned buttons. She teetered to the blackboard, hands buried in the folds of her skirt. After a wide-eyed glance at Miss Wells, she pointed at the top name.

Alma bit down to stifle a giggle.

"Mary is already taken," the teacher said. She smiled again, close-lipped this time, the rest of her face strangely void of expression. "Choose another."

The girl dropped her hand and turned toward her desk. Before she could move, Miss Wells grabbed hold of her and spun her back to face the list of names. With trembling finger, the girl pointed again at the name *Mary*.

Without warning, Miss Wells raised her ruler and slapped the Indian's hand. The sharp sound of wood against skin ricocheted from wall to wall, reaching Alma before her eyes could fully make sense of what had happened. The entire class arched back in their seats. Whispers flooded the room.

"Silence, class," Miss Wells said, and turned back to the girl. "Now, my dear, select a *different* name."

The girl cradled her hand, a long red welt appearing atop her skin. Her dark eyes darted about the room. Her mouth hung agape. She looked confused, afraid, as if never before struck.

Alma's mouth went dry, the last of her giggles long dead in her throat. She scooted to the edge of her seat, watching the patience drain from Miss Wells's face with each passing second.

"Pick a name or I shall be forced—"

"She doesn't understand!" The words flew from Alma's mouth before she realized she was speaking.

The teacher's sharp gray eyes turned on her. "This does not concern you."

"If you just show—"

"Your father told me I'd see no trouble from you. Have I been misinformed? He'd be so disappointed."

Alma sank down in her seat. "No, ma'am." She dropped her eyes back to her slate, but her heart continued to push against the walls of her chest.

At the front of the classroom, the Indian whimpered. Her boots shuffled back and forth atop the floorboards.

Again Miss Wells addressed the girl. Her voice, at once both sweet and menacing, made Alma's skin prickle. "You have one more opportunity to select a—"

Ignoring the niggling voice inside her head, Alma's feet found the floor and propelled her toward the blackboard.

"You look like an *Alice* to me," Alma said, pointing to the second name on the board and nodding.

After a moment, the girl raised her hand and gestured to the same name. "Awlis."

Alma smiled. "Al—"

Miss Wells's ruler smacked against the blackboard.

Alma jumped. Alice cringed.

"Return to your seat, Miss Alma."

"I only wanted to—"

"You're not to rise again until the lunch bell, and you shan't be joining the others at recess."

Her shoulders fell. What a nasty old ninny Miss Wells was for punishing her so when all she'd done was help. She trudged to her desk at the back of the room. Several sets of deep brown eyes followed her—curious, but otherwise cold. She picked up the heavy chalk to continue her lines, but could not pry her attention from the blackboard.

After her demonstration, the girls seemed to catch on. One after another, they shuffled up to the front of the room and, without pause, pointed to the name below the one previously selected. The girl Alma remembered from yesterday, the one with the doll, chose the name *Margaret*. Another girl, whom Alma guessed to be her age as well, selected *Rose*.

When all sixteen girls had picked new names, Miss Wells turned to the boys. Despite his shorn hair and new military-style suit, Alma recognized the first boy to rise by his bright, foxlike eyes. He crossed to the blackboard with the same pluck he'd shown climbing from the wagon. Mimicking the girl who had gone before him, his outstretched finger moved toward the next name on the list, *Ruth*.

Alma winced and waited for Miss Wells's ruler to rise. But the boy's hand stopped short. He dropped his arm and cocked his head.

The grandfather clock sounded in the foyer, each clang echoing through the silence.

Alma teetered on the edge of her seat but dared move no farther.

Miss Wells turned the ruler over in her hand, its sharp edge scratching against her dry palm. Otherwise, she didn't move—not a blink, not a breath. Even her placid expression seemed chiseled in stone.

The boy's gaze cut sideways, eyeing the wooden stick, then back to the board. He swung his hand to the list of boys' names and pointed at the top one.

"Harry." Miss Wells laid aside her ruler and inked the name into her ledger.

CHAPTER 4

Philadelphia, 1906

"You know this man? This Harry Muskrat?"

"Yes." Alma handed her husband another square of folded newsprint. The ink was smeared where she'd worried it in her hands on the walk over to his office. "This article mentions his time at Stover. That's how I know he's the same man of my acquaintance."

She sat perfectly still as he scanned the article, forced her breath to come in even draws, forced her feet not to tap, her hands not to stir, forced her face to mimic his impassive expression. A faint, musty smell hit her nose—that of the towering bookshelves lining the room. Most days she hardly noticed. Today it dredged up unwelcome memories of Stover and her father's study. She sought distraction in the spicy scent of her husband's Bay Rum aftershave, in the whir of motorcars and clink of carriages on the street below, but to little avail.

"Indicted for murder." Stewart shook his head and slid the newspapers across his desk. "Dreadful, darling. You must be—"

"Harry would never do something like this."

He leaned back in his leather-upholstered armchair and worked a hand across his chin. "I didn't know you kept in contact with any of your former . . . er . . . classmates."

Alma swallowed and looked down. The tea stain upon her dress had set a faint sepia color, like an aged photograph. She hid it beneath her folded hands. "I don't." It had been easier that way, after what happened. "We, that is, Harry and I, lost touch when I returned to Philadelphia."

"That was what, fifteen years ago? How can you be certain the intervening years have not entirely changed this man?"

"Changed him how? Into a murderer? That's preposterous." She stopped and tried to swallow the rising hysteria in her voice. Her husband's face maintained its reserve, but his hands—fingers locked and knuckles tensed—hinted at apprehension.

She inhaled deeply and continued with more calm. "Harry was gentle, ruled by reason. He was smart, sophisticated . . ."

"Civilized?"

Alma cringed at the word. "Would you ask that of a white man?"

"I would ask that of anyone accused of murder—white, red, yellow, or black."

Silence crept between them. Stewart straightened the papers on his desk, aligning each corner with careful precision. He repositioned his pen squarely upon its tray. "Darling, life can change a man."

"But murder?" Frustration drove her from her seat to the window. She could feel tears mounting with each blink. As before, Harry's face surfaced in her mind. Innocent. He was the only one among them who'd always been innocent.

Outside, the street-side oaks trembled with a breeze. The morning's golden rays morphed and scattered through the leaves. Fall was coming. She'd felt its cool breath on the back of her neck as she hurried to Stewart's office. She saw its hand in the pallor of the leaves. "I cannot let him hang."

"If he's innocent, the courts will acquit him."

Alma turned back to him. His tone was matter-of-fact, his steady gaze earnest. How could he be so unmoved? She yanked off her gloves and paced the length of the room. "What if he needs something? Money. A lawyer."

"The court will appoint him a public defender."

"Won't you at least look into it?"

"The case is being tried in Minnesota."

Alma waved her hand toward the brass-and-wire contraption on his desk. "Can't you use that telephone machine?"

His lips flattened. "I don't see what we can do."

"Please, dearest."

The hard lines of his face softened. He lifted the phone's receiver from its cradle. "Hello, Central? Can you put me through to the Federal Courthouse in St. Paul, Minnesota?"

A pleasant female voice chirped out a response and the line went silent for a moment. Alma seated herself before his desk and scooted closer, trying again to be still.

"Hello?" Stewart said when the line went live again. "May I please speak to the district clerk?" A muffled response. More silence. "Stewart Mitchell, Esquire here, I'm trying to reach the attorney assigned the case of Mr. Harry Muskrat. . . . Not involved directly, no . . . I just told you, I'm a lawyer. . . ." Alma shifted in her chair as the clerk's voice sounded in the earpiece. "Yes, a phone number will do." Stewart jotted down the exchange and returned the earpiece to the switchhook.

His grip loosened from around the brass stem. A long breath whistled through his nose. His eyes probed Alma's, as if to gauge her resolve. She nodded with such vigor her hat slipped forward over her eyes. She repinned it atop her chignon as he reconnected with Central. "Tri-State 5400, please."

Alma leaned in, balancing on the lip of her chair. On the other end of the line, the man's voice was squeaky, his vowels broad and pitch lilting. The cadence struck her like a long-forgotten song. A shiver skittered from the nape of her neck down her spine and through her limbs. She had laughed, as a girl, the first time she'd heard people speaking that way. Not today.

Unable to decipher the man's muted words, she watched her husband's face. At first, his expression was convivial. He introduced himself and explained the reason for his call. He nodded as he listened to Harry's lawyer, and Alma found herself nodding in unison, hoping any moment he'd hang up and exclaim the conviction had been a mistake, the charges dropped. But then his brow furrowed. His head stopped bobbing. Alma stilled too. Her hands grew cold.

"I see, I see," her husband said into the receiver. And then another pause. His lips pressed together. The creases in his forehead seemed to deepen with each passing second. "He won't say anything?" Stewart asked. "Not one way or another?" His chin jerked back and eyes widened. "I see." Alma held her breath. More nodding, this time slow and somber. Stewart thanked the man, hung up, and pushed the phone away. His gaze fell to his hands, which he folded atop his desk.

"Well?" Alma asked.

"I'm afraid the circumstances surrounding your friend's case are rather bleak," he said, not meeting her eye.

"What does that mean?"

"The prosecution has at least one witness who saw your friend in proximity of the agent just before the shooting."

"That could be just . . . just coincidence."

"And the sheriff's report said a trader had recently sold Mr. Muskrat a gun of similar description to that found at the scene of the murder."

Alma pushed back her chair. "That doesn't prove anything."

"True, it's circumstantial, but—"

"These backwoods lawmen are trying to frame him." She threw her gloves down on his desk and stood.

"Why would they do that, Alma? That's perjury."

"You don't know what kind of twisted justice these men are capable of." Her hand fluttered to her throat. "Being Indian is sin enough for them."

Stewart blinked at her. She wished for once he'd get angry, too, leap to his feet with indignation. Instead, he rose slowly, crossed to where she stood, and took her gently by the shoulders. "Darling, you mustn't let this upset you so."

"He'll die, Stewart!" A twinge of guilt twisted inside her as her voice echoed through the room, undoubtedly audible throughout the reception lobby and neighboring offices as well.

Stewart flinched and dropped his hands from her shoulders. "If he does hang, it will be his own doing."

"How can you say that?"

"Your friend hasn't said one word about the murder—not to the sheriff, not to his lawyer, not to anyone. He's not talking at all." He stalked to his desk and sat heavily in his chair. "The arraignment is tomorrow. His attorney is going to enter a guilty plea."

Alma groped for the back of her chair, her fingers digging into the velveteen upholstery as she steadied herself against the sudden ache and nausea. When she was ten, she'd fallen off her horse onto the hard, dirt-packed road. For a moment all went black. She knew nothing but pain and air-starved panic. Then the world came back into focus—each color a shock to her eyes, each sound a sting to her ears. She'd rolled over and retched until there was nothing left in her stomach but bile. Now, hearing those words, Alma felt the same sensation. She couldn't let him die. Couldn't bear more loss. More guilt.

When she looked back up at Stewart, it was through bleary, tear-rimmed eyes. "He needs a better lawyer, one he can trust."

"I'm a patent attorney," he said. "I have no experience defending murderers."

"Accused murderers."

"My license to practice law doesn't extend beyond Pennsylvania."

To this she only huffed.

Her husband sighed and ran a hand through his sand-brown hair. "Help me understand, Alma. Who is this man? We've been married five years and you've never once spoken of him. Why does this mean so much to you?"

Alma turned back to the window. True, she'd spoken little of her life in Wisconsin. It was easier to live as if those memories belonged to someone else. She'd told him of her family's move west when she was seven to open an Indian boarding school. She'd told him of her return to Philadelphia at seventeen to live with her aunt. Of the decade in between, he knew nearly nothing. Much of her longed to tell him—of Harry, of Margaret, of them all. How freeing it would be. The words perched on her lips, but she drew them back with a sharp inhale. He could never know. Not all of it.

Another gust of wind stirred the trees, plucking the first of fall's leaves from the boughs. She watched them swirl and scatter to the ground. The sinking feeling she'd felt at breakfast overwhelmed her again, as if time were folding in on itself and drawing her with it. "Is there no one from your past for whom you would dare the impossible?"

For several heartbeats, there was only silence.

"Perhaps I could appear pro hac vice."

She turned around. "What does that mean?"

"With the public defender's permission, I can appeal to the court to assist with the case even though it lies beyond my jurisdiction."

Alma rushed around his desk and sank onto her knees before him. "Really? You'll do that for him?"

He took her hands and kissed them. "Not for him, darling. For you. Give me a day or two to clear my schedule and make the necessary arrangements. Then we can go to St. Paul and see what we can do."

"Thank you, dearest!"

"I can't promise success." He kissed her cheek and helped her to her feet. "First, I'll need to get his attorney to change the plea. Then we need to get Mr. Muskrat talking."

"I can help with that," Alma said quickly. "He'll speak to me."

Stewart reached into his drawer and produced a small notebook, his eyebrows already pinched in concentration. "We may even need him to take the stand. He does speak English, your friend?"

A phantom smell of tallow and ash invaded her nose, spreading over her tongue and seeping into her taste buds. "Of course he does. The only language permitted at Stover was English."

CHAPTER 5

Wisconsin, 1881

A loud whack brought silence to the room. Alma flinched and glanced up from her stew. Miss Wells stood at the end of the dining table, her ruler flat against the wooden surface.

"English only, children," she said.

"But the Indians still don't know any English," Alma mistakenly said aloud.

Miss Wells turned and flashed that crooked-toothed smile Alma had come to hate. "Then they should refrain from speaking altogether."

Alma slumped, leaning her cheek against her palm, and returned to her dinner. For several minutes, only the clank of dinnerware and the rhythmic click of Miss Wells's footfalls echoed off the dining hall's whitewashed walls.

Six long tables crowded the room—four on one side where the boys sat and two on the other side, nearest the main door, for the girls. Miss Wells paced the wide aisle in between, her overly starched skirt rasping atop the floorboards. At the front of the room another door flapped back and forth between the dining hall and kitchen, its hinges squeaking anytime someone passed through. At least once every night a howl rattled the conjoining wall when Mrs. Simms dropped a pot or singed a finger on the stove. The Indians would all giggle, Alma with them, and for a moment she didn't feel so alone.

The wooden bench upon which she sat was hard and splintery and made it impossible not to fidget. To her right sat Margaret. The Indian gripped the handle of her spoon flat against her palm the way a bandleader held his baton. Lumpy brown stew sloshed over the edges as she brought it to her mouth. Only two nights ago, Alma had shown everyone at the table the correct way to hold the utensil.

"Like you're holding a pencil," she'd said, raising her arm and taking an exaggerated bite.

A few of them had tried to mimic her for a short while. Others, including Margaret, ignored her completely. Maybe they'd never held a pencil either. She'd have to demonstrate that too.

"It took you months to learn how to use a spoon, kitten," her father had said when she complained.

But she'd been just a baby then and didn't remember it anyhow.

Now, a full six days since the Indians' arrival, she was growing tired of being an example. Maybe if they listened more, tried harder.

The hum of voices rekindled throughout the room, whispers in funny-sounding languages Alma didn't understand. As the voices grew louder, Miss Wells's lips flattened and her nostrils flared. "English only," she repeated, this time from across the room by the boys' tables.

The din waned but did not fully dampen. Another crack rang out.

"Silence." An edge rose in the teacher's voice. Alma's muscles tensed.

The room quieted save for the songlike voice of Margaret. Miss Wells stalked across the room, grabbed the girl's collar, and pulled her to her feet in a firm, fluid motion. "I said quiet!"

She dragged her to the front of the dining room and released her collar. Margaret looked from side to side, pallor overtaking the color in her cheeks. Miss Wells yanked over a chair. Its legs scraped atop the floorboards, sending a shiver down Alma's arms.

"Climb up and stand before your classmates," the teacher said.

When Margaret did not move, the teacher grabbed her arm and bullied her onto the seat. "Don't move," she said, and retreated into the kitchen.

Margaret turned toward the swinging door and stuck out her tongue. The other children laughed. Alma, too, but with a niggling unease.

When Miss Wells returned from the kitchen, all quieted. In her hand she held a thick slab of lye soap.

The smirk fell from Margaret's face. Her eyes grew as round as wagon wheels. "Awegonen i'iwe?"

Miss Wells took advantage of the girl's gaping mouth and shoved in the soap. Margaret tried to spit it out, her throat convulsing as she gagged, but Miss Wells kept her hand flat against her face.

Alma winced, imagining the bitter taste, remembering the way her hands burned and tingled after using it to scrub her skin.

Margaret tried three more times to spit out the soap. Each time Miss Wells stymied her efforts, her long, bony fingers digging into the girl's cheeks. Margaret's face twitched as if she were fighting back the urge to vomit. Lamplight glistened in her glossy eyes. But she did not cry as Alma surely would have. Her hands became fists at her sides. A deep breath whistled in through her nose, and the grimace smoothed from her face. Save for the blinking of her eyes and rise and fall of her chest, she did not move.

Miss Wells dropped her hand. Her nails had left crescent imprints around Margaret's mouth. "All right, everyone, continue on with your meal."

No one, not even Alma, moved. Her hands knotted in her lap; her eyes hung on Margaret.

"Eat!"

Alma snapped to attention.

The teacher smoothed back her hair and took a deep breath. "Eat. The soap stays in her mouth until every last bowl is cleaned."

The Indians sat still as figures in a tintype, their eyes wide and fixed. Clearly, they did not understand.

Saliva dribbled down Margaret's chin. Already her lips looked red and puffy. Alma picked up her spoon and sank it into her lukewarm stew. The sound of metal scraping over the bottom of her bowl echoed through the silence. Careful not to slurp, she forced down the slimy food. Another scrape. Another mouthful. Her hand trembled. Thirty-seven pairs of eyes followed her spoon from bowl to mouth. They still didn't understand. She glanced up at Margaret, who stared back with a sullen, accusing expression. To her, Alma must seem a traitor, mean and unfeeling just like Miss Wells. After this, they would never be friends.

She spied the boy named Harry seated across the room. His hands were clenched in fists atop the table, his expression frantic, angry.

He looked ready to spring from his seat and tackle Miss Wells. Alma locked eyes with him and shook her head slowly. She waved her spoon, then brought it to her mouth. Harry's eyes narrowed. His face remained hard, his hands flexed and still. Another slow, deliberate bite and Alma had to look away. He didn't see she was only trying to help. None of them did.

Then, from Harry's direction, came the drawl of metal. "Eat," he said loudly.

Alma sat stunned. Aside from the classroom drills of *hello, good morning, yes ma'am, no ma'am,* and *thank you,* none of the children had uttered a single English word.

He swallowed a spoonful of potatoes and broth, then dished up another. "Must eat."

One by one, other spoons joined the clamor.

When Harry's gaze once again met hers, his clever eyes regarded her in a way others didn't—no fear, no suspicion, but plain curiosity, as if she were the strange and exotic one. As if she were a riddle he could not quite puzzle out.

That night, like every night since the Indians' arrival, choked sobs filled the dormitory. It started the moment Miss Wells dampened the lamps and left the room. One girl at first, then another, until every bed rattled with the sound, as if sobs were contagious.

Even Alma felt the pull. Her throat tightened and tears threatened if she blinked. She knew they missed their homes, their parents, the siblings they'd left behind. But this was a better place for them. Papa had said so. Clean clothes, healthy food, beds, hairbrushes, and learning.

She rolled over onto her side and squinted through the darkness. One bed over lay Margaret, curled into a ball beneath the blankets. Her body quaked as she cried. She'd thrown up the minute Miss Wells removed the soap from her mouth after dinner. The teacher made her clean up the mess before permitting any of them to leave. At this, Margaret's cheeks turned red to match the blisters forming on her lips. She grabbed the sodden rag Miss Wells threw at her feet and hung her head, but not before Alma had seen a tear sneak from the corner of her eye.

Now, Alma reached beneath her mattress and pulled out Margaret's doll. It soothed her to hold it, to stroke its soft leather body and trace the embroidered flowers on its dress. The very secret of it delighted her. She'd hidden the doll the day of the fire. The following afternoon while the Indians marched, she'd sneaked into the dormitory and mended its torn seam. Her stitches were ragged, the thread several shades too light, but she loved the doll anyway. In the cover of darkness, she fingered the black wisps sewn onto its head. Coarse and thick like real hair.

Her dolls were much prettier, of course—white porcelain skin, pink lips in the shape of a bow, thick curls that sprang back when you pulled them. The special ones, the ones her mother kept tucked out of reach, had real glass eyes the same shade of blue as her own. Instead of nubs, they had proper hands with fingers you could count.

But Margaret's doll was soft. Its brown leather body felt like real skin when she held it against her cheek. She'd never owned a doll so suited for play—one that would not chip, crack, or scuff. She twirled it atop her bedspread, as if her mattress were a parquet dance floor, then hugged it to her chest. The smell of smoke and pine sap clung to its skin.

A hiccup-like sob drew her attention back to Margaret. She tried to ignore the sound, plugged her ears with her pillow, and hummed a soft tune. Her mother had taken the doll for a reason, just as she'd taken the Indians' clothes and her father their hair. It had to be a good reason, for why else would they do it? Something about the Indians forgetting their old lives and starting anew.

Through the soft down of her pillow she could still hear Margaret crying. The sound gnawed at her. Maybe she should return the doll—just for a little while—just until Margaret forgot her homesickness and the blisters on her lips healed. Then Alma could have it back and they'd both be happy. She squeezed the doll one more time, then whispered, "Margaret."

The girl didn't answer. Alma leaned from her bed and poked the girl's shoulder.

Margaret started and rolled around. She looked at Alma through puffy eyelids. Her breathing was ragged and snot ran from her nose. Her lips looked like breakfast sausages.

Alma smoothed the doll's hair, straightened its dress, breathed a final whiff of its woodland scent, and then held it out. "Shh! Keep it secret."

At first, Margaret did not move, but peered at Alma with suspicion. Then her hand crept forward. She grabbed the doll and shrank back into the shell of her blankets. Only then did her expression soften, her swollen lips trembling as if attempting a smile. She wiped her nose with the sleeve of her nightshirt and rolled around.

Immediately, Alma felt the doll's absence, wished she too had something to hold on to. But they were friends now, she and Margaret. Weren't they? The hope was enough to lull her to sleep.

CHAPTER 6

Wisconsin, 1881

Reveille sounded at first light. Alma winced and yanked her quilt over her head. But the horn's sharp notes were insistent, like needle pricks against her eardrums. Her father had assigned a boy named Frederick the duty of awaking the school with this noise every morning. He'd never even held a horn, had shaken it at first as if it might rattle. Silly boy. She could do much better. But Papa said it wasn't her place. The horn was ugly anyway, worn and rusty from Mr. Simms's days in the war with the Mexicans.

When the clamor ended, she slid from her bed and splashed her face with icy water from the washbowl on her bed stand. The ceiling creaked with footfalls of the boys shrugging off sleep in the attic dormitory. She brushed her hair smooth and traded her nightshirt for her school uniform.

The other girls bustled between their washstands and bedside trunks. Bedsprings squeaked as they tucked the corners of their sheets under their mattresses and smoothed the wrinkles from their quilts. They took turns weaving each other's hair into tight plaits. Alma could braid her hair all by herself . . . but never quite as neat as the other girls managed.

Stupor thawed from the room, and whispers rose above the sound of morning chores. It was a strange mix of heavily accented English and Indian gibberish, none of which was directed at her. Even Margaret still kept her distance. Alma perched on the edge of her bed and pretended not to mind, attacking her already gleaming boots with polish.

Boot heels clipped down the hallway and the room went silent. The girls scrambled into place at the end of their beds: backs straight, hands clasped, chins up, eyes down. Alma stood, too, her posture straight but less rigid. She watched Rose struggle with her buttons, securing the top one just before Miss Wells strode into the room. Alma's mother sauntered in a few seconds behind, still dressed in her sateen robe and lace-trimmed nightshirt.

"If you'll be so kind as to attend to that side of the room, Mrs. Blanchard, I'll inspect this side," Miss Wells said.

Her mother yawned and gave a lazy wave of assent. Usually Miss Wells managed morning inspection alone, but Alma had overheard her father encouraging her mother to "suffer more involvement with the pupils." So a few times over the past week her mother—a rare sight before the noon hour—graced their company.

Miss Wells, however, did not appear grateful for the help. The sharp features of her oblong face were pinched. Her gray eyes darted hither and thither, as if to catch any offenses before Alma's mother had a chance to overlook them. She marched the length of the room and stopped at the far-most bed.

May, whom Alma guessed to be the youngest of all the girls, was the teacher's first victim. Miss Wells examined the corners of her bed, the alignment of her quilt, the neatness of her trunk, even the cleanliness of her washstand.

All the while, May stood still as a stone figurine at the end of her bed. Only her coal-black eyes moved, following Miss Wells out the very corner of her sockets, fleeing down to the floor when the woman came to face her.

Miss Wells took the girl's chin in hand and turned it into the light. She inspected the smoothness of May's hair and neatness of her uniform. At a tap on the wrist, May extended her hands and splayed her fingers. The teacher scrutinized each nail for dirt, then turned May's hands over and examined her palms. The entire drill progressed in silence.

Alma saw May's bunched stocking and grimaced. Even though she was angry with the lot of them, Alma took no delight in what was surely to come.

"It appears you have not bothered to properly garter your stocking." The teacher's voice was sweet as honeycomb, a sound that made the nape of Alma's neck tingle. "What have you to say for yourself?"

May stared wide-eyed at Miss Wells and said nothing.

"Your stocking, Miss May."

The girl bit her lower lip and looked over her heavy black uniform. She smoothed her skirt, checked to see that the buttons on her sleeves were fastened and her boots laced, then turned back to Miss Wells and shook her head.

The teacher huffed and pointed to the slack fabric bunched around the girl's ankle.

May bent over and fought with the stocking until it lay smooth and securely fastened above her knee. When she looked back to the teacher, her face was hopeful, her eyes pleading.

"Ten demerits," Miss Wells said. She made a note in her ledger and moved on the next girl, ignoring the way May's carriage wilted.

If she didn't know the word *stocking,* May clearly knew what *demerits* meant: scrubbing the floors while the other children got to play in the yard. Alma couldn't help but frown with her. The factory-made stockings provided by the Indian Bureau fit May like an elephant's hat would fit a dormouse.

Miss Wells followed the same routine for each girl: leering over every inch of their bed, washstand, and uniform. By contrast, Alma's mother drifted down her assigned row of beds with little care. She seldom touched anything, and never the girls themselves. Whenever she encountered something overwhelmingly amiss, such as the water stains on Alice's dress, she flapped her hand in the offender's direction and said in a flat voice, "Demerits here, I should think."

Inspection was almost over when Alma saw a sliver of black fabric peeking from beneath Margaret's pillow. At first, she thought it just a shadow, but then her every muscle, from toes to forehead, clenched. The doll!

She tapped her foot and cleared her throat softly. When Margaret looked over, Alma nodded toward the pillow.

Margaret's eyes doubled in size. She started to shuffle backward, but Alma's mother had already reached her for inspection.

"Come forward, little girl. Stand up straight."

Alma's clasped hands squeezed so tightly her fingers lost feeling.

The seconds limped by. She followed every flicker of her mother's crystal-blue eyes: up and down the length of Margaret's dress, a glance at the nightstand and washbowl, to and fro from one corner of the bed to the other, then back to Margaret's face.

"Neat enough, but do stop fidgeting."

Alma exhaled and snuck Margaret a little smile.

Her mother sashayed onward, then paused and wheeled back. "What do we have here?"

Alma's heart echoed each step her mother took toward Margaret's bed.

"This is entirely unacceptable." Her mother brushed past the Indian toward the head of the bed, the pillow, the doll . . . the nightstand?

"A mat of hairs has been left here in your comb. Disgusting. Uncouth. Miss Wells, demerits here for this one."

This time, Alma had no chance for relief. Her mother whirled away from the nightstand and froze. Her dainty mouth fell open. Her porcelain skin flared red. She reached out and pulled the doll from beneath Margaret's pillow. "Where did you get this?"

Margaret looked like a baby bird caught in a tomcat's claws. Her eyes began to water and her lower lip trembled.

Alma's mother brandished the doll above her head. "You sinister little devil! You'll suffer more than demerits for this."

She grabbed Margaret by the collar of her dress and dragged her to the potbellied furnace in the corner of the room. The fire had dwindled through the night, but flashes of light still showed through the grate as the embers continued to smolder. She opened the door and threw the doll inside. Sparks swirled. Yellow flames gathered, consuming the doll and its beautifully embroidered costume. Margaret and Alma whimpered at the same time.

"Hold out your hand," her mother said, then more loudly, "your hand!"

Margaret raised a trembling hand. Her breathing had quickened and sweat glistened at her hairline. Alma's mother gripped the girl's wrist and thrust her hand toward the flames.

Sharp inhales sounded around the room. Even Miss Wells seemed surprised, though her lips trembled with a smile.

Margaret shook her head frantically. Her tears sparkled in the fire's light. She opened her mouth, but no words came out. Then, as her fingers neared the mouth of the furnace, she screamed.

The sound jolted Alma from her silence. "It was me, Mama."

When her quiet voice did not draw her mother's attention, she gulped and hollered over Margaret's cries. "It was me! I didn't burn the doll as you asked."

Her mother spun round. "What?"

"I . . . I just wanted to play with it."

Her mother dropped Margaret's hand. She no longer seemed to blink or even breathe but stared at Alma with a gaze that could quicken the dead.

"Mama, I didn't mean—"

"Silence." She strode across the room to Alma's nightstand and grabbed her silver-handled brush. "Bend over your bed and lift your skirts."

Alma looked down the rows of gaping faces and felt her cheeks burn.

"Now, young lady." Her mother's voice was steady, but knife-sharp. "Let these Indians see what happens to bad little girls."

With every step Alma took toward her bed, she regretted saving Margaret's doll. She hated Stover and wished her family had never come. She drew her skirt up over her backside and braced her hands on the mattress.

The back of the brush struck her bottom, stinging her skin through her thin cotton drawers and driving her forward. She balled the quilt in her fists and clenched her teeth. Her mother paddled her again. And again.

Ten strikes later, Alma's legs wobbled and tears streamed down her face. Her mother cast the brush onto the bed and stalked away. Alma stood and straightened her skirt, keeping her head down to hide her red, puffy face. She never wanted to see her mother or another Indian ever again.

Stares and whispers kept Alma's embarrassment aflame all day. Why couldn't the Indians just ignore her like they usually did?

When evening finally came, Alma lingered in the parlor as the others marched to bed. She waited until all was quiet, then hobbled upstairs. Her backside still throbbed from the morning's punishment.

A sliver of light shone beneath the dormitory door. Alma could hear Miss Wells pacing the room, counting heads. She sighed and slumped against the wall. Fresh tears sprang to her eyes—hot tears, full of hate and frustration. She couldn't bear it, not a single day more. She felt lonelier here surrounded by the Indian children than she had in Philadelphia all alone.

The footfalls stopped and the somber drone of evening Scripture began. "The word of the Lord came to Jonah . . ."

Ugh. Alma knew that one already. The Indians had probably never seen a whale, wouldn't know what the story meant. True, she hadn't either. But she'd seen the skeleton of one laid out in a museum. Surely that counted.

"Jonah rose up to flee unto Tarshish from the presence of the Lord, and . . ."

Run away, that's what she'd do. Run away and find a new mother and real friends.

When the footfalls stopped and the somber drone of evening prayers began, Alma turned the knob and opened the door just a crack. She slipped in and crept to her bedside. With Miss Wells's gaze upon them, not one of the sixteen girls dared look up. She sank onto her knees beside her bed. While her lips mouthed the last verse of prayer, her mind swirled with plans of flight.

After the teacher damped the lamps, Alma slid into bed, still dressed in her day clothes and boots. She would slip out as soon as the other girls were asleep. Maybe she'd join a troupe of actors, wear face paint and pretty costumes. Maybe she'd steal onto a steamboat and sail down the Mississippi. Anywhere would be better than here.

In time, rustling fabric and whining bedsprings settled. Slow, even breaths sounded through the room. Alma was just about to rise when the floorboard creaked beside her.

She cracked open one eye and spied one of the older girls, named Catherine, creeping toward the window. The girl's quilt hung over her shoulders like a shawl. She coaxed the window open without a sound and slipped out onto the roof.

Next, Alice tiptoed past, then Rose and Margaret. Had they stolen her idea? Were they running away too?

Alma remained motionless, her eyes combing over the other

beds. Sleeping forms rose and fell with silent breaths. No one else had awoken.

She looked back to the window. Alice and Rose had already vanished onto the roof. Margaret gathered up her nightshirt with one hand and grabbed the window frame with the other. A breeze fluttered her hair, carrying with it the scent of the lawn and trees, the rocks and dirt, the moonlight and stars. A slight leap and out she climbed, into the open.

CHAPTER 7

Minnesota, 1906

Endless miles of baled hay and swaying cornstalks at last gave way to the stone, brick, and steel of St. Paul. Inside the dining car, Alma's teacup chattered atop its saucer in time with the rocking train. The toast on her plate lay half-eaten and her soft-boiled egg untouched. She stared out the window at the small houses and tenement buildings lining the track. Every so often, the gray water of the Mississippi bullied its way into view between gaps in the transitioning landscape. At this distance, the river's surface appeared smooth, like a vein of painted glass in a decorative window. But Alma knew better. She had looked upon those same waters countless times as a girl. She knew their unforgiving and unyielding currents.

"La Crosse is what—a hundred miles downriver?" Stewart asked.

Alma tore her gaze from the window and looked at her husband. His soft eyes calmed her—not the blue of her parents' nor the inkybrown of the Indians', but hazel. Even in the harsh incandescent light of her aunt's parlor that first evening they'd met, his eyes had struck her. She could stare into them forever without reminder of things past. Here especially, so close to her childhood home, she needed that refuge. "A hundred and fifty."

"Did you come here often?"

She shook her head. "Only once. Mother preferred Chicago."

"Isn't that twice as far?"

"Yes, but twice as fashionable."

Stewart chuckled. "She's still living in La Crosse, isn't she? We could stop by on our return home."

"No," she said, on top of his words.

"You don't think she'd like to meet me?"

Alma clutched her teacup to silence its clattering. Her mother would love to meet him, to show him off to all of her friends. "See, my silly daughter's made something of herself, after all," she would say.

His tidy hair and correct posture, his tailored suit and silk tie, his silver tiepin and cufflinks—that was all she would see. Not the tender, honorable man beneath.

She shifted atop the velvet seat cushion. It no longer felt soft, but coarse and prickly. "I'd hate to take you away from your practice any longer than necessary."

His lips flattened. "And your father? Shouldn't you like to visit his grave?"

"No." Even to her own ears it sounded like a lie.

He crossed his legs and looked out the window. Minutes passed in want of a word, a touch, a glance. But Alma didn't trust herself. Her shaky voice, her watery eyes, her sweat-dampened gloves all would beg more questions, elicit more deceit.

"Union Depot can't be far off," Stewart finally said. "I'll return to our sleeper and instruct the valet about our luggage." He stood and grabbed the book he'd been reading over breakfast: *A Treatise on the Law of Capital Offenses.*

She touched his hand with the tips of her fingers. "Stewart . . . thank you."

He mustered a smile and exited the dining car. He would never admit to weariness, but she could see the lines around his mouth, the way the rest of his face refused the mirth of his smile, as if it had been painted on atop an otherwise somber expression.

Four days had passed since she'd first read of Harry's trial in the morning papers. Stewart's face had looked weary even then, but now, watching him walk away, she saw the fatigue in his step, in the slant of his shoulders. He loved her so. And this was how she repaid him?

Outside, debarking passengers bustled about the depot. Coaches, wagonettes, and the occasional automobile crowded the curb. Horns honked. Horses whinnied. Train whistles blew.

She and Stewart found a quiet corner on the platform. He withdrew his pocket watch from his waistcoat and sighed. "I had hoped to go to the hotel with you, but my appointment with your classmate's lawyer, Mr. Gates, is at eleven. I'd best head to his office straightaway."

"That's all right. I wanted to go see Harry, anyway."

His hazel eyes fixed her with a concerned look. "Alone? Shouldn't you like to freshen up first at the hotel? I can join you this afternoon and we can go together."

"I doubt anyone at the jail will take offense to my traveling clothes." She straightened his tie and patted his chest. "Besides, dear, it's the twentieth century. Women travel alone all the time."

He shuffled a foot atop the wood platform. "He's not being held in the city jail, darling, but several miles southwest of here at Fort Snelling."

An army fort outside the city? The idea seemed archaic. Harry wasn't some rabble-rousing warrior in the like of Geronimo or Crazy Horse. "This isn't a military matter."

"The crime occurred on federal trust land—"

"The Indians own the land. The government parceled it out under the Dawes and Nelson acts. Father spoke of it often."

He smiled that tired smile. "Yes, but not all of it was allotted. And even that which was remains in trust for twenty-five years."

"Oh." It seemed Stewart had done more than brush up on criminal law in the past few days. "What about bail?"

"The judge refused to set bail. I'll speak to Mr. Gates and see if we can't get your friend transferred to the city holding facility. Until then, why don't you—"

"Wherever he is, I'll see him today."

Stewart pursed his lips, but led her to the line of waiting cabs. "Are you sure?"

She squeezed his hand. "I'll be fine. I'll meet you back at the hotel in time for dinner."

He paid the driver and helped her into the brougham. "I hope he opens up to you. We need his cooperation."

"He will."

His face was stoic as the carriage pulled away from the curb. He checked his watch again, then disappeared into the thick of towering buildings and streetcars. Her heart squeezed. Stewart deserved better. Could nothing in her life remain unsullied?

She sagged, resting her cheek against the cold glass window. Once again, that wide gray river meandered into view, an unwanted companion as she headed south toward Fort Snelling. The first white settlers had adopted the Ojibwe name: *Mizi-ziibi.* Harry had told her that. She'd never expected to see its broad waters again. She'd never expected to revisit any of this. She slipped a hand into her purse and withdrew a necklace of strung porcupine quills. At its center hung a beaded medallion sewn onto leather backing. Her fingers traced the intricate design of beads, each painstakingly inlaid to form the image of a sun. Their bright coloring belied the years. Belied all that had happened. A sob built in her throat and she thrust the necklace back in her handbag.

She closed her eyes and breathed deeply. She could do this. Harry would talk to her, clear up all the confusion about the murder. He would go free; she would go home. Stewart would still love her. A day, maybe two and she could return to her dollhouse life.

CHAPTER 8

Wisconsin, 1881

Alma threw off her quilt and hurried to the window. She watched the girls scurry across the roof and clamber over the ledge one by one until only Margaret remained.

Grabbing either side of the window frame, Alma lifted her leg and swung it over the sill. The night air raked over the exposed skin of her neck and face. Her heart sped. "Wait!"

Margaret spun around, eyes wide and mouth agape.

As Alma scrambled over the sill and through the window, her knee caught on the hem of her skirt and she lost her balance. She tumbled toward the shingled roof. Margaret rushed forward, breaking her fall.

"Thanks," Alma said, wary to let go of the girl's arms. The slanting roof felt slick beneath her feet. The flat, solid ground seemed impossibly far away.

She'd never been on a roof before, and the thrill of it dampened her fear. From this height, she could see for miles. Dark trees covered the landscape, rising and falling with the hills and bluffs. The last of fall's leaves trembled with the breeze. Goose bumps tented her skin. A smudge of light lit the horizon in the direction of La Crosse. The only other illumination came from blinking stars and the thin sliver of a moon hanging above the trees.

Margaret pulled free from Alma's grip and frowned. She nodded back toward the room and then tilted her head to the side, cradling it against her palms. "Sleep."

Alma glanced over her shoulder through the open window. She could just make out the tidy rows of beds and the scrolling design of the damask wallpaper. It was warm inside. And safe. Part of her wanted to creep back, lie in her bed with her quilt pulled high, and forget all plans to run away. But then she'd wake up tomorrow to the same lonely life. "I'm coming with you."

Margaret's lips pinched into a scowl. "No. No come."

"Yes, I am."

A cross between a sigh and a growl sounded from Margaret's lips. She turned her back on Alma and stalked toward the edge of the roof.

Alma inched behind, her feet once again unsteady. "Wait."

Margaret did not. She dropped to her knees and inched backward over the ledge. Her legs grasped the corner post of the porch below, and she slid down until her feet hit the railing. From there, she jumped to the ground, landing with a crunch on the dry grass.

Looking down after her, dizziness stirred in Alma's stomach. She closed her eyes and sucked in three long breaths. Walking about the roof was one thing. Climbing down was something else entirely. Suppose she fell and ripped her stocking. How furious her mother would be. Not at all beseeming a young lady, she'd say. And Papa, how the glint in his eyes would fade.

But Margaret had made it look so easy. Pushing aside her doubts— she was running away after all—Alma sat down and swung her legs over the ledge. Margaret hissed at her from below and pointed again toward the dormitory. Alma ignored her. She rolled onto her stomach and inched her torso down off the roof. Her legs dangled, searching for the corner post. Her foot touched something hard just as her hands slipped from the shingle overhang. She careened downward, her stomach lodging in her throat, until her flailing legs found purchase around the beam. She twined around it and slid down. Slivers of paint poked through her dress, prickling her skin as they peeled away from the post and fell like snowflakes to the ground below.

When her feet found the railing, she felt the tug of both laughter and tears. She'd done it! She clambered down the half wall of the porch to the ground, landing on her hands and knees. The grass was cool and brittle. It crackled as her fingers spread and closed, spread and closed—the sound, the sensation somehow exhilarating as if she'd never felt grass before. No one stood over her telling her not to dirty her hands or her dress or her shoes. No sharp *ahems*. She could run if she wanted, and jump and scream—though she'd better not, at risk of waking the house—but she could, if she really wanted to, and that was enough.

Margaret's footsteps whispered toward her, and Alma's fingers stilled. If the Indian had been mad before, now she'd be furious. Bracing herself for more reproof, she leaned back on her haunches and glanced up. Margaret's face was contorted, but not with the scowl Alma had expected. Instead, her clamped lips held back a laugh.

"What's so funny?" Alma asked.

Margaret pointed at the roof and flailed her arms. A giggle burst free from her mouth.

"I could have fallen." Alma stood and brushed the dry grass and paint chips from her dress. "Broke my arm or worse."

Margaret made a wide-eyed face and clawed at the air, still laughing.

"What do you expect? It's my first time climbing from a roof." Alma locked her arms across her chest as Margaret continued to chuckle. "You do all kinds of funny things like . . . like holding your spoon wrong and wearing your boots on the opposite feet, and I don't laugh at you." Well, maybe she had—a little. Just to herself. That was quite different from laughing in someone's face. She turned to stomp away, but Margaret grabbed her hand. Despite her flushed cheeks and leaking eyes, her face held a look of contrition. She smiled, not a sneer or smirk, but a friendly smile. Alma found herself smiling too.

Hand in hand, they ran to the edge of the yard where the other girls had gathered. Strands of hair, freed from their long braids, fluttered around their faces in the night's breeze. When they reached the other girls, Alma noticed a lumpy pillowcase slung over Alice's shoulder. Bare feet peeked out from beneath the hem of her nightshirt. Before Alma could ask about the pillowcase's contents, Catherine bullied forward. "Yah thau·tú·ʌyakohlʌ túhne?"

Alma had no idea what the words meant, but she could tell from the rancor in Catherine's voice, from her leering eyes and flattened lips, that Alma's presence wasn't welcome.

"Shaa. Giganoondaago," Margaret said, followed by more indiscernible words.

"Listen, I think we should—" All four sets of eyes turned on Alma. The remaining words dried up in her throat.

Catherine put her hand out, palm toward the ground. She swung it quickly so the palm faced upward, then flipped it back again. "Tah! Né·ka²i·kʌ atwa²kánha tehanahalawʌlyehe²."

Alma looked back and forth between the two arguing Indians. She was not entirely sure they knew what the other was saying, but with unflinching eyes and set jaws, neither looked ready to back down. The knot in her stomach returned. She took a step back, but Margaret, who still had hold of her hand, pulled her forward. Margaret extended her other hand, palm out, two fingers pointing upward, then raised her hand until the tips of her fingers were as high as her head. "Nindaangwe."

Maybe Catherine didn't know the word, but she understood the gesture. Both girls were quiet for several moments. Then Alice lifted the silence. "Yukyaláhse², ʌwg·tú·ʌyakohlʌtú·ne² né·tsyatʌ·ló·."

"Khe·lé·ki²wah," Catherine said with a huff. She turned and stomped into the forest. Rose and Alice followed.

Margaret lifted her chin and smiled. Keeping hold of Alma's hand, she started into the black tangle of trees behind the other girls.

Little of the moon's meager light penetrated the woods. The leafless branches, like long, twisted claws, hovered over them, shuddering in the breeze. Alma opened her mouth, the words *let's turn back* poised on her tongue, but she stopped. Nothing of the spooky forest seemed to bother the other girls. They walked on with steady, almost beaming expressions, their footfalls quiet and graceful.

Alma plodded beside them, her feet snapping every felled branch, tripping over every exposed root, crunching through every drift of leaves. Catherine snickered at the noise. Rose and Alice shook with suppressed giggles, but Margaret only clutched her tighter.

The farther they went into the forest, the more Alma's skin bristled with misgivings. Maybe they'd better not run away after all. Nothing but barren trees surrounded them in all directions. The smell of rotting leaves hung in her nostrils.

A high-pitched shout cut through the quiet of the forest. Alma froze. It sounded like the voice of a boy, young like her and possibly in danger. Her eyes combed the darkness, her ears alert for any other sounds.

The Indian girls laughed at her startled expression.

Margaret tugged her onward in the direction of the noise. Alma's heart clamored, but her feet obeyed.

The cry came again, this time descending through a series of notes, more like a chant than a scream. Another voice joined with the first. Whoops and hollers cut in and out. A low, resonant sound pulsed behind the voices, steady and rhythmic.

Through the trees, Alma saw the glint of firelight. Dark figures danced in a circle around it. A sudden cold flooded her body and her hands trembled.

Night witches!

She'd read about such monsters in her fairytale picture books. Again her feet stalled.

Margaret squeezed her hand and smiled. Her teeth were brilliant in the moonlight, small and straight save for a gap between the two at front just breaking in. She and the others weren't scared. How bad could whatever awaited them be?

Alma shuffled forward, glued to Margaret's side. The forms around the fire took on shape and detail.

Not witches—Indian boys.

Ten of them clustered in a small clearing around the blaze. Some sat on fallen logs or leaned against nearby trees. The rest jumped and stomped, circling the fire in time with the song. Though they moved to the same tempo, each boy's dance was unique. Some crouched low to the ground, arms extended, step heavy. Others kicked up their knees, springing from one foot to the next. One boy brandished a long stick. Still another moved his hands through the air as if he were pulling back the string of a bow.

The girls were not running away after all. Relief more than disappointment lit Alma's heart. The fire, the dancing, the song all seemed so welcoming. She decided she'd not really meant to run away either.

Alma recognized a boy named Walter seated on the ground drumming on a hollow log. Frederick, the tallest and lankiest of the boys, sang out the strange tune. Harry spun and shuffled in the fire's glow, his eyes squeezed shut, his movements trancelike. She could not recall the other boys' names, but could picture where they sat in class. Like the girls, only the oldest had come.

Catherine, Rose, and Alice skipped into the clearing and sat beside the fire. The boys continued dancing and drumming, acknowledging the newcomers with little more than a nod. But when Alma emerged through the trees, close on the heels of Margaret, Frederick's high, clear voice fell silent. He stared wide-eyed in her direction, his mouth agape. The drumbeats died too. One dancer stopped. The rest, still lost in motion, slammed into him.

"Tāeh!" one of the boys said, jutting his chin out at her. "Awānaetonon!"

"Kauqui nahkma ne?" another asked.

A flurry of words Alma did not understand piled up from every direction. Anger flamed in the boys' faces. They closed in around her and Margaret, sneering, shouting, and throwing fiery gestures.

Alma clung to Margaret's arm. Both girls cowered and shuffled backward.

One of the boys hissed in Alma's direction. Another spit at her feet. The fight between Margaret and Catherine had been nothing compared to this.

Harry broke through the jumble. He held his hand out, palm forward, and brought it down sharply. "Bizaan." His voice was even and commanding. He stepped in front of them and faced the gang of boys. "Bizaan. Onzaam sa naa. Gaawiin da-zanagizisii."

Murmurs rose above his words. Someone stomped. Arms flew up, pointing toward the woods.

Harry stood his ground. "Nishiime." He pulled Alma forward, flush beside him.

From the back of the crowd Frederick nodded. "Nishiime." He made the same two-fingered gesture Margaret had signed earlier.

A few other boys also appeared to understand and backed away, but those who remained glowered in Alma's direction. Harry put his hand out in front of him, as if to keep them at bay. She could see the profile of his face, chin raised and jaw set, eyes steady.

"Friend," he said in slow, clear English.

"Friend," Margaret echoed, her accent thicker, but her voice just as pointed.

Friend. Alma couldn't stop the smile that spread across her lips. The boys' grave faces softened.

One by one, they shrugged and returned to the fire. Frederick took up song again.

Her heart retreated from her throat. She followed Margaret to the log where the other girls sat.

Harry perched beside them.

"Thank you," Alma said to him. "You speak very good English."

Harry smiled but shook his head. "No. No good English."

He turned his gaze toward the fire; Alma did the same. The logs crackled, and sparks drifted upward. Dust swirled around the dancers' feet. The biting night air no longer bothered her. Guilt and worry fled her mind. Her heart beat in time with the straight, steady rhythm of the makeshift drums.

A nudge drew her back to her companions on the log. Alice opened her pillowcase to reveal a stash of apples. She tossed one to Alma.

Undoubtedly, the apples had come from barrels in the cellar. Alma hesitated, the fruit inches from her mouth. Her father's voice filled her head. *And the Lord saith thou shalt not steal.*

This didn't feel like stealing, though. Hadn't the Indian Bureau sent the apples for them to eat? Why must they only eat them at someone else's behest? She took a bite. And another. Juice rolled down her chin and she wiped it away with the back of her hand.

When she finished, Alma tossed the core into the fire and turned to Harry. "What's the word for apple in your language?"

He drew his dark eyebrows together and shook his head.

"Apple." She pointed to the leftover fruit in Alice's pillowcase. "In Indian."

"Ah! Mishiimin."

"Mishiimin," she repeated.

A giggle came from Margaret's direction. Alma remembered several times when she'd seen Harry and Margaret whispering together in the hall or at the edge of the yard. She pointed back and forth between them. "Are you from the same tribe?"

Harry nodded. "Anishinaabe."

Alma puzzled at the word. Her father had made her learn the names of all the tribes sending children to Stover. Anishinaabe was not one of them.

"White man say Chippewa." He pointed to Margaret. "He my . . . sister."

Alma giggled. "*She's* my sister. That's what you say for girls."

Harry's cheeks colored slightly and he bobbed his head.

She looked back and forth between the siblings. They shared the same almond-shaped eyes, the same round faces. Margaret was taller, though Alma suspected Harry to be older. Both had the same plump shape. Her mother would call it pudgy. Alma thought it handsome.

"Anish . . ."

"Anishinaabe," Margaret prompted.

Alma frowned. Why would her father call Indian tribes by something other than their real name? She pointed to Rose. "Anishinaabe?"

Again Margaret giggled and shook her head.

Rose leaned forward. "Ho-chunk."

Margaret nodded in the direction of Alice and Catherine. "Naadawe."

"You say Oneida," Harry said.

"OnΛyoteˀa·ká·," Alice said, making sounds from her throat and nose Alma had never heard before.

Looking from one smiling face to the next, Alma's head swam. The Chippewa, who were really the Anishinaabe, called Alice's people Naadawe. White people called them Oneida, and they called themselves OnΛyoteˀa·ká·. Then something else occurred to her.

"What was your name before Harry?"

Confusion clouded his face. She pointed at herself. "Alma." Then directed her finger at him.

"Harry."

"No, Anishinaabe name."

His eyes brightened. "Askuwheteau. It mean . . . he looking over . . . he watch." He waved his hand over the camp.

"He who keeps watch?" Alma asked.

He nodded.

"Asku . . . wet . . . toe." She stumbled over the syllables. "I'll call you Asku for short."

Despite Asku's puzzled look at the sound of his new nickname, Alma took his silence for assent. She turned to Margaret. "What's your Indian name?"

The girl shook her head.

"Gigagwejimig ezhinikaazoyan," Asku said to his sister.

"Oonh! Minowe."

"Minowe." Finally a name Alma could easily pronounce. "What does it mean?"

Minowe blushed. She looked down and started to sing. Alma leaned closer. The words and tune were unfamiliar, but Minowe's voice was beautiful. The drumming slowed, and Frederick quieted his cry. The dancers stopped.

Minowe's voice filled the clearing, not loud, but bright and full. The melody had a slow, simple phrasing, like a lullaby. All the forest seemed to listen.

When the song ended, the boys whooped and hollered. Rose gave Minowe a one-armed hug. Alma clapped.

"Your name means to sing, then?"

"Yes, ma'am," Minowe said with the same straight face she used in class when addressing Miss Wells. They both laughed. "What Alma mean?"

Alma paused. Her name had come from a great-aunt whom she'd never met. If it had some meaning, she certainly did not know what it was. She looked down and toyed with the cuff of her sleeve. "It's just a name."

"We give you Anishinaabe name." Asku leaned forward, resting his chin in the palm of his hand. After a moment, he pointed to a cluster of aspen trees, their pale bark silver in the moonlight.

"Azaadiins," he said.

CHAPTER 9

Minnesota, 1906

The brougham stopped before a large, two-story building built of pale yellow stone. A clock tower topped its grand façade. Farther down the road, brick barracks lined the street. Soldiers marched around the manicured grounds. The seasoned boys, back from the Philippines or Cuba, moved with confidence and efficiency. The others, newly recruited from farms or immigrant slums, blundered through their steps. To Alma, all of them looked young.

The drilling, the uniforms, the regimented order reminded her of Stover. Little brown boys and girls marched to and fro in her memory, their breath a visible cloud in the slanting light of dawn. She shuddered and pushed the thought from her mind.

The cab agreed to wait. She climbed the stairs to the administrative headquarters. In the foyer, she stopped a soldier and asked for directions to the holding cells. The young man's eyes drifted downward from her face, then sprang back a moment later. His cheeks reddened when she repeated her question.

"Don't reckon I know what you're after, ma'am. Let me show you to the major's office."

In the presence of the major, the young soldier straightened. The blush disappeared from his cheeks. He hung back by the doorway, eyes fixed on the polished wood floor, offering nothing in the way of introductions. Alma sighed and approached the major's desk. "I'm here to visit one of your prisoners."

The man stood and smoothed his uniform. Bronze pins and embroidered insignia emblazoned the khaki-colored wool. "Prisoner?"

"Harry Muskrat. A Chippewa from the White Earth reservation."

"Ah, the Indian." He sat back down and motioned to the plain, straight-backed chair in front of his desk. "What's your business with him?"

Alma sank into the chair and took a moment to arrange her skirt. "He's an old acquaintance."

"Acquaintance?" Like the younger man before him, his eyes rolled down her silk traveling dress, then up to the wide-brim hat pinned atop her hair. He leaned back in his chair with a smirk. "Forgive me, ma'am, but you hardly seem the type to have history with the redskins. You from a church or one of those do-good ladies' societies? I assure you, ma'am, this heathen's soul is beyond saving."

"I am not from any church or women's organization, Major. As I said, I am a friend. Mr. Muskrat is a U.S. citizen. The army has no business holding him, let alone barring visitors."

"He killed a federal agent."

"Then it's a federal issue, not a military one. He's being tried in federal court, is he not?"

The major's face hardened. "What makes you think he's a citizen?"

"All Indians who claimed their land allotments and adopted civilized habits were granted citizenship."

"This redskin's no farmer. He's landless, a vagabond. A drunk. That ain't no civilized life."

Alma's fingers clenched around her corded purse strings. This man knew nothing of his prisoner. She'd heard that hardship had driven a few Indians to lease or sell the land they'd been given, but with his skills and intelligence, Asku was impervious to such hazards. "He's a citizen and I would like to see him."

Silence hung between them. The soldier behind her shifted his weight and the floorboards creaked. The major glared in his direction. "Sergeant Brooks, take Mrs. . . ."

"Mitchell."

"Mrs. Mitchell here to the ordnance depot. I believe her Indian's being kept in the round tower."

"Yes, sir," the sergeant said.

"Thank you." Alma rose and followed the sergeant from the room, hurrying to shut the door behind her before the major could change his mind.

They walked down a broad dirt lane bounded by barracks, warehouses, and artillery sheds on one side and open fields on the other. Trees stood at random intervals, casting a checkerboard of shade upon the lane.

The farther they walked, the fewer soldiers they passed. Alma shuffled to keep up. "Where are we going again?"

"The ordnance depot." He turned and winked at her. "That's officer speak for the old fort."

"Old fort? Why keep prisoners there?"

Sergeant Brooks shrugged. "Don't rustle up many Injuns these days. There was that uprising a few years back on the Leech Lake reservation, but don't think they arrested any of them bucks."

Alma fought back a scowl. "I see."

"In sixty-two they held hundreds of them Sioux Indians on that there island." He pointed to a lonely patch of land caught at the intersection of the Minnesota River and the Mississippi.

"How old *is* this old fort?"

"Built clear back in 1819," he said, walking with plumbed pride. His chest deflated when he saw Alma's frown. "Don't worry. It's been fixed up a bit since then."

"What happened to them?"

"Who?"

"The Sioux."

He shrugged. "A few of them was hanged, I think. Some starved. Nasty winter that year. Eventually thems that weren't no threat were sent back to their reservation."

Alma's feet slowed. The island's dense foliage hid whatever imprints the teepees and fire circles might have left, as if nature had swallowed all memory of these people. She paused a moment more, then rubbed the chill from her arms and hurried after the sergeant.

A round structure—like the ruins of a medieval castle—became visible at the end of the drive. Long, narrow musket holes cut through the stone walls, and battlements crowned the roof. "Is that the round tower?"

"Yup, there she is."

Inside, the round tower looked more like a storehouse than a defense post or prison. Crates and boxes lined the walls. Odd bits of furniture lay dust-covered and jumbled. Stairs leading to a second story circled around a great stone column in the center of the room.

At first, the room appeared vacant; then Alma heard a faint snoring. A soldier—so small and narrow through the shoulders Alma first thought him a child—sat on the bottom step, cradling his head atop his knees.

Sergeant Brooks's cheeks flashed crimson. "Attention!"

The tiny soldier sprang to his feet, swaying slightly and rubbing his bloodshot eyes. "Private Robinson, at your service."

Brooks glared at him. "This woman wants to see the prisoner."

"The Indian?"

"Yes, the Indian. How many prisoners ya got?"

"Well . . . um . . . just the one, sir."

"Very well, then. Where's the visitors' log?"

The private's eyes darted about the room. "He ain't had no visitors yet, sir . . . but I'm sure there's a log around here somewhere."

Alma waited while the men rummaged through piles of clutter. Her gaze drifted up the winding stairs and her heart bounded. She fidgeted with her hat and smoothed the wrinkles from her dress.

"Here it is, ma'am. Just sign here."

Alma took the fountain pen he offered and signed the blank sheet of rumpled paper. Halfway through, she frowned and crossed out the lettering. The black ink seeped and spread. "Forgive me, I, um . . ." She steadied her hand and started over. "Blanchard was my maiden name."

Neither of the soldiers appeared to care. The private grabbed a ring of keys and started up the stairs. "Just a warning, ma'am, he don't talk much. Might not know any English, come to think of it."

Alma smiled. "His English is impeccable."

The second floor was nearly bare. Narrow beams of light spilled in through the embrasures, illuminating a hidden army of dust in the air. Rusty metal bars cordoned off a quarter of the room. At one end of the cell lay an empty cot with a chamber pot tucked beneath. A tray of stale bread and mushy beans sat untouched upon a small table nearby. And there, in the corner, facing away from them in a simple, straight-backed chair, was Asku. Alma's breath hitched. Gray trousers and a dirty white shirt sagged against his bone-thin frame. A long black braid trailed down his back. Though he must have heard their footfalls, he did not turn around. She rushed to the iron bars. "Asku."

Little more than a whisper escaped her throat, but Asku turned around. She swallowed a gasp. The face of a stranger stared back at her. Deep lines cut his forehead and fanned from the corners of his eyes. His chapped skin looked several shades darker than she remembered. A dull expression hung from his face.

Then his eyes brightened, like dying embers coaxed back into flame. The boy she remembered shone in those eyes—curious, precocious, gentle. He rose from his chair, hastily buttoning his cuffs and wiping his trousers. "Azaadiins!"

Azaadiins. She'd almost forgotten the sound of the name. Her name. "Gigwiinawenimin, Asku." *I've missed you.*

"Gimiikawaadizi." He wrapped his hands around the bars just below hers. "How beautiful you look."

The private rattled his keys against the bars. "None of that funny Indian talk. I thought you said he speaks English."

Asku glowered at the guard. Gaunt as Asku was, he still towered above the private. "I do."

The small soldier puffed out his chest, but took a step backward. "Let's hear it, then."

Alma flashed the private her prettiest smile. "Might I have a chair to sit on while we talk?"

He looked around the empty room.

"I saw one downstairs," she said, batting her eyes for good measure. "Would you be so gallant as to fetch it for me?" He stalked toward the stairs, and she turned back to Asku. "Are they treating you all right? You're so thin. They haven't hurt you, have they?"

He stroked her gloved hand with his index finger. "No, Azaadiins. They have not mistreated me."

"I read about your case in the paper, my husband—"

"Turn, nishiime. Let me look at you."

Alma blushed. She stepped back from the bars and did a quick spin. "I came right from the train depot. I hope—"

"Time has not touched you. You're the same girl of my memory."

She reached into her purse and handed him a small package. "I brought you something."

He peeled away the paper and twine. *The Return of Sherlock Holmes.*"

"I know it isn't much. I hope you haven't read it."

His fingers trailed across the silk-wrapped cover, as if it were the soft skin of a lover. He opened the book, brought the pages to his nose, and inhaled. "Thank you."

Footsteps banged up the stairs. They both straightened. The private returned dragging a wooden stool. "Will this do, ma'am?"

"Yes, thank you."

Asku carried his chair to the edge of his cell and she joined him sitting, the folds of her skirt spilling around her down to the dirty floor. The rusty iron bars seemed to widen the inches between them.

"You're married now?"

"Yes, that's in part why I came. When I—"

"What's his name?"

"Stewart. Stewart Mitchell."

"How long have you been married?"

"Five years. He's a lawyer, you see, and—"

"Children?"

She looked down at her clasped hands and shook her head. "No."

"Nashke." He touched her hand through the bars. "You'd be a good mother."

Alma forced a smile even as her stomach knotted. Asku was wrong. She had nothing to offer a child. "My husband and I took the first train from Philadelphia when we learned—"

"Philadelphia. Minowe told me you left Stover after—" He stopped, and she was grateful. "A city of such culture suits you."

Alma rubbed her arms. The afternoon warmth seemed to falter, the light filtering in through the narrow, paneless windows becoming sickly. "I never needed fancy things. I could have been happy anywhere."

"But you're happy now."

"Yes."

He regarded her a moment, then frowned. "You never could lie well, Azaadiins."

"How can I be happy when you're imprisoned here?"

He started to withdraw his hand from the bar, but she grabbed it fiercely between her own. "Asku, I know you could not have killed that man. My husband and I are here to help. To get you set free."

Asku stiffened. The joy her visit had brought bled from his face. Even his voice lost its lightness. He got up and walked to the lone window within the cordons of his cell. "Those days in the classroom, in the wood shop, marching around the grounds . . . Did you ever stop and think what they were doing to us was wrong?"

Alma blinked. What did this have to do with the murdered Indian agent?

"To rob us of our homes, our families, our language, our way of life."

She shifted. The rickety stool creaked. "I . . . I guess I never thought on it."

"You never wondered"—he clasped his hands so tightly his knuckles cracked—"if perhaps the harm outweighed the good?"

"We were so young."

"That was the point. To blot out our inherent wickedness before the stain had a chance to set. Your father's very words."

"You know he meant well."

Asku turned. "How do you yet defend him?"

"I . . ." Alma felt a hand around her neck—her own hand—clutching at her collar, pressing into the soft flesh around her windpipe. How dare Asku say such things. "Nothing meant more to him than that school. Besides, what other choice was there? Imperfect means toward a perfect end."

He laughed a hollow laugh and gestured to his meager cell. "Is this the end of which you speak?"

"This is all a mistake, Asku!" Heat flamed up her ears. "That's why I'm here, to make this right."

"Some things cannot be made right."

"Not true." She stood and clenched the iron bars. Rust chipped off onto her gloves. "What happened to you? You were happy at Stover."

"That was not happiness. That was survival."

"Now who's lying?"

He shook his head. "If I were happy then, I was a fool. . . . Perhaps we both were."

Alma's jaw slackened.

"Thank you for your visit," he said without expression. "I do not want your husband's help."

"What are you talking about? They mean to hang you." She rattled the prison bars. "You're innocent! I can sort this out for you."

His eyes, the dark, foxlike eyes she loved, grew cold and dull. "I've had enough help from the white man." He looked past her and called for the guard. Footfalls sounded on the stairs, and he still did not look at her. "We're done here, Private. Please escort Mrs. Mitchell out."

"Asku, wait—"

"I wish you well, Mrs. Mitchell." He dragged his chair to the corner and sat down, angled away from her, still as death.

Her mouth went dry. She shuffled backward, unable to pry her gaze from the stranger in the tiny cell.

What had happened to her beloved friend?

CHAPTER 10

Wisconsin, 1881

Miss Wells strode down the aisle, her horsehair crinolette rasping against her cotton skirt, her heels like a hammer atop the wooden floor. She rapped her ruler on the edge of the desk Alma and Minowe now shared. "On your feet, Margaret. Let's hear your numbers."

The girl flinched and slowly rose to her feet. "One, two, dree, four, five . . . er . . ."

"Six," Alma whispered without looking up from her book.

"Six, seven, eight, nine, ten." Minowe sank back into her seat beside Alma the moment she finished speaking.

"Adequate, but not exemplary." Miss Wells's eyes flickered to Alma and narrowed. "Perhaps next time you can complete the recitation without Miss Alma's help."

Alma clamped her lips around a laugh. She glanced at Minowe and saw the same pent-up laughter building behind her cheeks.

"All right, class, pull out your slates. Write out numbers one through ten. Copy them five times before the end of the period."

Minowe picked up her chalk, and Alma turned back to her book. She knew Miss Wells would quiz her about the reading at the end of class, but her attention drifted from the book's pages to the windows.

A fresh powdering of snow had fallen during the night. She couldn't wait to don her overcoat and race outside. The Indian girls played a game with sticks and twine—*pupu'sikawe'win,* Minowe called it—no matter the weather. Now Alma played as well.

Of course, the snow had put an end to their nighttime excursions into the forest. Mr. Simms would undoubtedly notice footprints leading to and from the school.

After lunch, the boys marched outside for woodworking instruction with Mr. Simms while the girls cleared the tables and headed for the kitchen.

With her arms elbow-deep in a bowl of minced meat and breadcrumbs, Mrs. Simms divvied up the chores. Alice and Catherine washed the noontime dishes while the littlest girls dried. Others set to work peeling potatoes and churning butter.

Alma, Minowe, and Rose—whom Alma now called by her Hochunk name, Hįčoga—stood on stools at one end of the large, wood table in the center of the kitchen. A mound of dough towered before them, which they were to knead and shape into rolls.

Alma loved this time of day, no matter what her assigned task. As long as they did their work and kept their voices to a whisper, Mrs. Simms never yelled at them for talking and giggling.

With an apron tied about her waist and her hands dusted white with flour, Alma grabbed a handful of dough and pressed it down onto the table. She flattened and folded, flattened and folded, then formed a small ball and placed it into a large pan greased with lard. Her next one came out oblong and lumpy—more the shape of an animal than a roll. She laughed and nudged her friends.

"Look. A rabbit."

Minowe raised her eyebrows. Hįčoga shrugged.

Alma formed two long ears and a round tail. "See?" She hopped the sticky dough across the table.

Hįčoga giggled. "Wašjįgéga."

"Waabooz," Minowe said.

Alma repeated both words. It had taken her days to get the nasally *i* sound in Hįčoga's name right, to mimic the long vowels frequent in Minowe's words, but she loved learning, loved the game of piecing together the syllables and guessing at the meaning, loved that language—hers and theirs—was something they could share.

"Rabbit," the Indians said together, struggling, just as she did, with their pronunciation.

Minowe took her roll, shaped wings onto either side, and moved it through the air. "Bineshiinh."

"Wanįk," Hįčoga said.

"Bird!" Alma shouted, loud enough to catch a raised eyebrow from Mrs. Simms. "Sorry," she mumbled. Her friends laughed.

Hįčoga went next, creating a sticky blob neither Alma nor Minowe could guess at. She grabbed a new piece of dough and formed four legs and a round body. Then, after a quick glance in Mrs. Simms's direction, Hįčoga bared her teeth and growled. A bear! *Hųčga* in Ho-chunk. *Makwa* in *Anishinaabemowin*.

The game continued until only a few sticky streaks of dough remained where the giant mound had stood. Alma scraped what she could into a final ball, sculpting legs, a thick tail, and upturned snout—a wolf howling at the moon. She held it up for the girls to see.

Hįčoga scrunched her face, and Minowe poked at the now-sagging form. Alma readjusted the neck so the head once again turned upward and made a quiet howling noise.

Hįčoga clapped. "Šųkčąk!"

Alma echoed the Ho-chunk word, still stumbling over the nasally vowels.

They both turned to Minowe. She took the lump of dough from Alma's hand and studied it, then shook her head. Alma and Hįčoga howled together, faces raised toward the ceiling, lips drawn into an O.

"Ma'iig—" Minowe stopped mid-word and let the mushy figurine drop to the table.

"Are you girls speaking Indian?"

At the sound of Miss Wells's voice, Alma snapped to attention, dropping her face and clasping her sticky hands together.

"Need I remind you such speech is forbidden? Perhaps demerits or—"

"No," Alma said.

Miss Wells's eyes flared at the interruption. "Excuse me?"

Alma's knees knocked against the leg of the table. "We . . . um . . . we weren't speaking Indian. I was teaching them English." She nudged Minowe in the ribs. "Tell Miss Wells some of the words I taught you."

"Bird," Minowe said without looking up. "Rab . . . rab . . ."

"Rabbit," Hįčoga chimed in. "Pig, mouse."

"And those other—"

Mrs. Simms cut her off. "Can I fetch you something, Amelia?"

Irritation sparked in Miss Wells's eyes, but she fashioned a thin-lipped smile. "No, thank you. I just came to return my teacup." She placed her cup and saucer by the sink, then turned back to the girls. "Leave the teaching of English to me, Miss Alma."

That evening, Alma's father called her into his office. He sat behind a massive desk like the proud captain of a ship. Neat stacks of paper rested to one side. An inkwell and a worn prayer book sat on the other.

Even back in Philadelphia, she never ventured uninvited into her father's study. Yet almost every night he'd beckoned her in, sat her on his lap beside a warm fire, and read her stories from among his grand collection. Before they'd start, he'd let her choose a lemon drop or peppermint stick from the jar of bonbons kept high up on his bookshelf. The sweet flavor filled her mouth as his words had filled her ears.

Tonight, Alma bounded in and saw her mother seated in one of the two velvet armchairs opposite the desk. Her exuberance dwindled. This was not going to be one of those beloved reading nights.

She scooted into the free chair beside her mother and folded her hands in her lap. Her feet hung several inches above the floor, but she resisted the urge to swing them.

Her father adjusted his spectacles and looked down at her. "How are you taking to life here at Stover, Alma?"

"Fine, Papa."

"I know it's a great change from our life before. And these past months have been busy ones." His eyes flashed toward her mother. "Things will get easier."

"They'll be putting up the holly wreaths and mistletoe in the display windows of Wanamaker's soon." Her mother's voice ached and her gaze was distant. "If I had any say in the matter, we'd never have left Philadelphia." She sighed and massaged her head, her thin frame sinking back into the upholstery. "Such is a woman's fate."

"We both—"

"Get on with it, Francis. I have a headache."

The corners of his lips turned down, and he looked back to Alma. "Miss Wells tells me you're doing well with your studies."

Alma's body tensed at the mention of Miss Wells.

He continued. "But she says you involve yourself too much with the other students."

"I'm only trying to help."

"Thank you, kitten, but Miss Wells has a great deal of experience working with . . . um . . . uncivilized youth. She left her position at Carlisle to come help us found this school. She does not need your help."

Alma fought back a frown. "Yes, sir."

"I know we've placed you in a position of intimacy with these Indians. You study beside them, eat beside them, sleep beside them in the dormitory, but remember: You are not one of them." His hand found the prayer book on the desk and rested lightly upon it. "You are an example to them of goodness, of manners and civility."

"Can't I be their friend, too?"

Her mother and father answered at the same time—him with a nod, her mother with a sharp "no." Their gazes locked.

Alma squirmed on the sidelines.

"Their vile habits are bound to rub off," her mother said.

"It's those very habits that they're here to correct. Think of how they'll benefit from her company."

Her mother pointed a long manicured finger at her husband. "I'll not have you sacrifice our only child to this horrendous Indian experiment."

"They can be saved, Cora!" Her father's voice shook, his fingers clenched around the prayer book. "Saved from their own primitiveness, brought into the folds of productive society."

Alma sank down and slid back as far as she could in her chair.

"What will the people of La Crosse think when we have a daughter wearing buckskin rags and feathers in her hair?" her mother said.

"Come now, my dear, you're being overly dramatic."

"What about the doll incident? And you have not seen her running wild with them at recess, sticks in her hand like some barbarian huntress."

He raised an eyebrow in Alma's direction. She shrank down even farther into her chair. The fire crackled. Wind rattled through the leafless trees outside, kicking up the fallen snow and throwing it in swirls against the window.

Her father set down his spectacles and rubbed his eyes. "Games, Cora, they're just games. We'll teach them new games. American games."

Her mother huffed and turned away, staring off into the fire. Her voice came as a whisper. "Your self-righteous ideals will be the ruin of all of us."

"Cora—"

She waved him off with a flick of the wrist, as if dismissing a tiresome maid.

Her father's face fell. After a pause, he straightened and looked back at Alma. "You will be eight in a few weeks. I trust that's old enough to tell the difference between right and wrong. Our job here at Stover—and it is all of our jobs, even yours—is to teach these Indian children the ways of the Christian world. Yes, you may be their friend, but you must not join them if they fall back into the folly of their heathen ways. You must be a constant light. Do you understand?"

His words, like his gaze, lay heavy upon her. "Yes, sir. I do," she said. But she didn't—not really. What was so vile about their language? So barbarian about their games? What was so wrong about being Indian?

"Myself, your mother, Miss Wells, we cannot be around every moment of the day. If you see things—misbehaving, thievery, lapses into their tribal ways or language—you must tell me."

Alma bit her lip.

"Come here." He scooted back from his desk and patted his knee. Alma slid from her chair and climbed onto his lap. The smell of orange-blossom cologne and tobacco clung to the wool threads of his suit jacket and his neatly trimmed beard. She breathed in deeply, wishing to trap the scent forever in her lungs. "You're getting so big, kitten. Soon you won't fit on my lap at all."

"Yes, I will, Papa."

He squeezed her close, then drew back. "What we do here, Alma, it's for their own good. Will you be part of that?"

His blue eyes glowed in earnest. She thought about the sneaking out, the stolen apples, lying to Miss Wells that very afternoon. It hadn't seemed bad at the time, but here, seated on her father's lap, guilt clawed at her. She swung her legs and chewed the soft skin at the base of her nails. Finally, she nodded.

A smile fought its way onto her father's tired face. "Good girl." He set her down on the rug and reached for the jar of bonbons on the top shelf of the nearby bookcase. "One little treat, then off to bed."

"Can I have two? Please."

"All right, two."

He held up the glass lid, and Alma fished inside, her fingers brushing candy sticks and sugar drops, paper-wrapped taffies, molasses pulls, and caramel creams.

"You spoil her, Francis," her mother said, still looking at the fire.

With a long stick of peppermint in hand and a roll of taffy between her teeth, Alma traipsed through the dimly lit foyer and up to the dormitory.

The room was dark and quiet when she entered. Miss Wells had already made her rounds and extinguished the lamps. Alma laid the candy stick on her washstand and tugged off her boots and stockings. Her sticky fingers breezed through the long line of buttons at the front of her dress. She threw on her nightshirt and worked her hair free from its braid.

A chill stole through the thin cotton covering her skin. The curtains on the far wall billowed. She crept to the open window and heard her friends' whispers coming from outside on the roof. She hurried back to her bed and grabbed the peppermint stick—her friends had probably never tried candy before. They'd love sugary sweetness. She was just about to draw back the curtain when the echo of her father's words stopped her. Even if they weren't sneaking away, they weren't supposed to be out on the roof. And the whispers she heard were not in English.

Her chest tightened and she retreated from the window. She'd promised to be a good girl, a dutiful daughter, to report such misbehavior. Her feet shuffled back another step. She should go straightaway and tell her father. It was for the girls' own good.

Outside, the whispers cascaded into laughter—soft, quiet, free. Alma stopped. She felt stretched, like a fought-over toy that eventually breaks in two. Could her father be wrong? Surely not all the ways of the Indian were bad. And he did say they could be friends.

Wind ruffled the curtain again, carrying with it Minowe's songlike voice, Hįčoga's ever-present giggles. Alma glanced at the door behind her, allowing her father's words to roll once more through her mind before tucking them aside.

She tiptoed to the window and climbed out. Afternoon sunlight had melted the snow from the roof, but the frosty night wind bit her skin. Her friends sat a few steps off, pointing up at the black sky. Alma settled beside them and broke her candy stick into three pieces. Minowe drew her into the warmth of her thick quilt.

Hįčoga continued the story she'd been telling. She spoke Ho-chunk mostly, tossing in an occasional word of English. It didn't matter to Alma that she couldn't understand. She followed Hįčoga's hand as the Indian pointed at a cluster of stars that hung like shiny dewdrops in the night sky. The animation in Hįčoga's face, the feeling in her voice conveyed the story.

Minowe spoke next, gesturing to a group of stars Alma knew to be the Big Dipper. "Niswi giiyosewininiwag . . ."

Alma remembered *niswi,* three, from a few days before. Judging from Minowe's arms, one outstretched, the other tucked in close beside her ear like she held a bow, the following word was hunters.

Alma listened to Minowe's voice and stared up into the blackness, imagining the three hunters wending their way through the sky.

". . . makwa . . ." Minowe said amid a string of other words.

Alma leaned her head against her friend's shoulder, thinking of sticky fingers and dough animals. *Makwa.* Bear.

How could Papa fault her? The words and stories may be different, but the stars remained the same.

CHAPTER 11

Minnesota, 1906

Stewart had already unpacked and dressed for dinner when Alma arrived at their suite in the Ryan Hotel. She hurried out of her traveling clothes and grabbed the least wrinkled evening gown from her trunk.

Who was that man in the tiny prison cell? Not the sweet, courageous boy she remembered. Not the bright, intrepid youth who'd set out from Stover bound for greatness. She threw the gown over her head. The world darkened. Trapped inside the tight, slick fabric, she battled the folds of taffeta silk, searching for the neck hole and sleeve openings. The more her limbs fought, the more bunched and constricting the fabric became. For scant reason, tears sprang in her eyes. She couldn't even liberate a hand to wipe them away. Asku had been so happy to see her. At first. She'd believed time had left their friendship intact. How quickly that belief had changed.

At last she burst free, the navy silk falling into place around her. After rushing through her buttons, she snatched a brooch from her travel case and brought it to the lace yoke. Her fingers slipped. The pin gouged her thumb. Tarnation!

"Are you ready, darling? The dining hall shall close soon."

Stewart's voice from the parlor made her jump. She sucked the blood from her thumb and secured the brooch's clasp. The white lace was unbesmirched, but her finger throbbed. "Coming."

The Ryan's grand dining hall sat just off the lobby with a bank of windows overlooking the bustling street. Glass sconces lined the walls and a great chandelier with dozens of glowing bulbs hung from the ceiling.

Despite the late hour, the room swelled with patrons, all dressed for show. The familiar spectacle felt strangely foreign. The newly polished silverware glinting in the light, the melody of clanking china, the smell of sauce soubise wafting from the kitchen—this was her life. How different it might have been, though. She usually guarded against such comparisons, tucked that vision of another life deep within her bones. But seeing Asku brought it all back into relief.

She and Stewart followed the maître d'hôtel to a table at the far wall situated with some privacy. Her head continued to buzz as the waiter came and Stewart ordered dinner. Hands concealed in her lap, she picked at her nail beds, ignoring the pain and echo of her mother's reproving voice.

How would Stewart take the news that Asku had declined their help? He'd taken leave from work, traveled with her all this way—and for what?

"How was your meeting with your friend?" he asked.

Here was her chance to reveal the bitter news. The words readied themselves on the tip of her tongue. Just tell him. Instead she said, "You first. How'd things fare with Harry's lawyer?"

Stewart straightened, taking on that sedulous persona he donned at the office or the marbled rooms of City Hall. She'd always enjoyed watching him work—the steady rise and fall of his chest, the way his eyes flickered across the pages of some dossier or legal brief, the occasional scowl or thin-lipped smile, the way he groped for his pen and fell into a flurry of writing when struck with an idea. However unglamorous all that patent and antitrust business might be, he believed strongly in what he did. Once he took on a project, he never erred or faltered.

"First, the good news." Stewart sipped his iced tea. "Mr. Gates is amiable to me appearing pro hac vice on the case. We submitted the motion this afternoon. I'm confident the judge will sign off."

"And the bad?"

He glanced at the nearby tables and lowered his voice. "The case was mismanaged from the start. The original police report listed several witnesses, but only one—another employee of the agency—was ever interviewed. There was never any investigation into the relationship between Mr. Muskrat and the victim, and his link to the murder weapon is tenuous at best."

"I knew he was innocent."

"Perhaps, but proving that won't be easy. Onus probandi hardly matters in a case like this."

"Onus what?"

"Sorry, darling—burden of proof. Usually that lies on the prosecution, but, well, with Mr. Muskrat being Indian, I fear that burden rests upon us."

The waiter appeared with their soup. Stewart thanked him and resumed. "Every man in that jury will come to the trial already biased. At best, they'll think him a wild curiosity. At worst, a blood-hungry savage."

"But that's not true at all. If they knew how smart and kind and—" She stopped, realizing her voice had begun to tremble.

"That's what we must show them."

"How?"

"Mr. Muskrat will have to take the stand, speak about his time at Stover and Brown. We'll get him a new suit. A haircut, a shoe shine . . ."

Alma lost track of her husband's words. Around them, most dinner guests were sipping their cordials and scraping the last of the mousse from their dessert cups. She felt the target of their errant gazes, the topic of their whispers, as if everyone knew her secret and was waiting for her to interject, waiting for her to admit Asku wanted no part in their attempts to save him. She picked up her spoon and cut a lazy pattern through her bowl. Hunger hadn't touched her in days. She ate now for pretense and to spare Stewart worry, but the terrapin soup sat like a stone in her stomach.

"It's an Algonquin word, terrapin," she said over him.

Stewart gave her a quizzical look, then glanced down at his bowl.

If only they were back home in their quiet parlor, or out for a stroll along Chestnut Street, so happy, as they had been, in each other's company that the rest of the world fell away.

"Are you done, ma'am?"

Alma nodded up at the waiter and he whisked away her bowl. He had a maestro's grace, but a farmer's rough hands. How long until that part of him, the toil of his youth, faded completely? Perhaps it never would. She thought of Asku's hands—cracked and calloused but nevertheless clean and manicured, as if he, too, were torn between competing identities. *Robbed,* he'd called it. But how could he say that? Her own hand found its way to her lips and she bit down hard on skin aside her nail. Like their adroit waiter, Asku had been given a chance at a better life. Where had it gone wrong? "I don't know if Harry will agree to testify."

"What? If he's afraid of speaking before crowds, I can coach—"

"That's not the reason. He's quite good in front of crowds, actually." She smiled, remembering how clear and eloquent Asku could be, but her lips quickly slackened. "He doesn't want our help."

Stewart's brow furrowed. His hazel eyes blinked. "I don't understand. Why ever not?"

"He didn't say." A little lie, but how could she tell Stewart that Asku no longer trusted the white man? "He wouldn't speak of the murder at all. Turned me out before I could persuade him of our intentions."

"He does realize the severity of the charges?"

"Yes."

Stewart pinched the bridge of his nose. "Mr. Gates said he'd been uncooperative, but I thought with you here . . . I thought you were friends."

"We were. We—" Damn her eyes. Alma fished inside her handbag for her hankie and blotted an errant tear. "We are."

"We can't do this without his cooperation."

"The truth is on our side. Isn't that enough?"

The quiet that followed made Alma's skin itch. The waiter returned with their main course, and the silence continued. Stewart cut his roast duck into small, precise squares. He took one bite, chewed for several seconds, then put his knife and fork down, as if he could stomach no more. "Tomorrow I'll book our return passage to Philadelphia."

"We mustn't leave. Not yet."

"Without Mr. Muskrat's assent, there's nothing more we can do."

Leave Asku to die? A sudden hysteria gripped her. Asku may not want their help, but he needed it nonetheless. "What about the insufficiencies in the investigation? You said yourself there were witnesses yet to be interviewed. And the murder weapon."

"The trial date is set. There isn't time to—"

"I can speak on Harry's behalf."

"One testimony is hardly enough to sway a jury."

Alma's skin flushed with desperation. It was all she could do to keep her voice below a shriek. "How can you countenance this injustice? Harry is an innocent man. You might as well hang the noose yourself."

Stewart balled up his napkin and threw it atop his uneaten duck. "Enough of this, Alma. Who is this man to you?"

"I told you. A friend, a classmate."

"Were you lovers?"

"No," Alma said, louder than she intended.

"You haven't kept in contact?"

"What? You think I've been carrying on an affair with a man a thousand miles away? Before today I had not seen or spoken to Harry in over fifteen years. If I'd passed him on the street I wouldn't have even recognized him, he's so altered."

"Then why all this?"

"I . . ." How to put into words what she hardly understood herself? "He was my father's favorite pupil."

"Alma, you hated your father."

Not always. Not before that night beside the elder tree. "And the brother of my closest friend."

"Another friend of whom you never speak."

"Must you attack me like you do those men in the courtroom? Like I'm some criminal?"

"Darling, that's not what I meant." He reached for her hand, but she pulled away.

The waiter returned and cleared their plates. When he asked if they wanted dessert, they both shook their heads tersely and he left them to their silence. Stewart batted crumbs from the heavily starched tablecloth. Alma crossed her arms over her chest and gnawed again at the skin alongside her nails. How dare he riddle her with such questions. A friend on trial for murder—wasn't that explanation enough? Never mind that there was more. Much more. She peeked up at him and felt her heart snag. "I'm sorry."

Stewart said nothing but reached across the table and drew her hand from her mouth. Though his face remained hardened, he stroked her ragged cuticles with the pad of his thumb.

"It's a dreadful habit, I know. Mother used to rub soap around my nails to stop me. It worked. For a while."

Another silence.

"I may have been estranged from my father, but I never lost faith in his principles. Everything he stood for is on trial here as well. If we fail, if Harry dies, my whole life has been . . . a lie."

"Your life is with me, back in Philadelphia. It has nothing to do with this anymore."

A knot formed at the base of her throat. If only that were true.

Stewart sighed. "We'll need to gather more evidence, letters of witness that speak to his character." He pushed back from the table. "We'll take the train tomorrow to La Crosse."

Alma froze. "Why?"

"There must be someone there who'll write on his behalf. Your mother, an old teacher?"

Miss Wells was headmistress now at Stover, or so Alma had heard. And she'd always been fond of Harry. But to go back, to see the town and school again. Alma swallowed. "Wouldn't it be easier to send a wire?"

"And risk a delayed response? We can be there and back in a single day." Renewed determination animated Stewart's face. "After we obtain character letters, I'll ask the judge for a continuance to delay the trial a few days. I need more time to sort through all the evidence."

Alma bit her lip. She could end this still. One word and they'd pack their trunks and return home tomorrow. No visit to Stover. No more stirring of ghosts. Life would return to normal. But Asku would hang.

She tugged at the constricting lace about her neck. "Tomorrow, to La Crosse, then."

CHAPTER 12

Wisconsin, 1888

Alma filed out of the church behind her parents. Her father stopped beside Reverend Thomas at the base of the stairs in the shadow of the building's tall spire and struck up a conversation about the morning's Scripture. Alma nodded at the reverend and slipped away through the crowd.

The morning sun painted the churchyard golden, but its rays offered only a memory of summer's warmth. Orange and red leaves dappled the surrounding chokeberry hedge and overhanging trees. Children skipped across the yard chanting rhymes or playing tag. Adults milled about in small clusters, the men speaking of rains up north and the river's rising water, the women of quilting bees and bake sales. Nearly fifteen now, Alma wandered listless among them. The children's games seemed silly, while the adults' conversation droned tedious and dull. Finally, she spotted Lily Steele across the yard and hurried over. They linked arms and strode together at an easy pace, catching up on the week's worth of happenings.

"You're coming to the piano program tomorrow, aren't you?" Lily asked.

"I don't know if I can."

They passed a group of boys, and Lily gave a gentle toss of the head. Her blond ringlets caught the sunlight as they moved, drawing attention to her lovely face and long white neck. It was a practiced move to be sure, but judging by the boys' ogling gazes, it worked to good effect. "You simply must come. Everyone's going."

Everyone, of course, meant La Crosse's fashionable set.

"Including my brother."

Alma looked down to hide the rush of warmth invading her cheeks. Edward Steele. For months she'd sneaked glances at him over the worn pages of her prayer book. To see him twice in so many days, perhaps even to sit beside him . . . but then . . . "Tomorrow's the start of the new term and I—"

"The Indians are coming back? So soon?"

"Six weeks seemed a terribly long time to me."

"I would have welcomed the break." Her doll-like lips puckered.

"Yes, it's just, it's such a big schoolhouse, you see. And to be there by oneself—"

"Father says it's unnatural, teaching the Indians. Living with them like equals. You really should stay with us and attend school here in La Crosse. Mother just adores you. We could practice our lessons together, and pin each other's hair, and make . . ."

The picture Lily painted was a lovely one. Music concerts and soirées. Alma's Indian friends weren't acquainted with the latest hairstyles or dresses. Only Asku read and wrote at her grade level and could help her with her arithmetic and essays. And yet, when she was with her friends, none of that mattered. And she had missed them. Dreadfully.

She spied Asku through the crowd. He alone had forgone going home and instead spent the time apprenticing with a local farmer. His skin had deepened to the color of rosewood from his weeks in the sun. His clothes were just as neat, his hair just as tidy, his eyes clear and beaming. He waved boisterously, his entire arm flapping through the air. She raised her hand to return his wave, but after a sidelong glance at Lily, cringed back, offering little more than a nod. Asku's smile faltered. Though the sight of it squeezed her heart, she waited until the Steeles' carriage pulled away before searching for him again.

However suitably dressed, the lone Indian in a sea of white faces was easy to spot. He stood beside Mr. Coleman, the farmer with whom he'd apprenticed, and his wife. Their two small children hung about Asku's feet, tugging his shirtsleeves and hugging his legs.

"Harry's been such a help around the farm this summer," Mrs. Coleman said when Alma approached. "Your father does good work there at Stover."

"Thank you," Alma said.

Mr. Coleman clapped a hand on Asku's shoulder. "I never thought I'd welcome a red man into my home."

Alma watched Asku's jaw clench and his eyes narrow. The movements were slight, subtle, little more than an aberration. When he spoke, his voice rang light and steady. "Thank you for the opportunity."

Instead of waiting for her father to finish his conversation with the reverend and ready the carriage, Alma and Asku decided to walk. She whispered this to her father, who distractedly waved his assent.

Much of the church crowd had already dispersed. The dusty street leading from the city lay nearly empty. Asku walked a pace apart, his duffle slung across his back. To talk to him, Alma had to crane her neck and speak over her shoulder. "Sorry about before. Not waving, I mean."

"It's all right."

"It's not that I'm embarrassed of our friendship. Only I . . ."

"Boonendan," he said. *Forget it.* "I understand." But his step still seemed weighted, the soles of his boots never quite clearing the ground.

"Bet I can beat you to the tracks," she said.

Asku looked up and at long last grinned.

They broke off running at the same time, laughter rising between their brisk inhales. After a few strides, Asku pulled ahead. Alma hitched her skirt above her ankles and dashed behind him. With each breath, her lungs fought the rigid stays of her corset. Her boot heels caught in the road's every rut and divot. Dust swelled in Asku's wake, stinging her eyes and scratching her nostrils. They had begun the year nearly the same height, but over the months he'd grown at least half a head taller. The soft fullness of his frame had melted away into long, corded muscle.

"You dawdler! Come on," he said, disappearing behind a bend.

Alma scowled and pressed onward.

Several twists in the road later, Asku came back into view. He stood where the road crossed the railroad tracks at the far edge of town, brushing the dust from his clothes with an ear-to-ear grin. Despite the stitch in her side, Alma sprinted the last stretch. When she reached her friend, she stopped and bent forward, wrapping her arms around her waist and panting.

"Not fair," she said when at last she could speak. "You're not wearing ten pounds of silk."

"No, but I was carrying this." He tossed her his duffle.

Alma staggered back beneath the bag's weight. "How many sets of clothes do you have in here?"

"It's books." He took back the bag and slung it over his shoulder. "Your father let me borrow a few before I left."

"How many is a few?"

Asku chuckled. "Ambe." *Let's go.*

They skirted the eastern edge of town following the railroad tracks that wended northward. With arms outstretched for balance, they shuffled side by side atop the iron rails, or leapt from tie to tie to see who could jump the farthest. The blue-gray waters of the Mississippi winked at them from the far western horizon. At State Street they headed east, fields of windrowed hay flanking them on either side, then cut diagonally between a break in the bluffs on a narrow wagon road.

The sheer faces of craggy rock gave way to rolling hills overlain with trees. With the sun directly above them, they stopped beside a small stream to rest. Asku unwrapped a wedge of cornbread and handed a piece to Alma. She sat on a flattened boulder at the edge of the water and devoured the bread in three bites.

"Hungry?"

Embarrassed, Alma straightened and brushed the crumbs from her skirt. She tossed her head, hoping for the same graceful effect Lily had achieved, but succeeded only in wrenching her neck and entangling her hair. Hopefully, Asku hadn't noticed. "Are you glad you stayed the summer with the Colemans? I mean, instead of going home?"

He shrugged.

"Do you miss it, the reservation?"

"I miss my family. The sound of drum circle and my grandfather's stories . . ." He seemed to lose himself amid the memories, his eyes going uncharacteristically blank, the rise and fall of his chest slowing. A moment later he blinked, squared his shoulders, and said as if by rote, "This is better. The way of the future for my people."

A gust of wind whipped by, rustling the trees and sending a shock of orange and yellow foliage showering down around them. Alma laughed, if just to lighten the mood, and stood, shaking the leaves from the folds of her skirt.

Asku moved beside her, their faces only inches apart. He smiled and plucked a leaf from her hair. He held it out between them, twirling its stem between his fingers, his brown eyes locked with hers.

Alma's throat went dry, as if a chunk of cornbread had lodged there and would not go down. A strange electricity hummed in her core—at once both pleasurable and disquieting. Part of her ached to lean in closer, to touch his hand, his cheek, his lips. Would the heady sensation surge or diminish? After a moment's contemplation, she took a step back. Asku was like a brother to her, after all. With forced levity she plucked the leaf from his hand and declared, "Wiigwaas," recognizing the jagged edge of the tear-shaped birch leaf.

Asku looked down, the corners of his mouth dropping slightly, and nodded.

Before coming to Wisconsin, Alma had known little about the varying types of trees. Aside from Fairmount Park, Philadelphia had few trees to speak of and she saw them all the same. But her Indian friends called each type of tree a different name—*mitigwaabaak, aninaatig, wiigwaas*—and taught her to identify the shaggy bark of the hickory, sweet sap of the sugar maple, and saw-toothed leaves of the white birch. Azaadiins, the name Asku had given her their first year together at Stover, meant "little aspen."

She dropped the leaf in the stream, watched it sail away atop the glassy water toward the Mississippi, and then turned back to Asku. The short brim of his cap cast a shadow over his downturned face, but she could still read the somberness in his expression.

Half an hour later, they rounded the final bend. The thick fringe of trees cleared, and the school's brick façade appeared before them. A wrought-iron arch rose above the rutted road where the browning lawn butted up to the tree line. Block letters crowned the arch: STOVER SCHOOL FOR INDIANS. Alma passed beneath, but Asku hesitated. He had the wary look of a fox again, his eyes sweeping the full length of the arch.

"Father commissioned it at the start of summer," she said. "Eventually, he wants to put a matching fence around the entire grounds."

"To keep the Indian in or the white onlookers out?"

Alma shrugged. "Both, I guess."

Asku ran his hand down the side of the arch and nodded. "Minwaabaminaagwad," he said, and stepped through. "It looks good."

They walked in silence down the remaining drive. Aside from the fresh coat of white paint gleaming from the pillars, the scene reminded her of the first day she had ever met an Indian.

Mrs. Simms clucked around a long table heaped with food and pitchers of lemonade. Miss Wells strode around the house carrying a tidy stack of uniforms.

"Five new pupils this year," Alma said. "Another Anishinaabe. One from Oneida and three Menominees."

"Soon we'll run out of space."

"Father's already talking about adding new buildings."

A call from Mrs. Simms cut short their conversation. "Harry, dear, come help me move this table out of the sunlight. The butter's melting and dribbling all over the linen."

Asku set his duffle at the base of the steps and jogged over to Mrs. Simms while Alma went inside to change out of her church clothes.

These past weeks, when the creaking wood floors of Stover were largely silent, Alma had slept in the small bedroom across from her parents' room at the opposite end of the hall from the girls' dormitory. This morning she had awakened early, taken her black school dresses from the carved armoire in the corner of her temporary bedroom, and moved them back to their rightful place in the simple chest resting at the foot of her dormitory bed.

Though she had drawn back the drapes and flung open the window before leaving for church, the dormitory still smelled musty. In the golden afternoon light the empty room begged for life, for rumpled bed covers and furniture set askew, for laughter and whispers and pattering bare feet.

Alma hurried through the buttons trailing down the bodice of her gown and threw open the lid of her bedside chest. The inside was empty. She glanced at the washstand. Her silver comb and mirror were gone as well. Holding the front of her dress closed, she leaned out the window.

"Mother!"

"What's happened to your Sunday dress? The hem is caked in mud!"

Her mother's voice behind her made her start, and she whirled around. "I—ah—"

"Your father should never have let you walk back from town alone."

"I wasn't alone; Harry was with me."

Her mother's eyes bulged. "You're far too old to be gallivanting about with young men, Indian or not."

Alma swept the folds of her soggy skirt behind her in a futile attempt to conceal the full damage of her afternoon romp.

"Don't stand there by the window in a state of undress. Go change. And be sure to bring your skirt to Mrs. Simms forthwith for cleaning."

"I can't find my uniform. I moved it here this morning, but my trunk's empty."

"You'll be staying in your own room this year."

"What? No!"

Her mother's expression hardened. "Like it or not, you're a young lady now, Alma. It's not proper for you to be living like a common boarder among these Indians."

"What about being an example?"

"You can do that from a distance."

"I promise, Mother, I won't go walking alone anymore. I'll behave like a lady. Please, I'll be so lonely in my own room."

"You've become too familiar with these savages."

"They're not savages. They're my friends."

Her mother's expression turned rueful. She cupped her hands over Alma's cheeks. "I know this pains you, dear, but it's high time you cultivate more respectable friends—friends equal to your worth and breeding. Like Miss Lily Steele. She's a fine young lady. And no doubt able to keep her skirts above the mud."

Alma sulked past her mother and down the hallway to her new prison of a room. She had plenty of "respectable" friends. Why did it suddenly matter if she had Indian friends, too? She cast off her muddied dress and donned her uniform. That word Lily had used—*unnatural*—came to her mind. Was it true? She closed her eyes tightly and imagined something wonderful happening—her father bringing home a litter of kittens or a brand-new pair of ice skates. It wasn't Lily she'd run and tell, but Minowe and Hičoga. And now, sleeping by herself in this awful room, she'd miss out on their late-night stories, the funny faces they made when Miss Wells turned her back during morning inspection, the secrets whispered through the darkness in their unique blend of Indian and English.

The sound of approaching wagons rattled her window. Alma's spirits buoyed at the sight of her friends. Natural or not, she didn't care. She bounded down the stairs and out to greet them.

Minowe leapt from the back of the first wagon. Though they'd been apart less than two months, her friend looked different. Her soft form had filled out, her hips wide, her chest round and full beneath her blouse. Her bronze face had thinned, drawing attention to her lovely, wide cheekbones and darkly lashed eyes.

Alma felt a tickle of envy. "Gimiikawaadizi," she said, trying not to let it show in her voice. "How pretty you look." A tight hug and the feeling left her.

They found Hičoga and all exchanged quick accounts of their weeks apart. Then they walked arm in arm toward the picnic. When Alma explained her exile from the dormitory, her friends immediately offered suggestions on how she could escape to join them on the roof or at their secret stomp dances in the forest. Maybe she wouldn't miss too much after all.

Out of the corner of her eye, she saw two boys—no older than six—hanging back from the crowd gathered around the picnic spread. Judging by their shaggy hair, bright clothes inlaid with ribbons, beaded moccasins, and wide, fearful eyes, they were among this year's new enrollees.

She left her friends and walked toward the boys. Crouching before them, she offered each a hand.

"Pōsōh," she said, greeting them in Menominee. It was just a guess, but since that was the only tribe to send more than one new student this year, it seemed like a good one. Before she could finish her introduction, a shadow fell over her. An older boy she didn't recognize stood above her. Thick black hair brushed his shoulders. He wore a red shirt—the same vivid color as a nearby maple—and navy brocade vest. A beaded belt cinched his waist. From his neck hung a necklace of alternating beads and quills. He put his hands on the younger boys' shoulders and pulled them back.

"Kēcīskiw," he said to them. *Enemy.*

Alma stood, wincing at the word. The newcomer's dark walnut-colored eyes narrowed into slits. Her father rarely accepted new students above the age of ten. Slower to learn and harder to train, he said. But this boy was at least her age, probably older.

Alma felt small beneath his stare. Her fledgling smile garnered only a deeper scowl.

He steered the younger boys away, giving Alma a wide berth, as if her skin seeped poison. Stunned, she watched them go, his condemnation haunting her ears.

CHAPTER 13

Wisconsin, 1906

The short carriage ride from the train station to her mother's residence stirred in Alma a faint nausea. Sweat dampened the velvet lining of her hat. La Crosse, though yet familiar, had altered much in the past fifteen years. Pavers now lined the sidewalk. A drugstore and soda fountain replaced the chandlery. Half a dozen more church spires pierced the horizon. But the saddlery remained. And Mrs. Westin's dress shop. Even the Wallis Carriage Company still stood, though its windows were cracked and the storefront sign faded.

Alma closed her eyes and fought back the rising bile.

Upon arrival, a maid led her to her mother's parlor. Eyelet lace shrouded the windows. The sun sneaked through, but only in winks and fits. Rosewood and lilac perfumed the air. As a girl, she'd loved to creep into her parents' bedroom and sit at her mother's vanity. She'd dip her fingers in the various jars of cream, pat her face with powder, and sniff the glass vials of fragrant oil. Looking into the vanity mirror, she'd imagine herself a grown woman—beautiful and elegant as her mother, wearing the same floral perfume. Now the scent only added to her queasiness.

A familiar settee rested in the corner. Alma sat down and clasped her hands to keep from fidgeting. Countless times she'd sat upon this very settee, Minowe and Hičoga beside her, their heads bent over their needlework, trading whispers and laughter. The seat was harder now than she remembered and new upholstery covered the cushion.

Its cherrywood legs and armrests gleamed with polish as they never had at Stover.

Alma looked up at the sound of footfalls. Time had spared her mother the worst of its ravages. Eyes just as blue, skin just as fair, she glided into the room with the same graceful step Alma recalled from childhood. She appraised Alma from the doorway, her face like the china figurines atop the mantel, frozen and dispassionate.

"Where's your husband?"

No niceties, then. No warm hello. No tearful embrace. Alma hadn't expected such a welcome, wouldn't have known what do with such tender familiarity, but she felt its absence nonetheless. "He sends his regards."

In truth, Stewart had insisted upon coming, had fretted so over her traveling alone, but she'd convinced him he needed to work on the continuance motion with Mr. Gates. She couldn't let him see her like this, so frazzled and exposed.

Her mother sank into a nearby armchair. "I'd hoped to meet him, this man who forgives all sins. Or didn't you tell him?"

Alma's jaw clenched. "I am not here to talk about my husband. I need a favor."

"Fifteen years and she comes begging favors." Her mother said this with a snicker, addressing no one but the stale, overly perfumed air.

Alma struggled to keep rein of her tongue. "I trust you've heard about Harry. My husband is helping with his case. We need you to write a letter on his behalf, a testimony of character. Have you paper and pen?"

"Surely you can spare a moment for pleasantries. Tea?" Before Alma could respond, her mother continued. "Something stronger, I should think."

She poured two copitas of sherry and returned to her chair.

Alma hesitated. It was hardly one o'clock. But her mother drank half the glass with her first sip. "You remind me of your father. Always trying to help these people no matter what they do."

Was that a compliment? Alma didn't think so. Even if it were, the comparison sat uneasy upon her. There was little remembrance of him here in this house: none of his books or mementoes, no smell of tobacco or pomade, his blue cap and saber missing above the mantel.

Alma's heart ached at their absence. She swallowed a mouthful of sherry to fortify herself. Another for good measure. Yet even as she set her copita down on the side table her hand trembled. "I'm nothing like him."

Her mother shrugged. "You certainly don't get it from me."

"Does that mean you won't write the letter?"

"It broke him, you know." There was a pity she'd never heard before in her mother's voice. A sadness unfettered by her usual contempt. "He put on his suit and his glasses and sat in that musty old office every day until he died. More Indians came and went. But he was never the same."

The warmth of the alcohol in her stomach faded. "Mother, please, I'm here to talk about Harry."

The woman stood and poured herself another drink. "Made the local paper three days running, this murder business. In truth, I was surprised I even remembered him—so alike they are, and after all these years. He always seemed so . . . mild to me."

"He was. And smart, and mannerly. You commented on it often."

Again her mother shrugged.

"He's innocent."

"What does your husband think of all this? Traveling such a distance to defend a stranger."

"He's happy to do it. He wants to ensure justice."

The smirk on her mother's face made Alma feel like a child again, caught fibbing about broken chinaware or torn stockings. "He loves me."

Why then the timidity in her voice?

"Hmm." Drink in hand, her mother crossed to the window and drew back a corner of the curtain. Light spilled in around her—so much so that Alma had to squint. Her mother looked out unperturbed. "The foolish things we do for love . . . I know you think I was cold back then, cruel even, but I was just preparing you for life's tragedies. I'm sure you see that now."

Alma opened her mouth but found her tongue too heavy for words. Was she better prepared, as her mother said? Would life have crushed her otherwise? She didn't feel strong or resilient, but she was here, wasn't she? And would carry on to Stover and wherever else she might have to go to prove Asku innocent.

At last, her mother let go of the curtain. "I'll write this letter for you, Alma, but don't ruin what you have in search of what you've lost." She threw back the last of her sherry. "Trust me, that's no way to live."

With the sun still high in the sky, Alma passed beneath the familiar arch with its wrought-iron lettering: STOVER SCHOOL FOR INDIANS. Buildings of every shape and sort crowded the once-open and rustic grounds. The forest had been beaten back, and what lawn remained was cut to haunting precision. More than her mother's graying hair, more than La Crosse's expanded Main Street, Stover's transformation shook her. She felt transparent, ungrounded, like her memories had no anchor and would flit away into oblivion.

"How many students attend school here?" she asked the young boy in uniform who met her in the drive.

"One hundred and sixty-three, ma'am," he said in very precise English. He pointed out the separate boys' and girls' dormitory buildings, a mess hall, laundry, and gymnasium. The old schoolhouse still stood, though according to her guide, only as an administrative building and staff quarters. She watched the boy as he led her there: his stiff, mirthless walk; his serious demeanor. He seemed a man of forty, not a boy of ten. Had they been so staid and formal when she was a girl here? Her memories were of laughter and games and running.

And yet, there was something of Asku in this boy. His tidy appearance, his inquisitive eyes.

"What's your name?"

"Benjamin Franklin Redtail, ma'am."

Alma smiled. "What tribe do you come from?"

"I'm an American, ma'am. Uncle Sam is my father. The United States is my tribe."

She bent over and looked him in the eye. "Yes, but before that?"

He paused a moment, glancing between her and the faded brick schoolhouse. His hands wiggled and tugged at his cuffs. "Ho-chunk."

"Hąhó, then."

His eyes went wide and he ducked his head down like a turtle pulling into its shell.

With effort, she smiled again. "I'm sorry. I'm not trying to get you in trouble."

He nodded and started up the stairs to the schoolhouse entrance. Asku's words came back to her, ringing like tinnitus in her ears. *Did you ever stop and think what they were doing was wrong?* Now, as before, she struggled for an answer. If assimilation had failed even him, how could there be hope for this boy? She took a deep breath and mounted the steps. No. It may have failed others, but not Asku. Freeing him would prove that.

The old house, with its polished floorboards, broad foyer, and double-wide staircase, revived a feeling of circumspection. Her chin lifted and back straightened as if a stack of books rested atop her head. Her feet whispered over the rug as if her mother were listening. Benjamin Franklin Redtail straightened, too, his face grave, his little hands no longer twitching.

"I can find my way from here," she said, and headed alone to her father's old office. It was hard not to think of him as she'd seen him last, standing in the doorway, his face ragged, his boots caked in dried mud. The tenderness and nostalgia she had felt for him at her mother's quickly died.

The door to the office was open, but Miss Wells was not inside. The same oak desk sat in the center, surrounded by the same varnished bookshelves she remembered from childhood. Yet the space seemed more spartan than it had in her father's time. No fire in the hearth. No candy jar tucked between books on the shelf. The walls were bare save for sixteen photographs—each in a simple brass frame—hanging in a grid upon the far wall.

Her eye caught on the first photo, and the breath froze in her lungs. She crossed the room in three swift steps and pressed a gloved hand against the glass. Her fingers caressed the outline of each figure, her memories giving them life and color. Asku in the center, shoulders back and head high. Alice and Catherine holding hands to the side. Frederick, barely able to suppress a grin. And there at the edge, hair tousled, not quiet in line with the others—

Tears blurred the image, but she could not look away. Her fingers pressed more firmly as if a thin pane of glass were all that separated them.

"Such nice photos, are they not?"

Alma startled and spun around, furtively wiping her eyes. Miss Wells stood before her. Alma's pulse hitched and the blood crept from her limbs, as if she were a girl again awaiting reprimand. "Miss Wells," she said with forced levity. "Pleasure to see you again."

"Likewise." Miss Wells crossed the room and thrust out her hand just as Alma began to curtsy.

Flustered, Alma rose and shook hands. Her old teacher's grip was firm and brief. Blue veins showed through her thinning skin. She turned to the wall of photographs. "A wonderful chronology of the school's success."

Alma swallowed. "Yes."

Miss Wells straightened the picture Alma had left askew. "And Harry, one of the brightest boys I ever taught." She paused, examining each of the other faces in the photo. When her eyes lit upon the last figure, her mouth pursed and the lines about her forehead deepened.

Alma braced for whatever snide comment the woman might utter. But when Miss Wells turned around, her eyes flashed with pity. A moment later, it was gone, the stony woman Alma remembered returned.

"I need a letter for Harry, for the trial, one that speaks to all the good qualities he fostered here."

Miss Wells crossed to her desk and opened the top drawer. "I thought someone would come." She glanced at Alma, then back to the tidy stacks of paper within the drawer. "Though I didn't think it would be you."

"You'll write it, then?"

"I've already prepared such a letter."

"You have?" Thank God. Each passing moment here cut a fresh wound.

"Of course. I hate to think what it would do to the school's reputation if Harry's convicted."

Alma flinched. Was that the reasoning behind her ready aid? Surely she still cared for Asku, believed him innocent. The woman's cool, businesslike expression unsettled Alma. Miss Wells had devoted her entire life to saving the Indians. But had she ever truly cared for Asku, for any of them?

Besides, the school had survived worse scandals.

"Ah, here it is." Instead of handing the letter to Alma, she slipped it in her pocket. "Would you like to see the grounds?"

"I . . . um . . . Benjamin pointed out a few things. And I've a train to catch at five."

"Only a brief tour, then." She marched from the room before Alma could protest.

They left the old schoolhouse and crossed the yard. Alma's step faltered as they passed the wood shop. It was silent now, though the blare of machinery and drum of hammers echoed from her memory.

"We use the old shop for storage now," Miss Wells said. "And see our lovely little bandstand." She pointed to a gleaming white platform with a hexagonal roof.

It hurt her eyes to look at it. Hadn't the archery target once stood there, nestled amid the trees? She could still see the faded bull's-eye, still smell the pinesap, still feel the snowflakes melting upon her cheeks.

"Are you coming, Mrs. Mitchell?"

Alma startled. That name sounded so foreign in this place. She tore her gaze from the bandstand and followed Miss Wells toward a large, boxy structure.

"This is our new classroom building," the woman said, pride evident in her voice. "We've come a long way since our provincial beginnings."

The interior was divided into four classrooms, each with several rows of desks and a large blackboard at the front. The Indian children kept to their work—reading, arithmetic, writing, and penmanship. The youngest ones, sequestered in a classroom of their own, chirped back simple phrases at the teacher. They were tiny, these children. Their legs dangled beneath the desks' tops, feet far above the ground.

"They're so young," Alma said.

"No younger than when you were a student."

Could that be? It all looked so different from here on the outside.

"It's better to get them at this age. They're more moldable."

Alma frowned. Her father had said the same thing, hadn't he? Asku had reminded her as much. Funny, when she'd heard the words through a child's ears, they hadn't seemed so self-righteous. Now they made her shudder.

A final glance around the room and she noticed the ruler resting on the edge of the teacher's desk. Her heart sped reflexively and her hands burrowed into her skirts. Many teachers struck their pupils, she reminded herself, at white schools and Indian alike. But for such trivial offenses? For not speaking English? For choosing the wrong name from the blackboard?

"You look troubled," Miss Wells said.

They were back outside now in the blinding sunlight. Alma blinked and shielded her eyes. "No, it's just . . ." She gestured about the yard. "Is this really what's best for them?"

"They certainly cannot live as they once did. Godless. Landless. For better or worse, Mrs. Mitchell, that time is gone."

"Yes, but—"

"They're clothed, they're fed, they're learning skills to help themselves prosper. Have you a better solution than that?" After a pause, Miss Wells pulled the sealed letter from her skirt pocket and handed it to Alma. "It's people who fail the system, not the other way around. You'd do well to remember that."

CHAPTER 14

Wisconsin, 1888

Great Father Cleveland's portrait had replaced that of President Arthur above the blackboard. The varnish on the desks had begun to wear, and the black lacquer on their iron legs peel. That air of confusion and fear, so palpable to Alma that first year, had ceded to the listless ease of routine. March, sit, stand, recite. At times, her Indian classmates still resisted, rebelled, but in quiet, secret ways perfected over the years.

Today, being the first day of the new term, however, the first day after the Indians' return from their first visit home in seven years, the mood of the room felt more spirited. Voices rose above a whisper, conversations ran on until Miss Wells's ruler smacked against the blackboard. She grouped the returning students according to aptitude and set them to quiet study.

Alma sat in the back of the classroom next to Asku. *Robinson's Textbook of Progressive Practical Arithmetic* lay open between them. In a matter of minutes, he had read the chapter introduction and moved on to the problem sets, tidy rows of equations covering his slate.

Alma's slate, however, remained blank. Her eyes drifted over the numbers in the textbook, but the scene at the front of the room pulled at her attention. The five Indians new to Stover stood in line before the blackboard. The boy from yesterday, the one who had branded her enemy, towered above the others. His hair, now shorn short like the other boys, had a tousled, wild look. While the little ones wavered from foot to foot, fidgeting with the brass buttons on their uniforms or wringing their hands, he stood unperturbed, his gaze moseying about the room.

One of the five, an Oneida girl Alma guessed to be about seven, spoke a few words of broken English. At Miss Wells's instruction, she stepped to the board and chose the name Bertha, then went to sit with a group of second-year students copying lines from a grammar book.

The teacher moved on to the next in line, one of the small Menominee boys. When she asked his age, he drew his lip between his teeth and shook his head. "No English."

She placed him and the other two smaller boys in a cluster of seats at the front of the room after directing them to the board to select their new names. Only the tall one remained.

"Do you speak any English, young man?" she asked.

Nothing in his posture changed—no pull of the lip, no turn of the head—nothing to indicate he understood or even heard her words.

"I know the nuns run a school on your reservation. Am I to believe a boy your age speaks no English?"

Still no response.

Miss Wells pursed her lips. "Have you a Christian name?"

Silence.

Her nostrils flared around a deep inhale, giving her face the look of a rabid dog. Only upon exhale did her features recover their stoic disposition. "Very well, I shall choose one for you." She glanced at the board and scratched a name down in her ledger. "Henceforth, you'll be known as George. Now take a seat with the other first years."

He stood defiant for another second. Miss Wells's fingers wrapped around her ruler, the tendons beneath her pallid skin taut as piano strings.

Alma leaned forward, elbows atop her book, the tip of her braid swinging over her inkwell. Perhaps the boy truly did not understand. Miss Wells pointed again at an empty desk. George yawned, then sauntered over to his assigned place.

"Are you ready to turn the page?"

Alma jumped at Asku's voice. "I . . . umm . . . give me a minute."

She forced her eyes back to the textbook and grabbed her chalk. Numbers swam like fish in her head, slippery and evasive as she tried to focus.

"Imbecile," Asku whispered.

"I'm going as fast as I can, Mr. Top-of-the-Class."

He laughed. "Not you. The new boy."

"Maybe he doesn't understand English." She glanced sideways at her friend. His eyes narrowed, trained on the new boy slouched among the younger kids several rows in front. It was a look she'd not seen him wear before—one of annoyance and contempt. He shook his head but said nothing more.

Alma reeled in her attention and finished the problem sets on the first page with Asku waiting beside her. His eyes turned to her and softened, lingering on her face. Even with her focus trained on the page, she could feel their intensity. Her corset, still new and uncomfortable, grew impossibly tight. When she squirmed and straightened he looked away, but a small part of her missed his attention.

She'd just flipped to the next page when a shriek sounded from the kitchen. Giggles erupted around the room, but a stern look from Miss Wells quickly silenced them. Another scream rang out, followed by the thunder of clanking pots.

The teacher huffed and rose from her desk. "Miss Blanchard, attend to the class while I check on the welfare of Mrs. Simms. I venture a squirrel has found its way into the pantry again."

Alma frowned and stood. The moment Miss Wells's skirts swept across the doorjamb, Minowe's hand shot up. "I have a question, Miss Blanchard." She drew out the final words with mock emphasis.

"Me too, Miss Blanchard," Frederick said across the room. As chuckles rose from all around, Alma's cheeks colored.

"Me three, teacher Blanchard," Hįčoga added.

Alma picked up the ruler that lay at the edge of Miss Wells's desk and smacked it against the palm of her hand with exaggerated force. "Sīsīsī," she said. "Here, here. Hush now."

More laughter.

The ruckus died and the students returned to their work. At the front of the class, the new students struggled over their slates, trying to copy their new names. Alma knelt beside one of the little Menominee boys, newly christened John. He held the chalk in a death grip between the tips of all five fingers, pressing so hard atop his slate the stick broke in two. Alma picked up one of the splintered pieces and demonstrated the correct grip.

"Nice and easy," she said, writing out the letters of his name. "You don't have to press so hard."

John took hold of the chalk, imitating Alma's grip, and drew a squiggly *j* onto his slate.

Alma patted his arm. "Paēckeqtam. Good."

As she stood up and dusted off her skirt, she noticed George's dark eyes trailing her movements, his jaw set in a scowl. He lounged in his chair like a dandy at a horse race, legs extended full length beneath the desk and crossed at the ankles, arms folded across his chest.

"Do you need help?" she asked, crossing to his desk. Miss Wells had written *George* in tidy block letters across the top of his slate. The space below, where he was to copy out his name, remained blank.

"It's easy. Let me show you." She reached for his chalk, but he nudged it away with his elbow. The thin white stick rolled off his desk onto the floor. Alma frowned and bent to pick it up.

His boot slammed down, just missing her fingers, grinding the chalk into pale dust against the floor.

She looked up, mouth agape. Surely he'd not meant to—He met her stare with a smug grin, his dark eyes sinister and challenging. A string of indecorous words flew to mind, but the clap of Miss Wells's footsteps in the hallway silenced her.

"Nothing but a furry vermin, as I suspected," Miss Wells said, entering the classroom. Her gaze settled on Alma. "Is everything all right?"

Alma rose, straightened her shoulders, and smoothed back a ringlet of hair that had fallen across her hot face. She glanced at George. His hateful expression made her shudder. Part of her wanted to tell and watch him work off demerits, but then, that's what he expected of her, to stand in solidarity with the frightful Miss Wells. "George accidentally dropped his chalk," she said in a forced, singsong voice. "I'm afraid it shattered. He'll need a new piece."

Back at her desk, Alma tried to catch up with Asku, but her thoughts refused taming. How dare this new boy dislike her so! They'd only just met yesterday. And she'd been nothing but nice to him and the other newcomers. Asku was right; the boy was an imbecile. Yet she couldn't stop staring.

Supplied with a fresh piece of chalk, George continued his stoic protest. After instructing him once again on his assignment, Miss Wells grew impatient. Her cheeks flamed with color; her words became clipped.

"Insolence in this classroom will not be tolerated." She grabbed George by his suit collar and pulled him to his feet. Alma saw his hands clench into fists, then slowly release. Though he was nearly the same size as the teacher, he let her tug him to the back of the room. She kicked his feet together and forced his arms out like a scarecrow. To Alma's surprise, he did not resist.

"There. Now you're to remain in this position until the end of class."

George smirked.

"Oh, one more thing." Miss Wells turned to Alice, who sat three desks over from Alma and Asku in the back row. "Alice, please retrieve two prayer missals from the bookshelf."

Alice hesitated, but a withering look from Miss Wells brought her to her feet. She delivered the heavy volumes to Miss Wells, flashing George an apologetic grimace before returning to her seat.

Miss Wells thrust a book into each of George's hands. Sinew bulged at his wrists. His outstretched arms teetered. Alma braced herself, expecting any moment for him to throw the books loudly to the ground. But he did not.

"Faces forward, students," Miss Wells said. "Back to your studies."

Fifty-four grim faces turned forward. Chalk murmured against slate. Textbook pages fluttered. Behind her, Alma could hear George's breath growing labored as the minutes ticked by. Halfway through her assignment, she stole a look back in his direction. Sweat beaded on his forehead. His skin flushed deep red; his outstretched arms trembled. His expression, however, remained composed, his stare fixed and determined.

Alma shook her head and turned back to her equations. Eventually he would break, if not today, then tomorrow, and be better for it in the end.

CHAPTER 15

"Beautiful building, isn't it?" Asku's lawyer, Mr. Gates, hopped up the steps to hold the door.

Alma looked up. She had to hold her hat in place and tilt her head all the way back to see the crest of the red-tile roof five stories above.

Mr. Gates smiled, displaying a neat row of small, yellowed teeth. "Brand new, you know. Laid the last stone only four years ago."

Stewart tarried street side, neck craned, mouth slightly agape. In his upturned eyes, Alma saw that glimmer of boyish glee. It infected her, pulled at the corners of her lips, just as it had the first time she saw it, early in their courtship when he'd invited her to the symphony. They never made it to the concert hall, waylaid by every building of architectural merit along the way. Structure, proportion, angulation—these words had meant nothing to Alma, nor held any particular interest. But the tenor of his voice was as pleasing as any orchestra, and his face, more animated than yet she'd seen, stirred in her a common delight.

It'd been so long since she'd felt anything like it. The emotion lightened her step like a strong wine. "Perhaps you should have been an engineer or architect," she remarked between Broad Street Station and the Academy of the Fine Arts building.

He smiled, his cheeks lit with a touch of embarrassment. "In fact, patent law is much like the two. . . ." And from there went on to explain with similar rapture the care and invention it required. At some point he took her hand and held it in the crook of his arm—she didn't notice precisely when, only that it had felt right resting there.

Now, watching him at the curb, she fought to hold that shared delight, but it slipped from her grasp as quickly as it had come.

"Impressive!" Stewart said, finally mounting the steps toward the entrance.

"Impressive," she echoed. On another day, she might have meant it. But today, still frazzled from her trip to Stover and with so much riding on the judge's decision, the massive granite building with its towers and turrets, dormer windows and gables made her feel small and anxious. She took a deep breath and passed the threshold.

Inside, the Federal Courts Building opened up into a grand interior courtyard. Sunlight streamed in through skylights more than a hundred feet above, splashing against the marble walls and columns. People of all standings bustled by—men sporting finely tailored suits, youths in grease-stained uniforms, families dressed in homespun cotton.

Mr. Gates gestured to the glass and mahogany elevators at the far end of the hall. "Are you coming, then?"

Alma reached back and found Stewart's hand. He stroked her fingers, then tucked them into the bend of his arm. She could tell his initial frustration over Asku's declination had faded along with the deep-set exhaustion around his eyes. In its place, a quiet but steadfast resolution had settled.

On the third floor, they waited for nearly an hour on one of the polished wooden benches in the hallway outside of the judge's chambers. Mr. Gates filled the time with a constant stream of banter. Stewart offered the occasional *ah* and *how interesting,* while Alma managed only a distracted nod. She adjusted and readjusted her hat, straightened her gloves, smoothed her green rep day suit, and tried not to think of Asku in his tiny cell. His coldness gnawed at her. Had she been wrong this entire time? Had Stover really done more harm than good? She thought of little Benjamin Franklin Redtail, of all the children she'd seen on her return visit. They were well fed, well clothed, learning useful skills and trades. But had any of them smiled, just once, during her stay?

A clerk greeted them without apology for the wait and showed them to the judge's chambers. A dusty yellow globe on a brass chain lit the windowless room. Disheveled bookcases stood against the wall. The smell of smoke and mildew choked the air.

Behind a broad oak desk sat Judge Baum. "You'd better have a good reason for this disruption. I've piss-little time between hearings," he said without looking up, then bit off a large chunk of ham sandwich. A cigar smoldered in the ashtray beside him. His shirtsleeves were rolled up to his elbows, and his jacket hung on the back of his chair.

The clerk cleared his throat.

Judge Baum's eyes widened when he glanced up. He swallowed his sandwich, wiped his hands on a handkerchief, and stood. "Madame."

"Your Honor, this is my wife," Stewart said.

Alma dredged up her best smile and bowed. "Thank you for seeing us."

The judge did not return the smile. "Get her a chair, Fitzsimmons," he barked to his clerk as he yanked down his shirtsleeves and shrugged on his jacket. Then he turned his scowl on the two lawyers. "Well?"

Mr. Gates's gaze fell to the floor while Stewart adjusted his necktie and stepped forward. "Pardon the intrusion, Your Honor, we're here regarding the case of Mr. Muskrat."

"I know who the devil—forgive me, ma'am—I know who you represent, Mr. Mitchell. How many Philadelphia lawyers do you think I have running around here?"

"We've come to ask for a brief continuance."

"How brief?"

"Three weeks."

"What in tarnation for?" The judge winced apologetically at Alma, then turned back to her husband. "Mr. Muskrat won't even open his mouth to assert his own innocence." He took a long pull on his cigar and blew a cloud of smoke in Stewart's direction. "He's all but hanged himself."

Alma's hands curled around the armrests, her nails digging into the wood. This man cared nothing of the trial, felt no stir of gravity or urgency.

Stewart waved away the smoke. "Seven people were claimed to have seen Mr. Muskrat within the hours surrounding Agent

Andrews's murder, but only one was interviewed." Her husband withdrew a sheet of paper from his bag. "Furthermore, numerous complaints had been filed against Mr. Andrews over the years. I'd like a subpoena to review the agency's records and investigate these complaints."

"Just what are you hoping to get out of this, Mr. Mitchell?"

Stewart glanced back at Alma. "Proof of his innocence. Reasonable suspicion that someone other than Mr. Muskrat might have committed the crime."

The judge took the paper from Stewart's hand with a dark chuckle.

"Your Honor, this is life or death for this man. Due diligence is required."

"And how do you expect to uncover this proof? Travel up to the red man's reservation and play detective?"

"I just want to interview the other witnesses."

"Look at these names, Mr. Mitchell. Mis-sah-bay, Oge-mah-we-guan . . . these are backwoods, teepee-building savages. You speak Indian? Or were you expecting to converse with them in your Harvard English?"

Stewart's face hardened and the tips of his ears grew red. "Princeton, Your Honor, and I do not—"

"Nindanishinaabem," Alma said, standing. The men turned and stared. "I speak Chippewa. A little, anyway."

The cigar dropped from the judge's lips. His face pinched with suspicion. "That sounded like more than a little to me."

Alma glanced at Stewart. He rattled his head and blinked several times, his dark pupils crowding out the hazel of his eyes. She should have told him beforehand. But when? How does such a thing come up when you keep your past so hidden? Before she could telegraph her apology, he looked away and cleared his throat. "My wife was . . . er . . . formerly acquainted with the defendant. She wanted to speak on behalf of his character. We have letters from her mother and Mr. Muskrat's former teacher as well—all attesting to his good nature."

The judge leaned back in his chair and pursed his lips. He looked first at Alma and then turned his glare on her husband. "I'm not inclined toward leeway in my court, Mr. Mitchell. I'd just as soon have this whole business done and behind us. There's little you could produce that would sway a jury toward a verdict of innocence. People want to feel safe in their beds at night, not afraid a wild Indian is going to come and kill them while they sleep." Alma opened her mouth to protest, but the judge waved her off. "I know, most of that business was done half a century ago. They're nothing now but a beaten and dying race. Still, the law must be upheld." He handed the witness list back to Stewart, nodded for the clerk to open the door, and picked up his sandwich.

Anger flared inside her. This was not justice. She crossed the small chamber and gripped the edge of the judge's desk. "Have you even looked at the case?"

"I beg your pardon?"

"It doesn't make sense. Mr. Muskrat is not the blanket Indian you described. He's smart, educated. He wouldn't kill someone in plain sight, then carelessly discard the murder weapon."

Stewart touched her arm. "Alma, dear—"

Judge Baum sat forward, rolling his cigar between his thumb and forefinger, an air of amusement lighting his expression. "It's all right. Go on, Mrs. Mitchell. What do you think happened?"

"That he was set up. That the reservation police picked up the first Indian they saw just to close the case."

The judge snickered.

"I know Harry Muskrat. He's a good man. And I've dealt with hayseed sheriffs before, too. I know what they're capable of." She leaned forward over his desk, ignoring the stench of smoke and cured meat. "You speak of upholding the law, yet you'd sooner hang a man than entertain questions about his guilt."

"You're the only one who questions his guilt," the judge said, but the snide quality to his voice was gone. "How did you come to know this man?"

She let go his desk and straightened. "My father ran a government boarding school for Indians."

"I take it Mr. Muskrat was a student there?"

"For nine years."

"And he did well?"

"He was the brightest student ever to attend the school. He graduated valedictorian and went on to study at Brown. And he was well liked, beyond academics. Faculty, students, even the townsfolk were fond of him. It's all here." She handed over the letters.

"How did he end up back on the reservation?"

"I don't know . . . we lost touch, I'm afraid."

"I see." The judge unsealed the letters and glanced over their contents. Alma watched him read—the back and forth of his eyes, the grind of his teeth as he chewed on the butt of his cigar. Surely this would sway him. His nose twitched. An eyebrow rose. Alma held her breath.

"His history is very interesting, Mrs. Mitchell, but nothing in these letters precludes him murdering that agent. I've seen plenty of good, intelligent people commit crimes."

"We just need a little more time!" She winced at the shrillness of her voice. "Your Honor."

"Have you ever been to a reservation? Rough places."

"Like you said, the Indian Wars were done a long time ago. They're farmers now. I'm sure we'll be fine."

The judge sat back in his chair, silent. Alma could hear the surge of her pulse in her ears. Again he looked between her and Stewart, and for a brief moment, as their eyes met, his gaze softened. He sucked a long drag off his cigar and blew the smoke off to the side.

"All right. I'll give you ten days, Mr. Mitchell. After that, no more blasted motions or delays."

"Thank you, Your Honor," Stewart said.

Alma smiled, a true smile. "Thank you."

The judge snorted and returned to his lunch. Between mouthfuls of sandwich he said, "Temper your zeal, Mrs. Mitchell. You might not like what you find up there."

CHAPTER 16

Wisconsin, 1888

"You took plenty time," Hįčoga said when Alma arrived at the rendezvous point behind the large maple at the edge of the yard. "We were about to leave without you."

"I had to wait for my parents to sleep," she said, panting. "Father only just snuffed out his candle." Her less-than-graceful climb down from her bedroom window had left her palms scratched and the pads of her feet stinging.

Minowe snickered. "Next time we leave you for the Windigo."

"I'm not afraid," Alma lied as they started into the woods. Though she could easily find the secret clearing, she would hate to brave the dark forest without them. Tales of this man-eating monster were popular around their bonfires, and she often thought she heard his cry lurking in the wind. But tonight, Alma's anxiety ran deeper even than the Windigo. She, Minowe, and Hįčoga did everything together. To be left behind, to trudge along without them and arrive alone, that would hurt her more than any spirit could.

Moonlight cut through the canopy and revealed a teasing twinkle in Minowe's eyes. Hįčoga flashed her dependable grin. Alma's unease retreated and she pulled her friends closer. The promise of winter hung in the chilly air. The musty smell of fallen leaves swirled about them.

"What were you all giggling about during study hour?" Alma asked. "I heard you clear from the parlor."

Hįčoga's smile broadened. "Someone put chalk dust inside

Aní·tas's ledger book. When she opened it, the dust spilled out all on her dress."

Alma stifled a laugh. Walter had christened Miss Wells Aní·tas— the Oneida word for *skunk*—several years back when she'd given him thirty demerits for *accidentally* lighting fire to a textbook. The name stuck. "She must have been furious. Who did it?"

"No one owned to it," Minowe said. "We all of us got ten demerits."

A frown swept Alma's face. George. "When are you going to stop defending that boy?"

Hįčoga shrugged. Minowe stared forward with a moony expression, as if she'd hardly heard Alma's words.

"Father ought to send him home. He's an utter dunce."

"No," Minowe said. "He's much brave."

"Brave?"

"Weyi," Hįčoga agreed.

Alma shook her head but let the subject drop.

A low, steady rhythm sounded in the distance. With each step, the drumbeat swelled, accompanied by familiar, high-pitched chanting. Alma's heartbeat quickened, matching the lively pace. Firelight broke through the thickness of trees, and dancing shadows stretched along the ground like spokes on a giant wheel. Dust clouds bloomed as feet struck the earth in time with the song.

When they entered the clearing, Alma squinted in the bonfire's sudden brightness. Smoke perfumed the air. Chatter buzzed over the song and the crackle of the fire. The tone was light, the words an easy tapestry of Indian and English. Back at the schoolhouse, the watchful gaze of adults followed them everywhere—from morning bed inspection to evening prayer. Here in the forest they mingled freely, not as schoolmates but as siblings, cousins, and friends.

A steady stream of dancers stomped and shuffled around the fire. Others lounged at the periphery. A Ho-chunk boy had sneaked a flute from home and played along with the drums. Dried gourds rattled in time with the music.

Minowe pulled Alma into the circle of dancers. They shuffled side by side, bouncing with the song's rhythm. Minowe moved like an eagle, her arms spread wide, her quilt stretched like wings, its colored pattern feathers fluttering through the air. She kicked up her knees, twirling as she moved.

Alma hitched her nightshirt above her ankles and followed after her friend, losing herself in the song. Here her dance was free, unscripted, nothing like the measured movements of the waltz or polka her mother insisted she learn. Her skin, numb from walking through the frigid forest, began to thaw. She threw her head back and drank in the full moon's brilliant glow.

Without warning, a hand circled around her arm and yanked her from the thick of dancers.

"You don't belong here," George said, loud enough for the entire camp to hear.

What? Alma rattled her head. He spoke English?

Silence spread through the clearing. The singers dropped out one by one. The drummers' hands slowed. The dancers' feet deadened. All faces turned toward her and George. Minowe, hitherto beside her, shuffled back into the crowd.

Alma pulled free from his grasp. "Who are you to say who may attend?"

"You are no Indian." He turned to the crowd. "Who invited this wayāpeskiwāet mūhkomāniahkiw, this paleface?"

The fire answered with a pop and crackle, a nearby owl with a lonely hoot. Her friends, however, said nothing.

"I have as much right to be here as you." Her voice sounded thin, but she held George's stare, stilling her trembling hands into fists.

"Get out of here. Awānaetonon! Go home to your white man's school."

Alma opened her mouth in reply, but her voice found no hold. Tears threatened in her eyes. She cast a desperate gaze at Minowe. Her friend's eyes darted to the ground, her silence as biting as a hundred hateful words. Never before had Alma felt so alone.

Then a voice rose from the gaggle of onlookers. "I invited her." Asku pushed forward, moving between her and George. "She stays."

George closed the distance, bringing his face only inches from Asku's. They stood equal in height, Asku slim but solid, George broad and gangly. "She'll betray us. The white man always does."

"She is Azaadiins—friend and sister to us. Our secrets are her secrets."

"Wanātesew," George said, turning to the crowd with a sneer. "He is foolish, the white man's pet."

A few chuckles rose from the silence. Alma's heart skittered in her chest.

"And you live in the past," Asku said. "I learn the ways of the white man so the Anishinaabe have a future. You are gagiibiingwe— blind—if you do not see it."

The crowd grew quiet. A few heads bobbed in agreement, but otherwise no one moved. The air seemed thick, electric, too dense to breathe. George glared at Asku, but finally stepped back. He turned to Alma and held out a closed fist thumb-side down. Firelight glinted in his narrowed eyes. He extended his fingers and said, "Yōm wāpahtah!"

She'd never heard the phrase before, but judging by his scowl and the gasps of the other Menominees, it was hardly a friendly remark or gesture. Her knees softened, but she refused her feet a backward step.

George turned and stalked toward Frederick and a group of older boys a few paces off.

A solitary drum broke the uncomfortable silence, joined quickly by another. The flute and rattles caught the beat, breathing life back into the singers and dancers. Asku took hold of Alma's hand and led her to a nearby log.

"Thanks for standing up for me."

"Always, Azaadiins."

The scuffle had made a briar of her insides. She wrapped her free arm around her stomach, nursing a faint nausea. Could what George said be true? Was she the outsider, the interloper he claimed her to be? Save for those few weeks when the Indians first arrived, she'd never felt like one. Their stories were her stories. Their language her language. She kept their secrets and they kept hers.

Why, then, had only Asku spoken up?

He squeezed Alma's hand, pulling her from her reverie. His grip was soft, tentative. The same jolt she'd felt that day by the stream hummed through her. But the effect was short-lived and weaker than before. The heat that radiated from his hand reached no farther than her skin. She pulled free and looked away.

"What you say to make Tshikwā'set so angry?" Alice asked, coming toward them.

"Me? He began it."

Alice flashed a sheepish smile and tossed her a few warm acorns. Minowe and Hįčoga joined them too. Alma rolled the acorns round and round in her palm. Where had the girls been a few moments before when she needed them? In their position, she would have stood beside them and spoken up.

Minowe inched closer to her on the log. She leaned her head on Alma's shoulder and squeezed her hand. "It's hard for Tshikwā'set . . . er . . . George, not having come here when he was young."

Alma trained her gaze on a small fir tree across the clearing. She didn't care about George's reasoning or his real name. How could Minowe, of all people, have said nothing? They'd been the closest of friends for years. George wasn't even of her tribe.

Minowe squeezed her hand again, a small, wordless token of apology, and Alma's anger tottered. She remembered the way she ofttimes felt in town, the awkward pull between the white friends whose approval she so craved and her Indian friends whose company she truly enjoyed.

After a heavy moment, she laid her head on Minowe's and returned the squeeze. The blistering loneliness she had felt standing alone before George slowly faded. Once again, the fire's warmth embraced her. The lively music pulsed through her veins.

George was wrong. Indian or not, she did belong.

CHAPTER 17

—➤◆◄—

Minnesota, 1906

Alma tried to sleep, but the stars whispered to her through the train window. The three hunters roamed the dark sky chasing after *makwa,* the bear. *Jiibay-miikana,* the Path of Souls, stretched like eyelet lace across the blankness. Her friends' voices rang in her ears—Minowe's melodious tone, Hįčoga's giggles. Memories of the cold night air prickled her skin, and she could almost see the fog of their breath drifting up from their rooftop hideout to the inky heavens above.

Beside her on the train, Stewart slept. His hair, the color of a wet beach, had fallen across his forehead. The lines around his eyes and those cut across his brow had smoothed. She alone had carved them into his skin and was glad the damage was only transitory. She traced the outline of his handsome face with the tips of her fingers, gently so as not to wake him. He would forgive her this—the trouble of it all, her secrets. Wouldn't he?

Just after dawn, they alighted at the tiny town of Detroit Lakes and hired a rickety wagon to take them to their hotel. Twice along the short ride down Main Street, Alma saw hand-painted signs in the storefront windows: NO INDIANS ALLOWED.

In their hotel room, Alma splashed some water on her face and pinned back the locks of hair that had fallen out of place during the sleepless night on the train. The lumpy bed in the center of the small room tempted her, but they hadn't time to tarry. She lingered a moment more before the washstand, her hands clutching the sides of the chipped porcelain basin. The woman that stared back at her in the filmy mirror on the wall looked haggard—dry lips, bloodshot eyes, lackluster skin. She bit her lips and pinched her cheeks until they colored. Better, yes, but fleeting. She looked away before the pallor returned.

At the front desk she and Stewart inquired after a horse and buggy to take to the reservation. The young clerk scratched his head. Dandruff showered down from his rumpled hair. Or were they nits? Alma shuffled backward, fighting back a grimace.

"We got a buggy you can rent, but it's a long way to the reservation," he said.

"Twenty-two miles. I know," Stewart said. "Have you a good horse?"

"Good enough. 'Cept . . ." His eyes darted to Alma. "Wouldn't linger there after dark. A man was kilt there not long back. Shot by one of them Injuns in cold blood."

Alma clenched her teeth, barring passage to the sharp words readied on her tongue.

"I'm aware of that, thank you," Stewart said. "Show us to the buggy and hitch the horse, if you please. As you say, we've a long ride ahead of us."

"Ain't got nothing against them Chippewas," the clerk said as he led them to the barn. "Heck, we've even had some famous chiefs stay here. Hole-in-the-Day, Little Wolf, and the like." He turned to Alma. "Don't worry, ma'am. We boiled the sheets and scrubbed down the floors right after."

The road to White Earth snaked northward through dry, golden prairie. Lakes winked in the morning sunlight, roped together by winding streams. An occasional hill swelled above the flatlands. Pine forests, far to the east, painted the horizon a cool blue-green. Farms lay scattered across the land like fallen leaves, windrows of hay and rows of cornstalks bounded by unspoiled meadows. Still, for all the beauty, she couldn't sit still.

"Nervous, darling?" Stewart asked.

"Why ever would I be?" He loosed a hand from the reins and laid it on her jogging knee. She stilled.

"Neither the judge nor that young hotel clerk seemed to think very highly of the reservation."

"I doubt Judge Baum has ever been to a reservation. And that boy? A ninny."

"Alma, it's not like you to be so unkind."

"Well, he is. You'll see. White Earth will be like any other rural community."

The wagon rattled onward and they crested a low hill. Alma squinted into the distance, hoping to see a collection of roofs or a spire-capped water tower on the far horizon. Only prairie and a patchwork of trees stretched before them.

Stewart was right; she was being unkind. But a decade and a half had passed since the Dawes and Nelson acts divided up the reservation into allotments. Surely the Indians' farms were prospering. By now, not only Asku and Minowe and Frederick, but hundreds of Anishinaabe children had been educated at schools like Stover. They could read and write, had profitable skills and genteel manners.

Again Asku's words nettled her. *Did you ever think what they were doing to us was wrong?* No, their visit to the reservation would prove that. Why, then, was she so nervous?

"Are there others from Stover you expect to meet at White Earth?" Stewart asked.

Her knee itched to bounce, but the weight of his hand kept it still. "The reservation is far too large for social calls."

"Perhaps they might help with the case."

"What time is it? Are we close?"

"They could show us about the reservation. Answer questions about Agent Andrews."

"There's no one!" She turned her head and stared across the prairie. "The time, please."

His hand left her leg. His pocket watch snapped open and closed. "Half past eleven. We've a ways yet to go."

An hour past noon, several miles into the reservation, they arrived at a small village. Log cabins and a few shotgun houses lined the rutted throughway. Shirts and trousers billowed from backyard clotheslines, and animals brayed in the barns. Farther down the road, the houses gave way to a spattering of shops, a two-story town hall, and a steepled Episcopal church.

Stewart stopped the wagon in front of the general store. Several Indians tarried about the entry. A strand of fish hung from one man's shoulder. Others carried sacks or small crates filled with supplies. Birch bark baskets and cradleboards swayed on women's backs. A group of men lounged against the storefront, talking between drags on their cigarettes.

"Pardon me, where can we find the Indian Office?" Stewart asked.

The Indians' banter ceased and their eyes turned wary. No one spoke.

"Perhaps I should speak slower. In-di-an Off—"

Alma put her hand on his arm and turned to the Indians. "Aani-indieteg Ogimaawigamig?"

Surprise cracked through their guarded expressions. Murmurs rolled among them. After a moment, one of the men nodded toward a homestead-style building farther down the road and said in clear English, "That way."

Stewart tipped his hat and urged the horse onward. "Much obliged."

They passed by a large storehouse, another barn and stable, and a four-room army barracks. Shutterless windows gaped at her from the rustic buildings, their roughly fashioned doors crooked and unpainted. Utilitarian, she decided. Economical. She would not allow the word *bleak*.

"Aaniin. That's the customary Chippewa greeting, by the way," she said.

Stewart repeated the word, stumbling through the syllables. "What does it mean?"

"It's a shortening of aaniin gidoodem—what clan are you from?"

His eyebrows pulled together in confusion.

"You can just say boozhoo."

Again that puzzled expression. Then he smiled. "Ah, like bonjour. From the fur trading days."

She nodded.

A flagpole stood before the agency building, the Stars and Stripes whipping in the breeze some twenty-five feet above. A similar flag, she remembered, minus a few stars, had flown proudly over the gabled roof at Stover.

Beside the flagpole, the white clapboard agency gleamed so brightly in the afternoon sun Alma had to squint. New shingles hung from its roof. Behind it stretched a fallow field dotted with canvas tents and teepees—twenty or thirty structures in all, and more under construction. She frowned. Surely they didn't live here, like this.

Stewart tethered the horse and helped her from the buggy. "It still surprises me when I hear you speak their language. I never knew you were so close to these people."

She squeezed his hand and said with manufactured lightness, "How boring you would find me, if you knew all my little secrets."

"Secrets?" He laughed weakly. "I dare say, the past week has brought surprises enough to last a lifetime."

Inside they passed by an unvarnished bench and two mismatched chairs to a long counter. A small picture of President Roosevelt hung in a cheap tin frame, lonely on the wall.

Beyond the counter, the office was a hive of activity. Stacks of paper and worn ledger books claimed every available surface. Survey maps plastered the walls. The air smelled of stirred-up dust and mildewed paper. One man, a half-breed guessing by his high cheekbones and broad nose, huddled over a spread of documents. Another, the only woman in the room besides Alma, thumbed through a cabinet of folders. Several other workers bustled between desks and file drawers. No one looked up in greeting.

Stewart rapped gently on the counter. "I'm looking for Deputy Agent Taylor."

"Can't you see we're—" A burly white man, seated at a nearby desk, glanced up at Stewart and stopped mid-sentence. His eyes flickered to Alma and seemed to stall. He stood, but without hurry, smoothed his jacket, and straightened the gold-plated star pinned above his breast pocket. "What can I do for you?"

The other employees came to attention as well. Alma's skin tingled beneath the intensity of their collective gaze. Stewart repeated his request.

"He's head agent now," the man with the star said. "Is he expecting you?"

"I'm afraid not. Our trip was too sudden to announce by letter, and I was told you have no telephone."

"Nearest telephone's back in Detroit Lakes. I'll tell Agent Taylor you're here. What was your name?"

"Stewart Mitchell. I'm here regarding the murder of Mr. Andrews."

"You a lawman?"

"I'm one of the attorneys involved in the trial."

Alma looked around the room. Stewart had not even mentioned which side of the case he represented and already she felt a crackle of tension.

Her gaze stopped on the half-breed. He was the youngest of the employees, more a boy than a man, and the first to return his attention back to his work. He wore his thick black hair short, parted at the middle, and slicked down with oil. His brown eyes were light, his skin the color of pale clay.

The man with the star emerged from a door at the back of the room and waved them forward.

A young man greeted them inside the office. "Welcome, welcome. I'm Agent Taylor." He shook Stewart's hand and nodded at Alma. "Have a seat. This is Sheriff Knudson."

The man with the gold badge bobbed his head. He closed the door but remained in the room, leaning against the far wall.

Alma sat in a high-backed wooden chair, feeling caged in the small room. Daylight dribbled in through the milky glass of the lone window. The agent's musky cologne permeated the stale air. Her eyes drifted from the window to a waist-high bookshelf topped with a mantel clock and matted tintype.

"That's my pappy," Agent Taylor said, smiling at Alma. "Fought with Custer and Colonel Mackenzie during the Great Sioux War."

Alma shifted in her chair. The man's vivid blue eyes and sharp face unnerved her. He leaned back in his chair, still smiling, and laced his hands behind his head.

Stewart cleared his throat. "You served under Mr. Andrews as deputy agent before the murder, is that correct?"

Mr. Taylor brought his hands around to his lap, but remained relaxed and easy in his chair. "Yes, that's right. For goin' on three years."

"And, Mr. Knudson"—Stewart swiveled around to face the sheriff—"you completed the investigation against Mr. Muskrat and executed the arrest?"

Sheriff Knudson nodded.

"Mr. Muskrat offered no defense or alibi," Agent Taylor said. "He'd bootlegged a gun same as the one shot Agent Andrews just a few months prior. What more questions could you have?"

"Did he admit to the crime?"

"No," the sheriff said. "He ain't said nothing at all."

Stewart unbuckled the flap of his satchel and withdrew several sheets of paper. "Seven people were listed as witnesses to the crime, but only one interview was filed with the report. Do you have summaries or transcripts of the other six?"

The sheriff took the top sheet of paper from Stewart and frowned. His rough, weather-beaten skin reminded Alma of Mr. Simms. "I only interviewed the one. Abe Johnson. He's a worker at this here agency and one of my deputies. Heard the gunshot from his kitchen window and saw Mr. Muskrat fleeing into the woods. No need to interview the others."

"From what distance did he see Mr. Muskrat?"

"Pardon?"

"How far from Mr. Johnson's window to the woods?"

The sheriff shrugged. "Fifty yards. A hundred tops."

"That's quite a distance. Especially in the dark."

"You city folk might not know, but the moon shines real bright out here in the country."

"It was a new moon that night," Alma said.

They all looked at her.

In the days after learning of Asku's trial, reading and rereading those articles, she'd thought back to where she was the night of the murder. What banality had occupied her time when a thousand miles away all this trouble had begun for Asku? It was a Sunday. She and Stewart attended a dinner party thrown by one of Stewart's colleagues who'd moved to the suburbs. She'd thought of every laugh, every smile, over and over again until it made her sick. She remembered the hum of the electric hansom that carried them home. "Watch your step, ma'am, it's mighty dark," the driver had said. And later, after she and Stewart had made love, she remembered lying awake staring out the bedroom window at the moonless sky.

"I grew up in the country," she now said to the sheriff. "It's black as perdition on a moonless night."

"You accusing Deputy Johnson of lying?"

"No," Stewart answered. "But if you didn't question the others, how do you know they were even present at the time of the crime?"

"It happened right in front of the general store. Mr. Larson hadn't closed up yet, so naturally he's a witness."

"And these others?"

"I'm sure you saw on your way over here, the way them Indians loiter about the shop front. Them there's the names of the usual riffraff who hang about piss-drunk on turpentine and gin."

"You never verified that they were actually there?"

Again the sheriff only shrugged.

Stewart's jaw muscles tightened and his nostrils flared. Alma watched him wrestle back the uncustomary tide of anger. When he spoke, his voice was steady and controlled. "I'd like to interview them myself, then, if you don't mind."

"Best'a luck with that."

"Excuse me?"

Agent Taylor laughed through his nose. "Won't find them very willing. One, they don't speak much English. Two, they're mighty mistrusting, these Chippewas. Hell, they'll probably think you a missionary, bringing the missus along and all." He turned to Alma. "To what *do* we owe the pleasure of your company?"

"Probably never seen a real red man before," Sheriff Knudson said before she could answer. "If you were hopin' for feathers and buckskin, you'll be sorely disappointed."

"Actually, I—"

"Is that why you came? To see the noble savage in his natural habitat?" Agent Taylor picked up a stamp from his desk and twirled the wooden handle between his fingers. Ink had stained the rubber seal black. "I'm afraid the sheriff is right. All we have here are would-be farmers and inebriates. Perhaps you'd—"

"Mr. Taylor, I've met and known dozens of Indians. Mr. Muskrat was my friend. I've come to see why the investigation against him was so grossly mismanaged."

The smirk fell from the agent's face. "I see."

"To that end," Stewart said, handing Mr. Taylor another sheet of paper, "it says here that numerous complaints had been filed against Mr. Andrews while he was agent here. I've a subpoena to examine all the agency's records."

Agent Taylor dropped the stamp. It landed on the papers Stewart handed him, leaving behind a messy streak of ink. The corner of his mouth twitched, making his neatly trimmed mustache look like a fuzzy caterpillar inching atop his lip. "The records won't show you nothing. The Indians complain because they don't want to work. They're indolent, Mr. Mitchell, born and bred lazy as sin. They complain because they want everything handed to them without a drop of sweat on their part. They complain because they want to dance their heathen dances and practice their devil magic." He slammed his hands down on the desk. "That's why they file complaints, Mr. Mitchell. That's why the old Muskrat shot and killed Agent Andrews. That's the reality here." He shoved the white pages Stewart had presented back across the desk. "You with your papers and your tailored suit can't do nothing to change that."

Alma leaned away, the wooden chair stiles digging into her back. Stewart didn't move. "I'll tell you what I can do, Agent Taylor." He brushed an invisible fleck of dust from his sleeve, then neatly stacked the papers and returned them to his satchel. "Tomorrow when I return, if you or the sheriff bar me access to your files or impede my interviews with the witnesses, I'll return to Detroit Lakes and telephone St. Paul. The judge will have you both arrested for delaying and impeding a federal trial."

Agent Taylor gave a false chuckle. The color had leached away from his face, leaving his skin sallow. "You can kick up a fuss all you want, Mr. Mitchell, but tomorrow's Annuity Day. The rolls and records you're after will be in use. Official government business."

Annuity Day. So that was the reason for all the tents and teepees, the reason the agency workers were in such a dither when she and Stewart arrived.

Stewart stood. He held his hand out for Alma, but his hazel eyes remained fixed on the agent. "We'll conduct our interviews tomorrow, then. The day after, your records had better be on hand." He buckled his satchel and tucked her arm into the crook of his elbow. "Good day, gentlemen."

CHAPTER 18

Wisconsin, 1888

Outside, the bugle sounded. Rhythmic footfalls marched over the icy crust of yesterday's snow. Alma lifted the curtain shrouding her bedside window and peeked out. Down in the yard, the Indians' cheeks were scarlet. Their breath hung in the air. Sweat trickled down their temples, even in the cold. Most kept perfect time and formation—march, half step, hold time—their lines wrapping and weaving throughout the yard. But the newer students stumbled. They slowed when they should quicken, stepped right instead of left.

George in particular stood out. His knees never rose as high as the others; his arms never swung as straight. His feet struck the ground off tempo. She watched Mr. Simms box him over the head, messing his already untidy hair. To this, George only smirked and quickened his pace a half beat too fast.

He wore that same mischievous smile as he sauntered behind his marching classmates into the classroom after breakfast. Beneath the desktop, Alma's hands clenched. She hated the way he flouted the rules. She watched him sink into his seat at the front of the class, beside the younger children. He'd kept up his charade of ignorance, convincing even Miss Wells he knew no English. Liar, she wanted to shout when he bungled easy phrases or ignored simple directions. But she kept her mouth shut, grinding her teeth till her jaw ached. The others thought him clever, wily, brave. It was for them she remained silent.

Only Asku shared her indignation. He slid behind their double-wide desk and handed her a history text. "He's up to something."

Alma placed the heavy book atop the desk but didn't open it. "If he doesn't want to learn, why is he here?"

"The sisters at the missionary school on his reservation kicked him out. So the agent sent him here."

She almost laughed. "The agent can't force someone to come. Enrollment at Stover is voluntary."

Asku's bright eyes dampened. He shook his head and looked down at his book. "They have their ways."

"What do you mean?"

"The agent controls the food, tools, and money granted to us in the treaties we signed with the Great Father. We can no longer roam to hunt and fish as we please. Without government rations and supplies we have nothing."

Alma bit her lip. "But . . . you wanted to come, didn't you? And Minowe?"

His expression grew distant. "In the beginning I was . . . unsure. Our father wanted it. He knew the world was changing." Asku paused. "Mother disagreed. She cut away her hair, streaked her face black with ash in mourning." He smoothed a hand down the open page of his textbook. "I see my father's wisdom now. The way of the white man is the way of the future."

Alma nodded halfheartedly. She looked back at George, her throat growing tight. Had his mother cried over his departure too? He sat uncharacteristically straight in his chair, his eyes fixed on the blackboard, where Miss Wells had written out each grade's lesson plan. His uniform never looked crisp and neat like Asku's, but, for once, it didn't bother her. Perhaps he was trying.

She turned her attention toward her studies—a chronological history of England's monarchs. Asku was already several pages ahead of her, but she could catch up. That he had progressed so far so quickly impressed not only her but the entire Stover staff, and she wondered briefly before opening her book if she would fare as well were the text before her written in *Anishinaabemowin,* not English.

Three paragraphs into her study, a low buzzing noise snagged her attention. She looked around the room for the offending bee or horsefly. Seeing none, she returned to her book.

Amid the sound of chalk scratching over slate and the occasional flutter of a turning page, the buzz continued. Alma found herself reading the same passage about Richard I over and over again.

With a huff, she looked up again. By now, the noise had caught the attention of Miss Wells. The teacher's thin lips curled slightly. She strode along the near wall, shaking out the checkered window drapes. Her bones stood out beneath her dry, pale skin as she moved—those of her wrist, her hands, the sharp vertebrae of her neck.

A soft giggle drew Alma's attention forward. A few of the first years leaned toward George, shaking with suppressed laughter. Alma sat forward to get a better look. Beneath his desk, George held a small cream-colored box. Whenever the buzzing began to taper, he gave the box a gentle shake and the noise flared.

Miss Wells walked from the bank of windows to the front of the class, striding so close to George the hem of her skirt brushed his gangly leg. She cocked her head, clearly alert to the proximity of sound, but did not see the paper box hidden beneath his desk.

She shook her head as if to dislodge the low, persistent noise from her ears and straightened. "All right. First, second, and third years, eyes on the blackboard."

The buzzing continued as Miss Wells chalked out a series of short phrases on the board. Alma could see the teacher's shoulders bunching with tension. Her lettering grew dark and cramped, her fingers throttling the chalk.

By now most of the students had seen the box. They craned, twisted, and pointed behind the Skunk's back, their lips clamped, holding back laughter.

Had it not been George's doing, Alma might have laughed too.

Miss Wells turned around and the class went rigid. The older children dropped their heads over their textbooks. The younger ones fixed their gaze forward. George cradled the box between his knees and folded his hands atop the desk. The humming quieted.

Beside her, Asku remained lost in Plantagenet history, but Alma gaped at the scene at the front, her face angled down to feign study, her eyes straining upward.

"Who can read the first line for me?" Miss Wells asked.

As usual, no one volunteered. Indolence, Miss Wells frequently complained. But Alma knew the Indians simply preferred not to stand out or appear conceited.

The teacher's face soured. "William, please rise and recite the first line."

The young Potawatomi boy stood on command. His cheeks grew flush. He fidgeted with the hem of his suit coat, rolling the coarse fabric between his thumb and forefinger. After a heavy silence, he began, "God b-b-bless our se-chul."

"We learned this word last week." Miss Wells's words came more clipped than usual. "Sound out the letters."

William's face turned from pink to crimson. "Sss . . . chhh . . . oool?"

"School. The last word is *school*." Aní·tas slammed the edge of her hand atop her palm like an ax. "As a second year, you should know this word by now. Repeat the phrase in full."

"G-g-god b-b-bless our s-k-k-k—" William stopped and took a deep breath.

Alma bit her lip and looked down. William never stuttered when he spoke in Potawatomi.

Renewed buzzing broke the painful silence.

"Sk-k-k—"

"School!" Miss Wells shouted.

The class jerked to attention. Alma blinked and swallowed. The teacher smoothed her hands down the front of her dress and breathed in deeply through her nose. She turned back to the board and wrote the word *school* in big letters. "Everyone take out your slates and write out this word a hundred times."

"There isn't room," Catherine said.

"Write. Small."

George shook the box again.

Miss Wells spun around, eyes bulging. "Where is that noise coming from?"

After a moment, she seemed to catch the sound's origin and crossed to George.

As she neared, George let his arm fall to his side, the white paper box cupped in his hand. Walter, seated directly behind him, grabbed the box and hid it in his lap.

"Show me your hands, young man," Miss Wells said to George.

He placed his hands, palms up, atop his desk. The corners of his lips twitched, as if fighting back a smirk.

The Skunk's eyes narrowed. She pursed her lips and moved on to Walter. "Hands."

Having passed the box behind him to Frederick, Walter produced his hands.

Giggles erupted like popping corn around the classroom. Miss Wells raised her head, her gray irises blazing like a firebrand, and the room went silent.

The buzzing box passed covertly from one student's hand to the next, always a step or two ahead of the fuming teacher. When Aní·tas reached them, the Indians would hold up their empty hands and shrug, their round faces beaming with a practiced look of innocence.

The prank continued for several minutes. Gone was the pretense of study. Miss Wells stalked up and down each aisle. "All of you— fifteen demerits, unless someone tells me who is making that hideous noise."

Without even a twitch of a smile, Alice raised her hand. "I don't hear no noise, Miss Wells."

The teacher's lips turned purple. Her neck muscles bulged beneath her sallow skin. "It's *any* noise. I do not hear *any* noise."

More hushed laughter. Even Alma had to bite down on her tongue to keep from giggling. She felt a tug on her sleeve and turned. From across the aisle, Minowe thrust the offending box in her direction. Alma's eyes widened and she shook her head.

"Odaapinan," Minowe hissed. *Take it.*

Alma's gaze flickered to Miss Wells. She had resumed her desk-by-desk inspection, winding her way toward them. Any moment she would look up and see the box in Minowe's outstretched hand.

With a scowl, Alma snatched the box and hid it in her hands beneath her desk. It was made from thick foolscap paper. George had probably filched the paper from her father's office. Alma pulled back one of the side flaps and peered inside.

A hornet!

She slapped her palm over the opening to keep the insect from flying out and looked up. George leered at her from the front of the room. He lounged like a tramp behind his desk, arm lolling over the back of his chair, legs protruding into the aisle.

A sharp pain stung her palm. She clamped her lips around a scream, but a tiny squeak escaped. George smirked. Miss Wells spun toward her.

"Miss Blanchard, whatever is the matter?"

Alma fumbled with the box flap, closing it just before the hornet escaped. "What? Um . . . nothing's the matter."

The insect buzzed angrily in the box. The teacher stepped forward, her eyes hungry like a bloodhound tracking a scent. "Do you hear that?"

Alma looked past the teacher at George. How had he even found a hornet midwinter? His smug expression made her blood crackle. She could show the box to Miss Wells, tell her George was to blame for the entire escapade. The thought brought an inward smile. But his was not the only face turned in her direction. The entire room, all her friends and classmates, stared, watching what she would do.

She shoved the box between her legs, burying it in the folds of her skirt to muffle the sound. "A horsefly was buzzing at the windowsill a while back." With a quick squeeze, she crushed the box between her knees. The noise deadened. "It must have flown out into the hall."

Miss Wells tilted her head, as if combing the silence for some lingering trace of sound. After a long moment, the madness drained from her face. "Back to your studies, class."

Everyone turned forward, save for George. Alma held his stare, matching his scowl with a smug smile. She tossed the crumpled box over her shoulder, sat up extra straight, and dusted off her hands with exaggerated show. His frown deepened a moment, then morphed into a lopsided grin. He chuckled silently and turned forward while Alma preened.

CHAPTER 19

—————⟫•⟪—————

Minnesota, 1906

The small gathering of tents and teepees she and Stewart had seen on the edge of White Earth Village the day before had grown into a bustling encampment. Mule-drawn carts and rusted buggies choked the thoroughfare. Their shaggy horse lurched and ambled as people on foot, even those carrying heavy packs or canoes, passed them on either side. How would she and Stewart find the men they needed to interview—the "witnesses" listed in the investigation report—amid this crowd?

Something else unsettled her as well. Minowe. It was impossible not to think of her. She must be here. Alma scanned the swarm of faces. Would she even recognize her after all these years? The thought brought an unexpected surge of sadness. Would the laugh lines around Minowe's mouth and eyes now be permanent fixtures? Would the luster have vanished from her skin the way Alma's had? Would her gap-toothed smile give her away or be locked behind a scowl? Alma squared her shoulders and raised her chin. It didn't matter. She had enough trouble beating back the past without thinking of such things.

At last they reached the livery. She and Stewart left the wagon and walked the short distance to the agency.

"Let's start by finding the arms merchant," Stewart said, scanning the crowd. "A white man will be easier to spot."

He started toward the cluster of booths that had risen at the far corner of the field like the trading posts of old. Alma hesitated, pulling back on his arm, her attention captured by the goings-on before the office. "Just a moment, dearest."

A long table had been set up with a muslin tarp stretched overhead to block the sun. Sheriff Knudson and his deputies hovered beside a heap of broadcloth-wrapped bundles. He looked in Alma's direction and tipped his hat, his aspect smug and vaguely menacing despite his full-toothed grin. She ignored the prickle of hairs rising beneath her collar and nodded back.

Agent Taylor sat drumming his fingers atop the table. If he saw Alma and her husband, he made no show of it, even as she pulled Stewart forward to get a better view of the proceedings.

A line of Indians had formed—if one could call so lively and unruly a gathering a line—stretching deep into the adjacent field. People stepped in and out as they spotted friends and family. They hugged, laughed, cooed over the little ones strapped in cradleboards on their mothers' backs. A young man had lured a cluster of blushing girls with his flute. Farther back in line, a rattle sounded. Above the songs, Alma heard fragments of jokes, stories, and gossip. Those who had food or tobacco shared it readily, and the fragrant scent wafted above the gathering.

Yet beneath the conviviality, Alma sensed the crackle of discord. Whispers, sidelong glances, even the occasional sneer. Those with lighter coloring or facial hair congregated together. Their collared shirts and calico dresses looked less worn than the beaded buckskin and broadcloth their counterparts wore. English and French peppered their speech. The divide, subtle as it was, surprised her. Had Asku or Minowe hinted at such things as children? Not that Alma could remember. It was her world—the white world—that cared about class and blood quanta.

"Next," the agent hollered over the din, drawing her gaze forward.

An older man shuffled to the table. Crevasses, deep as dried riverbeds, furrowed his dark brown skin. Morning sunlight glinted off metal cones dangling from his ears. When asked his name, he replied, "Niski'gwun." *Ruffled feathers*. The mixed-blood she'd seen yesterday, *James,* the agent called him, handed the man a fountain pen and pointed to an open ledger. Niski'gwun fisted the pen the way her classmates had when they first arrived at Stover, and scratched an *X* beside his name. Ink smudged onto his fingers. He wiped them on his weatherworn trousers before reaching for the silver Agent Taylor had counted out for him. Niski'gwun picked up the coins one at a time with a shaky hand—one, two, three, four, five—and stowed them in his jacket pocket.

Agent Taylor sighed. He shooed Niski'gwun toward the stacks of bundled goods and flagged the next Indian forward. This man approached with his wife and small son. Unlike the older Indian, whose long gray hair was bound in several braids, he kept his hair cropped and fashionably parted to the side. He gave Christian names for himself and his family and signed his name in clear script. Five coins to him, four to his wife, and two for the small boy.

"Only this?" the man asked.

"Now, now. You know y'all received more than your due back in the nineties. Won't be paid back in full for a couple of years yet."

"Your mistake, not ours."

Agent Taylor kept one hand atop the metal cashbox. The other fell to his side, dangling next to the pistol holstered at his hip. "Get along now."

The family collected the money and then their rations. Before walking away, the wife peeked inside her bundle, opening it just wide enough for Alma to spy its contents: a length of green calico, a spool of thread, a comb, a few packets of seeds, a sack of flour, and a tin plate and matching bowl.

The woman reached inside and rummaged through the goods, her face coloring with disappointment. Her son skipped beside her and held up the new blanket he'd received. "Look, nimaamaa."

"It is good." Her voice cracked. She smiled for the boy, even as tears built on her lashes.

Alma watched them go with growing unease.

"Come along, darling," Stewart said. "The longer we tarry, the busier the merchants become."

She knew he was right, but her feet refused to move, her eyes refused to waver.

The family stopped before another table just beyond the cover of the agency's tarp. A man stepped from the shade. Though he was well dressed in a silk shirt and fur-lined coat, the gold tooth that flashed when he grinned hinted at meaner beginnings. He, too, had a cashbox and ledger, but Alma didn't recognize him from the agency.

She watched as the father laid the family's coins—all eleven dollars—on the table. The gold-toothed man consulted his ledger. After a quick count on his chubby fingers, he slid two coins back to the father. The rest he tossed into his cashbox. Alma's stomach roiled—the clanking silver, the man's glinting smile. What right did he have to this family's money?

"Just a merchant settling accounts."

Alma startled. Sheriff Knudson had sidled up beside her and was staring in the family's direction. "You looked worried is all, ma'am."

Again something about him reminded her of Mr. Simms—the gravelly voice, the calloused hands, the scent of stale sweat. She couldn't quite place it. For all his rancor, Mr. Simms had been harmless. But Sheriff Knudson? A shiver spread through her limbs, but she didn't slink back, didn't shy away when his watery gaze turned upon her. Harmless. Still she was glad when Stewart stepped between them and tucked her hand into the crook of his arm.

"Shouldn't Agent Taylor oversee such transactions?" he said. "Dollar to your dime your merchant is violating anti-usury laws."

"You don't strike me a bettin' man, Mr. Mitchell."

"This, Sheriff, is not a gamble."

He chuckled. "You gonna get a subpoena for thems records, too?"

Alma felt Stewart's muscles tighten, but when he spoke, his voice was even. "Excuse us. We've a botched investigation to attend to." He tugged lightly on her arm. Reluctantly, she followed, glancing back over her shoulder as the merchant's box jingled with another deposit.

The field beyond the agency had the feeling of a county fair, and Alma's step lightened. Wild rice simmered over cook fires, perfuming the air with its nutty aroma. Boys hurled sticks and squatted together with round stones in a game akin to marbles. Her gaze snagged on a troop of girls running to and fro. Each brandished two long sticks above her head. A loop of twine with two thumb-sized billets spun through the air from one girl's stick to another. Alma paused, watching them scamper through the browning grass.

"Pupu'sikawe'win."

"What, darling?"

"Oh, it's a game. I used to play it when I was little." Minowe had taught her, passed her the billets when no one else would, despite Alma's dubious ability to catch them.

Alma turned away, but their laughter followed. Only after she reached the commotion of the merchants' stalls did it finally subside. She welcomed the escape.

Indians crowded the tables, inspecting the wares. She stood on her tiptoes, craned her neck, and finally pushed into the crowd to see what lay for sale. Bolts of fleece and broadcloth. Checkered quilts and calico bonnets. Farther along, an assortment of beads. She lost Stewart, but went on. The arms merchant must be here. Fry pans, buckets, shovels, candles, oil lamps, soap, buttons. Hunks of salt pork surrounded by a swarm of flies. Someone stepped on the hem of her dress. Another elbowed good-naturedly past. More bolts of cloth. Saddles and harnesses. Plow blades and seeders. Nuns handing out wooden rosaries. A few stalls down, the Episcopals peddling prayer books.

Alma disentangled herself from the mob and watched from the periphery. Some bartered in English. Too much. Too high. Others pointed and shook their heads. They traded not only in coin, but also with animal pelts and jugs of maple syrup. She caught glimpses of other deals too—those conducted furtively beneath the tabletops. Flashes of silver exchanged for jars of tawny-brown liquid.

But no guns.

Perhaps the man who claimed to have sold to Asku wasn't here.

A hand clasped about her arm. Alma jumped.

"Just me, darling," Stewart said.

"I don't see anyone selling firearms."

"Technically, it's illegal to sell guns to Indians living on the reservation. But I think I've found him." Stewart nodded to a nearby table. Steadying herself against him, she rose onto her toes again and scanned the booth. A hodgepodge of hunting knives rested atop a worn velvet drape. Stacks of lead bars teetered beside a pyramid of cans. DuPont Gunpowder, their labels read. The man behind the counter wore a collared shirt, yellowed from too many washes, under a buckskin jacket. A graying beard covered his face.

When the Indian in front of them stepped away, Stewart shouldered forward with unexpected pluck, pulling her along.

"You two stand out like bacon in beans," the merchant said. "How can I help ya?"

"Are you Lawrence Filkins?" Stewart asked.

"That's the name my mother gave me. Most people call me Larry."
He stuck out a grease-stained hand.

To her wonderment, Stewart didn't hesitate, but took the man's
hand and shook it vigorously. "Pleasure to meet you, Larry. Did I see
you here at the June fourteenth celebration?"

"I come out for all the gatherings."

"To sell your wares?"

"Yep, don't recall seeing you, though."

Alma looked down, hiding her flushing cheeks beneath the wide
brim of her hat. They *hadn't* been here in June. What was Stewart playing at? A row of steel arrowheads caught her eye. How long
since she'd shot a bow? It seemed like another lifetime altogether.
The newly polished metal shone like snowflakes against the dark
velvet coverlet. She reached out and stroked the cold steel.

"Careful, ma'am. Thems sharp."

Alma pulled her hand away and forced her gaze back to the man's
weather-chapped face. "I know."

"You . . . er . . . looking to buy arrowheads?"

"No," said Stewart. "I'd like to buy a pistol."

Alma feigned a cough to cover her surprise. Was this Stewart's
plan? He'd never told a lie in his life. Why not just come out and ask
the man about Asku and the gun?

Larry's eyes narrowed.

"You sell knives, percussion caps, lead for making bullets." Stewart rattled a hand in his trouser pocket. Coins clinked and jangled.
"Surely you sell guns."

Several moments passed. Alma waited for Stewart to drop the
ruse, but his earnest expression never cracked.

At last Larry said, "What type of pistol you looking to purchase?"

"What types do you have?"

Larry leaned forward to survey the surrounding crowd, then bent
down and retrieved a bundle from beneath his stall. He unwrapped it
atop the knives and arrowheads, revealing a small cache of revolvers.

"These here are pretty old. I've got a better store back in Bemidji—
some of them new self-loaders. But you might like this .22 Rimfire or
this Starr Single Action."

Stewart picked up one of the guns. He spun the cylinder and
squinted at the sight. The gray steel looked strange in his hands, at

odds with the smooth kid leather of his gloves. Alma choked back nervous laughter. Had her husband ever even held a gun?

"What is this, a .44?" he asked.

"Yep."

"What about a .38? I'm looking for a Colt Lightning model."

Larry stroked his beard. "Had several of them a while back. Sold my last few over the summer. You don't want that model nohow. Trigger mechanism's a bit temperamental. How about this Colt Single Action?"

Stewart handed the gun butt-first back to him. "You do most of your business here on the reservation, Larry?"

He nodded. "Got my official trader's license."

"But you're not licensed to sell guns."

"Pardon?"

"Selling guns to Indians is illegal." Stewart's tone had changed from genial to icy.

Larry frowned and hastily bundled the revolvers. "I only sell to white folks like yourselves."

"You told Sheriff Knudson you'd sold a Colt Lightning to Harry Muskrat at the June fourteenth celebration."

"Can't always tell if thems Indians or not. He spoke real slick English."

"Yet you believe you could recognize him among a lineup of other Indians?"

"Course I could."

Alma's stomach fell, but Stewart pressed on. "And the other Colt Lightnings you sold over the summer? To whom did they go?"

Larry hid his cache back beneath the table. When he rose up, he squared his shoulders and glowered in their direction. "Just what are you getting at?"

Alma shuffled backward. Stewart did not move. "Nothing, Mr. Filkins. You've been most helpful. I'll see you in St. Paul."

Stewart clasped Alma's elbow and steered her through the crowd. She fixed her face with a calm expression in case Mr. Filkins was eyeing their departure, but inside she felt gutted.

"That was dreadful," she said, when they'd cleared the booths. "Do you think the prosecution will call him as a witness?"

"If they don't, I will."

"He can identify Harry," she all but yelled.

Stewart faced her and took her hands. "He's an illegal arms trader who just admitted he sold several guns of the same model that killed Agent Andrews on this reservation over the summer. Not only does that make him an unsympathetic witness, it widens the suspect pool."

His step was jaunty as they continued on from the merchants while Alma's feet were heavy, her insides entangled. She glanced over her shoulder at Mr. Filkins. He was holding up a curved knife for a new customer, making skinning motions through the air. A knife made sense here on the reservation. A rifle, too. But a revolver? Why had Asku bought such a gun?

CHAPTER 20

Wisconsin, 1889

The wind blew unseasonably warm. An Indian summer, Alma had heard the townsfolk call it.

Hidden between rows of billowing sheets, she and her friends pushed back their sleeves and unbuttoned their tight collars. They hiked up their skirts, allowing the breeze to kiss their calves and ankles through their stockings. The earthy smell of browning grass and perishing leaves mingled with the crisp scent of soap. Calls and laughter rang from the yard beyond.

"Waú," Hįčoga said. "How come the boys get to play their sports while we're stuck doing chores?"

Alma let her head fall back and closed her eyes, relishing the sun's warmth like a stolen gift. "Is it so different back home on the reservation?"

Minowe laughed. "Gaawesa. Not at all."

Another rush of wind stole past. Alma's dark silk dress drank in the heat, but this particular breeze, stealing over her sweat-dewed skin, hinted at the lurking autumn. A chill worked down her body. She opened her eyes and pulled a sheet down from the line.

Hįčoga and Minowe seemed in no hurry to return to their work. They pulled aside one of the hanging sheets and peered at the boys running about the yard.

"Your brother's grown p'įžą," Hįčoga said.

Minowe wrinkled her nose. "Handsome?"

"Ho. Frederick too," Hįčoga said.

Minowe rose onto her tiptoes to see over Hįčoga's shoulder. "Frederick looks like a spider, all arms and legs. Too . . . too . . . what do you call it, Azaadiins?"

"Gangly," Alma said. Her friends laughed at the word.

"Gangly," Minowe repeated. "Tshikwā'set is much beautifuler."

Alma buried her face in the sheet she was folding to smother a laugh. "Beauty is more a feminine quality."

"What mean I to say, then?"

Alma glanced beyond her friends at the pack of boys. In her estimation, Asku was more regal than handsome. He sat apart from the others, reading beneath the boughs of a tree, shoulders squared and back straight even in repose, dark eyes ever shrewd. She turned to the others. Frederick had grown so lanky he seemed to trip instead of walk. Walter looked more a boy yet than a man, his cheeks full and ruddy. Her gaze flickered to George, then quickly away. "Well-favored, that's an expression you could use."

The boys clumped around a large ball. Frederick tossed it to Walter, who then hurled it forward through the air. Dozens of arms shot up. George's hand emerged above the rest, fingers splayed, sweat glinting off his skin. He grasped the ball and hugged it against his chest, then barreled through the crowd.

She'd welcomed his departure at the end of summer term when he returned home for the rice harvest. Though his disruptive antics had eased with time, she was ever on guard around him, her stomach tight and tongue ready. He'd made ready friends among the other Indians, making it impossible to avoid his company. Still, she never addressed him, never applauded his stories, never laughed at his tomfoolery.

His return for a second year of schooling had surprised her, though she knew better now than to assume his enrollment voluntary. He continued to sit at the front of the class, sequestered with second-year students half his age and a third his size, feigning illiteracy. Yet instead of balking at the charade, she felt a tug of admiration for his pluck. Three days into the new term, when a sparrow erupted from the flour tin, showering the kitchen in white and sending Mrs. Simms into hysterics, Alma caught herself smiling. When a screw came loose from the classroom furnace, causing the pipe to rattle with every breeze, Alma swallowed a chuckle.

Now, she watched him fight his way through the cluster of boys. He had grown nearly as tall as Frederick, but his shoulders were much broader, his arms ripe with muscle. She'd spent a year glaring in his direction, but never really noticed the exuberance of his smile, the way his cheekbones sharpened his face, the contrast between his burnt-sugar skin and midnight-black hair.

Alma's fingers drifted to the nape of her neck, winding about strands of hair that had broken free from her chignon. "You could also say comely, dapper, pleasing to behold . . ." The sound of her trailing voice, suddenly deep and breathy, made her straighten. She looked away and busied herself with another sheet. So what if he was—well—all those things? She spread her arms and pulled the linen taut, continuing to shake the fabric long after the wrinkles had fallen out, as if the action might jog her senses.

Hįčoga grabbed the far end of the sheet and brought the corners together. "What about you, Alma?"

Her head snapped up while her stomach plummeted into her knees. "What about me?"

Her friend tugged the sheet. "Aren't there any boys from La Crosse you fancy?"

Alma grabbed the corners of the sheet from Hįčoga and finished folding it herself, drawing out the silence as she smoothed out the fabric and arranged it in a perfect square.

Minowe nudged her and giggled. "What about that blond boy from town?"

"You mean Edward Steele?" She tried to keep her voice light, casual, but it was impossible not to smile when she said his name. "P'įžą, I suppose."

Hįčoga snorted. "We heard about your last call at the Steeles' for days. Edward said this. Edward did that."

Minowe clutched her breast. "Oh, Edward!"

Alma bunched up a pillowcase and threw it at her. They all laughed.

It was true. He was always the highlight of her visits. The elder Mr. Steele owned the largest lumber mill in La Crosse. They were New Money, but had more than enough of it for her mother to overlook their undistinguished pedigree. Edward had inherited his father's strong features and his mother's fair coloring. He was confident and witty and ever in good form. Alma leaned against the clothesline crossbeam and looked up at the azure sky. True, there was haughtiness to his demeanor. He berated the maids and talked ill of the cook staff. Every conversation circled round to his latest hunt or billiard match. But he had more than enough good qualities to make up for that; she was sure.

Minowe sat down on a wicker basket piled with folded laundry, and Hįčoga reclined against the opposite pole. Enough sheets still hung around them that Alma dared lift her dress and petticoats a few inches above her ankles again. They made sense together, she and Edward. A suitable match, as her mother would say. Everyone had imperfections.

An egg-shaped ball covered in strips of worn leather flew through a narrow break in the sheets. It struck the ground and bounced to a stop at Alma's feet. George barreled through the sheets after it, stopping short when he saw the girls.

Alma gasped at the intrusion and pushed down her skirts. Her fingers fumbled to button her collar. "Can't you keep your horseplay away from our work?"

George smiled a crooked smile. His steady gaze unnerved her. "You hardly appears to be working."

Minowe and Hįčoga giggled, but Alma scowled. She reared back and kicked the ball straight at him. George ducked. It soared just over his head and above the laundry line, arching downward into the yard beyond.

He swiveled his head to follow its trajectory, then turned back to Alma. "Bully, you should join on the team."

"I thought we palefaces were forbidden from your mamāceqtaw practices."

Usually he grimaced when she used Menominee words. So, of course, she did so at every chance. This time, however, his mischievous smile did not falter. "It's a mōhkomān game."

A white man's game? Alma had never seen it played before. "And yet you deign to participate?"

George shrugged. His dirt-streaked shirt clung sweaty to his chest. "Not so much fun as pākahatuan, but Mr. Simms took all our sticks."

Alma covered her mouth and feigned a yawn, but George continued, shifting his gaze to her more enrapt companions. "Football, they call it. They're playing it all over—even at Carlisle. How can big chief Blanchard object?"

Minowe's cheeks had taken on a pink glow. She leaned forward as if the conversation were somehow interesting. Alma noticed she'd not bothered with her top two buttons, leaving the delicate curve of her collarbone plain to view. "Where did you get the ball?"

"Mrs. Simms."

"Poppycock," Alma said. "She hates your silly games as much as we do."

He turned back to her with a glint in his eye. "It's true. Frederick asked her to set aside . . . what's the word . . ." He tapped his finger against his lips in mock concentration.

Alma rolled her eyes.

"Pig's bladder. That's the word."

Her stomach turned. She wiped the tip of her boot in the brown brittle grass.

"Sure you don't want to play, Miss Alma?" he said with a laugh.

She tried to fashion her usual sneer, but managed only a half-hearted frown. Turning her back to him, she yanked another sheet off the line. Insolent boy. A constant burr inside her stocking. Yet she found her ears straining to catch his voice amid the clamor of the game, found her eyes drifting toward the playing field. Only because she hated him, of course. Only because she hoped he'd stay away.

CHAPTER 21

—————————⟫•⟪—————————

Wisconsin, 1889

"Can I turn around yet, Mother?"

"Be still while I finish with these buttons."

But Alma couldn't. Her heels danced. Her knees bounced. Her fingers played amid the silk flounces cascading about her hips. Her mother had laced her corset so tight that Alma managed only shallow inhales. A wink of cleavage showed above her collar. She tugged down on the lace, only to have her mother reach around and yank the frilly décolletage up again. "If you'd stopped fidgeting, I'd be done by now."

It took all Alma's will, but she stilled and glanced out the window. Outside, the snow cover sparkled orange in the setting sunlight. They mustn't be late. She couldn't bear to miss a single dance.

"There. Turn around."

Alma spun around and looked in the oblong mirror above her mother's vanity. A smile blossomed across her reflection. She ran her hands down the smooth bodice of her dress and swished her heavy skirt. The silk danced and rippled, flashing from soft rose to shiny gold in the lamplight.

Her mother gave the bustle a final fluff and her steel-blue eyes softened with approval. "Parfait." She retrieved a small bottle from the vanity and removed its crystal stopper. A bouquet of rosewood and lilac bloomed in the air. She dabbed Alma's neck with a few drops of oil. "You mustn't let any gentleman sign your dance card more than twice."

Alma fingered her pearl necklace, still lost in her reflection. "Mm-hmm."

"Save a dance for Mayor Donelson's nephew, Mr. Ellis. He runs his own iron factory in Milwaukee, you know."

"Huh? Oh, yes, the mayor's nephew." She tore free from the mirror and hurried to her room.

Her mother followed, hovering like a mosquito, fussing over this ribbon or that bit of lace, her voice a constant buzz. "Avoid lingering by the refreshment table, someone's bound to spill punch on your dress. . . ."

Alma collected her gloves, fan, and reticule. A splash of primrose in the small, handheld mirror atop her desk made her stop and admire her dress anew. Edward would be there tonight. Would he ask for a dance? Her stomach thrilled at the thought.

Laughter rang down the hallway followed by echoes of her friends' voices. She spun toward the lighthearted sound and found her mother still standing in the doorway. "One more thing, dear." Her face was drawn, her eyes once again chilly. "I know you fancy the Indians your friends. Such . . . *associations* cannot be helped here at Stover, but there's no need to appear overly familiar. Certainly not on occasions such as tonight."

"Ignore them, is that what you're suggesting? Pretend we came by separate carriages? They are my friends, Mother, and I—"

"You're a young woman now, Alma. You must exemplify taste and circumspection in your acquaintanceships. Indians do not fit within those parameters."

Alma frowned. "Says who?"

"I don't say these things to hurt you, dear. I just . . ." She straightened Alma's pearls. Her voice was unusually husky. "I had to settle. I don't want that for you."

Alma swallowed her brusque reply. A twinge of sympathy surged as she watched her mother glide away to collect her own adornments. Never before had she imagined her mother as a young girl—beautiful, rich, and full of hope. She'd seen the embossed dance cards tucked away between layers of tissue paper in her mother's closet. Every dance spoken for. At what point had she settled? Marrying her father? Coming here to found Stover? Somehow it was hard to picture her—even at sixteen as Alma was now—carefree and gay.

Sleigh bells sounded from the front yard, pulling her from such weighty thoughts. Alma grabbed her fur-trimmed coat and hurried to the stairs. The younger Indians—those too small to attend the ball—huddled on the landing, peeking between the rungs of the banister. Confusion and awe played across their shadowed faces. Alma knelt among them and admired the spectacle below.

Minowe, Hįčoga, and several of the older girls waited in the foyer. How beautiful they looked—their skin lustrous against their pale-blue dresses and elbow-length gloves, their sleek hair bound in elegant twists.

Footsteps thundered from the attic dormitory and the boys jostled past, taking the steps two at a time, with seemingly little care for their newly pressed suits. George glanced back at her and smirked.

That rogue. She shooed the younger children to bed and started down the stairs. Why ever had he been allowed to come? Surely he had some antic in mind to disrupt the evening.

The foyer was a jumble: her father and the boys donning overcoats, hats, and gloves; her mother, Alma, and the other girls with their cloaks and tippets. Shoes squeaked atop the floorboards. Petticoats rustled. She found herself pressed uncomfortably close to George. Nothing was amiss in his attire—not his usual open collar, rolled-up pant legs, or wrinkled shirt. The deep green cravat about his neck drew her gaze to his face and carefully parted hair. More shuffling. Someone bumped her from behind and she tottered forward, her hand reaching out for balance and landing squarely on his chest. Their eyes linked for a heartbeat, then, in tandem, flashed to her hand. She pulled back and muttered an apology to her feet. The front door opened for their departure and winter air stole in. Alma welcomed the cold rush over her skin and hurried out into the night.

Light glistened from every window of the Donelson mansion, refracting through the frost-covered glass. The inside was even more magnificent. Garlands of evergreen festooned the walls. A bushy fir tree towered behind the receiving line. Hundreds of tiny candles twinkled from its limbs. Red and gold ribbons wound through its boughs alongside strands of beads and popcorn. Small lace bags filled with candies and nuts hung from the branches.

Beside the great tree sat a wicker basket replete with programs. Alma took one for herself and each of her girlfriends. They flitted down the long, marble-tiled hallway into a grand ballroom. At one end, a string quartet played a gentle prelude. At the other end stood several tables draped in brilliant white linen and laden with sweets. A large crystal punch bowl sat in the center with dozens of tiny cups nestled around it.

A low murmur rippled across the room when they entered. The music sagged. Throats cleared. The Indians shuffled to one corner of the room, but Alma hesitated. Heat flooded her cheeks. She followed the stare of the crowd, their cocked heads and discreetly pointed fingers, and noticed for the first time how simple her friends' gowns appeared amid the splendor, how sharp the contrast between the pale cloth and their dark skin.

Her slippers felt gummed to the floor. Sweat bled through her satin gloves. Should she follow the Indians or seek out her other friends amid the crowd?

Before she could shake her paralysis, the mayor's nephew, Mr. Ellis, approached and asked for her dance card. Thank the stars! She would have given him every dance, had he asked.

Conversations rekindled around the room. Another gentleman stepped in behind Mr. Ellis and penciled his name upon her card. In the corner, a small crowd of revelers had formed around the Indians. Dance cards passed to and fro. The squall inside her quieted. She caught Minowe's eye and smiled. Her friend grinned back with undiminished glee.

When Alma turned around, Edward Steele stood before her, resplendent in his black dress coat and white necktie. His oil-slickened hair shone like spun gold in the twinkling light of the chandelier.

"Don't you look the part of an angel this evening, Miss Blanchard," he said, his voice just above a whisper. He took her hand and kissed it, then teased away her dance card. "You've already given away the first dance, I see."

She opened her mouth, desperate that some charming or witty phrase might form on her tongue. "I . . . you . . ."

"I'll have your second dance, then, and the finale." He took a step closer and handed her back her card. "You do galop, don't you?"

The closeness of their bodies, the musky scent of his eau de cologne—Alma could only nod.

"Good. I've been told I'm one of the finest dancers in the city. I'm sure we'll make a handsome pairing." With that, he spun around, leaving her still searching for words.

By the time the music swelled for the first dance, Alma's card was full and the abashment she'd felt at their arrival forgotten. One song rolled merrily into the next. The grand chandelier sparkled overhead, casting a brocade of jaunty shadows on the dance floor. Freshly cut evergreen boughs perfumed the air. Alma hoped the night would never end.

As she danced, she stole glances over her partners' shoulders at her Indian friends. In the blur of movement, they were almost indistinguishable from the other guests, their homespun clothes and brown complexions but a splash of color against the gay backdrop.

The mayor's nephew arrived for his appointed dance winded from the previous go about. A tinge of purple colored his face and beads of sweat glimmered along his hairline. Dutifully, she took his hand for the polka, breathing through her mouth so as not to gag from the pungent scent that filled the air between them when he raised his arms. Halfway through the dance he was panting, frothy spittle flying from his mouth every time he attempted conversation.

"Mightn't we rest a moment, Mr. Ellis," she said at last. "I . . . um . . . am feeling rather faint."

His face sagged with relief. He accompanied her to a line of chairs at the edge of the dance floor and hovered over her, chest heaving, chewing his lip as he scoured the ceiling.

She saved them both by asking, "Would you be so kind as to get me a glass of punch?" When he retreated to the refreshment table, Alma sucked in a full, deep breath of unsoured air.

"I think it's despicable," she heard a man say from the alcove behind her.

"Despicable?" another voice echoed with a trill of amusement. "What do you think, Miss Downey?"

At this, Alma glanced over her shoulder. Her friend Annabelle sat on a velvet tuffet with a plate of cookies on her lap. Karl Dressler stood beside her and Paul Van Steenwyk leaned against a nearby wall, swirling the punch in his glass.

"I . . . um . . . it is rather shocking, I suppose," Annabelle said.

Paul gave an impatient frown. Everything about him oozed languor—his sloppy posture, his crooked, but expensive tie—as if he found the privilege that came with being heir to La Crosse's biggest bank tedious. "Yes, but shocking in a good way or a bad way?"

"A bad way." Her tone was hesitant, more like a question than a statement.

Karl tugged on the sleeves of his ill-fitting suit and turned to Paul. "You think it's all right that they're here? Dancing about as if they're the same as us?"

"They certainly don't dress like us," Annabelle said with a coquettish giggle. "Just look at those homespun dresses."

Alma cringed and turned away. Hadn't she had the same ugly thought when they first arrived tonight? She hid behind her fan, hoping the passing dancers wouldn't notice the blotchy coloring creeping up from her bosom or the sudden moistness infecting her eyes.

"Beneath such triflings, though," Paul said. "Are they not the same as us?"

"Certainly not," Karl said.

Paul laughed as blithely as if they were speaking about a game of horseshoes. "Here, let's have Edward settle this. Edward!"

Alma heard his confident footfalls and took cheer.

"What do you think of the mayor's red guests?" Paul asked.

Of course he would defend her friends, and do so gallantly. His charm, his wit, why, any who listened would—

"Well, I certainly wouldn't deign to dance with one," Edward said.

Alma's fan slipped from her grasp. It tumbled to her lap and then flapped to the floor like a lame bird. Had she heard right? He'd never maligned Indians before.

"Nor me," Karl said, and she could hear the vindication in his voice. "Lice, fleas—who knows what sort of miasma they carry."

"Oh, me neither," Annabelle said quickly.

"Well, I for one enjoy the spectacle," Paul said. "These parties can be so drab."

Alma reached down with a shaky hand and groped for her fan. Spectacle? Is that what this was?

Annabelle spoke again. "You don't think they're . . . dangerous?"

"Good heavens, no."

"I'm not so sure," Karl said.

"You needn't worry, Miss Downey," Edward said in the same solicitous tone he'd addressed Alma. "These Indians are *civilized*. At least that's what old Mr. Blanchard would have us believe."

Above their ensuing laughter, Alma heard a soft crack. She looked down to see the ribs of her fan snapped, its delicate silk leaves crumpled in her hand. Their words demanded censure. But even when she'd settled on what to say, she found her frozen vocal cords a traitor to the cause. As much as she hated Edward in this moment, some part of her still craved his approval and affection.

"Your punch, Miss Blanchard."

She jumped a little at Mr. Ellis's voice. "Oh . . . ah . . . thank you."

She drank in silence, the sweetness hardly touching her tongue. The song ended and dancers shuffled about, looking for their next partner. Mr. Ellis had signed for her next dance as well, but she silently rejoiced when he'd begged off and slipped out to the veranda. Perhaps she'd take some fresh air, too, or try another glass of punch in the hopes of settling her roiling stomach.

As she stood, she recognized a new voice behind her. "Miss Downey? I believe this is our dance."

"I . . . I . . . you must be mistaken."

"My name is right there on your card," George said.

Annabelle's voice quavered. "No. I . . . er . . . promised this dance to . . ."

"Me," Edward said. "I'm in line for this dance."

Noise filled the ballroom—clanking glasses, boisterous footfalls, the whine of strings as a musician quickly retuned his instrument—but Alma could hear nothing but the silence behind her. She turned.

"There you are, George." The sound of her own voice—loud and steady—came as a shock to Alma's ears. "You promised me this schottische, remember? Surely Miss Downey here wasn't trying to cut in."

The rosy color in Annabelle's cheeks ripened to scarlet. She looked from George to Alma to Edward with a befuddled expression. "What? No. I . . ."

The lively song began. Without daring a glance at Edward, Alma held out her hand and prayed George would take it before the others noticed her trembling. A few more notes sounded and his fingers closed around hers.

"You didn't have to do that," he said when they reached the dance floor. "I didn't need your saving."

"I wasn't saving you, I was saving Miss Downey."

He smirked and slid his arm around her back. The tiny hairs on her skin enlivened. She found the new and pleasant sensation distracting and altogether unwelcome. She stepped when she should have hopped, then hopped when her feet should glide.

George bore her through the fumble, never losing his place in the dance. "I thought you were a more better dancer."

She flushed. "Maybe if I had a better partner—"

"Like that dandy back there?"

Alma's throat tightened. "No, not like him." She should have said something earlier to those gossips, intervened sooner. What was the point of fitting in if it felt so awful? "Actually, you dance better than I expected. Of course, your form is too rigid, but the steps are correct."

"You mean I dance well for an Indian."

"No, for an obstinate brute who never cared to learn."

A grin flashed across his face. "You would not care to learn with a partner like Aní·tas."

She thought of Miss Wells—a common fixture at the Saturday socials during dance instruction—and joined George in smiling. "True."

Their eyes met and quickly retreated. They finished the schottische in silence, Alma praying for the end. But when the final note played and George let go her hand, she found herself wishing for a few more bars.

"Good dance, Azaadiins," he said.

She couldn't decide whether the remark was sincere or sarcastic, but he'd never called her that before, her Indian name. The sound tingled in her ears.

A smooth, confident voice intruded. "Pardon me, sir, but I believe the honor of Miss Blanchard's final dance belongs to me."

Alma turned to see Edward Steele standing beside them. She noticed for the first time the way his flattened lips resembled a catfish's. And his eyes, too small and far apart, had a fishy aspect as well.

George met his smug stare, remaining beside Alma a moment more before striding away.

"The gall," Edward said as he pulled her close and swept them into the tide of dancers.

"Surely you don't begrudge him a simple dance."

Edward's jaw tightened even as he smiled down at her. "Of course not."

Before, such a smile would have melted her. Now, it only strengthened her resolve. "You're a hypocrite."

His graceful step faltered. "I beg your pardon."

"What do you have against the Indians anyway?"

He blinked and seemed to chomp upon his words before speaking. "These ingrates are already a headache for my family, hemming and hawing about selling their lumber." The honey was gone from his voice and in its place straight bitters. "What do you think happens when they return home from your father's school filled with ideas of equality?"

"It's their land."

"Says who?"

Alma's temples pounded and her carriage stiffened. How had she ever thought him debonair and handsome? She looked away and waited for the song to end, *accidentally* treading upon his toes every chance she got.

CHAPTER 22

⇒►◦◄⇐

Minnesota, 1906

The gun merchant was right, she and Stewart did stick out. It seemed a pall followed them through the crowd as they searched for the witnesses on Stewart's list. Games paused. Conversations stopped. Eyes tracked them.

Alma looked around. All the other whites on the reservation were peddling something: goods, religion, the government's brand of rule and order. Carpetbaggers, the lot of them. No wonder the Indians were skittish.

The climbing sun warmed the air, but Alma clutched the lapels of her duster closed. She should have worn a different shirtwaist. A slimmer petticoat. A less ostentatious hat. She'd never expected to feel like a *biiwide* here, an outsider, but she did. Was this how Asku felt that summer he'd stayed in La Crosse with the Colemans? Was this how Minowe and Hįčoga felt dancing at the mayor's Christmas ball? Alma smoothed the flyaway curls at the nape of her neck, but they sprang back into fuzzy ringlets before her hand left them. When had the air turned so muggy?

Minowe had always wanted curly hair. One night they stayed up long after evening prayers, rolling her dark hair in strips of muslin pilfered from the sewing closet. The next morning when they unwound the rags, the curls fell from her hair before Alma could fix them with bandoline and pin them in place. She'd laughed at their failed effort, laughed as Minowe snatched up the muslin and threw it in the potbellied furnace. With such perfect hair—so thick, smooth, and glossy—why would she want pin curls in the first place?

Now, Alma's laugh was quiet and bitter. How foolish she'd been. Keeping one hand on her lapels, she clasped Stewart's arm. With his patent-leather shoes, double-breasted overcoat, and shiny brown derby, surely he felt out of place too. But then, he'd never nurtured any false assumptions of belonging.

It didn't help that she could feel Sheriff Knudson watching her. Undoubtedly the Indians noticed, too. Even when Alma asked in *Anishinaabemowin* about those named on the list, she met with polite resistance. No. *Gaawiin.* I don't know who or where they are.

Stewart's patience was flagging. She saw it in his tight jaw and pinched lips. He'd taken to folding the sheet of paper with the witnesses' names again and again after each failed encounter, until the list was so creased the names were nearly illegible. At last, someone admitted he knew one of the witnesses. He nodded toward the village center and suggested they try the cemetery.

In quiet shadow behind the Episcopal church lay four rows of crosses. The air smelled of newly trimmed grass and the wooden markers were freshly whitewashed. Drying bouquets of wildflowers—primrose, spurge, aster—dotted the graves. She'd known their *Anishinaabemowin* names once too. Offerings of corn and wild rice also lay beneath a few of the markers.

"I don't see Mr."—Stewart glanced down at the list—"Mr. Zhawaeshk. Or anyone else for that matter." He pulled off his hat and blotted his brow with a hankie. *SJM.* She'd embroidered it in navy-blue stitching at one corner the first year they were married. He owned other handkerchiefs—ones she bought from Wanamaker's with finer stitching and more elegant script—but he always carried this one.

"Perhaps he just left," she said. "Or went to gather flowers." Her voice lacked conviction. The one day of the year every Indian on the reservation came to town and they couldn't find a single one to offer clues about Asku's case.

A breeze stole through the cemetery, knocking askew one of the bouquets. Alma walked over and righted it. Several faded blue petals littered the ground. Another breeze and they tumbled away. DANIEL LITTLE SKY, the marker read, HUSBAND AND FATHER.

Alma stood and backed away. She hadn't told Stewart, but she'd taken his advice and visited her father's grave when she'd traveled to La Crosse. After calling on her mother and Miss Wells, she had a few spare minutes before her train departed for St. Paul and found herself wandering toward the old church. She passed a flower peddler along the way and bought a single white daisy. At the gravesite she stood dry-eyed and silent until the clock tower on Main Street struck quarter to four. Then she'd left, flower in hand.

At the time, she'd convinced herself that to weep would be a betrayal, that the sadness welling inside her was simply fatigue. But she knew now that was just another lie. The same lie she'd told herself for seven straight years, destroying every letter he sent, unopened. Even when her aunt had told her he was sick, dying, dead; even then she'd clung to the delusion that withholding her forgiveness hurt only him.

She wished now she'd waited in the foyer all those years before to hear his last words to her. She wished she'd read his letters and maybe even written one in return. She wished she'd cried for him, not just at his grave, but all those nights when her heart ached, cried for him when she heard the news of his death, instead of calmly sipping her tea and remarking about the weather. She wished she'd left the flower to decorate his grave.

"What's etched here beneath the name?"

Stewart's voice drew her back across the miles to White Earth. He was crouched down, studying another marker. She blinked and found her eyelashes clumped and sodden. For a moment she let the tears fall, one then another, hot and wet atop her skin. Then she fanned her cheeks and joined Stewart beside the grave. Carved just beneath the crossbar, clogged with beads of dried paint, was the image of an upside-down crane.

"It's his totem. His clan."

"They still follow all that?"

"Some."

Stewart rose from his haunches and stretched his arms, his neck and shoulders undoubtedly sore from the long ride in. "Let's get one of those new Franklin Roadsters when we return home."

"They're too loud."

He wrapped his arms around her waist and kissed her. "But they're fast."

Alma smiled, imagining them driving through the Pennsylvania countryside, engine rumbling, wind rushing at their faces, the smell of gasoline mingling with the scent of spring's first flowers. But the image faded quickly.

She pulled away and glanced above the steeple at the wide October sky. Already the sun labored in its descent. They had an hour, maybe two, before they must return to Detroit Lakes.

"Could he have meant another cemetery?" Stewart asked.

She'd not seen another church when they drove through town. Perhaps the Catholics kept a small plot behind the mission school. They checked there without success. No cemetery. No Zhawaeshk.

Alma sat on the edge of a water well and dropped her head into her palms. Asku had described visiting a cemetery once. Here, near the agency. But he hadn't spoken of crosses or headstones. She looked up and scoured their surroundings.

A spattering of trees skirted the schoolyard and beyond it a clearing bright with sunlight. Alma took Stewart's hand and led him through the pines and cottonwoods. A host of miniature houses crowded the clearing, their pitched roofs rising above the sedge and switchgrass. They were long and narrow, stretching three, four, five feet or more. Each had a small opening—a window perhaps—no bigger than a playing card, with a sill or small ledge jutting out beneath.

Stewart ran a hand over the rough-hewn wood. "What are they?"

"Grave houses," she whispered.

A belch startled her. There, a few paces off, sat a young man, leaning against one of the houses. Zhawaeshk. It must be him. Her hold about Stewart's arm eased. At last, someone who could answer questions about the night of the murder, who could help prove Asku innocent. She forgot herself in her relief and started toward him, only to stop after a few steps. In his hand the man held a jar of brownish liquid, just like the ones Alma saw passed beneath the merchant stalls. He'd painted circles around his eyes—a sign of mourning. Recent tears had caused the paint to run, streaking his cheeks black.

"Boozhoo," she said softly. "Zhawaeshk na gidizhinikaaz?"

He turned his head at her voice, blinked, and frowned. After a long drink from the jar he tried to stand, but his legs faltered. He collapsed onto one knee. Sharp-smelling liquor sloshed over the edge of the jar and onto the beaded cuff of his buckskin shirt.

Stewart frowned. He hesitated a moment, pulled fast his gloves, and then hauled the man to his feet. "Are you Mr. Zhawaeshk?"

The man shrugged free of Stewart's hold, planted a steadying hand atop the grave house, and took another swig. "Who is wanting to know?"

Stewart brushed off his coat, his frown deepening into a sneer. His father had drunk. He'd mentioned this to her only once, in a breezy, offhanded way, but she saw now the admixture of pain and revulsion in his eyes. She walked over and squeezed his arm, then laid a hand on the man's back. "Whose grave is this?"

He cast her a scowl over his shoulder, then took another drink. "Niwiiw. My wife."

Alma felt Stewart's arm tighten around her waist. His gaze softened. "When did she die?"

"What care you?"

"The paint around your eyes. It must have been recent," she said.

He wiped his nose with the back of his hand. "Berry-picking season."

"I wish her well on the Path of Souls," Alma said.

The man choked on his drink and turned to her with leery eyes. "How do you know of jiibay-miikana?"

"My friend Askuwheteau told me."

He snickered. "Askuwheteau have no friends."

That couldn't be true. Everyone at Stover had loved Asku. "You must be thinking of another man."

"Son of Odinigun, of the Gull Lakes Band." Another bitter laugh. "I know who you speak of."

"Whom," Alma said, as much from habit as from spite.

"You thinks I care of white man's words?" He thrust out his arms. His loose shirtsleeves fell back to his elbows, revealing several raised scars on the underside of his forearms. "I didn't care when the sisters did this and I don't care now."

Alma gaped. She'd heard of teachers striking students' forearms with switches; had seen Miss Wells do it once or twice with her vile ruler. But this? It must have taken dozens of strikes to leave such scars.

"I'm sorry, I didn't mean . . ." She turned her face away, but he pressed closer, shaking his bare arms before her.

Alma shuffled back, bumping hard into the eaves of one of the grave houses. The weathered boards whined and shuddered. The entire grave house swayed. She gasped and tried to steady herself. Her wheeling arm struck the roof boards, splintering the wood and knocking loose the nails that held one of the boards in place. It swung free with a rusty cry. Sunlight spilled into the opening. As she teetered backward she caught a glimpse inside, horrified she might see skull and bones or decaying flesh, but unable to look away.

Dirt. Only dirt.

Stewart caught her just before she fell and toppled the entire house. She covered her wide mouth with her hands. "Oh God."

The man's dark eyes went wild. "Awas! You don't belong in our sacred place." His fingers clenched around the jar like talons, sending a shiver through the amber liquid. His other hand closed into a fist.

Stewart stepped between them and squared his shoulders. "Now, see here. We meant no disrespect. We only wanted to ask you some questions."

"I will speak no answers. Awas! Go!"

Stewart's hands twitched at his sides. "I can get a subpoena for your testimony."

Zhawaeshk cleared his throat and spit. Wet mucus sprayed across Stewart's shiny leather shoes.

Alma had never seen her husband's face color so quickly. His jaw tightened. His nostrils flared. "Apologize, sir."

Zhawaeshk shook his head.

Stewart yanked off his gloves, stuffed them in his hat, and thrust them at Alma. Had he gone mad? Boyhood fisticuffs aside, he'd never actually fought a man—not that she knew of. True, Zhawaeshk was drunk. Even as he set his jar aside and tied back his hair, he swayed and fumbled. But he stood just as tall as Stewart and looked at least a decade younger. Where Stewart's hands were smooth and groomed, Zhawaeshk's were scarred and calloused. His mouth twisted with a sneer. He raised his fists. Stewart did likewise.

"Wait!" Alma pushed between them. "Stop. This is no place for such madness."

Zhawaeshk stood so close she could smell his sour breath, feel its heat on her cheek. The veins of his neck showed like cords beneath his skin. How slow they pulsed compared to her own frenzied heart. How calm and sinister he appeared—a man with nothing to lose.

Stewart's arm roped her waist, pulling her sideways, away from the fight. "Alma, please—"

Before he could finish, Zhawaeshk leaned in and jabbed Stewart in the mouth.

Her husband blinked and brought a hand to his lips. Blood smeared onto his fingertips. For a moment, he just stood there, eyes glassy, as if the whole scene were too absurd for his analytical mind to process. Then he pushed her farther aside and swung his fist at the Indian, striking him in the eye. Black paint smeared across his knuckles. The force of the blow seemed to surprise all three of them. Zhawaeshk stumbled back. Stewart shook out his hand. Alma sucked back a yelp.

Within seconds, Zhawaeshk steadied himself, his sneer gone, his gaze serious as the dead.

"Bekaa! Stop! Look." Alma pointed at the grave house behind Zhawaeshk, the one he'd been leaning against when they found him. In his backward stumble, he'd kicked a small hole in the base of the house with his heel. His drink had spilled, too, its foul contents seeping into the small birch bark–wrapped bundle beside it. The spirit bundle for his wife, Alma guessed.

Zhawaeshk flung himself to the ground and frantically dried the bundle on his shirt. Fresh tears rimmed his bloodshot eyes. He took the liquor jar and flung it far beyond the houses. A howl burst from his throat and he started to rock, beating his forehead against the grave house roof.

His sobs grated at her heart. She knew all too well the agony of such grief. She reached for Stewart's hand, but he gave no response to her touch. His fingers remained limp within her hand, his face drawn in openmouthed shock. His lip had begun to swell. Blood stained his jaw. At last, he reached for his hat, which she'd forgotten she still held, and turned to go.

"Wait." She turned to Zhawaeshk. "I know we shouldn't have come to you here." Her throat closed as she struggled to hold back her own tears. "We're desperate."

"Go," Zhawaeshk said.

Stewart tugged on her arm. "Come on, darling."

Her feet would not move. She looked over the low grave houses, each pointing west, directing the dead toward the hereafter. Despite the sunlight, her skin grew cold.

"It's not Asku's time."

Zhawaeshk looked up at her. "Perhaps it is. He's a hero now in the eyes of our people. Before, he was nothing."

"How can that be? Daga. Please. Help me understand."

Zhawaeshk turned from her and whispered something to the grave. He pulled a chunk of maple sugar and a few strips of dried meat from his shirt pocket. After laying them reverently upon the windowsill, he struggled to his feet. "Help me fix the houses and I will tells you all I know."

They found a few scraps of wood and a handful of rusty nails alongside the clearing. Hammering with flattened rocks, Zhawaeshk and Stewart squatted side by side and patched the houses. Alma stood beside them, holding Stewart's coat and jacket, handing them nails, and listening.

Zhawaeshk's tale pained her. Were it not for a few details she knew to be true, she'd have branded it all as lies. By his recounting, Askuwheteau had returned from Brown withdrawn and bitter. He was offered a job at the agency but refused, wanting nothing to do with the white man, nor the half-breeds who lived like whites in the village. But he had no place among those who still followed the seasons either. He couldn't hunt or weave a fishing net. Couldn't build a canoe or skin a deer. Many words he had forgotten. Everyone thought him *maminaadizi,* uppity. Laughed at his funny white man ways. He tried his hand at farming his allotment and failed. Too proud, Zhawaeshk said. Too angry to ask for help. He sold his father's allotment and squandered it on firewater. Would have sold his own, too, had they let him. He had no home, no people. Even Minowe kept away. He hung around town like a shadow, drunk and cussing the world.

"What about Agent Andrews? Was there bad blood between them?" Stewart asked. They were at the well beside the schoolhouse now. He drew up the bucket and handed it to Zhawaeshk.

The Indian drank, then looked around the empty schoolyard. The alcohol's hold seemed to have faded. He was jumpy now, restless. He peered down the thoroughfare, scanned the fringe of nearby trees, then rubbed his arms. "After this summer, when they divided up our timberlands, everyone have got bad blood with him."

Alma stood a pace off, her mind struggling to reconcile Zhawaeshk's story with her memories. But something now in his voice—the cut of anger, the hush of fear—commanded her attention. "Why?"

He hesitated, then spoke quickly about crooked ledgers and land deeds, secret deals with lumber companies, favoritism showed to mixed-bloods who'd be more likely to offer up the pine on their new allotments.

Perhaps that explained the tension she'd felt back in the annuity line.

"Was Mr. Muskrat cheated in these dealings?" Stewart asked. He'd taken a small notebook from his jacket pocket and jotted down notes as Zhawaeshk spoke.

"No, he could read the funny marks on those land maps, so he got a more better allotment. But afterward he spoke out for the rests of us. Said they should make the whole process over again so it were fair."

"And did they? Reallot the land?"

Zhawaeshk shook his head. "Plenty people were happy when Askuwheteau shot Agent Andrews."

Stewart's hand flagged. He stopped writing. "You saw him shoot the agent, then?"

Alma felt the world still. Insects ceased their humming. Leaves quit their chatter. Even her heart and lungs seemed to slow. Could it all really end here? Could Asku really have stolen upon the agent and shot him in the back? *Bang. Bang. Bang.* Each shot sounded in her mind. She could almost smell the gun smoke. Please, not Asku. Never Asku.

"No, I not saw him. We were behind the store with our drink. Askuwheteau got up and went away. Many moments later I heard gunshots. Agent Andrews was dead on the road. No one was there."

"So it could have been anyone?" Alma said, her voice a bit too loud, her tone more like a statement than a question. "Asku mightn't have had anything to do with it at all."

Zhawaeshk rubbed his arms again. His sleeves fell back, bunching around his elbows, exposing his scars. He looked at the angry raised lines and then back at Alma. "Askuwheteau have wounds like this too."

She bristled. What kind of picture did this man paint for Stewart? That of a louse, a drunk, a deviant. Asku was none of these things, not when she knew him. And he'd never been struck. Not once.

She started to speak, to protest, but Zhawaeshk waved her off. "Not ones you could see." He thumped his chest. "Here. On the inside. We all of us do."

CHAPTER 23

⟫•⟪

Wisconsin, 1890

The Christmas ball dominated conversation well into the new year. With each retelling, the evergreen in the foyer grew taller, the mayor's mansion larger, the food and festivities grander.

Routine had just begun to dull the excitement when a cry—shrill and urgent as the steamboat horns that blared from the Mississippi— split the January air.

Standing on the top stair of the root cellar, Alma's head whipped toward the sound. Mr. Simms rushed from the workshop across the yard, bearing a large sagging mass in his arms. George raced next to him, cradling the other half of the lanky object.

The jug of molasses slipped from Alma's hand. It crashed through the crust of snow and shattered on the frozen ground beneath. Alma's eyes flashed down to the dark liquid oozing between the shards of broken clay, then back up. Mrs. Simms shouted up from the cellar, but her words did not register. The men carried not an object, but a boy, his body limp, his head lolling like a marionette lost of its strings.

The breath in Alma's lungs froze. Her stomach twisted and tightened. The cook's heavy footfalls echoed behind her, ascending the cellar steps. "Heavens above, child, whatever is the—my God."

The woman's ruddy face went white. She stood rooted beside Alma as the men approached.

"Clear the counter, Martha," Mr. Simms shouted. "Then go fetch Mr. Blanchard. This boy needs a doctor!"

Her husband's electric words seemed to shock the life back into her. She bustled past Alma and rushed toward the kitchen, taking the icy steps to the back door two at a time. The men passed in a blur of red. It showed in their cheeks and frost-nipped noses. It colored the fronts of their shirts and stained their forearms. It dripped on the white snow beneath them.

Alma came to life and hurried behind them into the kitchen. Pots and pans lay scattered on the floor where Mrs. Simms had swept them. George and Mr. Simms laid the body down on the wooden counter. The boy's face was slack and ashen—Charles. He was a Mohican a few years younger than Alma. His stories by the bonfire silenced the night wind, and he stole apples even more deftly than Alice.

Her eyes moved from his face down his torso. When they lit on the twisted, mangled flesh that had once been an arm, she gasped and stumbled backward. Three fingers were missing from his swollen hand. Lacerations crisscrossed his arm, extending well above the elbow, exposing bright-red muscle and splintered bone. Blood was everywhere, spurting in some places, oozing slowly in others.

"Rags, Miss Alma, fetch some rags."

She heard Mr. Simms's voice like a distant echo. Her legs moved of their own volition to the cupboard. She grabbed a thick stack of fresh towels and staggered back.

The older man's burlap hands guided her fingers to the crushed arm. "Keep pressure there now." He tossed a few rags across the table at George. "You too."

Her hands trembled as the white linen bloomed scarlet. Warm liquid seeped between her fingers. Her stomach heaved and the room began to spin.

"Breathe, Azaadiins," George whispered. He moved his hands so the tips of his fingers overlapped with hers. He too trembled.

A few inches above their hands, Mr. Simms tied a thick strip of leather around Charles's arm. "Keep on the pressure until the bleeding stops."

Footsteps clamored in the hall and her father bounded into the room. "What's happened?"

"Accident with the lathe," the groundskeeper said.

Her father stepped closer to the table, then reeled back. "My Lord! Is he dead?"

"No, sir, but he's lost a lot of blood. Best we fetch a doctor and quick."

"Yes . . . yes . . . go saddle the horses. I'll fetch my cloak and be out presently."

Mr. Simms flew from the room, parting the cluster of gaping boys who huddled at the back door.

"Off with you," her father said to them. "Close down the workshop and retire to your dormitory. Prayer is what the boy needs now."

They shuffled outside with wide eyes and anxious, thin-lipped expressions. A group of girls had gathered in the hallway at the opposite door. Her father shooed them away in similar fashion, sending the newly arrived Miss Wells to keep them upstairs.

"You'll be okay, won't you?" he said to Alma and George. "Mrs. Simms is here."

Alma glanced over at the cook. The woman sat in the corner on an upended pail, her face the color of the whitewashed walls, her eyes glazed and vacant.

Without waiting for a response, her father left the room, his heavy steps muffled by the hallway rug.

Alma looked at George, the sight beneath her hands too gruesome to regard. Sweat beaded across his forehead. His disheveled hair fell forward, shielding his downturned eyes. She could hear Charles's raspy breath, uneven and urgent, as if he were drowning beneath a current of invisible water. She felt the spasms of his body, his skin cool while his blood ran hot. Her eyes remained anchored on George, not looking as much as clinging, desperate for refuge.

"How did this happen, George?"

He looked up. A glossy sheen covered his eyes. Taut jaw muscles bulged beneath his tawny skin. His breath quivered with each inhale. "I was . . ." He stopped, raked back his hair with a bloodstained hand, and then continued. "I was sanding wood. At the lathe. A leg. For to make a table. Charles came. The end of his shirt—by his hand—"

"His sleeve?"

George nodded. "It caught in the spindle, pulling him. And his arm. The belt ate his arm. Chewed and twisted and spit it out. I stopped. Took my foot away from the treadle. Too late." He lowered his head, shielding his face from her.

"This wasn't your fault. I've been in the wood shop before. It's too crowded. So much is going on all at once. Just last week Frederick cut himself on a saw blade and needed stitches."

"Plenty more than stitches is needed here."

"I know, but—"

Charles gasped. His eyes opened, wide and frantic. Alma took one hand off the wound and laid the back of it on his cheek. His clammy skin was cool against her fingers. "It's okay, Charles. The doctor shall arrive any minute. Shh, now. Be still."

She stroked his cheek and his breathing steadied. When his eyes fluttered shut, she looked back at George. "He's so cold."

George cleared his throat, regaining his composure. "Mrs. Simms, do you keep any blanket in the kitchen?"

The cook's frazzled-haired head popped up. "What, dear? No . . . no, I don't need a blanket, thank you. I'm just resting here a bit before I start dinner is all."

Laughter slipped through Alma's lips while tears mounted at the rims of her eyes. "I'll go fetch one from the trunk in the hall. I think the bleeding has stopped a bit since Mr. Simms put on that tourniquet."

Alma returned with a thick wool blanket and tucked it around Charles's body. Blood wicked into its fuzzy fibers.

"Like ink," she said aloud. "Mother will be irate over the stains."

Again, she wanted to laugh. What did it matter what her mother thought at a time like this? A smile twitched at the corner of her lips. She glanced at George. What must he think of her? But a crooked grin sprang to his lips as well. A fleeting moment and their smiles faded. Their eyes strayed away.

Through the silence, Alma listened, begging of each passing moment the sound of horse hooves. The angst of her younger self, waiting, listening for a similar sound, flashed in her memory. She had never dreamed the arrival of the Indians would lead her here: standing beside a broken body, across the table from the boy who called her enemy, her ears once again straining to hear the cry of wagon wheels through the empty air.

When the sound did come—snow crunching, hooves pounding like a frantic drumbeat—Alma released a heavy sigh. Her father rushed in, followed by Dr. Austin and Mr. Simms.

The middle-aged physician shooed Alma from the table. His alert, beady eyes scanned Charles from head to toe. He lifted the saturated towels from the wound. "If there's any hope of him living, I'll have to amputate. Open my bag, Mr. Blanchard, and retrieve my saw. We'll need water set to boil and fresh linen too." He flung the soiled rags on the floor. Blood spattered across the kitchen.

Alma's stomach turned. The glint of the long metal handsaw caught her eye; the room blurred and spun. She pushed through the back door and raced down the steps to the yard. Falling to her hands and knees, convulsions overtook her and she vomited in the white snow.

The sun had sunk behind the trees, but rays of light knifed through empty boughs, casting a barbed-wire pattern of light and dark across the ground. From inside came an arresting shriek. The kitchen windows rattled. Alma's stomach heaved again.

How long she remained there, hands and knees buried in the snow, Alma did not know. Eventually, the door behind her swung open and closed. Footfalls descended the stairs toward her. She covered her vomit with snow and wiped her mouth on her sleeve.

George offered her a hand and helped her up. The warmth of his skin made her entire body crave his touch. He sandwiched her frozen fingers between his own and brought them to his mouth. His hot breath began to thaw her.

On any other occasion, Alma would have pulled away. But it was not just her hands that were numb. Her entire body felt shrouded in fog.

Her mother's voice from within the kitchen startled her back to reality. "Great heavens! What's happened here? Where's Alma?"

She slipped her hands from George's grasp just as the back door whined open.

"Alma, come inside this instant."

She turned around and her mother gasped. "You're covered in blood. That's not your silk gown, is it?"

This time, Alma found no humor in the absurd exchange. "No, Mother, just my cotton work dress. I was helping Mrs. Simms in the cellar when . . . when the accident happened. I'll wash up at the well and be in presently."

Her mother frowned. "Very well. You too, George. You're absolutely gruesome."

The two of them plodded to the well. The air had cooled with the sun's retreat, creating a frozen crust atop the snow that crunched beneath their feet. Alma's legs felt heavy, each step a chore. She sank onto the lip of the well while George cast and reeled the bucket. They washed their hands in the frigid water without a word. Alma scrubbed hers frantically, rubbing the skin raw. George smoothed his together in slow, circular motions, his eyes fixed, distant.

She dried her hands on a patch of skirt not soiled with blood, vomit, or melted snow and started back to the schoolhouse. George did not follow.

"George—"

"Tɛ·h!" His voice bellowed across the open yard. He backhanded the water pail, sending it careening through the air. The pink-tinged liquid spattered over the snow. "The white man and his white man ways. This never would have happened if not for that!"

Alma staggered backward. "Accidents happen. It's not anyone's fault."

His dark eyes, made even darker by dusk's dim light, raked over her like talons. "No? The Menominee never made machines that eat boys' arms."

The blood flared in her veins. "You don't have doctors like Dr. Austin who can heal such injuries either."

"You know nothing of our maskīhkiw."

"I know Charles would lose a lot more than his arm if not for Dr. Austin."

George crossed the distance between them in two heavy strides. He stood so close the hot cloud of his breath engulfed her face. He pointed toward a lonely break in the trees. "If white medicine is so great and powerful, what happened to them?"

Even before her eyes followed the trajectory of his arm, Alma knew to what he pointed. At the far end of the yard, like a deep pockmark in the otherwise smooth line of trees, stood a small cemetery. Eleven headstones jutted from the earth. Each was identical in form, plainly wrought and inscribed.

Alma hugged her arms against her chest, her fingers pressed to bone. The first death had happened quickly, only a few months into Stover's first term. Pneumonia. ROBERT, JANUARY 1882, was the only epitaph. The boy's true name, his Indian name, had faded from her memory, but his copper face lingered. Death had come every winter since. She remembered every face.

When she spoke, her voice came thin, wavering, equal parts anger and sorrow. "And children don't die on the reservations? Death, I suppose, is also the white man's invention?"

"They die. They die in the arms of their mothers and fathers. Tshipe'kaino is performed in their honor. Here is a lonely death."

Alma blinked back the tears that returned to her eyes. "The Lord is always with us. We never die alone." But the words sounded like her father's.

"Whose Lord? The Indian does not want your God any more than he want your killer machines." He glared down at her a second more, then stormed back toward the house.

The cold twilight closed in around her, but Alma did not move. Her hands trembled and her chest heaved. She hated George—his arrogance, his pride, his refusal to cede even the smallest ground.

After several deep breaths, she mustered a semblance of poise and turned back to the house. Her eyes caught on the meager cemetery, pale headstones like ghosts at the edge of the woods. Their memory ripped through her, and though her feet moved toward the warm, gaslit rooms of the grand brick schoolhouse, her heart questioned their direction.

CHAPTER 24

─────►•◄─────

Minnesota, 1906

Alma looked back at the wide field beyond the agency as she and
Stewart rode from town. A large group of men squatted around a
blanket, whipping long sticks at shoe-shaped patches of buckskin.
The moccasin game. Asku had explained it to her once. A good
player could win a new shirt, headdress, or pony; a poor player leave
in want of the same. The men laughed and hollered. The hider shuffled bullets beneath the moccasins and a new round commenced.
Nearby, several women chatted beside a crackling cook fire. Children romped and dallied.

Then drums sounded—deep, resonant, staccato. The kind of beat
that captured the heart and overrode its rhythm. The sound was more
rich and commanding than the music made from hollow logs and
upturned pails Alma remembered from her youth. But the effect was
the same, the yearning immediate. The Indians would dance tonight,
sing and celebrate in firelight until dawn lit the sky. Alma imagined
herself among them—her body moving in time with the song, her
feet striking the hard ground, her lungs stinging from the smoke and
exertion. This life could have been hers, too. Yet when she closed her
eyes, the vision was hazy, blinking, like the lantern of a steamboat
obscured in fog.

Alma clutched the wagon's splintery sideboard and refused another look back. Her free hand found Stewart and nestled into the
crook of his arm. Here, beside him, was where she belonged.

Onward they drove, and the drumbeat loosed its grip, fading behind leaf chatter and birdsong. Though the sun had dipped west-ward, it promised enough daylight to see them back to Detroit Lakes. She recounted the day's events and, for the first time since their arrival in Minnesota, felt a sense of victory. They'd found only one witness, but Zhawaeshk's account of the murder seemed definitive. He'd come upon the body less than a minute after the shooting and had seen no one else on the road. From his telling, the others—the shopkeeper, the sheriff's deputy, the Indians who'd been gambling in the nearby woods—all arrived at staggering intervals afterward. None of them had actually witnessed the killing.

She turned to Stewart and smoothed his coat lapel, letting her hand linger a moment on his chest. His poor lip had doubled in size. She'd fix it up tonight with iodine and ice if the hotel could come by it. He'd been amazing today, surprising her at every turn. "How do you know so much about guns? Don't tell me you read all that in a book."

"No." He smiled, a rare sight these days, and ever so welcome. "Well, part of it I read. But my grandfather was somewhat of a collector."

"Really?" It was nice for once to feel like she wasn't the only one withholding bits of the past.

"He kept an old set of dueling pistols, a seventeenth-century musket, the flintlock rifle his great-grandfather used in the Revolution."

"Did you ever fire them?"

"I was forbade to even touch them." His handsome smile broadened; his gaze lifted toward the sky. "I did, of course, one night when all the grown-ups thought I'd gone to bed. I was five, maybe six. Nearly blew my foot off . . ." His voice drifted and he chuckled. "Grandma raged a fit over the hole in her Oriental carpet. . . . Needless to say, I got a good lecture about how gentlemen handle firearms."

Alma laughed, envisioning a young Stewart—inquisitive and precocious even then—sneaking into his grandfather's study. She thought of her own escapades, all the times she'd snuck around without her parents' knowledge, and felt a fleeting moment of kinship with her husband. Perhaps their childhoods weren't so different after all. Then, as always, her mind drifted to that last evening she'd ventured out in secret. Of course they were different—utterly and irrevocably so.

"Will you wire the judge when we return to town? Lobby for a mistrial?" she asked after several moments of silence.

"Not yet."

"What more evidence do you need?" She pulled away from his side and scrutinized his face. "Surely, you now believe Harry innocent."

"My beliefs matter little. It's the judge or, more likely, the jury we've got to convince." Stewart kept his attention forward, navigating around a shallow pit in the lane. "We can now cast doubt on the prosecution's version of events—who witnessed what, who had access to a gun—but none of that actually refutes Mr. Muskrat's involvement. What Mr. Zhawaeshk said about the recent allotment proceedings is interesting. Tomorrow we'll look more into—"

"But you do believe that he's innocent?"

He pulled his eyes from the road and gave her a quizzical look.

"You mustn't believe what Zhawaeshk said," she continued before he could give her an answer she didn't like. "About Harry being a vagabond and drunk."

Stewart's expression, now as it had been when Zhawaeshk told his tale, was inscrutable. But she knew his distaste for such behavior. He was puritanical in that regard. She knotted her hands and buried them in the folds of her skirt. Maybe then she wouldn't be tempted to chew through her leather gloves to get at the skin around her nails. Everyone made mistakes, had faults and secrets. Surely Stewart could see that. This wouldn't change his commitment to the case. To her. Would it? "All I—"

The horse lurched, throwing the carriage off-kilter. Stewart shook the reins, but the animal continued to hobble and slow, favoring its right hind leg.

"He's hurt," Alma said.

Stewart stopped the carriage and jumped down. When he approached the horse, it whinnied and shied away.

Alma winced. Her bookish husband knew little of animals. "Careful."

He bent down to examine the leg and the horse reared back, kicking up a cloud of dirt. The buggy swayed and nearly toppled. Alma grabbed the side and held her breath. Stewart staggered back, dusting off his coat. "Blast it! Are you all right?"

Alma stood. "Here, let me help."

"No." Stewart flung off his derby and shrugged out of his overcoat and suit jacket. "Stay in the wagon, darling."

Alma crossed her arms and remained standing. She couldn't help but smile as he rolled up his crisp shirtsleeves and inched toward the horse again, arms outstretched and fingers splayed. "Stay now." He patted the horse's back, then tugged lightly on its leg.

Despite Stewart's gentleness, the horse refused to raise his hoof. Instead, he snorted and whipped his tail at Stewart's face. Alma started to climb from the wagon when she heard the clamber of approaching riders. Four men drew up behind them, steam rising from their stallions' nostrils in the cooling air.

"Trouble?" a ginger-haired man asked. He was one of the men she'd seen yapping with Sheriff Knudson and handing out rations earlier that day.

Stewart took a deep breath and squared his shoulders. Alma could tell he hated being out of his element. "It seems our horse has gone lame."

"Might've thrown a shoe," the man said without even a glance in the animal's direction. "Don't suppose you've a hammer and spare."

The other men chuckled.

"No, I'm clear out," her husband said through gritted teeth.

"All the better. A city man like you." He sized up Stewart and snorted. "Course, there's a farrier back in the village. Doubt you'd make it there and back to Detroit Lakes before dark, though." His muddy-green eyes cut to Alma. "I'd hate for you to get lost along the way."

She shivered, but held his gaze.

"Saw you talking to Zhawaeshk over there by them funny houses they build over their dead. He tell you anything useful?" He opened a small tin and stuffed a wad of chewing tobacco into his mouth. He smiled at her then, his lower lip protruding, his teeth the color of dirty dishwater. She thought she might be sick. Had he been following them all day, lurking in the trees and brambles beyond the cemetery?

"What Mr. Zhawaeshk said is privileged information," Stewart answered for her.

The red-haired man swung his gaze back to Stewart. "That's right. You're here on official business." He tugged with exaggeration on his grimy bow tie. More chuckles from the other men. "They put a lot of stock in that down there in the capital? The testimony of a piss-drunk Indian?"

"Men of all color and station drink." Stewart looked down, rubbed the back of his neck, then glanced at Alma. "It does not entirely negate their worth or their testimony."

"Guess we'll see about that." The man readied his reins. "Best you continue on now, before the sun sets. You've a whip, doncha?"

Stewart hesitated. "Yes."

"Give 'im a good whacking and he'll get you back. Let the farrier in Detroit Lakes handle him tomorrow." He tipped his hat to Alma and spurred his horse, leaving a swell of dust behind him. The others followed.

All save one. James, the light-skinned Indian, hesitated, his eyes flickering between their wagon and his departing companions. The other riders disappeared behind a bend in the road, and James dismounted, cussing under his breath. "Merde."

"We're fine, thank you," Stewart said.

James gritted his teeth and shook his head. "You whip this horse back to Detroit Lakes and he'll never walk again." He stroked the horse's neck and whispered in its ear. "Steady, boy."

The beast's swishing tail stilled. Its ears relaxed downward and its breathing slowed. The Indian squatted and ran his hand down the horse's leg. When he tapped the back, the horse raised his hoof. "It's not a thrown shoe. Get me a stick."

Stewart gaped down at him.

"A stick," he said again, and let the horse's hoof fall.

"Ah . . . right." Stewart hurried to the edge of the road and pried a low-lying branch off a tree.

The Indian took the stick, snapped it in half over his knee, and whittled one end with a knife from his belt.

"I appreciate your help." Stewart raked back his hair, leaving the slick locks rumpled. "I'm afraid I don't know much about horses."

Alma watched the young man shape the wood into a small, narrow hook. His nails were neatly trimmed, but his fingers strong and calloused.

"You work for the agency, don't you?" Stewart asked.

He nodded, keeping his light-brown eyes trained on his work.

"What do you do there?"

"I'm editor of the *Tomahawk,* our weekly paper. And I translate from time to time for the agent."

"You're Chippewa, then?"

James raised an eyebrow in Stewart's direction, then turned his attention back to the horse. He peeled away a few more layers of wood and closed his knife. "Métis—mixed-blood. My grandfather was a French trapper."

"Did you know Harry Muskrat?"

To this, James said nothing. With one hand again bracing the horse's hoof, he scraped away clumps of mud from around the shoe. "Here's your problem." He held up a jagged stone. "Don't think it punctured or bruised the sole. Soak the hoof in warm water when you get back and he ought to be fine."

Stewart extended his hand. "Thank you."

"Yes," Alma said. "Miigwech."

James ignored Stewart's hand and tossed the stone far away into the prairie. Then he turned for the first time to Alma. His eyes narrowed. "You should go home."

Her skin burned. Was it the intensity of his gaze or the nagging feeling he might be right? "I can't."

He turned his back on both of them and mounted his horse. "There's more than Agent Taylor who don't want you snooping about here."

"We're not here to cause trouble," Stewart said.

James smirked. "That's what all you white men say."

"I beg your pardon." Without heed to his dirty hands, Stewart yanked down his shirtsleeves and fastened his silk knot cuff links. "We're here helping one of your own race."

"Helping? They say that too."

"And what?" Alma's hands clenched at her sides. "We should leave Askuwheteau to hang?"

Again, James's eyes narrowed over her. "Go home. You're chasing ghosts."

"Why did you help us, then?"

He shrugged. "Pity."

Stewart straightened his suit coat and donned his hat. "We don't need your pity."

"Not for you. For the horse." He rode off, his shadow long and spindly in the waning sunlight.

"Don't let him spook you, darling." Stewart climbed back in the wagon and took up the reins. "We'll show them all we have no intention of backing down."

She nodded, but could not shake the half-breed's words. Memories of her father's grave had surfaced today. But his was not the only grave, not the only cemetery whose white slab headstones haunted her.

Chasing ghosts. If he only knew.

CHAPTER 25

—————

Wisconsin, 1890

Days passed with their accustomed rhythm—morning lessons, afternoons of sewing, piano, and the occasional social call in La Crosse—but Alma stumbled through them like an unpolished dancer, languid and off tempo.

She visited Charles each afternoon in the infirmary, spoon-feeding him broth and relaying whatever bits of gossip she thought might raise his spirits. He rarely smiled. Pain and despondence deadened his eyes. George had been right on one account. Charles needed his family.

Today, on her way from the kitchen with Charles's lunch tray, she stopped at her father's study. "Any news of Charles's family?"

Her father looked up from the stack of newly opened letters on his desk. "What?"

"Charles's parents. It's been two weeks since the accident. Surely they're on their way."

"I thought it best not to worry them. Dr. Austin says the boy's condition is stable."

"They don't even know?" Her fingers clenched around the tray. "He'd benefit so from their company."

"What do you suggest? Have his family journey two hundred miles—in midwinter no less—when all they could do here is fret?"

She realized in that moment how glib her remark—the white man alone being able to heal Charles's injury—must have sounded to George that night by the well. Doc Austin saved the boy's life, it was true. His injury would heal. Nothing in the doctor's black bag could heal his melancholy, though. "Think of what comfort it would bring him to have his family by his side."

Her father's attention drifted back to his letters. "The Lord comforts his people and will—"

"I know. Have compassion on his afflicted ones." Alma sighed, still hovering by the doorway. "Couldn't we send Mr. Simms with the sleigh?"

He groped for his magnifying glass, speaking even as he read. "The school could hardly do without him for so many days."

"Oh, Father." She stomped to his desk, set down the tray, and grabbed his silver-rimmed glasses. Soup sloshed from the bowl. "Just use your spectacles."

"The writing here is terribly small. How is one ever expected—" He reached for his glasses, but Alma kept hold. At last, his eyes ventured upward. "Sit down, kitten."

She dragged forward a plain straight-backed chair. He took her hand and patted it. "You've always been such a sweet girl. Your concern over Charles does you credit. But he will be just fine. The Lord is watching over him. We are his family now."

"But his arm . . . perhaps if his parents cannot make the journey to Stover, Charles could be taken to them once he is well enough to travel."

Her father stiffened. "No, such talk is out of the question. If he were to go to the reservation now, it's likely he would never return. And what would he do there? Without an arm he would become nothing more than a beggar, wallowing his life away on the agency's doorstep."

Her father's blue eyes had grown wide and cold. She looked down. Her free hand fell to her side, her fingers sliding over the chair's unvarnished wood.

"But—"

"After Charles heals we'll start straightaway teaching him a skill, a trade he can perform, limited as he is. That's what's best for him, for his future, don't you think?"

"Yes, but—"

"Good. I know the event was traumatic. I'm sorry you were there to see it." He let go of her hand and turned his eyes back to the pile of correspondence. "Keep Charles in your prayers and encourage the other girls to do so as well. That's the best thing you can do for him."

A splinter pricked the pad of her thumb. She pulled it out and sucked away the blood. Why couldn't he see?

"The boy's soup, Alma, it's getting cold."

She returned the chair to its corner—this time without scraping its legs atop the floor—and crept from the room with Charles's tray. Before closing the door, she looked again at her father. He sat straight now, spectacles in place, his finger tracking his place on the paper. Naught but the dinner gong would break his attention. He'd grown stout these years. Veins the width of thread crisscrossed his cheeks beneath his waxen skin.

Inside the infirmary, Charles lay beneath a shrouded window in the corner. Two other beds crowded the tiny room. Other students, hacking and feverish, intermittently filled them. Today, they both lay empty.

Alma set the tray atop the bedside table and pulled back the curtains. Charles squinted in the onslaught of light and scooted up into a semi-seated position. His face had regained only a hint of color. The hollows of his eyes were dark and sunken. It was hard for Alma to look at him and not recall that night—the blood, the screams, the saw. For his sake, she hoped Charles remembered none of it.

She drew the room's lone chair up beside the bed and reached for the soup.

"I can feed my own self, Azaadiins."

"Yes, of course." She perched the food tray on a pillow atop his lap.

With a shaky left hand, he grabbed the spoon and sank it into the soup. His other limb was nothing more than a bandaged nub. Alma looked down but watched him eat through the corner of her eye. The spoon wobbled, but the yellow broth did not spill.

"I used to do everything with this hand until I came here and Miss Wells made me learn it all over again with my other. She's vicious with her ruler stick." A smirk flashed across his face. "She won't have no more choice now."

Alma had no reply.

He took a few more sips of soup. "Estotkeh auptoonnauwaukun? No words for me today?"

She bit her lip and thought back on the day's events. "Frederick and Walter got ten demerits today for speaking out of turn in class."

"Unnunnaumpauk?"

"No, in English. But it was supposed to be silent study. Walter slept through reveille and was late to drill practice. Fifteen demerits for that."

"I no miss that." Charles put down his spoon and leaned back. A grimace spread across his face with the movement.

Alma rescued the tray just as the soup began to slosh over the side of the bowl. Beads of sweat had broken out across Charles's forehead and his eyes remained scrunched shut. She fumbled in the bedside drawer for the bottle of laudanum and coaxed open his mouth. His lips puckered when the drops of reddish-brown liquid hit his tongue, then relaxed. The deep furrows around his eyes softened.

She put away the laudanum and continued, mostly to fill the silence. "I do have one bit of good news. Father received word today that the Woman's National Indian Association has awarded Asku a scholarship to continue his studies after graduation. I don't know if he's selected a college yet, but—"

"Azaadiins, can you sing at me?"

"Oh no, you wouldn't like that. I have a most unlovely voice. Let me get Minowe. She sings so well."

Without opening his eyes, Charles groped for her hand. "I no mind. Please, a song."

Her eyes traveled from his face to his gauze-wrapped stump and back. She sighed. "What shall I sing?"

"Anything."

She knew many piano melodies but few of the accompanying lyrics. Several church hymns came to mind, but she settled instead on a tune with more levity. Leaning in close, she took a deep breath and began to sing.

> *The girl that I lov'd she was handsome,*
> *I tried all I knew her to please,*
> *But I could not please her one quarter so well,*
> *Like that man upon the trapeze.*
>
> *He'd fly thro' the air with the greatest of ease,*
> *A daring young man on the flying trapeze.*

She stopped after the chorus. Charles's chest rose and fell with the heavy rhythm of drug-induced sleep. Was it folly to believe he would ever recover? Even with his ambidextrous skill, one limb could never match the speed and precision of two working in concert. Was Stover to blame and she by extension, or had fate eyed him for this tragedy since birth?

Alma shook her head and stood. These questions had plagued her since the accident and still she had no answers. Guilt gnawed at her. She knew he longed for other voices—those of his mother and father—and other words, Mohican words. Perhaps for now the opium could sweeten and transform her song, but it would not last forever.

The ceiling creaked. The other girls were undoubtedly gathering upstairs with her mother for sewing instruction. Six mechanical sewing machines now crowded the upstairs parlor—a far cry from the early days of simple stitching. The girls rotated between machine work, where they made new uniforms and linens to supply the school, and handiwork like crocheting, knitting, and detailed cross-stitch and embroidery.

The sway of the wrought-iron treadles soon hummed down from the rafters. She thought of the crowded parlor, her mother's reproving eye, the concerned looks passed between her friends after glancing in her direction.

She fled the infirmary, but instead of ascending the stairs to join in the needlework, grabbed her cloak from the hallway chest and hurried through the kitchen to the backyard.

Work had resumed in the wood shop. Steam billowed from the grease- and soot-covered engine along the shop's far wall. The usual din of hammers, saws, and spinning lathes reached her across the snow-covered lawn. She imagined the unvarnished floorboards, stained and warped with blood, now covered, forgotten beneath a blanket of sawdust. How could they all go on—her father, her mother, Mr. Simms—as if nothing had happened?

Around the far side of the schoolhouse, she found a measure of peace. Her breathing slowed and her heart regained a steady rhythm. The trees pressed in closer here than on any other side of the house, leaving but some thirty yards of clearing. She seated herself on a long wooden storage box nestled alongside the schoolhouse. Swollen gray clouds crowded the sky, dropping the occasional snowflake, but the eaves of the house shielded her from their assault.

In the open silence, she set about unspooling her thoughts. The hateful gossip at the dance, the recent accident, the cemetery whose headstones she could just make out through the trees. To all this, her father was blind.

Her eyes wandered the blankness of the clearing. A lone archery target stood nestled against the tree line. The painted rings had faded and the burlap covering had frayed. Two years back, the school had staged an archery exhibition at the La Crosse fair. Alma remembered the hearty applause. The lace-fringed hands of a dozen ladies had shot into the air at the offer of one-on-one instruction. She could almost smell the rich scent of popcorn and roasted peanuts that had wafted from the food stands. Were such carefree days gone for good?

She stood and heaved open the lid of the storage box on which she sat. Several dusty bows and quivers of arrows lay inside. She grabbed a set and fit one loop of the bowstring into the bottom nock. Next, she braced the bow against her leg and bent the upper limb forward. The stiff wood whined in resistance. Her hand slipped and the upper limb sprang back, missing her nose by only inches. She tried again, putting all her weight and strength into the endeavor; the loop slid into the nock.

Facing the target, she blew away the cobwebs from the feather vanes and positioned the arrow. The bow felt foreign in her arms. Her muscles struggled to recall the correct movements. She pulled back and shot. The arrow sang through the air, at first on target, then veering left, striking not the bull's-eye, but a nearby tree.

"Good shot."

Alma jumped at the voice and spun around. George stood a few paces off.

"What are you doing here?"

He looked down at the heap of wood scraps in his arms, then nodded toward a large stack of lumber piled along the brick wall.

"Oh . . . well . . . carry on," she said.

"What would your mother think? You holding the bow and arrow of the Indian."

She raised her chin. "Archery is a respectable pastime among ladies."

He snickered and walked past. Halfway to the pile he began to whistle. He tossed his load atop the waist-high stack of timber and turned around. Instead of retreating, he leaned against the brick wall, arms and ankles crossed like a train-yard hobo, and continued to whistle.

Confounded boy! She turned her back to him and marched to the tree line to remove her arrow. They'd said nothing to each other since the night of Charles's accident, but where she once found satisfaction in their enmity, the silence and retreating glances now perturbed her. She throttled the arrow, yanked it from the tree trunk, and strode back to her bow.

Clear as birdsong, George's whistle-tune filled the small yard.

She tried to focus on other sounds—the swoosh of her skirt over the snow, the occasional rustle of barren branches bending in the wind—but it was not enough to distract her from his song. Then the melody hit her. Her eyes went wide and heat rushed into her cheeks.

He'd fly thro' the air with the greatest of ease, a daring young man on the flying trapeze.

"You were listening?"

"Very funny song. What's a trapeze?"

"How dare you listen!"

His lips curved into a mischievous grin. "Why you never sing with Minowe and Hįčoga?"

"I haven't the voice for it." She shook her head. "That's not the point. I only sang to avail poor Charles. It has nothing—"

"I like your voice. Sing it again."

"Stop it, George." She turned away, facing the target, and nocked her arrow. "Leave me be. I haven't the stomach to quarrel with you today."

When he spoke again, his voice had lost its taunting edge. "No, truly. It is good what you do for him."

Alma shook her head. She waited to hear retreating footsteps, but George did not move. After several seconds of silence, she raised and drew the bow. A low chuckle rent her concentration. With bow upright and arrow poised to shoot, she spun around. "What?"

George raised his hands above his head, still laughing. "Your form, Azaadiins, it's very wrong."

He'd used her Indian name again. She lowered the bow. "I don't need your help."

He arched an eyebrow and took a step closer, his arms still raised.

Ignoring his approach, she turned back to the target. "I'm just a little out of practice."

Footfalls continued toward her through the snow. She drew back the arrow, but stopped when a hand came to rest on her hip.

The air in her lungs froze.

"Here." He guided her back leg around with his foot, aligning her body perpendicular to the target. He pressed down on her shoulders until her carriage relaxed. Then, mirroring her stance, he moved in close behind her. His left hand grabbed the bow directly below her grip. He matched the curve of her drawing arm with his, their fingers overlapping atop the bowstring.

The target, the trees, the cloudy gray horizon blurred. Alma blinked. George's breath tickled the back of her neck. They drew back together and loosed the arrow. It whistled through the air, arcing slightly, then descended toward the target. Alma pivoted around without waiting for it to land. George had dropped his arms but not backed up. She looked up into his face, only inches from her own.

Her mother's voice sounded in the back of her mind, badgering her about propriety and the precise distance of chaste interactions, but when his hand touched her cheek, tilting her head up toward his, she knew nothing but the contact of their skin.

Their lips pressed together. Had she started the kiss or had he? That thought, too, slipped from her mind. He cradled her head fiercely, the pressure of his mouth against hers alternatively rough and tender.

Then, suddenly, he broke apart from her, spinning round on his heels and strolling away. Alma remained frozen, the shock of the encounter rooting her to the ground. A strange mixture of panic and elation bubbled up inside her. The electricity of his touch was like none she'd ever felt. It lingered on her cheek and lips, buzzing like a delicious poison.

Before rounding the corner, George looked over his shoulder. He blinked, mirroring her own bewilderment, then shot her a pulse-quickening grin.

No sooner had he disappeared behind the brick façade than Alma heard the voice of Mrs. Simms.

"Alma!"

She hurried around the house to the kitchen.

"Heaven above, child! That's the third time I called you."

"Sorry, ma'am. I . . . I didn't hear you."

"What you doing yonder round the house anyway?"

Alma's chest tightened like a vise. She looked around for George, then remembered he had sauntered off in the opposite direction. Breath rushed from her lungs. Not only had he heard Mrs. Simms, but also had the good sense not to let her see him. "I wanted some fresh air."

"Mighty cold to be out after some air."

Alma danced past the cook into the kitchen. Was it cold? She hadn't noticed.

CHAPTER 26

Minnesota, 1906

She and Stewart made it back to their hotel just as the last rivulets of light drained from the sky. They'd spoken little since their encounter with James and the other agency workers. Alma couldn't quiet her thoughts, nor did she dare give voice to them. The few conversations Stewart sparked dwindled quickly, like fire set to damp wood.

Dinner passed much the same. She chewed her food, sipped her wine, but tasted nothing. A piss-drunk Indian—that's what the men had called Zhawaeshk. Would the jury see him any different? And the gunsmith—what would he do? She could picture him in court pointing his grubby finger at Asku. "That there's the man I sold the gun to."

Even if he sold other guns of the same model, even if his dealings were illegal, she and Stewart needed more evidence. Her husband tried to look unbothered, just as he had when the men rode up and asked him if he had a spare, as if a man of his station knew anything about shoeing a horse.

She needed to learn more about what had happened to Asku, what had transformed him from the boy she'd loved to the awful man Zhawaeshk described. But she needed to hear it from someone she could trust.

"Dessert, ma'am?" the hotel matron asked.

Alma shook her head. The knowledge of what she must do had set her stomach churning and she regretted eating anything at all.

"I wish we'd gotten more statements, but we haven't time to go in search of the other witness," Stewart said between bites of pie. "Tomorrow we must start on the agency's files."

"I could try to find them," Alma said. As well as a few witnesses of her own.

Stewart frowned. "Split up? I don't think it's a good idea."

"Don't worry, dearest. I speak the language, remember? And I shan't go far." She smiled as she spoke, hoping to give her voice a lightness that belied the sudden flush of dread. Seeing Asku had always been part of the plan, she'd counted on it, prepared for it. But the others? How would she keep the memories at bay? Already she felt them like a vine snaking around her.

"I don't like the idea. Going to La Crosse was one thing. It's proper city and you had family there. But White Earth?"

"I'll be fine," she lied.

In the quiet of their suite, Alma peeled off her evening gloves and rummaged through her trunk for her needlework. She'd never been any good, not like Catherine or Hįčoga. In truth, she rather detested the activity. But her hands felt charged, restless. She sat down on the lumpy divan and arranged her canvas and thread across her lap. Tomorrow she'd seek out May or maybe Peter. They were several years younger than Alma and had sat rows away at the front of the class. But that was the point, better to interview acquaintances than those formerly called *friends*. Less painful that way. Less chance they'd dredge up unwanted memories, unspoken names. Her hand slipped and she grazed her finger with the needle. No blood—only a sharp sting.

Stewart took her hand. She'd only dimly registered when he came to sit beside her with the town's single-paged paper. He kissed the red scratch upon her finger, and then with more force her palm, the inside of her wrist. She could hear the paper crumple in his other hand, watched as he tossed it aside. It drifted like a feather to the floor. His free hand found her waist and pulled her across the worn velveteen toward him. She closed her eyes and waited for that familiar spark, that warm tingle. Nothing came.

She clutched her needlework and stood abruptly. "I best put this away before I stick one of us again."

She hurried to the bedroom and cast the silly needlepoint into her trunk. What was wrong with her? All she could feel when he touched her was the winter-cold fingers of another. She stood before the vanity and unpinned her hair, glaring at her reflection in the filmy mirror. *Get ahold of yourself, Alma.* She started on the silk-covered buttons that ran down the back of her dress, but her fingers felt stiff and clumsy.

Behind her, the divan's seat cushion let loose a haggard whistle, and the sitting room door closed. Stewart's footfalls padded toward her.

"Let me help." He brushed her hands away and finished unfastening her buttons. His breath prickled her skin. Her dress fell away and she felt his lips brush the nape of her neck. They traveled downward over her skin while he slid the strap of her chemise from her shoulder. Again, Alma closed her eyes and tried to relax, but her muscles knotted beneath each kiss. His breath felt warm and sticky, his touch like the harassing tickle of a mosquito. He snaked his hands around her waist toward the hooks of her corset.

"Was this all a mistake?"

His face pulled away from the crook of her neck, but his arms remained encircled around her. "What?"

Alma wiggled free from his grasp and spun to face him. "Coming here. Do you really think we have a chance at proving Harry innocent?"

"Don't think about that right now, darling." He reached again for her waist.

"What if you don't find anything tomorrow at the agency? Suppose I can't find any more witnesses."

He succeeded in unhooking her corset and flung it to the corner. "Then we'll find another way."

The blitheness of his comment cooled whatever flame his touch had kindled. He reached for the other strap of her chemise, but she backed away, clutching the thin cotton to her breast.

"Alma, what's wrong?"

"I just . . . we should have found something more by now. I didn't think it would be this hard."

"It troubles you to be among these Indians again."

"What? No . . . it's just the circumstances."

"Why don't you ever talk about it? Your father's school. Your former classmates."

"How often do you speak of your friends from Princeton?"

He took off his tailcoat and tossed it over the back of a chair. "Rarely, but I wouldn't travel cross-country to exonerate one of them for murder either."

"You agreed to come!"

They both winced at the volume of her voice. The neighboring guests had probably heard her through the hotel's thin walls. Stewart moved beside her and sank onto the cushioned vanity stool. He pulled her onto his lap. This time she did not lurch away. "Darling, I know you're worried about your friend, but you've grown so cold and foreign."

"I'm sorry." She unfastened his bow tie and pulled it free of his collar. "I shan't let my temper go again."

"It's more than that, Alma." He tucked a loose curl behind her ear and traced the curve of her face. "You're fighting for friends I never knew existed. You speak languages I've never even heard of. You're laconic and melancholy. I haven't seen a true smile cross your lips in over a week." His featherlight touch moved down her neck, danced over her collarbone, and down. "Open up to me, darling. Help me understand why this all means so much to you."

So much of her ached to tell him, to rid herself of these lies, to feel his forgiving kiss and make love to him unhaunted by the memory of another. But she couldn't. The truth would break him as surely as it had broken her. She arched away and faked a yawn. "I'm tired."

His hand fell to his side and he released her from his lap. He retreated to the far corner of the room and dimmed the lights before undressing. But she had already caught a glimpse of his wounded face.

In bed, she curled up to the very edge of the mattress and clamped her mouth around a sob. Only her eyes had permission to cry. The day covered her like a dirty film. As she hugged her arms to her chest, she realized with some relief it was not Stewart who repulsed her but herself. As much as she feared losing his love, she feared even more that he'd realize her unworthiness and regret he'd ever loved her at all.

CHAPTER 27

Wisconsin, 1890

Mrs. Simms's voice hummed like a fly at the edge of Alma's attention. "Don't overdo it, ladies. Too much water and the crust won't come out flaky."

Alma nodded and drizzled another tablespoonful of liquid over the mixture. A tin of lard sat beside her on the vast counter. Flour dust hung in the air. It reminded her of falling snow and of archery and of—

"Tsk! That's too much." Minowe batted away Alma's hand and moved their shared bowl of pie dough out of Alma's reach.

Half a spoon's worth of water hit the counter before Alma stopped pouring. "Hmm?"

"Zhiishiib," Minowe said under her breath. Working beside them, Hįčoga and Alice both laughed.

"Did you call me a duck?" Alma asked.

"The duck is always fooled by the trickster. He's gullible. Foolish," Alice said.

Minowe threw a handful more flour into their bowl. "Stupid."

"I was just following the recipe."

Minowe shook her head.

Alma sighed and leaned onto the counter. Chin resting on hand, she stared forward at nothing in particular. The piecrust was safe in Minowe's expert hands. Her thoughts rolled back, cataloging every surreptitious touch, every secret encounter she and Tshikwā'set—of course, she used his Menominee name now—had shared over the past weeks. Before, when the very sight of him had vexed her, their paths had crossed continuously. Now that she coveted his company, their encounters seemed too few.

That morning in class, they had brushed past each other en route to their desks. Their eyes met, then retreated. His fingertips grazed the back of her hand.

"Azaadiins," Asku had whispered to her as she sat stunned several minutes into class. "Open your book. Miss Wells is on her way down the aisle."

She'd turned to a random page and pretended to read. "Miigwech. You're a godsend."

Now, hours later, the back of her hand still tingled with the memory of Tshikwā'set's touch.

The back door of the kitchen swung open and Mr. Simms stomped in, brushing snow from his woolen jacket as the door slammed behind him. "Them extra sacks of taters arrived from the Indian Bureau. Want 'em in the root cellar?"

"That'd be fine, dear," Mrs. Simms said.

Her husband opened the door a crack and shouted, "Down in the cellar, George."

Alma's head sprang up, her eyes fixed on the window above the sink. Tshikwā'set appeared in the yard, a large sack of potatoes flung over either shoulder. The door to the root cellar creaked open and he descended out of view.

Minowe nudged her. "Hand me the rolling pin."

Without taking her eyes from the window, Alma groped around the counter until her hand touched the smooth cylindrical pin. She held it out and Minowe took it with a huff.

George reappeared from the cellar and disappeared around the house. Alma frowned, but her eyes were rewarded a minute later when he reappeared carrying two more sacks. Despite the falling snow, he'd removed his jacket and rolled up his sleeves. The sleek, taut muscles of his forearms showed beneath his snow-kissed skin. Wisps of black hair, wet and glossy, fell across his forehead.

Perhaps it was the warmth of the oven Mrs. Simms had stoked for the pies, but Alma felt a flush of heat. Her eyes clung to Tshikwā'set, following his every step, taking in his expression of placid concentration.

He had just reached the cellar entry when Mrs. Simms's stocky form moved in front of the window, blocking Alma's view. Seven large jars teetered in the woman's arms. Her small eyes scanned the room, her fleshy face bobbing as she glanced at each pair of bakers. "Six, seven, eight, nine . . . We'll need more cherries. Alice, dear, will you go down to the cellar and—"

Alma's arm shot up. "I'll go."

She bounded out the back door with the cook's voice trailing behind her, "Very well. Two jars . . ."

Gray afternoon light spilled through the open cellar door, illuminating the dusty flight of stairs.

She left the falling snow and descended. The smell of wet earth, tinged with the scent of onions and brine, hit her nostrils. "Tshikwā'set?"

No answer.

"Tshikwā'set? George? Are you down here?"

Reaching the final step, she looked around, squinting as her eyes adjusted to the dimness. Stacked barrels cast oblong shadows against the clay walls. She pushed past strands of dried apples that hung like Spanish moss from the ceiling and ventured a few steps deeper into the room. Damp, stale air filled her lungs. A hand grabbed hold of her and pulled her from the waning shaft of overhead light into the darkness.

Alma screamed, but a calloused palm quickly covered her mouth, muffling the sound. Lips brushed against her neck and a soft *shh* filled her ears. Her muscles relaxed, but her heart continued to flutter. She turned around, facing the dark outline of her assailant. He leaned in to kiss her, but she pulled back. "You frightened me."

"You scare too easy."

His arms circled around her waist and drew her close. They kissed frantically, pausing only for breath. His hand flattened on her lower back, pressing her hard against him. Her fingers twined in snow-slickened hair. His lips, at once sweet and salty, tasted delicious against her own. After what seemed like forever and no time at all, they pulled their faces a few inches apart. Neither spoke.

Their chests heaved in concert together. She brushed the snow-wetted locks from his forehead and traced the line of his face with her forefinger. When she reached his lips, he captured her hand in his and kissed it.

"Tshikwā'set," she said just to feel the syllables tumble over her lips. "What does it mean?"

He considered for a moment. "Sound of the thunder."

She grinned. "Fitting."

"My mother took me before the awāetok because I had stopped attending to the Catholic school. She thought a spirit worked in me. I stood before the men of the medicine lodge and shouted I had no more need for the white man's education. My uncle, he was there, and gave me the name."

"And you didn't have to go back to the nuns?"

"In the eyes of my uncle and the awāetok I was already a man." Tshikwā'set paused. "The agent didn't agree. He came to our home with his fake lawmen, said I must come here. My uncle could do nothing."

"Here's better than the Catholic school, though, right?"

He shrugged. "You're a more better kisser than the nuns."

At that, she batted him across the shoulder. He staggered theatrically back, bumping into a stack of bagged turnips, pulling her down with him as he fell. Vegetables rolled helter-skelter. They laughed and kissed and laughed some more. His hand drifted from her waist up to her breast. It rested there a single, thudding heartbeat before she brushed it away.

Footsteps sounded above them. "Alma, dear, have you found those cherries?"

She and Tshikwā'set leapt to their feet and shrank back into the shadows. "Yes, Mrs. Simms. I had some trouble, but I . . . ah . . . I just found them. I'll be up presently." She pressed a silent kiss against Tshikwā'set's lips, grabbed two red jars from the nearby shelves of preserves, and hurried up the stairs.

That night, Alma lay awake in the darkness of her room. Behind her closed eyelids, she could see Tshikwā'set's handsome face. Her hand trailed over her cheek, down the length of her arm, and along the curve of her waist. She inched up the hem of her nightshirt. The sweep of soft fabric sent a delightful shiver over her skin. Her breath hitched.

The doorknob rattled and her door opened with a whisper. Alma froze. Cold air whirled in behind the faint patter of footsteps. Her hand shot toward the bedside table, groping for matches.

"Who's there?"

Before she could light her candle, the mattress sagged with the weight of a new occupant. She opened her mouth to scream, but the breath caught in her throat, allowing for only a meek whimper. Her heart flapped against her breastbone.

"Shh, Azaadiins!"

The familiar timber of the voice dampened Alma's anxiety. Her hand steadied enough to light the bedside candle. Not one but two forms appeared in the flare of yellow light.

"Waú! You could have told me you were coming." She pulled back her blanket and let Minowe and Hį̆čoga climb under. They squeezed in close to keep from falling off the narrow bed.

With Hį̆čoga lying between them, Minowe rolled onto her side and raised her head. "Okay, Alma. Speak it."

"What?"

"I told you she'd not tell," Hį̆čoga said.

"After Charles's accident you were . . . gigashkendam apane," Minowe said. "Sad."

Hį̆čoga nodded. "Gloomy."

"Now, since four weeks, you . . . you act odd. My brother says you don't study in class, at dinner you don't eat. You nearly ruined the pie today."

"You didn't even brings up the right jars from the cellar," Hį̆čoga added. "Who wants to eat a pie made of beets?"

Alma bit her lip. "Sorry about that. I've been . . . distracted."

"We know," Hį̆čoga said. "By who?"

"By whom. Who is a subject pronoun."

Hį̆čoga turned to Minowe. "Did we mistake and crawl into bed with Miss Wells?"

All three of them giggled into the pillow. Silence followed in the wake of their laughter. Minowe and Hį̆čoga wore expectant looks, their brown eyes anchored upon her.

Over the years she'd confided everything to them—from silly disagreements with her mother to the arrival of her monthly courses. And she'd meant to tell them about Tshikwā'set too. After their first kiss, the news had buzzed inside her all through dinner, but in waiting for the right moment, the right mood, and sufficient privacy, the evening had come and gone without it breaching her lips. So, too, passed the next day and the one following. She met Tshikwā'set again in the stables. They shared a hurried embrace in the stairwell. Notes—hidden between the pages of arithmetic and grammar books—passed between them in class. After each exhilarating encounter, each lingering stare, she'd set out to tell Hįčoga and Minowe. Each time the words stuck like honey to her tongue.

Even now, she struggled to name what she felt, to describe how one errant kiss had grown and deepened into so much more. "I think I'm . . . I've fallen in love."

Minowe gasped. Hįčoga squealed.

"Shh," Alma said, even as she giggled. "You'll wake the whole school."

"With who? I mean *with whom?*" Hįčoga half whispered. "That Mr. Ellis you danced with at the Christmas party?"

"Actually, it's—"

"Of course not that stinky man," Minowe interrupted. "It only can be that sun-haired boy." She turned to Alma. "It's Edward Steele you've fallen in love with, yes?"

Hįčoga spoke again before she could answer. "There was that other boy at the dance too. What his name? Van . . . Van—"

"Paul Van Steenwyk?" Alma scrunched her nose and shook her head. "No, not him. And certainly not Edward Steele." She drew the quilt like a hood over her head and leaned in close. "Tshikwā'set. I'm in love with Tshikwā'set."

The excitement drained from her friends' faces. Hįčoga's brow furrowed. Minowe jolted upright, losing her balance and falling clear off the bed.

Alma winced at the loud thud. "Are you okay?" She leaned across Hįčoga and offered Minowe her hand.

Minowe batted it away. "What you say?"

"I asked if you were okay."

"Before that," Minowe said, still seated on the floor, rubbing her backside. "You love Tshikwā'set?"

Alma nodded.

"Giiwanaadizi."

"I'm not crazy."

Minowe rattled her head. "Not many months ago you hated him."

"I didn't hate him," Alma said, though she could feel her skin flush with the lie. "We just didn't get along."

"Brute, you called him."

"And swine," Hįčoga added.

"Dunce. Scoundrel. Fop."

"Okay, okay. I may have said a few unkind words when he first came. A girl can change her mind." Alma sat up and traced her fingertips over the brightly colored squares of her quilt. "He's different now. I'm different now."

Minowe clambered from the floor and dusted off her nightshirt. Her fingers trembled and her skin looked greenish in the dim light. "Like I says, giiwanaadizi."

"What's wrong with us being in love?"

"Us?" Minowe snorted. "You think he love you, too?"

Alma's gaze retreated to the flickering candle. Wax dribbled down its sides, pooling in the brass drip pan. The camphor smell from the match head still lingered in the air. Did Tshikwā'set love her? He'd not said as much. Neither had she, though, not until just now. "What's wrong with you? I thought you wanted Tshikwā'set and me to get on better."

Minowe kept her distance from the bed, one foot shuffling back and forth atop the wool rug. She looked to be wrestling with some emotion—sadness perhaps, or anger—and Alma felt immediately contrite. "I'm sorry, I know I should have told you straightaway, I—"

"You're a gichi-mookomaan-ikwe. He's an Indian."

Alma's muscles tensed. "It never mattered before that I'm white."

Silence seeped between them like spilled molasses. Hįčoga, still lying beside her on the bed, broke the impasse. "When did all this happen between you and Tshikwā'set?"

"About a month ago."

"Waú!" Hįčoga batted Alma's shoulder with the pillow. "A month and you didn't tell us?"

"I wanted to tell you. I did. He kissed me and I—"

"'I hokiwąk?" Hįčoga's voice sparked with glee.

"Yes, we kissed. Can you believe it? Behind the schoolhouse by the old archery target." She lay back onto the bed and grabbed the pillow, clutching it to her breast. "It was wonderful."

"He kiss you one time. That doesn't mean he cares for you," Minowe said.

"Not just once. Dozens of times. Whenever we can sneak a moment." Alma's head sank into the mattress and she watched the candlelight dance across the plaster ceiling. "I feel like I can barely breathe without him."

Hįčoga giggled. "That's why you volunteered to go into the cellar this afternoon."

"It's impossible to find time alone."

Minowe hugged her arms around her chest and shook her head.

Alma sat up again, her stomach tightening. "I thought you'd be happy for me."

Silence answered her. She turned with desperation to Hįčoga.

"We are, but . . ." Her friend shrugged. "Your parents will be much angry."

Alma set aside the pillow. Cavorting with a boy, unchaperoned— her mother would faint if she knew. And Father? Student relationships were forbidden at Stover. Such foolery got in the way of one's study, she'd overheard him say on more than one occasion. If anyone found out, she and Tshikwā'set would undoubtedly be punished. Worse, he could be sent away.

"You mustn't tell." Alma looked frantically between them. The more people who knew, the greater the risk of discovery. "Not anyone, please."

Hįčoga nodded, but Minowe remained a statue, brow drawn, eyes inscrutable. Alma's heart climbed into her throat. "Nindaangwe, right?"

After a heavy moment, Minowe sighed. "Yes, of course you still my friend, Azaadiins. I won't tell anyone." She smiled—not her sunny gap-toothed smile—but a stiff, anemic approximation, then grabbed Hįčoga's arm. "Come on, we better go before Miss Wells find us out of bed."

"Miigwech," Alma said. *Thank you.*

BETWEEN EARTH AND SKY   189

Her friends tiptoed from the room. Hįčoga winked at Alma over her shoulder. Minowe did not look back.

She blew out the bedside candle and settled back beneath the covers. Though her friends' warmth still lingered on the sheets, the bed felt wide, open, and lonely.

CHAPTER 28

—————<——

Minnesota, 1906

Warmth came a weak and distant straggler behind the sun. Rain had fallen in the night and left the air dank. Alma kept her duster buttoned from hem to collar the entire ride to White Earth. Worry lines, something Alma had seldom seen before the ordeal of the trial, now seemed a permanent fixture upon Stewart's face.

The events of last night, his advance and her refusal, lay open between them like an undressed wound. She tried several times at light conversation and failed. Stewart sat silent, wringing the leather reins and tugging on his shirt cuffs the way he did when he was preparing to argue a big case. He'd grown up with a good name, but not always the fortune to match. His father, he'd told her, was an impulsive man known for both singing and shoddy investments. She imagined this nervous tic to be a vestige of one of those periods of dearth when the family couldn't afford new shirts for their growing boy.

When they reached the general store at the village center, Stewart slowed the buggy. She hated to part like this, in silence, without so much as a glance, a smile, a kiss on the cheek. She opened her mouth, but the words *I'm sorry* seemed insufficient.

"I still don't like you going alone," he said, facing forward.

"You said yourself we haven't the time."

"Perhaps one of Mr. Knudson's deputies should go with you."

"No one will be forthcoming with one of the sheriff's men present." A strand of hair fell into his eyes. She hesitated before brushing it away.

He captured her hand but seemed uncertain what to do next. Another day, without so much hanging over them, he would have kissed it. Today he settled for a light squeeze. "Be careful."

"I will," she said, when what she meant was *I love you.* "I'll meet you at the agency before noon."

She climbed from the wagon and watched him drive off. How much more could he forgive? Water splashed about the wheels and his form became ever smaller. She lingered a moment longer, then hiked up the hem of her skirt and crossed the muddy road to the general store.

Unlike yesterday, when the entire village buzzed with people, today the air was quiet. A few tents remained in the open field—most in some stage of dismantle. The merchants, with their tinware and cloth and guns, had left only bent stalks of grass and rain-filled imprints where their booths had stood. Even the stray dogs that had run about begging scraps of food had vanished into the great expanse of the reservation.

The porch that swept the length of the storefront too sat empty. The rusty hinges of the front door whined when Alma opened it. Flies buzzed in after her through a large tear in the screen even after the door had closed. Two rows of shelving ran the length of the small store. Sacks of flour, sugar, and coffee spilled into the aisles. She stepped over a jumble of shovels stacked upright against the wall and made her way to the front of the store.

A plump white man stood behind the counter. When he looked up, his full pink lips wobbled, as if caught between a grin and a scowl. "You must be that woman up from St. Paul. Agent Taylor's worked himself into a downright dither over you."

"No offense—Mr. Larson, is it?—but Agent Taylor can dither all he wants. I've got work to do here."

The shopkeeper chuckled—a deep, jolly sound—and winked a blue eye at her. "No offense taken, ma'am."

"Alma Mitchell." She extended her hand across the counter.

He wiped a palm on the faded apron tied high across his belly and shook her hand. "Pleasure to meet ya."

Behind her, the shop door creaked open. A woman with a cradle-board strapped to her back lumbered in. Alma's breath caught a moment, then tumbled free. The eyes, the mouth—it was not a face she knew.

Mr. Larson waved to the woman. "Boozhoo."

She smiled back and headed for a shelf crammed with various rolls of fabric and thread. Her dark eyes flickered warily to Alma as she shifted through the stock.

"You speak Anishinaabemowin?" Alma asked the shopkeeper.

He shrugged. "A word or two here or there. Good for business, ya know."

"Maybe you can help me, then." She took a folded piece of paper from her purse and handed it to him. "I'm looking for these men."

He squinted over the paper, running a finger down the list of names, and chuckled again. "Good luck. Ain't seen any of them around here for a while."

"Perhaps I could find them on their farms. Do you know where their land allotments are?"

"Men like these are still living like the old days. They don't farm or keep to their allotments. Besides, in all likelihood they've sold their lands."

"The government holds the land in trust. They're not allowed to sell."

Mr. Larson's smile dampened. He glanced over to the woman with the cradleboard, then back to Alma. "New law says they can. If the agent deems 'em competent. And these men had debts. Big drinkers, them five."

"Who bought the land?"

"Depends. If it were prairie, probably some Easterner wanting to try his hand at farming while the gettin' is still good. If they had timber lands, more likely than not was that greedy lumber company." He sighed and shook his head. "Ain't right, if you ask me."

"Where do they live if they haven't their own tract of land?"

"Here and there, I suppose. Drifting between kinfolk."

Alma frowned and took back her list just as the Indian woman approached. She laid a bolt of blue and white striped calico on the counter. Mr. Larson asked how much she needed in near-perfect *Anishinaabemowin*.

While he measured and cut the cloth, Alma's eyes drifted to the baby cooing on the woman's back. Everything about him was beautiful—his colorfully embroidered swaddling blanket, his fat cheeks and crescent eyes, his wild tufts of downy hair. He freed one arm from his wrappings and grasped playfully about the air. Alma couldn't help but reach out. He grabbed her finger in his chunky hand and giggled as she wagged it back and forth.

"Miikawaadizi," she said to the mother. "He's adorable."

The woman smiled, but shifted slightly so the babe's soft hand slipped away. She paid Mr. Larson for the cloth and turned to go.

"Here," he said, pulling out a red and white candy stick from a nearby jar. "For the little one."

Alma watched them leave with a curious ache between her lungs. She tried not to wonder if Minowe had children. Tried not to picture them with her lovely brown eyes and moon-shaped face. It took a moment to clear her head and remember why she'd come to the shop at all. "You're sure you don't know where I might find these men?"

Mr. Larson shook his head. "Afraid not."

She crumpled the list of witnesses and shoved it back into her handbag. If he couldn't help her, she had to find someone who could. She'd come this far, after all, roused so many memories. What was a few more? "How about a woman named Medwe-ganoonind? Do you know where she might live?"

Another shake of the head.

"May, that was her Christian name. Or a man called Peter. He went by—"

"Mrs. Mitchell, I wish I could help, but you'd have far better luck over at the Indian Office. They're the ones with the roll books, after all."

The thought of returning to that stuffy white building empty-handed made her stomach turn. "Just one more." Her mind dredged through the list of long-silent names. "Frederick. He's tall, mid-thirties. He called himself . . ." She couldn't remember his Indian name.

"I know half a dozen men fittin' that description. I couldn't tell you where any of them live, though." He gave her an apologetic smile, then grabbed a rag and began wiping down the scratched countertop.

Alma watched his movements, the light grip on the rag, the small circles he made over the wood, and thought back to the grand foyer at Stover. She could see Frederick bent over on hands and knees working off demerits. The scent of floor polish stung her nose. He must have hated the work, but in her mind's eye he was smiling, humming some tune.

"Nesayegun. That's what he called himself," she said to herself, turning to leave.

"What'd you say? Nesayegun? I think a fella by that name does some work over there in the agency wood shop."

"Really? Which direction is the shop?"

"It ain't steady work, mind you. Fixes things for the agency when they break or fall apart. He mightn't be there today. And he mightn't be the Indian you're looking for. But you can go check. Five buildings down on the right. Between the barracks and barn."

"Thank you, Mr. Larson. Thank you so much."

He blushed. "Ain't nothin'. Just glad to be of help. Good luck to ya."

Alma hurried down the road in the direction of the shop. Mud splashed and slurped around her boots. Though she had to hold up her skirts an inch or two higher than proper, she slowed only to navigate the largest puddles.

Little differentiated the dilapidated street-side barn from the wood shop. Dry, sun-bleached pine sided both buildings. The stench of dusty fur and manure rose from the barn. The shop smelled like a forest—earthy, with hints of vanilla. Its filmy windows rattled from the roaring machinery within. One of the large double doors lay ajar, exposing a sliver of the dim room within.

Her heart flapped like a moth inside a mason jar. Sixteen years stood between them. Life, with all its meanderings, seemed to shrink the friendship they had once shared. Would he even remember her? Her hand fluttered over her dress, her hair, her hat—smoothing, arranging, adjusting. Flecks of dried mud dotted the hem of her skirt and she suddenly wished she'd taken more care to avoid the puddles.

She knocked, but the sound vanished into the din. After a long inhale, she pried the door open a few more inches and slipped inside.

A light breeze stole in behind her, sending the carpet of sawdust swirling into the air. The burnt smell of tired gears and overworked rubber commingled with the bright scent of wood. Frederick hunched over a ripsaw, feeding a long piece of wood into its spinning teeth. The gust of air ruffled his cropped hair. He blinked through the sudden storm of sawdust, eyes fixed on his work, hands steady. Not until the plank was fully rent did he reach down and switch off the machine.

He straightened and wiped his brow with the back of his hand. Dirt and grease stained the rough pads of his fingers. He was just as lanky as she remembered, long cords of muscle roped around a narrow frame. He cocked his head toward the door, his face lined with displeasure. Though the sawdust had long since settled, he blinked again and burrowed his cracked knuckles into his eyes. "Azaadiins, is that you?"

"Frederick!" She swept across the room toward him, raising her arms for an embrace, but stopped short when his eyes flickered toward the open door. He wiped his hand over his leather apron and thrust it with stiff formality between them. Her smile dampened. "It's good to see you. You look well."

"So you're the gichi-mookomaan-ikwe causing troubles at the agency?"

"Word spreads quickly around here."

He shrugged and grinned. "Agent Taylor knows not the way of soft speaking."

"I'm here because of Asku."

Frederick glanced again toward the door. He nodded, but said nothing.

"Do you know what happened? Who really killed Agent Andrews?"

"Askuwheteau asked you to come?"

Alma dropped her gaze to the floor. Darned wool peeked through a hole in Frederick's worn but polished boots. He'd cuffed his pants to hide a tattered hem. "No, I came of my own accord," she said at last.

Frederick humphed. "I know nothing of the agent's murder."

The want of emotion in his voice made her doubt his words. "What happened to him after Stover? After Brown?"

"That's his story to tell."

"Please, Frederick. I've heard such awful things. That he's a lush, a hobo. That he lives alone without family or friend."

"Sounds apt."

Alma flinched. She steadied herself against the nearby workbench. Sap oozed beneath her hand, sticking to her glove. "I don't understand."

Frederick leaned back against the long ripsaw table and folded his arms across his chest. "I worked as a tradesman in St. Paul for three years after I left Stover."

"I remember. Father was so proud."

He huffed and shook his head. "I came home because my grandfather was sick. But I was too late. He died the night before I arrive."

"I'm sorry."

"While my grandmother and aunts made the body for burial, many people came offering their favorite tales and memories of my grandfather." His eyes, previously turned upward as if watching the memory play out in the shadowy rafters, swept downward and met her own. "I couldn't understand their stories, Azaadiins. I had lost the words, the words of my people. Nookomis, my own grandmother, was a stranger to me."

"But surely your language came back to you. And think of all the skills you had gained to use here."

"It did come back. After some while." He looked down at his hands and pried a splinter from the pad of his thumb. "Have you ever pulled back the husk of a corn and found that the inside is empty, all the kernels have been eaten aways by a worm or field mouse and only the cob is left? You can feel it when you hold it—it's lighter than the others ears, has trouble holding shape."

What was Frederick talking about? Corn and field mice? This had nothing to do with Asku or the murder. His eyes kept to the floor. One foot cut circles through the sawdust. Otherwise he was still. She started to speak, to steer him back on topic, but he continued. "That's what we're like, those of us returned from Stover or Carlisle or Haskell. Peel back the husk and we're empty, hollowed out. The Indian in us eaten away." He shook his head and drew in a long breath. "Some worse than others. When Askuwheteau came back he was nothing but husk."

"Why should that be? He did so well at Stover. All that knowledge, how could that make him empty?"

Frederick laughed and turned away from her. "Gaawiin ginisidotanziin." He picked up both halves of the sundered board and tossed them into a pile of similarly sized planks. The resulting clap echoed through the small shop, shaking the windowpanes.

Alma winced at the noise. "You're right, I don't understand. What happened to him here?"

"Not here. It happened to him when they cut his hair and burned his clothes. It happened when your father and Miss Wells tricked him into believing he could be white. It happened to him at Stover and followed him here. It follows us all."

"But you . . . you're prospering." She immediately regretted the choice of word. His mended clothes, his rough, overworked hands— this was not prosperity, not as she'd envisioned it as a girl listening to her father's oration.

"My people are Métis. Trappers and traders. I'd seen white men before I came to Stover. Heard a few words of English. Knew of your one God. Asku, his people were different. Traditional. Still followed the seasons. That's a more hard life to come home to and fit in."

"Even if that were true, I still don't see how that relates to the murder of Agent Andrews."

"Do you know the Anishinaabemowin word for reservation?"

She frowned. "Ishkonigan."

"But do you know its meaning?"

She thought for a moment, then shook her head.

"Leftovers." Frederick strode across the shop toward a trestle table. Worn tools and rusty nails littered its surface. "The white man has always been generous with what he doesn't want."

She started to protest, but what could she say? Sawdust settled on her tongue. The truth of his words was here all around her. And it had been true at Stover, too—the factory-made uniforms, the out-of-date textbooks, the skimpy food rations. But what did that have to do with the trial? "I know there's more to this, Frederick. Several of you here made complaints about Agent Andrews, about some allotment proceedings this past summer."

He shook his head and rummaged through a few old cans before retrieving a small hook-shaped tool. Without answering, he stalked back to the ripsaw. The splinters of wood strewn about the dirty floor crunched beneath his footfalls.

Alma sighed and hurried behind him. "Tell me about Agent Andrews, Frederick."

He spun around so quickly Alma nearly ran into him. His eyes had hardened into iron bullets and his nostrils flared. "Mii go izhi-booni'itoog. He's little different than any Ogimaa that come before or any that will follow."

Mii go izhi-booni'itoog. Leave it alone. But Alma could not. "I'm just trying to help."

A thin, tight chuckle slipped Frederick's lips. What echoed back from the rafters sounded like a wail. "We never wanted your help, Alma. Awas." He turned and hunched over the ripsaw, burying his attention in its greasy gears.

"But—"

"Awas!"

Go away! Alma shuffled backward. Tears built along her lower lashes. "Please. We were friends. Nimbeshwaji'aa."

Frederick looked up and sighed. "I don't know who killed Andrews. Maybe it was Asku. Maybe it was someone else cheated in the agent's dealings. Ask Minowe. She'd know more than me anyway."

Alma's stomach tightened. "I . . . we . . . maybe there's someone else, a friend of Asku's you could direct me to." She reached for the list of names in her handbag.

"You used to call her nishiime—sister."

Alma shifted and looked down at the scattered wood chips. "We grew apart the year after you and Asku graduated."

"Follow the road past the agency office, then head eastward into the prairie. There's a small trail. Maybe you see it. That will take you to her home."

"Is there no one else—" His hardened expression stopped her. She took a deep breath. "How far up the road to this trail?"

"Ningo'anwe'biwin."

"How will I know when I've reached her house?"

He turned back to his work without reply. For a moment a dead silence hung between them, then the ripsaw roared to life, echoing what Frederick had said.

Awas!

CHAPTER 29

———➤◆◄———

Wisconsin, 1890

"What a startling transformation that boy—whatshisname—George has made."

Alma halted at her father's voice, nearly dropping the crochet thread she'd fetched for Mrs. Simms to use until more kitchen twine arrived from the Indian Bureau. She flattened herself against the wall and peeked in through the cracked door of her father's study.

"Quite." Miss Wells relaxed opposite Alma's father in a plush armchair, her long fingers curled around a teacup. A wisp of hair had freed itself from her ironclad bun and danced about her face, transformed in afternoon sunlight from mud brown to spun gold. To Alma, she'd always seemed old. But looking upon her now, Alma realized she couldn't be more than thirty or thirty-five.

"He must have learned more from those nuns than he let on," Miss Wells continued. "I've advanced him three grade levels since Christmas."

"Remarkable. And not a single demerit, you say?" Her father stroked his beard, his eyes bright. "The Lord does produce miracles. You've done good work here, Amelia."

Color bloomed in the teacher's cheeks. "I, well, thank you. I'm sure I can squeeze more progress out of him before the term is out."

"It's settled, then. We'll graduate him with the others."

His words hit Alma like frigid water. The oxygen bled from the air. Surely she misheard him. She leaned in closer, her eyes reaching sidelong, her ear all but pressed to the door.

Miss Wells's fingers tightened around her cup. "He has a long way to go yet."

"We haven't a choice," her father said. "That was the deal the Indian agent brokered with the boy's uncle—two years here, until the boy reached eighteen. Our time is up. It would reflect poorly on our numbers if he doesn't graduate."

"The others are far more advanced—Harry, Frederick, Catherine— even that silly girl Alice reads better."

"But he can read." Her father's tone was matter-of-fact, his back straight and hands laced atop his desk.

"Yes."

"And write, and spell, and manage simple arithmetic?"

"Yes, but—"

"That's all he'll need."

Miss Wells sat up and brushed the wisp of hair back from her face. "After graduation, he'll go straight back to the blanket."

"You think? Return to his reservation?" Her father sighed and leaned back in his chair. "Hmm . . . you're probably right. At least we've reformed him from the troublemaker he once was. The agency will be grateful."

"Another year and he could be—"

"My hands are tied."

Alma sagged against the wall. Tshikwā'set graduate? How could that be? She felt a throbbing and looked down to see the thread unspooled and twisted about her index finger, leaving the tip fat and purple. Slowly, she unwound the thread. The pain flared with the sudden release of blood.

"A modest victory, I suppose." Miss Wells's petticoat rustled as she rose from the chair.

"But a victory nonetheless," her father said. "We cannot erase in one generation centuries of Godlessness."

Alma hastened from the door at the sound of approaching footsteps. She stumbled into the dining hall and sank onto a bench. Graduation was in June, only two months away. What would happen after? Would Tshikwā'set return home, back to the blanket, as they'd said? This was his home now, here with her.

She laid the mess of thread upon the table and nipped at her cuticles, ignoring the bitter taste of soap that spread across her tongue.

They sat here every evening during study hour, she and Tshikwā'set, feigning tutelage. When Miss Wells strode within earshot, they recited times tables or parts of speech. When she moved on, ruler in hand, to scrutinize someone else, they whispered about matters of the heart, their hands clasped beneath the table. His improvement in class had been part of the show, lest Miss Wells doubt the benefit of Alma's instruction. So in a way they'd brought the misfortune of graduation upon themselves.

"Keep that up much longer and your mother's bound to notice."

Alma looked up and saw Asku seated at the other end of the hall. She hadn't even noticed him when she came in. "Hmm? Oh." She dropped her hand from her mouth.

He closed his book and came to sit across from her. "What's wrong?"

"Nothing. It's just . . . don't you think Tshikwā'set should stay on another year? Father wants to graduate him." She set about untangling the thread, pulling it so taut the fibers burned across her skin. "I think it's a dreadful idea. His penmanship is awful, his spelling atrocious, his—"

"I say good riddance. It's not like he wants to be here anyway."

"Of course he does."

Asku raised a brow and she knew he'd heard the doubt in her voice.

A faint tap drew her eyes to the far window. Tshikwā'set smiled at her through the filmy glass and nodded toward the woods.

She stood and hurried to the door. "I . . . er . . . I think I hear Mother calling."

"You forgot your thread." Asku tossed it to her, then followed her eyes to the window. Outside, Tshikwā'set loped across the yard toward the shade of the trees.

Asku's gaze flickered back. He cocked his head and frowned. "He's going to leave, Alma."

She toyed with the end of the thread until it frayed. Was he right? She lobbed it back to him. "Give this to Mrs. Simms for me?"

Tshikwā'set waited for her several yards into the forest, standing in a shaft of spring sunlight. Stover's rigid schedule and strict routine made it easy for them to slip out together. They knew at any given moment where the adults ought to be, knew when roll was counted, knew when their absence would go unnoticed.

He removed his wool jacket and slung it over the crook of his arm. The same breeze that ruffled the budding leaves in the branches above tousled his sable hair. While most of the boys at Stover had taken to using Macassar oil to part and smooth their cropped locks, Tshikwā'set refused. No part of him, not even his hair, would submit to the white man's strictures. How he passed morning inspection, Alma had no idea.

"Took you plenty long." He wrapped an arm around her back and tried to kiss her, but she pulled away.

"Did you know my father has a mind you should graduate?"

"Me?" He blinked and glanced back at the distant schoolhouse, a smile creeping to his lips. "Really?"

"This pleases you?" She hiked up her skirt and petticoats and stomped off. The dark soil, boggy from the spring thaw, clung to the soles of her boots. Winter's debris lay strewn over the forest floor—snow-felled branches, decomposed leaves, weather-bleached pinecones. Though his feet made no sound, she knew Tshikwā'set followed but a step behind.

Her chest ached just beneath her breastbone. A dull, radiating pain she'd heard tell of in novels and magazine serials. Sick at heart. Flaubert, Haggard, Corelli—all their heroes and heroines suffered this affliction. To read of it was one thing, but to actually feel it—this new and persisting pain—how did one endure? Several minutes on and the sensation grew intolerable. She spun around. The thick fringe of trees hid all sight of Stover and its outbuildings. "Well?"

"Well what?"

"What do you intend to do?"

Tshikwā'set's expression became cloudy, inscrutable, his gaze probing. He inclined his head slightly, but said nothing.

"Askuwheteau has been accepted to Brown University. Did you know? Quite a prestigious school. In Rhode Island. It's all Father can talk about."

To this, he only snorted.

"And Frederick. He has work lined up with a carpenter in St. Paul."

"You want me to go to Minnesota?"

"No, you know that's not what I mean."

With two long strides, he shrank the distance between them to inches. He smelled of soap and sweat and wood chips. It took conscious effort from Alma to pull back instead of lean in. "You could stay here. Find work in La Crosse."

"Oh, nēnemōhsaew." His hands tightened around his jacket, released, and tightened again.

"What does that mean? That you won't go back to the reservation? That you'll stay?"

He didn't respond but grabbed her hand and pulled her toward a nearby break in the trees, where afternoon light spilled through the tangle of budding branches. A wide clearing stretched before them. Alma squinted as her eyes adjusted to the sunlight. At the far end, the tufts of grass and reeds gave way to a steep incline. A wooden façade jutted from the hillside, its thick logs weatherworn and faded.

At once, Tshikwā'set stiffened. His nostrils flared and eyes narrowed. He pulled Alma back into the shadows of the nearby trees and handed her his jacket. "Stay."

Before she could protest, he released her hand and circled around the clearing toward the wooden structure. Alma's pulse quickened. She'd never ventured so far in this direction. To the west of Stover, scattered farms buffered them from the city limits of La Crosse. But she and Tshikwā'set never sneaked out that way for fear of being seen. Here, to the east, she was less clear on the boundaries. Surely, they were still on government land. Who then had carved this dugout into the earth?

She watched as Tshikwā'set neared the dwelling. Her hands clung white to his jacket. He moved with feline grace—long, slow, fluid strides. A few feet from the gaping doorway, he stopped. He crouched to the ground and sifted through the brown clumps of grass, examining the dirt beneath. Then, remaining low, he crept toward the entrance.

"Don't go in!" she hissed to the yards of empty meadow between them.

He paused before the dark opening and glanced back over the meadow. His eyes commanded her to stay put. Then he disappeared inside.

With him lost to her sight, each moment seemed to stretch to infinity. A bird cawed, far in the distance. The grass rustled. Just when she decided some horror must have befallen him, he emerged unscathed into the light and waved her over.

"An old trader lodging," he said when she neared.

Alma glanced around the clearing. "Are you sure it's abandoned?"

"Long empty." He took her hand and led her inside.

The smell of must and damp earth hit her the moment she entered. She clutched Tshikwā'set's arm and let her eyes adjust to dim. The room was no bigger than her bedroom. Dried leaves and other bits of fossilized flora crunched beneath her feet. A series of roughly hewn beams supported the packed clay walls and roof. A straw pallet, limp and dust-covered, lay in one corner. Crumbling charcoal and scattered twigs cluttered the ground in the opposite corner. The ceiling above was blackened and concave.

Tshikwā'set walked over and poked at the crater. Bits of earth and debris showered down around him, filling the room with dust.

Alma gasped. "The ceiling's collapsing!"

But the downpour of earth had already stopped. He laughed and coughed at the same time. "No, nēnemōhsaew, that's just the chimney hole."

She arched her eyebrows and continued to stare with distrust at the dark soil above them. The dank air swirled cool around her and she shivered. Tshikwā'set pulled her toward him and wrapped her in his arms. She forgot the cold, her fear, and leaned her head against his chest. "Tell me you'll stay."

She rocked with the slow ebb and flow of his breath.

"I do not know."

Alma pulled away to hide her tears. How could she feel so much when he apparently felt so little? She hurried from the dugout into the blinding daylight. "Father, Miss Wells, Askuwheteau—they were all right. You'll return to the reservation, back to your old life, and I'll never see you again."

He came and stood beside her. The few inches between them felt like a chasm, widened by his silence.

A shadow fleeted over them. Alma looked up. A great eagle circled overhead, its wings golden against the blue backdrop of the sky. It dipped and soared effortlessly, cradled in the arms of the wind.

"Maeq-Awaetok, the Great Spirit, made the first man from a bear. But he was alone." Tshikwā'set pointed at the sky. "So the bear called to Kine'u, the eagle, and said, 'Come join me, brother.' And Maeq-Awaetok made the eagle a man, too."

Alma sucked in a deep breath and wiped her eyes. The eagle continued to circle high above them, as if it owned the whole sky. "Then what?"

"Nama'kukiu, the beaver, joined them as well. Noma'eu, the sturgeon. Omas'kos, the elk. Moqwai'o, the wolf. Ota'tshia, the crane. These became the clans of the Menominee people."

"Which clan do you belong to?"

"I am a Thunderer, of the Eagle clan. Some forget their clans now that we are caged on the reservation. But I will always be a Thunderer."

He sat down, then took his coat and spread it over the ground beside him. She knelt atop the navy-blue fabric and tucked her skirt around her. Her mother would notice a mud stain. More importantly, it gave her reason to look away. She felt foolish for reading affection in his touch, devotion in his kiss.

He brushed her cheek with his hand. "Nēnemōhsaew—"

"Stop saying that. I don't know what it means."

He laughed. "It is the name one calls his lover."

Alma's entire body hummed. "You love me?"

"Have I not showed you this?"

"You never said so."

"Why? Better to know through action, no?"

"Wouldn't you like to hear the words?"

He laughed again and shrugged.

Alma patted her hair and raised her chin. "Fine. I shan't say so either, then."

He leaned in and kissed her. She held out, fighting the urge to match the rhythm of his lips for five solid seconds, then gave in.

"I know you love me, Azaadiins." He kissed her once more, then laced his hands under his head and lay back atop the tufts of grass. "I feel it in your touch. I see it in your face when you look at me."

Her body went suddenly cold. "Do you think everyone else can tell?"

"No."

She wrung her hands and glanced at the sun, tracking its progression through the sky since their departure from the schoolhouse. "We're careful, right?"

He worked a finger inside the cuff of her sleeve and tugged playfully. "Nobody besides us two knows."

"Umm . . . I might have let a word or two slip to Minowe and Hįčoga. And Asku might know too. But they'd never say anything to anyone."

He snickered. She lay down beside him and rested her head on his shoulder. His soap and wood smell filled her senses. She could drink that scent forever and still desire more. With his hands behind his head, his shirt stretched taut over his chest. The outline of a necklace caught her eye beneath the white fabric. She ran her finger atop it. "What's this?"

He unfastened the top buttons of his shirt and pulled out a long pendant. Alma's eyes grazed the smooth dark skin of his chest before taking in the necklace. It was made with black beads the size of cherry pits strung between long pieces of porcupine quill. At its base hung a medallion of tiny colored beads threaded together to create the image of the sun. She remembered it from his first day at Stover when he'd stood above her and called her enemy.

"My father gave it to me before he died," he said.

He had told her of his father before, of his death in a lumber accident when Tshikwā'set was young. "You've kept it hidden all this time?"

"I saw they would burn my clothes, that first day I came, so I hid it."

"They never noticed at inspection? You'd get in so much trouble."

His lips curved into a wry smile. "Every mornings Mr. Simms and your father look me up and down. Every mornings, but they never see."

She traced the outline of the sun with her finger. "It's beautiful."

He flattened his hand over hers and looked up at the wide blue above them. She could feel the steady beat of his heart beneath her palm. "What are we going to do?"

"You could come north with me, to the reservation."

"I'm being serious. Please say you'll stay."

His jaw tightened and lips flattened. "It's not so easy. Our worlds are like the sky and earth, Azaadiins. They get very close, but never touch."

"We share in the same world, don't you see?"

"You say these words, but you've never lived anything but the ways of the white man."

"Are our ways so bad?"

He answered neither *yes* nor *no,* but pulled her tightly to his chest—so tightly she struggled to draw air. But it didn't matter. They were more than close. They were touching.

CHAPTER 30

Wisconsin, 1890

At the cry of the bugle, the Indians marched from the schoolhouse double file. Scarlet and blue banners festooned the veranda. The students paraded down the freshly painted stairs and across the yard.

Alma watched their synchronized approach from her seat at the piano, carried out to the lawn for the occasion. One hand shielded her eyes from the bright midmorning sun while the other rested atop the ivory keys.

As valedictorian, Asku led the march, his fox eyes beaming, his shoulders back and head held high. Her own carriage swelled at the sight. His gaze flickered in her direction and he smiled broadly. They'd chosen his suit together: a single-breasted morning coat and matching striped trousers, both light brown. She'd given him the silk cravat he wore as a graduation gift. Both pride and sorrow pulled at her heart. She'd never met a more intelligent boy—white or Indian. Nor had she known a more constant friend. Already she could foretaste the bittersweetness of his absence.

The other graduates marched behind him—Catherine, Frederick, Alice, and Tshikwā'set—all dressed in finely tailored clothes. The rest of the students followed, red corsages pinned to their black uniforms.

Tshikwā'set . . . the looming prospect of his departure panicked her. Since their afternoon in the meadow nearly two months before, she'd broached the subject of his future several times, but his response was always vague, evasive. He had siblings back on the reservation and his mother. They needed him, he said. But she needed him, too.

The company of Indians marched down the aisle, bisecting the throngs of seated commencement guests. Heads crowned in felt hats and flowery bonnets swiveled, following the procession toward the grand dais at the edge of the yard. Red, white, and blue flounces skirted the platform. Atop it stood an oak lectern flanked by chairs. Her father perched on the centermost chair to the right, so buoyed by pride she thought he might float away. Miss Wells sat beside him like a glacier, her face pinched as if it knew no other expression, despite the day's palpable excitement. Reverend Thomas and Mr. Chase—Superintendent of Indian Schooling, in all the way from Washington—joined them atop the dais. The superintendent's eyes wandered over the yard and great brick schoolhouse, resting finally on the bright blue sky above, even as the parade of students approached. His plump fingers fidgeted in his lap, giving Alma the distinct impression he cared little for pomp and festivity.

She turned her attention back to the students, who had now reached the base of the dais. They arranged themselves in three lines, the smallest children in the front, each spaced a uniform distance from the next. Alma marveled at the display. They had drilled this entry every day for a month until Mr. Simms had lost his voice from shouting out commands. The result was as near perfection as any company could perform.

Her eyes lingered on the back row, flashing over her friends' faces, until inevitably settling over Tshikwā'set. Something about him still whispered defiance. Whether it was his ruffled hair, his all-too-confident posture, or the sardonic curve of his lips, she could not tell.

Reverend Thomas approached the lectern and delivered the benediction. Alma peeled her eyes from Tshikwā'set and readied her fingers over the piano keys. When the reverend took his seat, she began to play. After a few bars, the Indians joined in with song.

Hail Columbia, happy land!
Hail, ye heroes, heav'n born band,
Who fought and bled in freedom's cause,
Who fought and bled in freedom's cause.

After "Hail, Columbia" ended, Alma moved right into "The Battle Hymn of the Republic," concluding her modest part in the commencement. She rose from the piano and took her seat beside her mother in the front row of the audience while the students marched around toward the back. Only the graduates remained—Asku, Frederick, Catherine, Alice, and Tshikwā'set. They took their seats atop the platform. Superintendent Chase delivered a short, generic address; then her father rose to the podium. His voice trembled with emotion, starting out quiet and ending just below a roar. The same words he had uttered a thousand times again passed his lips: progress, civility, triumph over savagery.

At the end, he wiped the perspiration glistening at the edge of his receding hairline and welcomed Askuwheteau to the stand. "And now it is my pleasure to present Harry Muskrat, a young man from the White Earth Chippewa reservation in Minnesota, and Stover's first valedictorian. This fall, thanks to a generous grant from the Women's National Indian Association and funds made available through Senator Dawes's General Allotment Act, he will travel to the great state of Rhode Island to attend the prestigious Brown University."

Asku stood and crossed to the podium. He moved with polish and grace, his posture without the air of haughtiness she saw so often in "well-bred" men. Despite his confident walk, his fingers curled and released at his side—his telltale sign of nervousness, one she knew no one in the audience aside from herself would recognize. Their eyes met and she smiled with full-toothed encouragement. His hands stilled and he pulled a slip of paper from his breast pocket.

"It is my honor to appear before you today under such great auspices. To this place, and its people, I owe an enduring debt. These walls have been my home for nine years, and I have passed here from a child to a man. From one who knew little of the world to one yet untested, but firmly set in the way of progress."

Asku's voice rang clear and steady. Golden sunlight lit him from above. His lively eyes swept the hushed crowd as he spoke, not once retreating to the unfolded speech atop the podium. Miss Wells's lips softened into a smile. Her father wiped a tear.

"I come from a great and proud people," Asku continued. "We have lived many generations upon this land. But if it be our destiny to continue, we must merge with the white man and meld to his ways. Like two forks of the same great river, our destinies lie intertwined. The course is set. We cannot uphold the past any more than we can reverse the water's flow." He paused. "Our hope rests in the future. A future made bright by unity with the white man. What we, the Indian, can offer we shall offer. What we can learn, we must learn so that both our peoples may prosper on this earth."

Asku smiled amid a swell of applause. A tide of handshakes, backslaps, and hugs carried him back to his seat. Alma leapt to her feet, and the rest of the crowd did likewise. Only Tshikwā'set seemed unmoved. His hands banged together a couple of times, then knotted in his lap. His eyes wandered the sky. She could read the war playing out inside him by the way his forearms tensed and knuckles blanched. He hated what Asku said, and yet . . . and yet he cared for her.

A listless Mr. Chase distributed certificates of accomplishment to all the graduates and the ceremony concluded. The guests rose from their seats and drifted toward the large buffet of refreshments Mrs. Simms had set up at the far edge of the yard.

Alma moved to follow, but her mother grabbed her arm. *Ahem.* She examined Alma's appearance with a roving eye. "You hit the wrong chord halfway through the first verse of the 'Battle Hymn.'"

Was that all her mother had taken from the ceremony? "I'm only the accompanist."

"The details matter, Alma. Let's just hope Mrs. Pierce did not notice or she'll have nothing else to say about the event. You know she fancies her daughter a better musician than you."

Alma's eyes drifted toward the cluster of people holding cups of punch and plates of cookies. As always, she sought Tshikwā'set. He stood in the shade of an oak tree talking with Mr. Wallis, who owned a carriage company in La Crosse.

"Alma! Are you listening to me?"

"Hmm? Oh, yes, more care next time." She hurried off before her mother spewed further admonishment, and slipped into the crowd, addressing no one until she reached Asku. "Your speech was wonderful!" She laced her arm around his and squeezed. "Gigiiminowe. Very eloquent."

He beamed. "Thank you. I had not expected such a crowd."

"Father's been waiting for this moment for nine years. I'm surprised he did not invite the entire state of Wisconsin."

They both laughed. She released his arm and they strode side by side to the refreshment table. The cups of lemonade and punch brought back memories of an earlier day, the sun slanting down on a similar spread, anticipation quickening her blood, waiting for the very first Indians to arrive. Her throat grew tight and tears caught in the web of her lashes. "How I shall miss you, Asku."

He grinned and handed her a drink. "Come east with me, then. Enroll at Vassar or Mount Holyoke."

"Mother says I already have more education than I shall ever need." Her eyes flickered toward the oak tree where Tshikwā'set still stood. "Besides, I think I should miss it here too much."

Asku followed her errant gaze to the oak tree. The rosy exuberance drained from his cheeks, leaving his expression wistful.

Alma bit her lip and hastened down the buffet toward a towering tray of butter cookies. "You'll meet hordes of terribly interesting people at Brown." She heaped a pile of cookies onto a plate and handed it to him. "The bustle of Providence will sweep you up, and you'll forget all about me and this little school."

Their fingers brushed as he took the plate. "No, I shall never forget you, Azaadiins."

Before she could reply in kind, her father parted through the crowd with Mr. Chase. "There you are, Harry! Allow me to introduce Mr. Chase from the Indian Bureau. Mr. Chase, our valedictorian, Harry Muskrat."

The superintendent's thick lips curled and his nose wrinkled. "Muskrat?"

"The muskrat is an honored animal among my people. He gave his life so that the world could be built anew after the flood."

"Hmm . . . interesting . . . Mr. Blanchard tells me you've been accepted to Brown. Bully for you, my boy! I'm a Yale man myself."

The man's watery gray eyes fell on Alma. The flat expression he'd worn throughout the ceremony livened. His thick lips, crowded between a graying mustache and beard, curved upward. "This must be your daughter." He raised his top hat, exposing a crown of baldness beneath. "Miss Blanchard."

Alma held back a grimace and bowed. Thankfully, her father steered the conversation back to Harry. Out of politeness, she endured a few more moments of the man's sideways glances, then flashed Asku an apologetic smile and slipped away.

She scanned the crowd for Tshikwā'set. He no longer stood beneath the sweeping arms of the oak. He was not by the refreshment table, nor had he sought shade on the veranda.

At last, she spotted him through the dense gathering, standing with Frederick and a few boys from La Crosse. Their eyes met and he inclined his head toward the back of the house. He'd made his decision.

Alma hesitated. Could she bear to hear he was leaving? Just when she'd screwed up enough courage to follow, Lily Steele captured her arm. "There you are, Alma. What a quaint little affair. Almost feels like a real graduation ceremony."

Alma grimaced. "It is a real graduation ceremony. They worked hard. They're going off to jobs, colleges." She slipped her arm free from Lily's grasp. "Now, if you'll excuse me, the . . . um . . . the cookies need replenishing." She hastened to the buffet, grabbed the tray with the fewest shortbreads, and sped around the schoolhouse.

The vast backyard was nearly empty. Mr. Simms lounged in the open doorway of the wood shop, arms crossed, his cloudy expression untouched by the day's gaiety. His hooded eyes followed the movement of the few guests who milled about inside, viewing the equipment and machinery. Alma wondered if they noticed the stain, the dark patch beside the lathe where Charles's blood had seeped into the floorboards. No, she decided. Her father was a man of details. He would have made sure it was covered for the occasion. The boy had recovered, after all. Still, Alma lingered, the tray growing heavy in her arms. Yes, he'd recovered, but he would never be the same.

A flash of movement in the kitchen window caught her attention. She hurried inside.

The large room, always a center of bustle and activity, for once lay still. Sunlight streamed in through the windows, casting the room in a golden glow.

"Tshikwā'set?" she whispered, setting the tray of cookies atop the counter.

He waved to her from between two towering cupboards. Stepping around the butter churn and a broom, she joined him in the small cranny.

"Before you tell me anything I have to—"

He silenced her with a kiss, his lips hungry, urgent. She forgot whatever it was she wanted to say and leaned into his embrace. When she was all but starved of breath, he pulled away. They crouched down for better concealment amid the jumble of kitchenware, their knees touching, backs pressed against the sides of cupboards. Tshikwā'set leaned forward and kissed her again.

Unease built in her stomach, even while his lips lingered over her own. A fierceness infused his embrace, an undercurrent of emotion she couldn't quite name. She pulled back. "You're leaving, aren't you?"

"Mr. Wallis talked to me today of his carriage works."

Alma spoke over him. "I knew when I saw your reaction to Asku's speech—"

"Mr. Simms vouched for my skill with the saw and the lathe and the—"

"I knew you'd made up your mind to return to the reservation."

"He hired me on at a dollar a day!"

Alma blinked. "What? You're not leaving?"

He shook his head. Her elbow struck the butter churn as she reached for him. It teetered but did not fall. They laughed, and when their laughter was spent, they kissed again.

"Where will you stay?" she asked.

"Mr. Wallis recommended a boardinghouse near of the shop."

Her smile faltered. "Do they take on . . . er . . ."

"Indians? Mr. Wallis seemed to think so."

"And Father could write a letter recommending you." She squeezed Tshikwā'set's hand. "You're really going to stay here in La Crosse?"

"Ēh, nēnemōhsaew. Yes."

Alma felt weightless. Sunlight fell like a halo around them, gilding the broom and butter churn and cupboards, erasing from view the dust and cobwebs. She leaned forward and rested her head against his chest. His heartbeat—a pace quicker than its usual steady rhythm—sounded in her ear.

"Shan't you miss your home?" she asked.

His chest rose and fell with a deep breath. "Every day. The smell of pine trees, the smiling faces of my brothers and sisters, the sound of the tāwāēhekan, our sacred drum." His arms tightened around her and he burrowed his fingers into her pinned-up curls. "But I would miss you more."

"We don't have to stay here forever. In La Crosse, I mean. We could settle closer to your reservation. Maybe Milwaukee or Green Bay. You could open your own carriage repair shop. I could work at a grammar school or teach piano."

Tshikwā'set's body shook with laughter. "You? A teacher like Aní·tas?"

"I wouldn't be so wicked as her." She scowled in her best Miss Wells impression. "But I certainly wouldn't tolerate troublemakers like you."

"That's not the life of you." His voice was thick, suddenly void of humor. "You were meant for big houses and fancy dinners, china and silver."

Alma lifted her head to meet his eyes. "I don't need all that finery."

"You don't want to marry some rich white man?"

"No."

The glint in his eyes faded, leaving them hard and weary as petrified wood. "You should, Azaadiins." But as he said this, his arms tightened around her. "We're not a good match, you and I."

"We're a perfect match." She pulled back slightly from his embrace. Why didn't he see that? What did it matter if they came from different worlds, so long as . . . She took a deep breath. "I love you."

For all their joking before in the woods, she'd never actually said the words. Now she felt suddenly wary and unclothed. Her heart pounded through the ensuing silence. Had he heard her? Did he feel the same? His actions spoke of love, staying here instead of returning to his home, but nevertheless she longed for him to say it.

The light around them faded, obscured by some fleeting cloud. Tshikwā'set's eyes dropped to the dusty floor and his brow furrowed. Despite the balmy day and warmth radiating from his body, Alma shivered.

Another moment of silence, then Tshikwā'set smiled—that

wry, crooked smile she so adored. He raised his gaze to hers. "Kemenīnemen. I love you, too."

Alma reached for him, not caring if she knocked over the butter churn or broom or even the entire cupboard. He loved her and he would stay. They kissed and huddled close until approaching footsteps outside shooed them away. Nothing of the rest of the day seemed to touch her—not Mr. Chase's salacious glances, not Lily's endless prattle, not the hours of cleanup after the guests had left. She watched the sun glide toward the horizon until it hung red and brilliant above the trees, its rays—for a fleeting moment—a bridge between earth and sky.

CHAPTER 31

Minnesota, 1906

Alma stood a moment in the middle of the empty road, her eyes adjusting to the bright midday light, her ears ringing from the blaring ripsaw, her nerves alight like an electric bulb. The hem of her skirt thrashed in the wind. How could Frederick be so cold? Didn't he still care? If not for her, for Asku. Find Minowe—that was his advice. Her jaw set and she shook her head. There had to be another way.

Clothes flapped on a laundry line at the back of a nearby house. Beyond the drying shirts and trousers, vines crawled across the yard. Yellow and green squash sat fat on the ground. Cornstalks rustled, their ears long since harvested, their leaves dry, brown, dead.

Peel back the husk and we're empty, hollowed out.

She turned from Frederick's workshop and marched toward the agency. The whine of the saw blade faded behind her. He was wrong. She remembered how he'd smiled on graduation day, how dapper he'd looked in his new suit, how he'd sat enrapt listening to Asku's speech. Something had been taken from them, yes, but something greater replaced it. A way to survive and thrive in the changing times. She'd lived that tenet her entire life, heard the echo of those words since her earliest days: her father's pontificating, Miss Wells's lectures, the rhymes they'd been made to memorize about Senator Dawes and his liberating legislation. It couldn't all be wrong.

The wind gusted again, stronger now, catching on the brim of her hat and yanking it free from her hair. She held it fast against her head and leaned into the gale. She forced Frederick's words from her mind, beat back thoughts of the depressing annuity line, and focused on the clapboard houses standing at intervals along the drive. Calico curtains fringed their windows. The scent of baking bread and roasting meat wafted toward her on the wind.

Laughter drew her eyes to a nearby schoolyard. Children ran about with sticks and balls, impervious to the wind, their faces lit with carefree smiles. Alma's step lightened. The quaint houses, the bustling school—White Earth Village was just like any other country town. A far cry from the sparse cabins and lone trading post her Chippewa friends had described to her a quarter century before. There might be problems, but the Indians were thriving here.

Inside the agency, the cheer she'd mustered quickly flagged. Stewart sat in one corner, all but the top of his head concealed behind teetering stacks of papers and ledgers. She'd feared Agent Taylor would try to hide or withhold documents despite the subpoena. It appeared now he'd chosen the opposite attack and provided every file and scrap on hand for them to sift through.

She hesitated before crossing the room, dreading more strained conversation, more tiptoeing around last night's argument. But when he looked up over the wall of paperwork, the flint was gone from his eyes. He grabbed a chair from the corner, brushed off the seat, and set it beside his own.

"Have you found anything?" she asked.

"Not as yet, I'm afraid." He gestured to the piles. Still more surrounded them on the floor. "Staggering really, the disorder of it all. I've managed to sort out most of the older documents. I shouldn't think we'd need anything before 1890. What did you learn from the store clerk?"

She peeled off her gloves and tossed them onto the table. "Nothing of import."

"You were gone quite some time."

"The clerk directed me to another man." For a moment, she could hear the ripsaw. "He hadn't any answers either."

Stewart sighed. "That's a shame. Witness testimony would strengthen our case."

"What about Zhawaeshk?"

Stewart nodded toward the ginger-haired agency worker they'd met on the road the night before. "He was right. When the jury learns

Zhawaeshk's a drunk, his credibility is lost." He raked back his hair and smiled weakly, his bottom lip still red and slightly swollen. "Let's hope we can find something here."

Alma eyed the stacks and felt a stir of panic. Asku's salvation lay here? In this mess? Stewart, however, seemed altogether placid. Scrounging for witnesses, scuffling among grave houses, settling lame horses—how trying yesterday must have been for him. Here, at last he was in his element. He needed only a housecoat and slippers, and the sight of him would be no different than a quiet, peaceful evening at home. His posture was straight as always, his notebook and pen arranged neatly, his attention already returned to the document at hand.

She pulled a thick file from atop one of the stacks. "What are we looking for?"

"I'm not entirely sure," he said without glancing up from his work.

Not sure? Dozens of piles and they weren't even sure what they were looking for?

"Don't worry, darling. I'll know when I've found it. Just set aside anything related to Mr. Muskrat or anything else that strikes you as odd."

The potbellied stove in the far corner hissed and crackled. The smoke smelled faintly of pinesap. She shrugged out of her duster and opened the folder. Inside was a collection of citations: heathenish dancing, destruction of property, plural marriage, conjurer's arts, improper gifting, lechery, and intoxication. Even offenses as trivial as long hair and infrequent school attendance had incurred a fine or reduction in rations. "This is ridiculous."

Several employees looked over with narrowed eyes and pinched expressions. She met their stare, then turned to Stewart. "What harm is there in dancing or gift giving?"

"Did you see Mr. Muskrat's name on any of those citations? Or anyone else cited multiple times?"

"No." In truth, she hadn't paid attention to the names, only the offenses. She'd danced those dances; helped her friends "conjure" medicines out of dogbane, wild peas, and snakeroot; taken their gifts and given gifts in return.

"Anything strange or suspicious, put in this pile," Stewart said, indicating a small stack beside him.

Everything was strange to her—not the acts themselves, but that the Indians' lives should be so regulated.

She came across a field service report about a young unmarried woman found to be with child. If the father were also single, the report recommended the couple be made to wed. Were he not single, more severe action—fines or even jail time—should be assessed, and the baby put up for adoption.

The paper crunched and rumpled under her tightening grip. To live under such scrutiny! To have such private matters discussed, debated, cataloged. And the baby. She stared forward at the far wall, the yellow maps bleeding into the white plaster, the cabinets and bureaus and tables and chairs all blurring into shapeless, nameless objects. This was not the life she'd imagined for her friends. Not the life promised them.

Hadn't it been that way at Stover, though? The litany of rules, the stiff punishment, the constant surveillance. She'd been a fool to think they'd be handed freedom after graduation.

"Find something?"

Alma straightened and looked at Stewart. "Hmm?"

"I know this is tedious, darling. Should you like to take in some air? Or I can see after some tea?"

"It isn't that. It's just, this is all so"—she waved a hand over the papers—"so bleak."

He teased the report from her fist and scanned its contents. "Yes, I've seen several of these field reports."

"What business is it of the agency's if they marry in the Christian fashion or not?"

"Surely you're not suggesting they . . ." He paused and lowered his voice. "Engage in amorous congress without official contract."

"What is making love if not an avowal of one's affections and devotion?"

He regarded her with a stunned expression. "Debauchery."

Alma dropped her gaze. Her cheeks burned. "I simply meant that they have their own marital customs."

"Customs forbade by the law. Laws policed by the agency."

His unimpassioned voice only enflamed her further. All logic, no emotion. Black and white without any gray. She stood and crossed to a nearby window. Water spots clouded the glass. She pressed her hand against the surface. How smooth. How fragile. She imagined her ungloved hand breaking through to the outside, the filmy glass cracking and splintering, its jagged shards red with her blood. She pressed a little harder.

A hand lit upon the small of her back. Stewart's. She'd know his touch if she were blind.

"I'm sorry, darling," he said quietly. "I know these people were your friends. I didn't mean to imply they were all criminals and debauchers."

Not just them—her too.

The glass was cool beneath her fingers. A touch more pressure and it would shatter.

At last, she pulled away—away from the glass, away from Stewart's hand. "I'm no help to you here."

"Nonsense. You're a great help."

She looked at the mountains of papers and ledgers and knew he was lying. There was only one way she could help: Minowe. "I'll just take a quick stroll about the yard."

"Don't go far."

She grabbed her coat, skirting his gaze. "I shan't."

CHAPTER 32

———⇒►•◄⇐———

Wisconsin, 1891

Despite the hearty fire crackling in the marble hearth, a chill lingered in the Steeles' parlor. It hung in the dour expression of the hostess and her daughter. It prickled across Alma's skin during the prolonged silences that riddled their conversation.

"There's a promise of snow in those clouds," Old Mrs. Lawrence said, waving a wrinkled hand at the gray sky peeking through the Oriental lace drapery.

Alma nodded in concert with the others and sipped her lukewarm tea.

"Probably the same storm that ravaged Dakota," Lily Steele said. Then, as if realizing her blunder, she bit her lip and dropped her gaze to the damask rug.

Alma set down her teacup and braced herself. Her silly friend had opened the door to the subject the others had been too decorous, but plainly fiending, to bring up.

"I heard the Indians' corpses are still there, lying frozen on the field, on account of the blizzard," Mrs. Lawrence's granddaughter said in a whisper, as if trading bits of post-soirée gossip.

Alma's stomach clenched.

"Ruth!" Mrs. Lawrence shot the girl a scandalized look.

Mrs. Steele straightened in her chair and raised her chin. The gaslit chandelier cast the sharp features of her face in a sallow glow. "Serves those savages right. However do you rest at night, Cora? Those Indian children might slaughter you while you sleep."

"It's been a trying few days." Alma's mother put a hand to her cheek and sighed. "Mr. Blanchard insists we have nothing to fear. Even in light of this uprising at Wounded Knee, he sees nothing but goodness in them."

"Murderous devils!" Mrs. Lawrence said.

Alma flinched at the old woman's words. Her fingers dug into the folds of her dress.

Mrs. Lawrence continued. "Have you any of those . . . those . . . what band are those hostiles from?"

"Sioux," Alma said.

"Does it matter what tribe they come from?" Mrs. Steele said. "Their malign traits are universal."

Lily glanced at Alma as she refilled the teacups. It was a look of pity, not solidarity. "It would be unchristian of us not to try, Mother."

"We'd be better off were they all dead," Mrs. Steele replied.

Alma reached for her tea with a trembling hand. The cup rattled against its saucer, liquid sloshing over the edge. She gave up and returned the teacup back to the table. "Women and children were among those massacred."

All five women turned cold, questioning gazes upon her.

"Are you implying the soldiers are to blame for this incident?" Mrs. Lawrence asked.

Alma's mother let out a trill of laughter. "No, of course not. A rancher's wife and daughter were taken after the battle in one of those retaliatory raids organized by the savages." She looked at Alma with piercing eyes. "Alma was just referring to those poor *Christian* souls."

Alma clenched her jaw, refusing to be cowed by her mother's stare.

"Good heavens, I hadn't heard that." Mrs. Lawrence clutched the satin bow about her gizzard-like neck. "Do you think any of the older boys at Stover might run off and join this red rebellion?"

"Believe me, we keep a very close eye on them. Mr. Simms has never failed in tracking down a runaway."

Ruth leaned forward in her chair. "Do you really think a full-fledged uprising is under way?"

"Don't you read the papers I pass you each morning, girl?" her grandmother said. "Those hostile bucks are burning schools, attacking wagon trains, pillaging the nearby ranches. I read just this morning the Governor of Nebraska called for troops to protect the settlers along the Nebraska-Dakota border. It's only a matter of time before the agitation spreads."

Mrs. Steele and her daughter both nodded, grave expressions cast upon their faces. With the sigh of a martyr, Alma's mother collapsed back in her chair.

"No need to worry, Cora," Old Mrs. Lawrence said. "The army will take swift care of them."

A sudden fear gripped Alma. These buzzards were not the only ones reading the papers. Her father had taken care to hide news of the Dakota fighting from the students at Stover, even from those who might have relatives among the dead. But what of Tshikwā'set?

Calls for safekeeping and worried expressions followed them as they left the Steeles'. Instead of steering the buggy toward Stover, Alma directed the horses downtown.

"Home, dear. I haven't the energy to visit the shops today."

"Mr. Simms asked if we would stop by the carriage factory and inquire about a part he ordered."

Her mother scowled but waved them onward. Traffic thickened as they headed west. Sprawling mansions gave way to single-story shotguns, ornamented coaches and buggies to surreys and mule-drawn box carts. Pillars of smoke rose from the mills and factories that lined the Mississippi. Locomotives blared their horns. All the while Alma's insides twisted with worry.

When they reached the Wallis Carriage Company, Alma left her mother napping in the buggy and hurried inside. Mr. Wallis greeted her from behind a small lacquered counter. Behind it, a variety of carriages stood on display. Her eyes moved beyond the shiny new models to an open door leading to the workshop. Six or seven young men labored over vehicles in various stages of repair. Among them she spotted Tshikwā'set. The tamponade around her heart eased.

"How can I help you, Miss Blanchard?"

"I . . . um . . . my father received a letter addressed to George. As Mother and I were coming to town today to call upon some friends, he asked me to deliver it." The lie left her mouth dry and her pulse unmeasured.

"Of course, I'd be happy to give it to him."

Her stomach dropped. "I . . . er . . . I hate to take you from your bookkeeping. I'll take it back."

The creases around the man's gray eyes deepened. He looked over his shoulder at Tshikwā'set and his expression softened. "All right, my dear. Mind your lovely dress. Floor's covered in sawdust."

The click of her boots over the floorboards heralded her approach, and the workers looked up from their hammers, trammels, and paint- brushes. Each one nodded when she passed. Though the clamor of their labor resumed, she knew their eyes had not left her.

Tshikwā'set sat on the stool at the very back of the shop, sanding down a long plank of wood. He, too, had glanced up at her approach, his unshorn hair falling over owl-wide eyes. He brushed the strands aside and returned to his work with a coolness that both alarmed and relieved her. Since his departure from Stover in July, they met with little frequency. Their paths crossed each Sunday in church, but there only a quick word or folded note could pass unnoticed between them. She'd never before come to the shop.

He stood, set aside his sandpaper, and wiped his hands over his cotton trousers. "You shouldn't be here, nēnemōhsaew," he whis- pered.

Alma opened her satchel and rummaged through its contents, feigning to search for the imaginary letter. "I had to see you. I was afraid news from Dakota had upset you."

His jaw clenched and his irises seemed to darken until they were barely distinguishable from his pupils. "Upset is not the word I feel."

"Just promise you won't do anything rash, reckless."

He glanced at his coworkers. "We cannot speak here. Remember the dugout we found last spring? Meet me there tonight."

"Okay, I'll try." At the bottom of her bag she found the dance card from a recent gala she'd attended. She folded it in half and handed it to him, just in case Mr. Wallis or the other workers were still looking.

Tshikwā'set arched a brow.

In a raised voice she said, "Father received this letter for you. Be well." She lingered a moment longer, loath to take her leave, then spun on her heels and walked away.

Thick, heavy snowflakes began to fall before Alma and her

mother reached the bluffs beyond La Crosse. Like frozen teardrops, they continued to float down from the angry sky through the afternoon and into twilight.

At supper, Alma peered through the frosted windowpanes across the dining hall, wondering if the storm still raged outside in the darkness. Voices whispered around her, quiet but electric. Minowe had noticed the copy of the *La Crosse Daily Republican and Leader* in the study when she came to remove the afternoon tea tray. THE MANIACAL ACT OF THE RED SKINS AT WOUNDED KNEE read the headline. She'd only managed to skim the first few paragraphs before Alma's father returned to the room, but now, the few details she had gleaned spread with hushed voices throughout the dining hall.

"Where's Wounded Knee?" a young Chippewa girl asked.

Minowe waited until Miss Wells moved beyond earshot. "Bwaan ishkonigan." *Sioux Reservation.*

Hįčoga leaned across the table. "Is it true, Azaadiins? Are hundreds dead?"

Alma pried her gaze from the window. Around the table, wide-eyed Indians stared at her. The fear and pain in her friends' faces left her breathless. Unable to hold their scrutiny, she looked down at the boiled potatoes and gristly meat untouched on her plate. "Yes."

"Women and children?" Hįčoga asked.

"Some," Alma said, then shook her head. "Many."

Whispers swarmed until Miss Wells rapped her ruler against the tabletop. "Voices, ladies. The dinner hour is for sustenance, not idle chatter."

Silence fell but did not last. No sooner had Miss Wells left to reprimand another table than Minowe spoke. "Who began it?"

"The papers say the U.S. cavalry were trying to disarm a group of captives when one of the Indians shot at them."

"And you believe it so?"

Alma looked back at blackness beyond the window. The inflammatory headlines and editorials she'd read in the papers, bitter words she'd heard today in town, the palpable distress building in the dining hall all tore at her, pulling her in divergent directions.

"It doesn't matter who started it," she said finally. "There was no need to kill innocent women and children."

"Ho," Hįčoga said in agreement.

"What means maniacal, anyway?" Minowe asked.

"Crazy. Violent."

Minowe's expression soured. "Is that how the white man really see us?"

"No." Her voice sounded hollow. "Well, maybe some, after an incident like this . . . those who are ignorant."

"*Us* maniacal?" Minowe shook her head, her dark eyes unblinking. Alma touched her forearm, but her friend pulled away. "Already so many dead. Do they want to kill us all?"

"Of course not." But again her words rang empty. She had nothing for their pain, their fear, their anger.

While the conversation continued around her, Alma retreated into her thoughts. She imagined Tshikwā'set sitting down for dinner at the boardinghouse where he rented a room. Did the others—the white boarders—get up and leave when he arrived? Did they break off their conversations and glare?

She thought too of Asku. Surely back East, at such an illustrious school as Brown, more mild temperaments reigned. With his gentle, curious nature, who could help but adore him? The depth of his bravery touched her—to travel so far from his home. If only she could see him, hear the clear, steady tone of his voice. Maybe then worry's hold would lessen.

A shrill whistle cry rent her from her musing. She looked to the front of the dining hall, where her father now stood beside Miss Wells. His face, just beginning to line with age, burned scarlet. He blared the whistle again and silence fell around the room.

"What's behind all this racket?"

No one answered.

His narrow eyes drifted over the rows of tables. When his gaze reached Alma, she held his stare. He must know news of Wounded Knee had finally broken at the school. Three of the children seated before him were Sioux, one from the Pine Ridge Reservation.

"They're worried about their kin. News of the—"

"Now's not a suitable time, Alma."

"But—"

He looked beyond her at the others. "If you cannot eat with proper decorum, you shall not eat at all. Take your plates to the kitchen and then go straight to bed. This meal is over."

Alma's hand tightened around her fork. Her sinews showed white atop her knuckles. "It was a massacre, Father. Haven't they the right—"

"Enough!"

She choked down her fury and followed the others into the kitchen. With her father standing watch, they washed the dishes in silence, then marched upstairs to their dormitory. She refused to look at him as they passed at the foot of the stairs. Seventeen now and he still thought her a child, oblivious to the world around her. She wasn't, though. None of them were.

At the second-floor landing, Alma grabbed hold of Minowe's hand and squeezed before parting for her room. Her friend's hand was cold and wrinkled from the sudsy dishwater. She squeezed back, but only weakly.

Inside her room, Alma waited and listened. Sneaking out tonight would be dangerous—the roof slick, the freshly fallen snow a canvas for her tracks. But after the angst she'd seen at dinner, she must go.

She paced her small room for over an hour until the downstairs lights no longer glistened upon the frozen yard. The stairs creaked; the hallway floorboards whined. Her parents' door opened and closed. For good measure, she waited another half hour, then donned her housecoat, wrapped the quilt around her shoulders, and snuck out through the hallway window onto the snowy roof.

Her first few steps found purchase on the snow-covered shingles. Then her foot caught a patch of ice. She slid toward the edge of the roof, arms wheeling, heels digging into snow. She slowed to a stop just before she reached the brink. Her body swayed, first backward, then forward as she overcorrected and toppled from the roof.

A drift of powdery snow broke her fall. The air flew from her lungs, leaving her gasping. She rose onto her hands and knees and listened. The schoolhouse remained quiet, a sleeping giant in the wintery night. After she caught her breath, she pushed herself up with wobbly arms. Her right knee had sunk through the snow and struck the frozen ground, tearing through her nightgown. Warm blood trickled down her leg.

She looked around the yard and listened once more. Melted snow dampened her gown, stinging her skin when the brisk wind licked over it. Clouds shrouded the moon; the forest before her lay black and ominous. The warmth and safety behind Stover's walls called to her, but she drew her quilt around her and trudged onward.

Though she had not visited the hillside dugout since she and Tshikwā'set had first discovered it last spring, her feet led her there without hesitation. The smell of smoke drifted among the snow-flakes. Light flickered from behind the tattered window covering and beneath the crooked door. She paused momentarily before entering. Someone else might have come to occupy the hovel—tramps from the train yard, hunters in search of winter game—but by now her entire body shook with the cold. Her knee ached and her fingers were numb. She pushed aside the plank of wood propped over the doorway and hurried inside.

As her eyes adjusted to the light, she saw Tshikwā'set squatting beside a small fire in the center of the room. He fed a few sticks and twigs to the blaze, then stood. Instead of moving to embrace her, he stalked the width of the dugout. "Do you know what they say in your newspapers?"

The tone of his words stung. They weren't her newspapers just because a white man had written them. The crackling fire promised warmth, but she moved no closer. "I've read some of what they say. Not everyone believes—"

"Murderous red devils, savage butchers!" He pulled a sheet of folded newsprint from his waistband and brandished it in her direc-tion. "Three hundred mamāceqtawak killed, their bodies left frozen in the snow, and we're the ones spoken of as butchers."

"Over two dozen cavalrymen were killed as well."

Tshikwā'set froze. His eyes narrowed over her. "Is that what we are worth? A dozen Indians for every one white man?"

"No, of course not, I was just—"

"A war of extermination, they're calling it." He paced again. "Do they expect that we just hang our heads and die?"

He shook his head. His chest heaved. After a moment of silence, his voice rose in a whoop. "Pīpiakotan! Pīpiakotan!" He repeated the phrase four times, the first cry long, drawn-out, the second short, clipped.

"Stop it!" She stomped her heel on the packed dirt floor. "No one is calling for a war."

He unfolded the paper, jammed his finger at a column of dark words, and began to read. "Our safety depends on the complete annihilation of the red man. To protect our civilization, we must wipe these untamable vermin from the earth."

She crossed the small room, grabbed the paper from his hand, and looked at the column's author. "It's just an editorial. The hateful words of some ignorant man."

"Words did not kill the Indian at Wounded Knee. White men's bullets did." His eyes darkened. "Well, we have bullets of our own."

Alma threw the paper into the fire. Sparks flew up, popping and snapping in the air, echoing the sounds of war and gunfire of which he spoke. The heat of the flames steadied her nerves. "Tshikwā'set, mayhem and violence won't bring about justice."

"Not justice. Revenge."

"Then more will die." He turned his head away from her, but she clasped his face between her hands and forced his gaze upon her. "There's no honor in that. Is that how you'd have your people remembered?"

Seconds passed, and his breathing slowed. He shut his eyes and leaned into her touch. "Your hands are so cold, nēnemōhsaew." His eyes opened and looked her over, as if seeing her for the first time.

She stepped back and smoothed down the locks of frazzled hair that had come loose from her braid. His gaze traveled from her face down her body, stopping at the bloody tear in her nightgown. "What happened of your knee?"

"I . . . er . . . I slipped from the roof."

A sudden clip of laughter filled the dugout. Alma frowned and took another step back. "It's hardly funny. I could have died."

But her words only made him laugh harder.

She turned from him toward the fire. Her fingers had regained some feeling, but her skin still stung with the cold. She removed the quilt from her shoulders and held it out in front of her, hoping the flames would dry it some before she had to venture back into the snow.

Tshikwā'set grew silent. She glanced back at him over her shoulder. The cheer had vanished from his face, but so, too, had the fury. With one long stride, he was beside her. He grabbed the quilt from her hands, flung it to the ground, and pulled her against his chest. When their lips met, she could feel his emotions spilling forth in their kiss—rage, sorrow, desire. Her heart bounded, at once urging her to flee and commanding her to stay. He slipped a hand between their bodies, grazing her breast on his way to the knot that fastened her housecoat. His other hand remained on the small of her back, pinning her against him. With each beat, her heart continued to battle—go, stay, go, stay. His lips moved from her mouth down her neck, wet and hot against her skin.

Go. Stay.

Within a minute, his deft fingers had pried apart the knot and both hands worked to disrobe her of her housecoat. He tugged the paisley ribbon from her braid and freed her dampened hair.

Go. Stay.

Her steadfast feet answered for her; her hands, moving to unbutton his shirt as he unfastened the top of her nightgown.

He pulled her to the ground atop the quilt and shrugged free of his coat and shirt. The fire continued to crackle and sputter beside them, casting a tawny glow on the wooden beams and dirt surrounding them. Outside, she could hear the wind howl. It ruffled the frayed window coverings and blew a few glimmering snowflakes beneath the door.

Tshikwā'set's hands traveled up her legs, pushing back the hem of her nightgown. Her skin tingled with his touch. His weight pressed against her. She closed her eyes and held her breath. Her body clenched at the initial wave of pain, then slowly relaxed. Their first movements were awkward, hesitant. Where to brace her legs; where to rest his elbow. Then their bodies found a common rhythm, and she arched into his embrace. The smell of sawdust lingered on his skin. Her tongue tasted the saltiness of his sweat as they kissed. Everything she had felt that day—all her fear and anger—receded to his touch.

Afterward, they lay side by side staring at the swirl of smoke escaping through the chimney hole. Alma knew she should feel guilty. This was not what good women did. She pushed down the hem of her nightgown and fastened the collar, but her movements were half-hearted, her capacity for guilt besieged by bliss.

Tshikwā'set rolled toward her. He propped himself up on one elbow and traced her collarbone with his free hand. "In Menominee culture, long ago, before the white priests came with their religion, a girl's aunt or grandmother looked of the other clans for a suitable boy for her."

"Why?"

"It's forbidden to marry within one's own clan. If the old women saw a boy they liked, they would speak with his family and arrange the match. Then the boy's family would take food and deerskins to the girl's family."

Alma's stomach fluttered. "And then?"

Tshikwā'set shrugged and kissed her throat. "Then she returned with the boy's family to her new home."

"That's it? No priest or elder? No formal ceremony?"

"No." Tshikwā'set rolled onto his back, resting his head atop his interlaced fingers. He lay quiet for several moments, then broke into laughter. "What would your father do if I brought him deerskins and say I was taking you for my wife?"

"I don't know, but Mother would kill you."

His laughter ebbed to silence. "I'll do it white man way, then."

Both panic and delight sprang inside her. She sat up and studied him. His dark eyes held a smile, but the rest of his face was serious. "You shouldn't joke about such things."

"You don't want to be wife of an Indian?"

"No, that's not it. I—"

He pulled her against his chest and began to nibble her neck.

"Stop! Stop," she said between giggles. "You'll leave a mark."

Rolling atop her and pinning her arms, he continued until water ran from her eyes.

Breathless and still laughing, she shouted out, "Of course I want to marry you!"

He stopped and leaned over her, hands on either side of her chest. His chin-length hair hung around his face, a thick black curtain obscuring his expression in shadow. She reached up and tucked the strands behind his ears. The glow of the firelight twinkled in his eyes. She no longer felt the cold of the storm, nor registered the cry of the wind, as if the world had shrunk to encircle only them.

"I'm saving every dollars I get. Some I send home. There's never enough food in the winter. Much fighting with the agent over our timber . . ." His eyes narrowed, clouded by thoughts beyond their warm little world. She trailed her hand over his cheek and along the taut muscles of his neck. His necklace swayed in the air between them like the lazy pendulum of a clock in need of winding. She ran her fingers down the strand of smooth quill and shiny black stones. When she reached the beaded medallion at its end, she tugged slightly.

Tshikwā'set blinked and his eyes cleared. He bent down and kissed her. "In springtime, nēnemōhsaew, I'll have enough moneys to speak my intentions to your father. The mōhkomān way."

A niggling unease lurked beside her joy. Her father would consent, but her mother? The drama she would make of it! Alma pushed the thought away and drew his face down to kiss her again.

At some point, she would have to brave the dark forest and bitter cold. At some point, before the light of dawn spilled over the horizon, they would have to let the fire die and part from the warmth of each other's bodies. But for now, she closed her eyes, tasted his lips, and let her mind believe nothing existed beyond the dugout walls.

CHAPTER 33

Minnesota, 1906

Alma hurried down the agency steps, letting the door slam behind her. She imagined the workers jerking upright at the sound and scowling. She imagined the stacks of paperwork teetering, a document or two cartwheeling free on the unsettled air. They weren't just citations, reports, and rolls; they were people's lives. She admired Stewart his objectivity, wished she'd been of greater help. But the faces behind the names haunted her, their voices a constant whisper in her ear. No, her only help now was Minowe.

When she reached the road her feet stalled. She looked right, then left and right again. Frederick had instructed her to follow the thoroughfare beyond the agency, hadn't he? So left then—north.

She took a step and hesitated again. How far had Frederick said to go before she'd spot the path off the road? *Ningo'anwe'biwin.* But what in tarnation did that mean? Her fingers clenched. She'd forgotten her gloves inside the agency and her nails bit into her palms. Why had Frederick been so cryptic, so utterly unhelpful? She knew she'd heard the phrase before, had once known its meaning, but couldn't pluck it from the threads of her memory.

No use standing around. The sun, now directly overhead, had baked the road solid. Alma's boot heels snagged on the wagon-wheel ruts and pock-like hoofprints that scarred the dirt, making her wistful of the morning's mud. She wrung her hands and muttered reassurances to herself as she walked. This reunion was not about them.

Minowe would see that. Surely, they could set aside the past, for Asku's sake.

After a few minutes, she stopped and looked around. Field and forest sprawled around her, a gradient of yellow and brown with a few sprigs and leaves still clinging to their summer green. Nowhere did she see a side path or fork in the road as Frederick described. Insects hummed in the air, jumping and flitting through the dried grass. Had she gone far enough? Too far? Maybe she'd been wrong; maybe this wasn't the way at all.

She spun around and marched back the way she'd come. She recalled seeing a small path through the woods, just beyond the schoolhouse. Perhaps that was what Frederick meant.

The path, wide and bright where it met the road, quickly narrowed. Towering bluestem and matted chokecherry bushes pressed in on either side. The charming houses she'd seen in town gave way to weary cabins. She studied the women tending their sparse gardens or grating their laundry against wooden washboards, but none bore any resemblance to Minowe.

Farther on she passed an old woman weaving pale rush stalks into a wide mat. Her cotton skirt was torn and threadbare, her wispy hair drawn into a knot at the nape of her neck. Several small children ran half-clothed through the yard. The sun beat off their beautiful brown skin, and their laughter lingered like drifting milkweed seeds in the air.

When she saw Alma, the old woman hollered to the children and corralled them about her. The wrinkles around her eyes and mouth deepened. The little ones peered at Alma between the fluttering rush strands and around the woman's wide-set haunches. Alma smiled and nodded in their direction. Renewed giggles bubbled up from the children. One gave a timid wave.

Alma thought to stop and ask the woman if she knew where Minowe lived, but the old woman's scowl kept her walking. At what point had she lost the warmth, friendliness, and curiosity so alive in her grandchildren? Maybe that wasn't fair. She looked old enough to remember the early treaties and ever-shrinking land. She would remember the Indian Wars too. Little Big Horn. Wounded Knee. Sugar Point. Perhaps she'd seen her own children taken, sent away to boarding school, and feared Alma had come to steal her grandchildren as well.

All for the best, Alma told herself as she continued onward. But those words, her father's words, had lost their steel. She passed more weathered cabins. More guarded glances. The old woman's scowl haunted her. She'd read about the wars and treaties as a girl. Growing pains of the burgeoning West. The right of the strong and civilized to conquer the weak. And yet, how different it must have seemed to this woman. How different it seemed to Tshikwā'set that night they'd met in the dugout.

A sharp pang gripped her, like her insides had been cranked through a wringer. What would Tshikwā'set think of her now—all her rationalizing and excuses? Alma shut her eyes and banished the thought. Her limbs felt heavy and her feet ached. Best return to the agency. Stewart would worry soon.

But she'd not found Minowe, not made any progress in helping Asku. She forced her weary eyelids open and pressed her muscles into action. Just a little farther.

The forest thinned. Tree stumps littered the landscape. Only the small, the gnarled, or the sickly still stood. Soon the stubble of trees opened to a bald patch of land where a small shack teetered in the wind.

Surely Minowe could not live here. Alma's whole body turned cold at the thought. She swallowed her discomfiture and forced a steady gaze. The shack sat without foundation directly upon the ground. Tarpaper covered the slab siding and shingleless roof. Square holes sufficed for windows, their rag dressings flapping each time a breeze stirred. She shuffled up to the door and raised her fist to the splintery wood. Her whole arm trembled. Her knuckles wore a sheen of sweat. She felt naked without her gloves, embarrassed, and decided it improper to call without them. But just as she stepped back the door opened.

A woman stood in the jamb, her calico skirt tied high about her waist to accommodate her growing belly beneath. Her deep-set eyes were too dark, her drawn lips too full, her russet skin too youthful to be Minowe. Alma exhaled, equal parts relief and chagrin. "I . . . um . . . pardon the disturbance."

A man appeared from the shadowy house and stood beside the

woman. His gaze swept the clearing before settling on Alma. He pulled a colorful strand of tightly woven beads from beneath his shirt. A wooden cross hung at its center. He held it out for her to see, then reached for the door.

"Wait, I'm not a missionary."

He frowned. "We have no money."

"No." Alma blushed and tugged at her brooch. "I'm not selling anything."

His eyes narrowed and he roped an arm about the woman, resting his hand just below the swell of her belly. Beneath the bluster, there was tenderness in his touch, intimacy, and Alma found herself reaching back, searching for her own husband's hand, but she met only air. "I'm looking for a woman named Minowe. I wonder if she might have a . . . er . . ." She glanced at the tarpaper siding, then down to the packed dirt floor. "A house nearby."

The couple said nothing. She groped for the *Anishinaabemowin* words. *House* came quickly to mind, also the verb *to search for,* but the phrase demanded context. Did she say *Niijikwe Minowe:* my friend Minowe? *Nishiime:* my sister, as she'd called her all those years ago? *Nimiigaadenimdimin:* my enemy? Alma settled for the less descriptive *Minowe izhinikaazo anishinaabekwe:* a lady called Minowe. She uttered only the first few words before the man cut her off.

"No one of that name lives around here," he said.

"Are you sure? I was told she—"

"Yes, we are sure."

Before she could say anything else, he pulled the woman from the jamb and closed the door.

Alma retreated from the clearing, tears smarting in her eyes. None of this was as she'd expected—the dreadful reservation, the hostility from a people she'd known to be nothing but warm and kind. Her pace quickened, despite the flush of fatigue. Frederick's words made sense to her now. Asku's anger. They'd been promised a future that had never come. Prosperity, equality—words she'd heard a hundred times. Lies.

And Tshikwā'set. Her throbbing feet beat faster. If he saw her now, how could he feel anything but disgust? Had he been right when he'd labeled her *kēcīskiw*—enemy? All those years after Stover, clouded in her own misery, she'd ignored the truth. No, not ignored it; she'd run from it. Was running still.

Alma's stride petered to a shuffle. Her breath came short and wheezing. A sticky spume had built at the corners of her lips. She pulled a hankie from her handbag and raked the cloth atop her mouth and tongue. Over and over again, as if she'd tasted something foul, as if wiping her skin raw could erase all she'd said and thought and done.

The wind blew and she wondered what it must be like for the couple in their tiny shack. She imagined the cheap framework whining, the rags about the windows beating this way and that. How cold it must be in the winter. How damp when it rained.

She glanced back over her shoulder, but the shack was gone from view. Scraggly trees and waist-high brush surrounded the faint trail. Something didn't look right. Had she taken the wrong path from the clearing? She'd meant to return the way she'd come, but nothing around her was familiar. Her hands grew clammy. The sun dangled just above the horizon. Had Stewart noticed she'd not yet returned from her "quick stroll about the yard"? Of course he had; that'd been hours ago. How worried he must be.

She turned around and retraced her steps. Not five minutes on, she met a fork in the road. Drat! Which direction had she come? On blind faith she veered right and continued on. And on. A blister formed on the back of her heel. Each step sent a shock of pain.

The sky bruised over and crickets stretched their wings. The air grew cold. Alma buttoned her duster and buried her bare hands beneath her armpits. To her right, the weeds rustled. To her left, a branch snapped. She jumped and glanced about. Nothing.

No need to fear, she reminded herself. How different was this from the countless times she'd sneaked into the forest as a girl? Yet her bounding pulse refused to slow.

A headwind harried her every step, tugging at her dress. It stole beneath her collar and rattled the overhead leaves. But then, carried on its swells, came a whiff of smoke. Alma hurried along the path toward the smell. She tripped, fell, and clambered to her feet without regard for her scraped hands or dirtied skirt. Her side stung with exertion, but she dare not slow and lose the scent.

She stumbled into a clearing. Twilight's fading glow lit the outline of a tiny house. This time she did not hesitate to knock.

"Please," she said when the door opened. "I'm lost."

A man stared down at her, his face obscured in darkness, his wide shoulders and set jaw backlit by the crackling fire within. Alma's heart crowded her throat. He moved slightly and the strand of colorful beads and wooden cross around his neck caught the fire's light. "Of course, ma'am," he said. "Biindigen. Come inside."

CHAPTER 34

Wisconsin, 1891

Alma inspected the partially set table, then smiled down at Mabel and Ada. "Very good. Now place the knife at the top of the setting just below the salt cup and the fork here to the left of the plate."

The two third-year students did as she instructed, finishing off the four table settings. The double pendant lamp with its lace filigree gas shades had yet to be lit, but enough of spring's afternoon sunlight spilled into the dining room from the hall to illuminate their work.

A shadow fell across the table. A soft *ahem*. "We're having a dinner guest?" Alma's mother said from the doorway. "I was not informed."

"Yes. George. He's . . . er . . . one of the former students here," Alma said. "He asked to call upon Father, and Father invited him for dinner."

Her mother shook her head. "Probably come to beg a recommendation for some position or other. I hope he is not in need of a loan. Wasn't the whole idea that they be self-sufficient?"

Alma bristled. "He does very well at the Carriage Factory. I'm sure his business with Father is something else entirely."

"Whatever it is, I shan't bother with my formal toilette. And there's no need to set out the china. Use the earthenware."

The two young girls began to remove the plates before Alma could protest. As she watched her mother saunter away, a burst of anxiety clutched her. What would the woman say when she learned the real reason for Tshikwā'set's visit? Alma gulped down a few breaths and turned back toward her pupils with forced ease.

She showed the girls how to fold the napkins and where to place the water and wine goblets. Her father insisted such domestic skills would prove useful to the girls someday, qualify them for service in even the most fashionable of houses. Alma knew the girls enjoyed the break from scouring pots or folding laundry, so she was happy to teach them. Still, she cringed at the idea of them making a living this way. Surely they'd been brought here to achieve something greater than servitude.

After a final survey of the table, she released the girls to play in the yard and hurried to her room. Excitement had returned, dancing in her stomach like a moth at a flame.

She pulled four different dresses from her wardrobe and laid each atop her bed. The occasion demanded modesty, nothing too fancy, nothing that would attract her parents' attention. She held up one of the gowns—dark navy with a buttoned collar—and looked into the mirror. Modest, yes, but too much like her everyday attire.

Next, she selected a peach-colored gown with lace trim and scooped neckline. Tshikwā'set had seen her in it last year on the way to the Steeles' spring ball. She remembered the way his eyes hung on her. "Keonāēsem," he had told her afterward. *Beautiful.*

Her cheeks flushed and she returned the dress to the bed. Though she longed to hear him breathe that word again, tonight called for something less ostentatious. She rejected the next dress for the same reason and settled for a gown of soft blue silk, simple yet handsomely crafted.

Gay cries sounded from the front yard. "George! George is here!"

Alma hurried with her petticoats and buttons, her feet hardly touching the floor.

The front door whooshed open and a mob of footfalls spilled into the foyer. The other Indian students had always adored Tshikwā'set, especially the younger ones with whom he had sat at the front of the class. The din quieted and she knew her father had taken charge, dismissing the students to their dinner-hour chores. Her insides continued to rattle. She tidied her hair with sweat-slickened hands, then flew from her room.

She and Tshikwā'set had planned for this evening for weeks. What he would wear, when he should broach the issue with her father, what he would say—they had scripted every detail. Her mother, of course, posed the greatest obstacle, but once given, her father would not lightly withdraw his consent, even in the face of his wife's hysterics. As long as George could consult her father alone and garner his support, all would be well.

She grabbed hold of the banister at the top of the stairs and took a deep breath. With each step she descended, excitement overcame her nerves. She reached the parlor serene and expectant.

"Good evening, Miss Blanchard," Tshikwā'set said with a bow.

His tense, upright posture made her smile. "George."

She sat down on the couch beside her father. Tshikwā'set sat opposite them, clasping and unclasping his hands. Sweat dampened his hairline. His face had the look of one about to retch, but his eyes were steady, confident, ever glinting with a hint of mischief. She longed to reach out and still his hands with her own, but kept them prisoner in her lap.

To all this, her father appeared oblivious. "George was just telling me about a new spring system they're using on carriages these days. Rubber tires, too, you say? Like those of a bicycle?"

"Uh . . . yes . . . it's something they're experimenting with."

"You don't say?"

"Some even talk of a motor engine."

"Oh yes, I've heard of that. A Motorwagen they call it, made over there in Germany."

"France too. Perhaps someday we won't need for horses anymore."

Her father laughed. "I wouldn't go that far, my boy!"

Each convivial word further quelled Alma's nerves. Tshikwā'set's hands relaxed and regained some of their color. She did not allow her eyes to rest on him for long, glancing back at her father whenever the older man spoke, but they lingered long enough for quick appraisal. His suit was clean and pressed, the shirt beneath so bright it must be new. He had not cut his hair, as she had prodded, but at least wore it neatly tucked behind his ears. His shoes gleamed from a recent polish.

Her mother entered the room just as the conversation waned.

Alma's father stood. "My dear, you remember George, don't you?"

After a sharp nod from Alma, Tshikwā'set rose to his feet as well. "Mrs. Blanchard."

Her mother neither bowed nor extended her hand, but acknowledged him with a flat smile. She took her husband's arm and they processed to the dining room.

Tshikwā'set offered his arm to Alma, and they followed behind her parents. His light touch and careful distance felt strange after all the intimacy they had shared. A year's worth of stolen moments—hurried kisses, covert glances, passionate rendezvous—flashed in Alma's mind. How freeing it would be after tonight to share their love openly.

They passed by the crowded dining hall, where the Indian students had gathered for supper. Despite her mother's protests, Alma still ate most of her meals seated beside Minowe and Hįčoga at the long wooden tables. She looked for her friends through the sea of gawking faces. Hįčoga wore a broad, playful grin and crossed her wrists in front of her heart. Minowe smiled, too, but it seemed forced, wistful. She'd worn that expression ever since Alma shared with them the true purpose of Tshikwā'set's visit.

Perhaps Minowe just missed her brother. Alma missed him too. Asku's presence had always stilled her, fortified her hope and courage. If only he were here tonight.

At the entry into the formal dining room, Alma paused and gave Tshikwā'set's arm a light squeeze. His muscles felt tense enough to snap. When he pulled out her chair, its legs scraped softly atop the floor. They both winced, though neither of her parents paid the noise any mind. The soft light of the chandelier illuminated Tshikwā'set's handsome but grave face. He sat down across from her more upright than she had ever seen him deign to sit.

Trays of food rested on the small buffet to the right of her father. "George, may I have your plate? Roast? Potato? Beans?"

"Yes, if you please."

Her father dished the food and handed Tshikwā'set back his plate. "Cora, my dear?"

Alma watched Tshikwā'set from the corner of her eye as plates passed to and fro, pleased he had remembered not to start eating until Father had served them all. Though she knew he disliked pomp and ceremony, he hid it well. Only the occasional heavy breath and clenching of his jaw betrayed his unease and nerves. Alma contented herself that these were things only a lover would notice, and smiled reassuringly at him whenever her parents looked down over their food.

"I'm so proud of you graduates," her father said, breaking the silence. "You here in La Crosse, Harry back East." He took another bite of roast and leaned back in his chair. "What a time he must be having at Brown. The philosophical debate, the sport and camaraderie, the libraries and club halls . . ."

"The sophistication of a *real* city," her mother added.

If her father heard bitterness in her mother's voice, he made no show of it. "What about the others in your graduating class? Do you keep in touch with them?"

"Frederick's faring good in St. Paul. Catherine has went home to the Oneida reserve, I think."

"A blanket Indian again," her mother said. "What a shame."

Alma flinched and looked at Tshikwā'set. His hands tightened around his knife and fork, and his forearms flexed.

"Catherine had such talent with sewing," Alma said with forced lightness. "You remember her lacework, don't you, Mother?"

"I suppose her skills were a huckleberry above the rest," she replied. "But I don't see what good they'll do her on that reservation."

"Perhaps she could open a shop in Green Bay."

Her mother dabbed her mouth with her napkin, then waved it in Alma's direction. "You're such an optimist, dear. I suppose you get that from your father. The world is not the rosy place you think it is."

Alma bit her lip and allowed the conversation to dwindle. Nothing but the tap of knives and forks over the glazed clay dishes sounded from the table. After a minute or two, her father wiped his mouth and pushed back from the table. "I must say, George, I quite expected you to return to the reservation yourself after graduation."

Tshikwā'set shifted in his chair. "It will always be my home, but there are things in La Crosse that I am fond of also." His eyes flashed to Alma. "I am grateful to Mr. Wallis for taking me on in his shop that I might stay."

"I ran into Mr. Wallis in town just last week. He speaks very highly of your work. Says you're never tardy or loaf about on the job."

"It is kind of him to speak so."

Her father leaned back, eyes twinkling. "You're a credit to this school, my boy! You and the others, I cannot tell you how much your success pleases me."

"Thank you, sir."

"Now tell me, George, there was something you wanted to discuss?"

"Yes, I . . . er . . . ." He glanced at Alma and her mother.

"Of course. Let's retire to my study. Ladies, if you'll excuse us, please."

Tshikwā'set rose behind her father. Alma locked eyes with him and they both drew in a deep breath. She smiled once more, a final token of encouragement. This was the easy part. Her father had devoted his life to saving the Indian. Clearly, he'd grown to like Tshikwā'set. She watched the men exit the room, then glanced up at her mother. The woman wore a tired expression, her lips downturned and eyelids droopy, as if the meal had sapped her of all energy.

"Not much of a conversationalist, that one?"

"He was just nervous."

"Why should he be nervous coming back to Stover? More of a simpleton, I should think."

"He's really very bright."

"Bright?" Her mother laughed. "He could barely string together more than two sentences."

Alma balled her napkin and threw it down beside her plate. "Not everyone has to be a prattling fop. Besides, English isn't the language he was born to."

"Come now. You can hardly count those funny noises they make at one another as a true language. It's gibberish!"

"Mother, how can—"

"You're far too impassioned about this, my dear. Your entire face is ruddy, even your ears. It's not at all becoming."

Alma took a deep breath. Engaging her mother like this would hardly benefit the situation. She needed the woman as sanguine as possible when her father broke the news. "You're right. Forgive me. Come, let me play something for you in the parlor."

"That would be nice. My nerves are a bit frazzled from all this tedium. Some Chopin would be love—"

"Alma Marie Blanchard!" Her father's voice bellowed down the hallway.

Alma cocked her head. His voice was like the shrill cry of reveille after a fitful night, confusing and illusory, and she wondered whether she'd heard the sound at all or just imagined so.

He hollered again, the dark timbre of his voice unmistakable. She stood and hurried toward the study. Her mother kept pace behind her. "Good heavens, what's he ranting about now?"

"Alma!"

What could possibly have gone wrong? Her throat squeezed around her voice. "Coming, Father."

When they reached the study, she found her father pacing before the crackling hearth. His head twitched from side to side. His lips moved without sound. Tshikwā'set stood near the doorway. His eyes blinked in rapid succession. His mouth hung agape. She took a step toward him, but her father looked up and pinned her feet to the ground with a wild stare.

Her mother too stood paralyzed at the doorway. "Francis, whatever has come over you?"

His eyes remained fixed on Alma. "George tells me you wish to marry."

She looked between Tshikwā'set and her father. "I do."

"Marry whom?" her mother asked.

"Tshikwā—George, that is." She took a deep breath. "I should like to marry George."

"This George? An Indian?" Her mother laughed. "Impossible, ridiculous." No one else joined her laughter. Her face turned pinched and waxen. "This is madness."

"She's confused is all." Her father turned to Alma, eyes suddenly pleading.

"You said but a minute ago how proud you were of George," Alma said.

"Proud? Proud! That is entirely irrelevant."

Alma straightened and looked her father directly in the eye. "I love him."

Her mother collapsed into an armchair and began to sob. "I told you something like this would happen, Francis."

He waved her off and continued to pace. "Unnatural. Unholy. Think of the disgrace you'd bring to this school. After all these years of work."

Alma shook her head. What had come over him? "You said yourself—"

"Enough!" He sliced the air with a wild gesture. "I'd sooner escort you to the grave than to the altar with this man."

Alma staggered back, clutching the doorjamb for support. Tshikwā'set moved toward her.

Her father's eyes widened with venom. "Don't."

For once, Tshikwā'set obeyed.

Silence choked them. Only the popping fire dared to sound. Then her father straightened, smoothed his coat, and rang a small silver bell. Abraham, a young Ho-chunk boy apprenticing as her father's assistant, hurried in through the parlor.

"Fetch Mr. Simms."

Abraham nodded and scurried away.

"Shut the door, Alma." A measure of calm had returned to her father's voice, but his jaw clenched around the words.

Alma refused to move, disbelief as much as anger anchoring her where she stood.

He shouldered past her and jammed the door into its frame.

Another whimper from her mother. Her father paid the noise no heed. "Have you made your intentions known to anyone else?"

"No," Alma said. "We wanted your blessing first."

He moved to his desk and began rummaging through the drawers. "And what about you, boy? Have you told anyone?"

"No, sir."

"Good. Then we can all forget this discussion ever happened."

"What?" Alma took a step forward. "No—"

At that moment, a knock sounded on the door and Mr. Simms entered. His wiry hair stood on end, and a day's worth of white stubble covered his sunken cheeks. "Something you be needin', Mr. Blanchard?"

"Escort George here from the grounds."

"Father! What are you doing?"

Mr. Simms looked between Tshikwā'set and her father with an arched brow. After a moment, he shrugged. "Come on, lad. Off with ya."

"No! You can't do this! Father, I love him." Alma ran to Tshikwā'set and threw her arms around him.

"It's okay, nēnemōhsaew," he whispered. "We'll find another way." He peeled her arms from around his neck and stood to face her father. His lips barely moved as he spoke. "You're a hypocrite, Mr. Blanchard. You say the Indian is the brother of the white man, but in your heart you don't believe."

"I have spent my life working for the advancement of your kind!" He slammed his hand down upon the desk. "Equality is one thing. Miscegenation is another thing entirely. The idea of you with my daughter! It's unnatural, criminal! If God had intended for the races to mix, he would not have put us down on separate continents."

"Then why are you here? If your God gave this continent to the mamāceqtawak, what right have the white man to be here at all?"

Mr. Simms grabbed his arm, but Tshikwā'set shrugged him off. His wide, dark eyes fixed on Alma. She brushed away her tears and stared back at him, saying with her eyes what her lips could not. His expression softened, just for a moment; then he shouldered past Mr. Simms and stomped from the house.

When the sound of his angry footsteps disappeared, Alma sank to the floor and wept. Her father glared at her, and her mother fixed her with an expression of disgust. "Think of the ruin you almost brought upon this family, Alma!" she said. "Do you think any eligible gentleman would be interested in you if he knew you have been consorting with some wild man from the woods?"

"I don't care about those men. I love Tshikwā'set."

Her father moved around his desk and helped her mother from the chair. On the way out of the room, he stopped and looked down at her. His face held none of its former kindness or affection. "I am gravely disappointed in you, Alma. You're not to see that Indian ever again."

Who was this man? Surely not her father. Not the man whose lap she'd sat upon listening to stories. Not the man who slipped her candies and swung her in his arms. Not the man who brought her among the Indians, dressed her in a matching uniform, told her she could be their friend.

"Please, Papa," she wailed, long beyond caring who heard. "Please!"

He closed the door on her cries. She lay for several minutes atop the scratchy rug, his words playing through her mind like an ostinato passage of music. Only the key was off, the piano untuned. This wasn't how the night was meant to end. This wasn't the man she'd believed her father to be.

Alma staggered to her feet. From the top bookshelf, his jar of bonbons caught her eye. She grabbed it and hurled it at the door. The jar shattered, sending a spray of glass and candy onto the rug. She watched them scatter, the peppermint sticks and toffee wheels rolling into dusty corners and beneath chairs. The dwindling firelight glinted off the broken glass, and licorice perfumed the air. The once-sweet smell made her ill.

She tramped atop the wreckage to the dented door, candy and glass crunching beneath her slippers, poking through their soft soles at her tender feet.

CHAPTER 35

Minnesota, 1906

Alma felt every bump and sideways jostle as the buggy rambled along the faint road toward Detroit Lakes. The same wind that had hassled her all day followed her still, its cold fingers sneaking beneath her scarf, nipping every inch of exposed skin. It cut through the trees, ripping leaves from the branches and sending them in an upward flurry before abandoning them to the ground. Its low howl made conversation impossible, but for this Alma was grateful. She could read the anger burning in Stewart's face.

He'd spent all evening searching for her through the village, had called upon the sheriff, the deputies, the agent, even the grocer to keep watch. When she'd ridden up on the back of the Indian's mule, he'd pulled her down and embraced her so fiercely she thought her ribs might snap.

Now, even though their shoulders brushed as the buggy rocked, he felt a mile away. The oil lamps they'd borrowed and fastened to the frame creaked and swayed on their hinges, casting roving pools of light on the uneven road. She should repeat her apology, take his hand, and swear she'd never be so reckless again. Instead, she sat motionless, letting the wind frazzle her hair and spoil the delicate silk blooms on her hat, searching the darkness for some mental foothold, some way to make sense of the day.

Dinner was nearly over by the time they arrived at the hotel. Alma's limbs felt as heavy as sandbags changing from her day clothes into eveningwear. Her head throbbed. The blister on the back of her heel had bled through her stocking, but she had not the time nor care to change them. Instead of remaking her hair, she smoothed back the fuzz around her temples with water and then tucked whatever errant strands remained behind her ears.

Stewart awaited her in the sitting room adjacent to their sleeping chamber. The anger that had brewed on the long ride home still showed in the hard angle of his jaw, the way he stared beyond her, through her, never quite meeting her eyes.

Downstairs, they took their places in the small dining hall alongside the hotel's only other guests, an older couple on vacation from Des Moines who were finishing the last bites of their gummy apple cobbler.

Alma tried to feign interest as the gentleman regaled them of his fishing exploits in the nearby lakes. Tepid pork and mushy potatoes slid tastelessly down her throat. Somewhere between two seemingly identical stories of "walleye so big they just about snapped my pole" Alma's mind drifted back to the shabby cabins and shacks, to the overlogged forests and barren farmlands, to the meager annuities and rations. The reservation wasn't even supposed to exist anymore. Assimilation, integration—lies her father had told, lies she'd believed. The truth mocked every moment she'd shared with her Indian friends, every laugh, every smile, every kiss.

"Alma . . . Alma." Stewart nudged her with his knee beneath the table. "They're asking how we met. Would you like to tell the story or shall I?"

It took a moment to clear the past from her mind. The flickering sconces, the cheap wallpaper peeling at the edges, the lingering smell of burnt meat from the kitchen—slowly the present took shape around her. She looked up at the old couple. Their pale eyes were expectant, their lips—hers thin and painted, his dwarfed beneath a bushy white mustache—curved with placid smiles. Inwardly, Alma bristled at their blithe dispositions. "You go ahead."

Stewart forced a tight smile and turned back to the couple. "It's not all that remarkable of a tale."

"Oh, go on," the woman from Des Moines said.

"I saw her first at one of those moving-picture shows."

The woman leaned forward. "I love those! Which film?"

"In truth, I don't remember. One of those French numbers—"

"*Cendrillon,*" Alma interrupted.

"I hardly watched it, you see." Stewart's gaze flashed to her but didn't stick. "I was completely taken by her. But the hall was crowded and she slipped away before I could find her." He folded his napkin slowly and set it beside his dinner plate.

In the silence, Alma wondered what he was thinking. She thought of the flickering lights, the black-and-white images dancing across the screen, the *oohs* and *aahs* of the audience. Did he wish now he'd saved his dime?

"It was months before I saw her again. This time at Fairmount Park. She was there alone, reading. I watched her for the entirety of my lunch hour, not taking a bite. But it felt bad form to approach without introduction."

"Indeed," said the woman. "Young men today are frightfully forward. No sense of taste and manners. I was telling my grandson just the other—"

Her husband broke in. "Let the man finish."

His wife simpered and fell quiet.

"I went to the library that evening and borrowed the very same book. Every day I went to the park, and when I saw her next, I held the book out as if reading, hoping to catch her eye."

Alma stared at her husband. He'd never told her this part before.

"And?" the woman asked, echoing Alma's curiosity.

"And . . . she walked right past me."

Alma looked down. Was he saying this to embarrass her? To make her seem cold and aloof? But when he spoke again the timbre of his voice was warm and unaccusing.

"What could I do but follow her home? The next day I returned and peddled my legal services to her aunt—trust and probate matters, land deeds. That sort of thing." This Alma remembered, his unfamiliar but pleasant voice in the hallway.

"You're a lawyer," the woman said. She turned to her husband. "He's a lawyer, John."

"Yes, but not a personal property lawyer," Stewart said. His expression had thawed now and his eyes softened. "I studied for hours every night before meeting her aunt just to figure out what the dickens I was doing." The couple laughed. Stewart glanced at Alma with a thin but genuine smile. "But I secured the introduction I'd been craving."

She couldn't help but recall that first meeting in her aunt's parlor. He'd shaken her hand with altogether too much vigor. The sweat from his palm stuck to her fingers. But his eyes were tranquil, his demeanor confident without being cocky. She had no intention of falling in love again, had not thought it possible, but it happened nonetheless.

Five years had transpired and even the day's worry and anger could not overshadow his love. She tried to return his smile, but found the weight of it too heavy to bear. She didn't deserve his affections, his unflagging kindness.

In the privacy of their own sitting room, Stewart poured them each a finger of corn liquor. The small glass decanter rattled when he replaced it atop the side table. After handing her a glass, he joined her on the divan. Though he rarely drank, Stewart threw back the liquor without a grimace. "What were you thinking today, Alma? What in God's heavens were you looking for?"

Not what, whom. "I . . ." She sipped her drink and winced as the liquor hit her tongue. It burned the length of her throat, settling uneasily on her stomach. She took another sip. "Harry has a sister. I went to see if I could find her."

"A sister? Why didn't you tell me this earlier? I could have come with you, interviewed her myself."

"No . . . er . . . she's very shy and not altogether fond of—" Of what? Men? Whites? What lie would assuage him? Certainly not the truth. Not that it was Alma who wasn't altogether fond of Minowe, that the conversation they were liable to have was not suited for his ears. She had no intention of bringing up the past, but something might slip. "Strangers, not fond of strangers."

"What did she have to say?"

"I couldn't find her. Ended up lost. I'll go back and try another way tomorrow."

"Certainly not." He stood and paced the length of the room before returning to the side table and decanter.

"I must. Please. I'm no use to you at the agency. All those ledgers and reports—I haven't any idea what's important."

"The reservation is dangerous." He poured another drink. "I half thought . . . half thought the sheriff might have . . ." He drained the liquor in one gulp.

"Dearest, it was nothing like that. I got turned around and lost my way. That's all. Tomorrow I'll be much more careful."

"No, you won't. You'll stay here."

Alma stood. He'd never presumed to tell her what to do before. Not like that. "I'm not some porcelain doll to be locked away in a china hutch. Harry is *my* friend and I shall do whatever it takes to see him free. Whether you approve or not."

Stewart slammed his glass down on the table. The decanter clattered. He refilled his glass, splattering the doily as he poured. He raised the drink to his lips, his fingers strangling the glass with such force she feared it might shatter, then lowered it as if he might say something. His jaw remained clenched, however. He stared at the wall, his hazel eyes distant, his nostrils flaring with each exhale.

Alma reached out to touch his arm, to stay his hand. He felt like stone beneath her touch, and she pulled away. She thought back to his face when he'd pulled her from the Indian's mule—his openmouthed relief, the way his eyes clung to her, unblinking, like she might again vanish.

"I have to do this. There's so much I've done wrong. I have to feel as if I've helped in this."

The glass remained at his lips, the light of the nearby lamp reflecting off its tawny surface. Had he even heard her, registered what she said? She always marveled at the control he exercised over his expression. A lawyer trick of his. Yet something always revealed his emotion—a slight lift of the shoulders when exultant, a quick tug at his shirt cuffs when uneasy, a splaying of his fingers when anger got the best of him. It was like a secret code between them—things other people missed that Alma never failed to notice. Not tonight, though. Tonight he gave her nothing. She clutched her arms about herself, fingers burrowing into her flesh. She could not bear the sudden estrangement, but would not back down. She must see Minowe. Alone.

His hand sagged. He unstopped the decanter and poured the liquor back. Its sharp scent perfumed the air between them. He unfastened his bow tie and walked past her into the bedroom. "Something is amiss with the account books and ledgers. I can't quite put my finger on it."

He spoke to her in the same cool, detached fashion he spoke to his clerk. But it was better than silence.

"What do you mean?"

"It has to do with this latest land allotment." He shrugged out of his jacket and unbuttoned his waistcoat. "Indians came up from Minneapolis, Chicago, even St. Louis to receive land, many of whom are not in any previous roll books. And the deed log looks as if it's been tampered with—names penciled in and later erased, names scratched out, names gone over in ink like they'd been penciled in beforehand."

"What does all this have to do with Harry?"

"I'm not sure. Maybe nothing. It looks like there was quite an uproar after the proceedings—numerous complaints, even a letter sent to Washington. Maybe Mr. Muskrat was among those speaking out like Mr. Zhawaeshk said."

Alma did her best to swallow the disappointment rising in her chest. She'd hoped for something more, something definitive.

He turned away from her and stepped out of his trousers. She saw his skin for only a second—the light freckles that dotted his back, the hair that covered his calves—before he donned his nightshirt. He'd dimmed his bedside light and climbed beneath the sheets before she'd even begun to undress. No advances tonight. No impassioned lovemaking where every inch of their bodies hungered for friction, where sweat slickened their skin and moans freely escaped their lips.

Her breast heaved at the thought of it. She wanted so badly to touch him, to feel the crush of his embrace, to know that everything would be all right. A chill took hold of her. A draft no doubt stolen in through the thin drapes and poorly seated windows. She stripped off her gown and unfastened her corset. Perhaps it was best. The distance. There were too many ghosts between them tonight.

CHAPTER 36

—◆—

Wisconsin, 1891

"Jaha! Who let you out of the house?"

Alma, treading carefully over the rows of black soil and budding sprouts, smiled at Hįčoga. "I escaped. Here, let me help you." She grabbed Hįčoga's seed bag.

"I thought *ladies* did not work in the field," Minowe said, coming up beside them.

"Mother thinks I'm napping. You know I'd be out here more if I could."

Minowe smirked and continued along the empty track of dirt. With each stride, she plunged the long stick she carried into the ground, poking a small hole in the loamy earth. "Aren't your fancy La Crosse friends coming this afternoon for tea?"

Alma followed after and sprinkled a few broad white seeds in each depression. "Mother invited them, not me."

Her friend snickered without looking back.

"Only one seed, Azaadiins," Hįčoga said from behind her. "Otherwise the plants tangle and choke one another."

"Oh." Holding the hem of her skirt above the ground, she bent down and fished out the excess seeds. "What are we planting, anyway?"

Hįčoga squatted beside her and covered the hole with dirt. "Wič'ąwą—winter squashes."

They continued for at least a dozen more yards, Minowe burrowing the hole, Alma dropping a seed, Hįčoga tilling over fresh soil.

The sun smiled above in the cloudless sky. Magpies chattered from the fence posts. A soft breeze carried cool air from the nearby forest. How good it felt to be out of the stuffy schoolhouse.

The days since her father's outburst in the study had stretched on with bitter tedium. True to his word, he guarded against any opportunity that might bring her and Tshikwā'set together. He forbade her to leave the schoolhouse, even for a walk around the grounds, unless in his or her mother's company. Under the pretext that Stover now had too many students to cart back and forth into town, he asked Reverend Thomas to conduct a special worship service in the school's dining hall each Sunday. He even bought two bloodhounds to prowl the grounds at night.

Her mother had made the weeks of estrangement from Tshikwā'set equally unbearable, disallowing all unnecessary contact with the Indians. No more common meals or afternoon chores. No more Saturday socials or evening study hours. In place of these activities, Alma languished in the stuffy parlors of the La Crosse aristocracy, sipping tea and chatting about a host of banal and insignificant topics. Her mother contrived any excuse to bring them into town, as if sudden immersion in white society would cure Alma of her wicked affliction.

Now, however, Alma hummed as she walked, careless of the mud that clung to her boots.

"What are you so happy about?" Minowe asked. "Two weeks ago you were crying. Now every times I see you, you're smiling, singing. Chirk as damnation!"

Alma laughed. "Where did you hear that expression? Mr. Simms?"

"Aní·tas teached it last class." She raised her chin, pinched her lips, and gestured with her stick in the same jerky manner Miss Wells wielded her ruler. "Copy these words upon your slates, class: Damn, dratted, damnation."

At that, they all laughed.

"You'd get more than a mouthful of soap for that," Hįčoga said.

Alma wiped the water from her lashes and swallowed down the last of her giggles. Her eyes hung on Minowe's gap-toothed smile— a rare sight these days and ever so dear. It drew her back across the years to that night, standing beneath the eaves of the schoolhouse, when first she'd seen it. And Hįčoga's laughter, so like a bell—she wished she could bottle up the sound and keep it with her forever. After a quick glance around the yard, she dropped the seed bag and grabbed their hands. Dirt roughened their skin. "I'm running away. With Tshikwā'set."

She'd met him surreptitiously in town a week and a half ago while she waited in the carriage for her mother. The street-side door of the carriage had opened soundlessly. Alma had blinked at the sudden flood of sunlight, trying to make out the lithe form that glided in. The carriage did not rock, nor the door creak upon closing. Even before her eyes adjusted, she knew who had entered. Only an Indian could move with such stealth.

Tshikwā'set placed his fingers over her lips. He closed the window coverings and sat down beside her.

"Tshikwā'set! How did you—"

This time, his lips silenced her. She threw her arms around him and kissed him back, not just his lips but his cheek and eyelids and neck. His fingers worked the buttons of her blouse until the swell of her bosom above her corset lay exposed. His mouth roved from her jaw to her collarbone, then downward. She shivered at the delicious feel of his lips against her skin.

Too soon he stopped. The recesses of her mind awakened and she buttoned up her shirt. "Mother ran into Mrs. Wright's shop for a fitting. She'll return any moment."

He nuzzled her neck, fighting her fingers as she tried to fasten the final buttons of her collar. Her hands abandoned their charge and wound into his hair. Against the renewed swell of passion, her mind fought for clarity. "Father didn't write to Mr. Wallis, did he? Recommending your termination. He said he would. You still have your job?"

"He did." His hand slid over her silk waistcoat and jacket, stopping atop her breast. "Mr. Wallis kept me on in spite of it."

Alma moved his hand back down to her waist. "He likes you quite well."

"He does." Tshikwā'set pulled back and looked directly into her eyes. "He's willing to help us."

"How?"

"Two weeks from today he has a shipment of wagon parts going to Milwaukee. He knows the foreman and said we could ride with the parts in the freight car. It's a late train, leaves the rail yard at eleven thirty. Come the following morning we'll be gone, but no one will think we went by trains."

"What will we do after we reach Milwaukee?"

"I have enough money to buy us tickets to Green Bay, and from there, a wagon to Keshena."

"The reservation? After my father realizes we've fled La Crosse, that's the first place he'll look."

"By time he arrives we'll already be married."

"Married? It won't be easy to find a willing pastor."

"I know a priest in Keshena who will do it."

Alma stiffened. "A Catholic priest?"

"Yes." His dark eyes roved her face and he cocked his head. "You still want to marry, yes?"

She bit her lip.

"Catholic, Presbyterian—does it matter so long as we have the white man's paper?"

Silence followed. She imagined the pain and fury in her father's face when he learned she had not only married an Indian, but had done so in a Catholic church.

Tshikwā'set's arms slacked around her. He sat up straight and leaned away. His handsome face bore a pained and bewildered expression.

Her heart clenched and she grabbed his hands. "Of course it doesn't matter. I love you and want to be your wife no matter who performs the ceremony."

Tshikwā'set's expression remained guarded. "Life on the reservation is not like here. We don't have balls and fancy dinners. Even with the money I've saved I can't buy big house or expensive carriage like this."

"I'd rather be with you than the richest man in Wisconsin." She leaned in and kissed him. His lips, at first stiff, slowly livened beneath hers until they matched her hunger.

"It won't be forever, nēnemōhsaew. I can cut timber until we're settled, then look for work in a carriage shop in Green Bay or Oshkosh. Maybe we can return to La Crosse someday and you can be with your family again."

A strand of hair had fallen over his face. Alma brushed the soft black lock back behind his ear. "You're all the family I need."

He drew her against his chest, but the squeal of nearby door hinges stopped them before their lips could meet. Her mother's footfalls sounded on the sidewalk.

"Two weeks. Meet me at the bottom of Grandfather's Bluff." He'd leapt from the carriage just as the door on the opposite side began to open. "Eleven o'clock, nēnemōhsaew. I'll be waiting on you."

Now, as she relayed the story to her friends, she expected to see the same unbridled excitement that hummed inside her lit upon their faces. Instead, the gleam vanished from Minowe's eyes. Hįčoga lost her grin. "Azaadiins, your parents will be so angry."

"Let them be angry. I don't care."

Silence fell between them. Even the magpies ceased their chatter. Alma's heart inched into her throat. "It's the only way Tshikwā'set and I can be together. Aren't you happy for me? For us?"

Hįčoga squeezed her hand. "Of course, but—"

"You won't be happy for long," Minowe cut in. She pried her fingers from Alma's and crossed her arms, her seeding stick trapped in the crook of her elbow.

"How can you say that?"

Minowe snorted and shook her head.

"What?"

Her friend started to walk away. "Nothing."

Alma grabbed her arm. "What's wrong with you? You've been against me on this from the start."

"You think because you dance sometimes with us around the fire, because you speak our words that you know what it is to be Indian."

"I'm not trying to be Indian. I just want—"

"Fancy dresses and parlor games won't do you no good on the reservation."

"I'm not without domestic skills." But in truth, she hadn't thought about that. The collar of her dress felt suddenly damp and sticky. "I can cook . . . a bit. And sew. And I can always tutor children on the piano if Tshikwā'set and I need money."

"Piano?" Minowe rolled her eyes. "You think we keeps pianos in our wigwams? In our shacks or agency-made cabins?"

"I . . . I didn't think . . . I'm sure—"

"And what about your wiisaakodewininiwag childrens? Half-breeds fit in nowhere. Not your world. Not his." She shrugged free of Alma's grasp. "Marry Edward Steele. Live in a big house on State Street. You'd be better happy there in the end."

"Waú!" Hįčoga said. "Not if she loves Tshikwā'set."

"She should love a white man."

The words struck Alma like a ruler against her knuckles. With Minowe's smirk came another slap. Had she always felt this way? Didn't she care that without Tshikwā'set Alma could hardly breathe?

"You sound just like my father."

"Maybe for once he's right."

"And what of us? I suppose we shouldn't be friends either, you being an Indian." Alma regretted the words the minute she said them.

Minowe winced and threw her stick to the ground. "Fine." Her voice was choked. "You thinks we were friends? We were never real friends, Alma. This, all of this"—she flung her arm toward the schoolhouse—"it's a lie. A lie you've tricks'd Tshikwā'set into believing."

"You're just jealous that we're happy together."

Minowe laughed—a fake, icy laugh. "Of all the things that happened to him here—the punishments, shamings—you're the worst."

She stomped off, leaving Alma with a mouthful of bitter words and tears stinging her eyes.

"Do you think that too, Hįčoga?" Alma asked after she found her voice.

"No, Azaadiins. Of course we're friends. Minowe too. She just . . ." Hįčoga paused and kicked at the dirt. "Living on the reservation won't be easy. They're not used to no waxopíni wí there."

"What about the nuns? They're white women. And surely some of the agency employees have wives."

Hįčoga shrugged. "It's different. You'd be the wife of an Indian. Many peoples—white and red—won't like that."

Alma squinted up at the sun. Only moments before its bright face had seemed so cheery. Off in the distance, she heard the rumble of an approaching carriage. "I love him . . . What would you do if you were in my place?"

Hįčoga bit her lip. After another drawn-out pause, the smile Alma cherished returned to the girl's face. "I'd run away too."

"Will you help me? I need someone to distract the dogs and keep them quiet while I sneak out."

"I can manage that."

"And afterward, you can't tell anyone where we've gone. Father will figure it out eventually, but at least Tshikwā'set and I will have a head start. After we're married, there's nothing he can do." The thud of horse hooves and cry of iron wheels grew louder. "I'd better go."

She turned to leave and saw the stick Minowe had thrown to the ground. Alma picked it up. Her fingers curled around the rough bark until they blanched. "It's not a lie."

Hįčoga eased the stick from her hand and burrowed a fresh hole. "Don't worry none about Minowe. She'll come around. First her brother left and now you. She just feels left behind. I'll bring her with me to help with the dogs. I know she'll wants to say goodbye."

"Bring her if you want. I don't care." Her shaky voice betrayed her. She took a step toward the house, then turned back. "It won't be forever. Goodbye, I mean. We'll see each other again, I'm sure."

Her friend flung another seed onto the earth and looked down, but not before Alma saw the doubt in her eyes.

CHAPTER 37

———⇒•⇐———

Minnesota, 1906

Alma alighted the carriage and shook the dust from her skirt. Stewart kept his gaze forward, the brim of his derby shadowing his face from the morning sun. He'd woken with a stiff, rigid manner and sat thus still. "Which direction are you going?"

She looked both ways down the thoroughfare. "North." She pointed in the direction she'd started off yesterday before turning around, the direction Frederick had instructed her to go.

"How far?"

Ningo'anwe'biwin, whatever that meant. "Um . . . no more than a couple of miles."

"And what's the name of this sister?"

A layer of dust had settled over her from the ride in and seemed to cover everything—her shoes, her skirt, her hair, her skin, even her tongue felt dry and gritty. She swallowed. "Minowe." How strange to speak her name aloud after so long, and yet so effortless, as if her lips had never forgotten the motion. "Margaret, that was her Christian name. Surely she's married now, but I don't know her surname."

Stewart exhaled, long and steady. He took out his handkerchief and dabbed the back of his neck. The white silk turned damp and brown. She watched him finger the blue initials hand-stitched at the corner before finally looking at her. "And you'll be back at the agency by—"

"By one. I promise."

He turned forward again and held his eyes shut through another long exhale. Then, without goodbye, he steered the horse and buggy toward the livery. It sickened her to watch him go. Her neck felt flush, but her hands clammy. They'd argued before, she told herself as she started off down the road. But this was more than an argument. Something had wedged between them. Something sharp and deep. Or maybe it had always been there—her past, her secrets—and only now lay exposed.

She glanced over her shoulder. The white agency building glared in the sunlight, painfully bright against an otherwise neutral landscape. She squinted and watched Stewart mount the steps. He was doing this for her. Whatever was between them, he was still here. After she got her answers from Minowe, after they freed Asku, she and Stewart could look forward again and let the past alone.

First she had to find Minowe. A dense fringe of grass and shrubs lined either side of the road. Beyond lay open field—some tilled, some fallow—with stands of birch and cottonwood about the border. But no path anywhere in sight.

Ningo'anwe'biwin. She unpinned her hat and wiped her brow with the sleeve of her duster. When had she heard that phrase? She caged her present troubles and thought back. Summer perhaps? Long ago. Warmth had hung in the air, the canopy of leaves above her full and green. Minowe was beside her and they trudged hand in hand behind a loping Asku. She'd been ten, maybe eleven.

"How much farther?" she'd asked.

Asku turned and grinned. "Ningo'anwe'biwin."

"What does that mean?" she asked Minowe.

Her friend puzzled a minute, working through the translation, then her face brightened. "From one place of rest to the next."

"Oh." Alma walked a few more feet, then stopped. "How far is that?"

Minowe shrugged.

Asku whirled around again. Light filtered through the trees, falling around him like a golden cloak. "About half a mile, Azaadiins. Come on. You can make it."

He seemed then as he'd always seemed to her: invincible, infallible. And Minowe . . . Frederick had been right. They used to be inseparable.

A cool fall breeze nipped at the back of her neck and rustled her skirt, sucking the memory of warmth from the air. Solitude stung her like a hornet's bite, a cruel reminder why she seldom tended the garden of her remembrance. She took a deep breath and continued down the road. Though her chest heaved and sweat returned to her brow, she doubted an Indian—unencumbered by heavy petticoats, a corset, and high-heeled boots—would yet require a rest.

After a few more minutes of travel, the tall roadside grasses parted to reveal a narrow trail. It snaked eastward through the prairie and disappeared into a sparse woodland. Alma stretched onto her tiptoes and looked down the main road. No other trailheads visible. Hiking her skirts, she clambered up the road's embankment onto the trail.

Alma's insides tightened as she tramped down the path. Every inch of her skin itched with the urge to turn back. Asku she could talk to. And Frederick. They'd both been gone before she and Tshikwā'set announced their plans to marry. What they knew, if anything, came secondhand. But Minowe bore witness to it all.

She stopped and shook the clenched-fist tension from her hands. Turn back now and Asku hanged. Her feet shuffled onward. She couldn't abide more sorrow and guilt.

The path dead-ended at several acres of downward-sloping farmland. Weeds and dry prairie grass overran most of the land. A few rows of corn stood like skeletons at the far end, bounded by sprawling squash plants and a leafy cluster of beet tops. Trees sprouted like whiskers beyond the modest stretch of crops, and farther on a small lake rippled in the afternoon sunlight.

She trudged across the field and around the tall cornstalks. A light breeze rustled their droopy, yellowing arms. Her heart inched higher and higher until she felt it pulse at the base of her tongue.

Clear of the garden now, she ducked beneath an empty clothesline into a barren yard. A small farmhouse stood at its center. Gray tarpaper clung to the frame like sunken skin. The breeze swelled and several torn swaths flapped back, revealing the studs and a helterskelter array of narrow cross boards beneath.

Alma climbed two stairs to a creaky porch. The eaves of the rusty tin roof shuddered above her. She hesitated before the door, her fingers loath to form a fist, her knuckles reticent to knock. At last she rapped. The rickety door shuddered.

No answer.

After several seconds of silence, she pulled back the flannel covering and peeked inside the paneless window. A wooden table stood in the center of the room beside a potbellied stove. Baskets of woven birch bark lined the walls, and five rolled rush mats rested against the far corner. The earthen floor looked newly swept, and a tidy set of tin dishes rested at one end of the table. No one was inside.

Should she wait? This mightn't be Minowe's house at all. Then she caught sight of a doll propped up in the corner, a cloth doll seated beside two others made of grass. Alma's immediately recognized the faded blue and white dress, the strands of yellow thread sewn on as hair. Minowe had made it when they were girls, not long after Alma's mother burned the Indian doll. Alma had made one, too, under Minowe's tutelage. Only hers had black hair instead of yellow. They'd taken greater care to hide them, stashing them beneath a loose floorboard beside Alma's bed.

What had happened to that doll? Perhaps it was still there in the dormitory, or in some dust-covered trunk. Minowe, she'd called her. Such a silly, childish thing to do, naming the doll after her friend. What had Minowe called her doll? Alma couldn't remember.

She seated herself upon the steps to wait. A tissuey layer of clouds grayed the sky, but the north wind lay dormant. She thought of yesterday's gale, how the house behind her must have shaken and rattled. A pang whispered in her heart. It was so tiny, the house, small enough to fit in her home's parlor with room to spare. She strangled back her sympathy. "I'm only here to talk about Asku," she would say, in the dry, matter-of-fact tone of Miss Wells when Minowe returned.

Minutes stretched and gummed together. With each snap in the trees or rustle of cornstalks, Alma's pulse quickened only to slow again when no one appeared. With time, the prairie grass and weeds blurred like a watercolor before her tired eyes. Her head grew heavy against her palm. Thoughts of quitting her post lazed through her mind when a thunderclap of tumbling logs startled her to attention.

Her head jerked toward the noise.

Minowe stood a few yards away, her face pale and wide, her arms limp as the last of the sticks and lumber fell to the ground. They rolled away from her feet like a rippling tide.

They stared at each other for several heavy seconds. Alma had never believed in ghosts. The temporal world haunted her enough. But seeing Minowe made her skin tighten and prickle, as if everyone lost in the past had emerged into the clearing with her. Minowe's starched black uniform was now a simple skirt and blouse—both patched and tattered at the hem. Her hair, once tied in a careful bun, hung long and plaited down her back. But her face, her eyes, her long arms and graceful hands were the same.

"You should not have come," Minowe said at last.

Though she'd practiced the lines, Alma's voice deserted her. "I . . ." She cleared her throat weakly. "I'm only here for Asku."

Minowe's eyes went glassy at her brother's name. Her lips compressed into a thin, sharp line. She looked away, blinking several times, then faced Alma with a hardened expression. "You can't help him."

"You're wrong. My husband is a lawyer. We're here searching for the truth."

Minowe snickered, her face contorting cruelly. She sank to her haunches and snatched up her fallen logs.

"Don't you care if he hangs?" Alma said.

"This does not belong to you." Her voice was low, hoarse, dangerous, but Alma paid no heed.

"He was my friend. Nisayenh, brother to me, too."

"Brother?" Minowe stood and stomped to the side of the house. She threw her cache of logs atop a stack of wood. They landed haphazardly, jutting out from the otherwise tidy pile, as the resulting clap echoed through the clearing. "You cannot say that. Not after these many years. After all you did."

"Me?" Alma tried to laugh, but it came out as a cackle. "I'm to blame for this?"

"Your father, that school, you all betrayed him."

"Who are you to speak of betrayal?" Madness edged her words. "You? Of all people."

Minowe flinched. "You never should of run away with him." Her voice broke and quieted. Her gaze retreated to the ground and she shook her head. "I told you so, but you wouldn't listen."

The dusty yard blinked in and out of focus. Alma closed her eyes and sucked in a deep breath between clenched teeth. "I'm not here to talk about Tshikwā'set."

"You thought nothing would happen." Another bitter snicker. "A white girl and an Indian."

Alma's pulse thudded against her temples. "Leave it alone, Minowe."

"You never really loved him. Just wanted to be one of us."

The words stunned her. Time stilled. She felt the sun beat upon her neck, felt the dampness beneath her arms and across her palms, felt her heart ache. She *had* wanted to be one of them, desperately; had hated always being the outsider. But her love for Tshikwā'set was more than that, far more. "This has nothing to do with him."

"No?"

Alma took another deep breath. Her fists trembled. "What do you know about the murder of Agent Andrews?"

"Nothing. I know nothing."

"If you don't help me, Asku will die. Is that what you want?"

Minowe's expression wilted. She brushed past Alma toward the front of the house. "I told you, this doesn't belong to you."

"You think I want to be here?" Alma grabbed Minowe's arm and spun her around. "To see you again?"

"Awas, then. Awas! Go back to your fancy house, with your fancy clothes, and your fancy lawyer husband." She yanked her arm from Alma's grasp and smiled a cruel, twisted smile. "Do you thinks of Tshikwā'set when you're in his arms at night? Say his name in accident? No." She stepped back and spit at the narrow patch of bald earth between them. "No, I bets you don't even remember Tshikwā'set's face."

Alma didn't blink, didn't breathe. She let her purse fall to the ground and slapped Minowe across the face. "Don't you speak of him! You have no right. Not after what you did."

Minowe shuffled backward, cradling her cheek.

Alma looked down at her hand. Despite the leather cushion of her glove, her palm stung. Her limbs still twitched with anger, but the outline of her fingers, her silk handbag below in the dirt, all blurred with tears. "I did love him. And I do remember. His face. His voice. Everything."

CHAPTER 38

Wisconsin, 1891

Alma took a parting glance around her room. Moonlight sliced through the gap in the curtains, illuminating the neatly made bed, bare vanity, and looming wardrobe. She thought back to the day her mother had moved her from the dormitory, separating her from the Indian girls, and how lonely the room had looked to her then. Two years later, it still felt lonely. She closed the door and crept down the hallway without looking back.

Two layers of stockings muffled her footsteps. Doubled-up petticoats ballooned her skirt. They simply would not fit in her crammed luggage. She'd struggled to close the brass clasps on her portmanteau suitcase and the seams of her carpetbag bulged. Both weighed more than the bulky sacks of flour Mrs. Simms stored in the cellar.

She was not going to chance another fall from the roof. She tiptoed down the stairs, boots slung over her shoulder, without eliciting a single creak or cry from the wood.

In the foyer she paused and glanced at the gilded hands of the grandfather clock. Five minutes before ten. She had little better than an hour to make it to the base of Grandfather's Bluff. The bags would slow her pace, but she could make it.

She turned down the hallway leading toward the kitchen. The dark corridor lay still and empty. She had expected to see light coming from beneath the door of her father's study. Most nights he stayed up late reading by the fire or shuffling through the piles of paperwork on his desk. Where was he tonight? She looked over her shoulder at the foyer and the cluster of rooms down the opposite hallway. Threads of moonlight filtered in through the foyer windows, otherwise all was dark.

Earlier that evening from inside her room, Alma had listened for all the familiar evening noises. She had heard the march of the Indians on the way to their beds, the sharp footfalls of Miss Wells performing her nightly inspection, the clink of glassware from across the hall as her mother sat before her vanity and daubed on her nightly regimen of lotions and perfumed beauty tonics.

Her father's routine had its own telltale sounds: the whine of copper taps as he switched off the last of the wall sconces; slow, heavy footsteps; soft self-mutterings. None of this she heard. After straining her ears for over an hour, she could delay her departure no longer. Between the arduous task of picking through her belongings for only the most practical and important and the excitement that flapped inside her chest, she must have missed her father's ascent to bed.

Another glance around the darkened first floor and she crept to the kitchen. Hičoga waited for her by the back door.

"Minowe's still mad?" Alma asked after glancing around the room.

Hičoga nodded.

She drew in a deep breath to push down her sorrow. Air filled her lungs, but she still felt empty. "Tell her . . . never mind."

The clock in the foyer sang out ten long chimes. She hugged Hičoga, threw on her boots, and hurried through the back door before her tears had a chance to well.

"Goodbye, Azaadiins," her friend whispered after her.

She raced across the yard to the cover of the woods. Amid the bramble and trees she turned back for one final look. The schoolhouse lay quiet and still, like a roosting owl. Even at night, the great edifice cast a shadow, swallowing the moon behind its boxy form. A darkened shape moved across the window in her father's study. Alma blinked and the apparition vanished. Unspoken goodbyes weighed upon her tongue. She swallowed the bitter taste and hurried on.

A faintly worn game trail wound through the trees. She followed it for a short distance, then broke away and veered right at the gnarled oak stump. Insects sang and deer mice scurried through the underbrush. In the distance, a coyote pup howled. After a few minutes, the sound of lapping water broke through the nocturnal chatter and the trees parted for a small stream. From here, she would chase the flowing water all the way to the base of the bluffs.

Sweat trickled down the back of her neck. Her arms ached from the weight of her bags. How many minutes had passed since she left Stover? Thirty? Forty? However much time had elapsed, she could not afford to rest. She ignored the cry of her aching limbs and listened instead to the music of the stream. Silver moonlight sparkled atop its glassy surface. Minnows schooled in the shadows of submerged rocks. An aspen leaf floated past, riding the gentle waves.

At this, she thought of Asku, the time the two of them had traveled together beside this very stream. Her heart felt raw as it always did whenever he crossed her mind. Would things have been different if he'd stayed? Could he have convinced her father to let she and Tshikwā'set marry? Could he have softened Minowe's anger?

She shook her head and sighed. Such questions were not fair to ask. He'd worked so hard to win a place at Brown. He belonged there. She pictured him strolling down the streets of Providence in a fine suit and bowler hat, lounging in smoky parlors engaged in heady conversation with his classmates. He and she were trading places, in a way, trading worlds, as Tshikwā'set would say.

The rolling forest began to thin. She could see the backside of Grandfather's Bluff in the distance. Her carefully guarded joy burst like wellspring. Tshikwā'set waited there. He'd take her hand and tomorrow they'd wed. She no longer felt the ache in her limbs. Her feet no longer plodded but skipped through the underbrush. A narrow road appeared through the trees and bowed toward her. She left the stream bank and scampered to the drive. Her heart beat lively now, and it took all her will to pause and listen before leaving the cover of the woods. So late an hour should bring few, if any, travelers, but she could not chance an encounter.

Behind her, the stream murmured along its course. Wind played the leaves like a symphony, stirring them to frenzy, then decrescendoing into silence.

She surveyed the road in both directions and then walked out of the bushes onto the level ground, laughing at her undue paranoia. Who would be out at so late an hour? And here, a good two miles from the nearest house.

The road skirted around the bluff, descending through the trees toward the plains and farmlands below. When she reached the westernmost side, the forest dwindled into scree and grass. At the bottom of the hill the road merged with several other small drives and cut across the flatlands toward La Crosse.

There, at the intersection, waited Tshikwā'set. She could see him clearly in the moonlight, clutching the strap of his canvas haversack, rasping his boot back and forth over the gravel. His tied-back hair had come loose at the front and fell like glossy feathers around his temples to below his chin. A rosy flush colored his cheeks. He tugged at his collar, opened the top button, then fastened it again.

Her lips parted and her entire body hummed. The last of her buried doubts and regret vanished. She ran toward him, dirt crunching beneath the soles of her boots. Tshikwā'set looked up. His entire face smiled and he jogged to meet her. His beaming eyes sent another thrill skittering deliciously over her skin. It mattered not if they made their home on a reservation or within a towering metropolis. It mattered not that she was white and he Indian. All that mattered was that they were together.

The final stretch of road cut steeply downward to the bluff's base. Alma slowed only enough to keep from falling. Her gaze flickered to the ground to maintain her footing. When she looked up again, Tshikwā'set had stopped some fifty yards away, his eyes wide and mouth gaping. He said something she could not hear.

A body crashed into her from behind, and a thick arm encircled her waist. She and her assailant skidded forward. Her bags fell from her hands and she wheeled her arms to keep from tumbling head over foot. The body behind her arched backward, pulling them both onto the ground.

Alma turned to her captor. In the pallid moonlight she recognized the trim beard and small blue eyes. "Father?"

How had he uncovered their plan? Her eyes darted back to Tshikwā'set as she tried to wrestle free. He sprinted up the road toward them.

A rumbling to the west caught her attention. A great glow moved in their direction. The yellow blur sharpened into several separate balls of light. The low rumble grew into a steady beat of horse hooves. Tshikwā'set stopped.

"Father, what have you done?" Alma whispered. She locked eyes with Tshikwā'set and screamed, "Run! Hide away in the woods."

He stood frozen for the span of several heartbeats. His eyes flickered to the approaching mob, then back to her.

"Forget me! Just go. Kēmēnon!"

Finally, he ran. The face of the bluff was too steep to climb, so he doubled back down the road and circled around the base toward the forest. Alma lost sight of him just as the riders reached the intersection. Four broke off and galloped after him while the others reined their horses and waited. Torchlight danced against the hillside.

Her father stood and pulled her up beside him. She fought to break away, but he grabbed hold of both her arms and wrenched them behind her back. "What devil has possessed you, daughter? Have you no shame for your sins?"

He muscled her down the road to where the riders tarried atop their steeds. She recognized the white hair and leathery skin of Mr. Simms. Beside him was Sheriff Gund. Alma's gaze flickered from his mustached face to the bullet-studded gun belt around his waist. Her heart tripped and sputtered. Her mouth went dry. Tshikwā'set ran fast, she reminded herself. And he knew the woods. They would not catch him.

She sucked in a deep breath and studied the other men. Mr. Coleman, the farmer Asku had done his first summer outing with, sat among the riders, as did Mr. Krause, the grocer, and the senior Mr. Steele, looking out of place in his posh chesterfield topcoat. The other two riders Alma did not recognize.

Mr. Simms dismounted. "Fetched the law, just as you asked, Mr. Blanchard."

"I see that," he said through gritted teeth. The anger in his eyes sharpened to alarm. "And several more along with it." He thrust Alma onto the old groundskeeper and approached Mr. Gund. "Sheriff, I appreciate you coming out at such a late hour. Mr. Simms might have misinformed you, but there's only one troublesome Indian I'm after. I dare say, an entire posse is not needed. Perhaps some of these gentlemen would rather return to their beds."

The sheriff looked off in the direction Tshikwā'set had fled. A stream of tobacco-stained liquid flew from his mouth. Then he turned back to her father. "It's a serious crime, trying to kidnap a white woman. Gotta be careful with these Injuns. They're slippery."

Alma's face twisted with a scowl. "He didn't kid—"

Mr. Simms's burlap palm flattened over her mouth and her father shot her a fiery glare.

"I only accuse the young boy of trespassing."

Sheriff Gund spit again, this time right at her father's feet, then nodded toward Alma. "Why she here, then?"

"I . . . you see . . . my daughter and I . . ." Her father broke into a lengthy explanation. He had little practice lying and it showed in this halting speech. His words faded to a hum as her eyes raked the dark woods into which Tshikwā'set and the riders had disappeared. Each passing minute bolstered her hope that he had escaped. When her attention circled back, the men's conversation had grown strained.

"You may be an Injun lover, Mr. Blanchard, with your school and all that. But I've gotta protect the interests of this town. Ain't that right, boys?"

"Don't want no red man seducing *my* daughter," one of the men Alma did not recognize said.

"Here! Here!" rejoined Mr. Steele.

The men's tempers had scarcely cooled when the other riders emerged from the woods. Four men—she counted them twice as their horses cantered closer. Her entire body breathed thanksgiving. He'd escaped. Then, as they ventured into the reaches of torchlight, she saw Tshikwā'set trailing behind them. Thick ropes bound his hands, and a grease-stained cloth smothered his lips. Alma's throat constricted to the size of a willow branch and her heart battered against her ribs. Blood trickled down his face from a gash above his eye. His clothes were dirty and torn, as if all four riders had wrestled him to the ground.

"I'll state again, trespassing upon the grounds of Stover is this boy's only crime," her father said. Alma could hear the nervous edge in his voice. He glanced at the bloody Tshikwā'set and winced. "To insinuate otherwise is an insult to my daughter's honor. Take him back to town, throw him in the jailhouse, and let's all of us to bed."

One of the men who had ridden after Tshikwā'set approached the sheriff. "Found him hiding out in an old trapper's dugout couple miles yonder. Put up some fight."

"I see that." The sheriff curled his lips and smoothed down his mustache.

"Let him go, please let him go," Alma screamed into Mr. Simms's hand.

"I'll contact the Indian agent in the morning," her father said. "He'll take the boy back to the reservation where he belongs."

"We also found this in that there dugout." The man thrust a silk ribbon up at the sheriff.

Alma blanched. She'd used that ribbon to tie off her hair the night she met Tshikwā'set in the forest, the night they'd made love and first talked of marriage. Tshikwā'set struggled against his bindings, the thick, fibrous rope cutting into his skin. The rider beside him kicked him with his boot heel square in the face and Tshikwā'set fell to the ground. Alma screamed again, tears smarting and stomach roiling.

The sheriff's eyes raked over her and he spit. He dismounted and stalked over to her. With a rough hand, he grabbed her long braid and held it up to the torchlight. The paisley ribbon fastened at the end of her hair matched cut and color the one taken from the dugout. "Still think your daughter ain't been seduced?"

"That, that proves nothing. I'm sure every girl in La Crosse has a . . . has a similar ribbon," her father said.

But Sheriff Gund was no longer listening. He released Alma's braid and pulled a thick coil of rope from his saddlebag. "String him up, boys."

A few of the younger riders cheered. Mr. Krause looked greenish; Mr. Coleman shook his head.

Frenzy gripped her. She bit at Mr. Simms's salty palm and stomped down on his toes. When he dropped his hand from her face she shrieked loud into the night. "Tshikwā'set! No!"

Her father spun around and smacked her. "Keep quiet, you sinful girl." Though his cheeks blazed red with anger, his eyes looked frantic, fearful. He scuttled behind the sheriff. "Please, you can't do this. There's no justice in this. It's against God's law!"

"You brought this upon yourself with that heathen school of yours."

A lone box elder tree stood at the base of the bluff where the road split. New leaves trembled on its skeleton-like branches. The sheriff tossed the rope to one of the men, who in turn flung it over a thick branch high in the tree. Alma fought and struggled. She threw her weight in every direction, but Mr. Simms's grip held. She clawed at his hands and forearms, leaving pale, ragged scratches in his suede jacket and gloves.

"If nothing else, this boy deserves a trial!" Her father's voice had grown thin and pitchy.

"This savage ain't no citizen," the man who'd found Alma's ribbon said. He grabbed the rope and began knotting a noose. His hands slid down the rough fibers, making an S, then coiling one end around it. Loop and tighten. Loop and tighten. Alma's insides wrenched as if he'd reached inside her, as if his fat, grimy hands were squeezing her viscera. Loop and tighten.

"Really, Sheriff, I must insist." Though he stood only a few feet away, her father's words sounded in her ears like a muffled echo. "In God's name, release—"

Sheriff Gund caught her father by the back of his coat and flung him to the ground. "Stay back, old man."

The men brought Tshikwā'set forward and forced him to his knees beneath the tree. They ripped open his collar. His quill and bead necklace—the one he had kept hidden his first day at Stover, the one Alma had felt against his chest the countless times he had held her in his arms—showed in the moonlight against his copper skin.

The man with the rope laughed and ripped the necklace from his neck. He cast it aside into the dirt and in its place fastened the noose. Several men gathered at the rope's end and the line grew taut. The branch above shook and groaned. Flecks of bark showered down like soot-blackened snow.

Alma thrashed and flailed. Several of her nails had broken off and her fingers were slick with blood. Bile burned her throat. She leaned over one foot and kicked back with the other. Her boot heel struck Mr. Simms's knee. His arms slackened and he fell backward, howling. Alma raced forward just as Tshikwā'set rose from the ground. His hands clawed at the rope about his neck. His body writhed. His face grew red with blood.

The world around her slowed. Though she ran as fast as she could toward him, the distance between them seemed to lengthen. Somewhere far off, a train hooted. They were supposed to be on that train, she and Tshikwā'set, northbound and away from here. They were supposed to marry tomorrow. They were supposed to live happily ever after, despite the odds, despite the color of their skin.

Mr. Coleman grabbed her from behind and wrapped her in his arms. "Don't look, Miss Alma."

She refused to turn away. Tshikwā'set's long legs flailed, the tips of his pointed toes grazing the long stocks of sedge and grass beneath him. Blood-tinged spit bubbled at the corners of his compressed lips. His once-beaming eyes now bulged from their sockets, no longer white and brown, but a crosshatch of red surrounding a pinpoint of black.

Mr. Coleman cradled her in a viselike grip, even as she struggled. Her braid had come undone and hair clung to the sweat and tears wetting her face. She pried at his hands, the last of her nails ripping off clear to the cuticle, staining his worn riding gloves scarlet. Only muffled noises reached her now: the men's laughter, her father's pleading, Tshikwā'set's wheezing breaths, her own high-pitched scream.

The moon gaped down. The elder shuddered. Tshikwā'set's arms slackened and fell to his side. Convulsions overtook him. The front of his trousers darkened and urine dripped down his legs.

Alma buried her face in Mr. Coleman's shoulder. His jacket reeked of horsehair and sweat. Her tears bled into the fabric. Some part of her brain remembered the need for oxygen and she lifted her head for a breath.

Though she could no longer see Tshikwā'set, his shadow danced upon the scree-covered bluff, danced a moment, and then went still.

CHAPTER 39

Minnesota, 1906

The midday sun brooded high above, casting not a shadow. The air about the house hung heavy, quiet, and still. Even so, Alma felt herself slipping, unmoored from the present. She rubbed her gloves back and forth over her skirt. The blood—she had to get it off her fingertips. Her stomach heaved and she spat bile onto the ground. It was Minowe's voice that reeled her back.

"When I told your father, I didn't think he would get the sheriff. I didn't know they would . . ." Minowe's hand fluttered to her throat and her voice dried up.

"Kill him?" The words rang through the yard. "String him up like an animal beside the road?"

Minowe flinched and dropped her head. Tears fell from her eyes onto the dirt.

Alma's hands curled to fists. Her nails bit into her palms, softened only by the thin leather of her gloves. She stamped to the nearby clothesline and curled about the post, lest she strike Minowe again. The splintery wood chafed against her cheek. How dare Minowe cry! How dare she pretend to have suffered when it was Alma whose life was ripped away. "Shut up."

Her sobs continued.

"Shut up!"

Minowe wiped her nose on the sleeve of her blouse. "I had no choice."

The meekness in her voice enraged Alma. She pushed away from the clothesline and spun around. The weathered post creaked and wobbled. "No choice?"

"I couldn't let you runs away together."

"It was nothing to you."

Minowe shook her head, slowly at first, then with violence. The sadness in her face flashed to anger. She bent down and scraped together a handful of dirt. It spilled between her clenched fingers like sand through an hourglass. "You stole everything! Our land, our game, our timber—even the language from our mouths."

She stalked to Alma and flung the earth at her face. It struck her like a thousand tiny pellets, stinging her eyes and choking her nostrils. Alma coughed and blinked. Fifteen years of pent-up rage roared inside her. "You harpy." She reached out and grabbed Minowe's collar. They tussled to the ground.

Minowe ripped off Alma's hat and with it a fistful of hair. Alma boxed her flat handed in the ear. All of her was dirty now, not just her face, and Minowe too. But her hands only clutched tighter. Minowe's fingers dug into her arms as they rolled and jostled, each trying to mount the other.

"I couldn't let you steal him, too," she said.

"Steal him? Steal him!" Alma clawed at Minowe's shoulder until the seam of her blouse split with a groan. "I loved him. I would have given up everything to—" She reared back with a clenched fist, but stopped short. Minowe's dark eyes seemed to look right through her, wild and reddened with tears.

Alma's hand went limp. How had she not realized it as a girl? The way Minowe had spoken of him, the way she looked at him, the countless times she took his side over Alma's. "You loved him, too."

Minowe pushed Alma off her and crawled away. A large swath of her blouse flapped down from the shoulder seam, revealing a thin, yellowed chemise. Her dark hair hung wild about her face. "I only meaned to stop you. To make you see the madness."

"Why didn't you tell me?"

"It isn't right for our kinds to mix." She began to rock, her hands scratching at her skin. "All I did was tell your father. You led them right to him."

"That's not true, I—"

"You could have saved him." Minowe fixed her with desperate

eyes. Her fingers dug deeper, drawing blood. "Why didn't you save him?"

It was like staring into a looking glass: the guilt, the pain, the same tears that wetted Minowe's cheeks streaming down her own. She pulled Minowe into her arms, stopping her frantic clawing. "It's not your fault."

Minowe fought and twisted. She shook and howled.

"It's not your fault!" Alma's voice carried through the clearing and echoed back. Minowe stilled. They held each other and wept. Watery snot dripped from Alma's nose, and her throat grew raw. When she closed her eyes she could still see the twisting shadow. Still hear the groaning tree branch. Still smell the torch smoke. It would be with her forever. And yet, here in Minowe's arms, she found solidarity in her pain, an acceptance and acknowledgment denied her all these years.

Through bleary eyes, she looked out at the spindly grove behind Minowe's house. Huge swaths of stumps scarred the earth, broken only by occasional birch or maple too small or crooked to have value as timber. Alma felt the same emptiness. Why did people always hurt the deepest those they loved the most?

Into the silence, Minowe said, "It won't bring Tshikwā'set back."

"What?"

"Saving Asku."

"I know that. I'm not trying to raise the dead. Just lay them to rest."

Minowe gave her a quizzical look. She stood and helped Alma to her feet. Dust covered them both head to foot. "Come, I'll tell you what I can." She led the way inside and built a fire in the stove while Alma took a seat at the table.

"Do you still keep in touch with Hįčoga?" Alma asked.

"Your father sent her back to the Ho-Chunk reservation after . . . after that night. Consumption took her a few years back."

"Oh." Alma felt like she had swallowed thorns. Her eyes retreated to the floor. She caught sight again of the dolls, the rag doll dressed in blue, the grass dolls, and one she'd not noticed from the window, its leather skin and embroidered dress so like that of the first doll she tried to save all those years ago. "Where are your children?"

"Day school." Minowe filled a kettle and set it on the stovetop to boil. "They're always trying to gets me to send them to the boarding school in Morristown, but I won't." She walked around the room, pulling aside the tattered window covering. Light spilled in, highlighting the sharp features of her gaunt adult face.

"Where's your husband? Does he work in town?"

"He comes and goes. Mostly goes." Minowe shrugged. "Do you have childrens?"

Alma looked down at the rutted tabletop and traced the path of a long scratch with her finger. "No."

The shrill cry of the kettle broke the ensuing silence. Minowe poured them each a cup of tea and then sat down across from her. From the nearby shelf, she grabbed a small cloth-covered parcel. Beneath the covering was a stack of tan granule bars, each the size of a deck of playing cards. She broke a small piece from the top brick and held it out. "Ziinzibaakwad."

Alma placed the hard morsel in her tea. A sweet, woody aroma blossomed up with the steam. As girls, Minowe had spoken often of maple sugar, bemoaning how flavorless white sugar tasted. Alma sipped her tea. The rich sweetness spread across her tongue. "Wiingipogwad. It's delicious."

A familiar gap-toothed grin spread across her friend's face. "You remember some of the Anishinaabe words."

"A few."

"This would please Askuwheteau." She sighed and the smile melted from her face.

"I went to visit him. In St. Paul."

Her eyes livened. "How is he?"

"He looked well," she lied.

"Your husband is a lawyer, you said?"

"Yes, he's taken on Asku's case, but we need your help to prove his innocence."

Minowe's eyes fell to her lap. She cradled her teacup but did not drink. "None of us are innocent."

Alma waited for her to say more, but Minowe remained silent, her gaze sweeping the room, restless, anxious, avoiding Alma's face. "Let's start with Agent Andrews. Can you tell me more about him?"

Her old friend's hand tightened around the cup, the tendons bulging beneath her dry copper skin.

"Several complaints had been lodged against him," Alma prodded. "What did he do?"

Minowe folded her arms, unfolded them, and folded them again. "He was a cheat. Always promising things—seeds, tools, foods—that came too late, too fews, or never came at all."

"And for that someone shot him?"

"No, we was use to that. But then he took our timber lands."

The story Minowe told filled the gaps between what she and Stewart had learned from Zhawaeshk and uncovered at the agency. The entire process had been corrupt from the start. Before the allotment, land speculators snuck onto the reservation to survey the land and spread their finding to those Indians willing to sell. An official land report went out before the allotment, but those who could not read English or understand survey maps could make no use of it.

"And Agent Andrews allowed all this?"

"He got a cut from every acre sold." Minowe explained how deeds were crooked, boundaries redrawn. The land was given out to whomever arrived first, with mixed-bloods and white Indians up from the cities camping out to get in line early. Agent Andrews said not to worry; there was land enough for all. But he'd miscalculated the acreage and hundreds of people—mostly the less educated, more traditional full bloods—walked away with nothing.

Alma was leaning in, her elbows propped upon the table, her tea long since cooled. "How do you know all this?"

Minowe pursed her lips and looked out the window. "I worked there for a time, at the agency. It's all filed away there, if you knows where to look. Most of it anyways. There were letters," she hesitated, "between the agent and lumber company . . . but I doubt if they're still there."

"You read them?"

"I wrote them, transcribed them, that is. I didn't make the connection between it all until after, though."

"Even so, surely he wouldn't be so bold?"

"If you ain't white and ain't a man, he assumed you had no sense."

A smile found its way to Alma's lips. "Miss Wells would smack you silly with her ruler if she heard you saying ain't."

They laughed together at this, sisters again for a fleeting moment.

"Would you help my husband find those files?" Alma asked when their laughter dwindled. "And make a sworn statement about those letters?"

Minowe rolled her mug back and forth between her hands, her face once again somber. "I don't know. They won't sell us back our timber. Give us back our lands."

"It might help Askuwheteau's case."

"How?"

"Any one of those people who didn't get an allotment has more cause to kill Agent Andrews than he did." Her mind was running now. Excitement edged into her voice. "Or someone from the lumber company. With the agent dead, they don't have to pay up."

Minowe continued to work the mug between her palms. Her eyes skirted Alma's, shifting about the room, and at last settling on the four small dolls in the corner. "I have to think of my childrens."

"You don't want their uncle killed for a crime he didn't commit."

Tears had returned to Minowe's eyes. Alma fished through her dirty purse for a handkerchief and handed it to Minowe.

A fragile smile broke the tears. "You broughts a silk purse with you to the reservation? Whatever for?"

"Well . . . for moments like this, I guess."

Minowe shook her head, laughing even as she cried. "You've become like your mother."

Alma frowned and straightened. "I beg your pardon."

"Only in little ways." Minowe wiped the last of her tears with Alma's hankie. "She was not all bad, your mother."

Alma looked down at her hands—not yet wrinkled or marked with age spots, but no longer as smooth and supple as they had been as a girl. "No, I suppose not."

Minowe held out the square of silk.

"Keep it."

Minowe breathed in deeply and smiled. Her eyes remained bloodshot and her nose red. Dozens of pin-scratch creases lingered on her skin—yesterday's joys and sorrows—and suddenly Alma found it difficult to remember the carefree face of her friend's youth. Her fingers fluttered over her own skin and she wondered if Minowe saw a similar battle-scarred stranger.

"You don't think Asku did it, do you?" Alma asked. "Killed Agent Andrews."

"Before the shooting people said bad things about him. They couldn't see he wanted to belong but didn't know how. Now they call him Wenabozho, a hero."

"Were they true? Those bad things?"

She shrugged. "Some. Most of them, I guess. But he came alive after this whole mess with the timber—like he'd been visited by a spirit or something—he stopped drinking so much, he set a council to get the allotment repealed, he wrote a letter to the head man in Washington and got nearly four hundred men to sign it. He was his old self again."

Alma cheered at this. That Asku, the old Asku, would never commit murder. She sipped the last of her cold tea. The sweet taste of *ziinzibaakwad* lingered a moment on her tongue, then faded. Out the window a veil of cloud shrouded the sun's face. "Can you think of anyone else who might have killed him?"

Minowe fingered her long braid, picking at the ragged ends. She opened and closed her mouth twice before finally speaking. "All this trouble Askuwheteau stirred up after the allotment. Agent Andrews began to change his mind. Thought about redoing the whole thing. Said as much in one of his last letters to the timber company." She looked straight at Alma. "I didn't read their reply, but I know it wasn't good. He cursed worse than Mr. Simms and kicked over his spittoon. Took me hours to clean up the muck."

"You've got to tell my husband about this."

Minowe grabbed a woven shawl from a nearby chair and draped it around her thin frame. "What's his name?"

"Stewart. Stewart Mitchell."

"Is he a good man?"

"Yes, honorable and diligent and—"

"I mean, is he good to you?"

Alma looked down at her empty cup. "Very. More than I deserve."

"Tshikwā'set would be glad of this."

She ached anew at the sound of his name, but the pain was less sharp, less debilitating, more like a remembrance of injury than a fresh wound. Was Minowe right? She'd never considered that even from the grave he might wish her happiness, might be willing to forgive, might never have blamed her at all.

"Bring your husband tomorrow," Minowe said, standing. "I'll tell him about the deeds and letters."

Alma started to leave, but stopped short of the door. She wrung her purse in her hands, watching the dust and dirt transfer from the silk to her gloves. "I . . . er . . . Stewart doesn't know."

Minowe nodded, no judgment in her look, only sorrow. "I won't tell him."

Outside in the muted daylight, she glanced again about the sparse land and back to the tarpaper shack. Minowe stood at the top of the stairs, the shawl about her shoulders somehow reminiscent of the quilts they'd clutched about them to keep warm those nights in the woods.

"It wasn't supposed to end up this way," Alma said. "I hate that I believed their lies—my father, Miss Wells."

"They believed them, too, Azaadiins. We all did."

CHAPTER 40

Minnesota, 1906

Back in the company of the wide, steel-blue waters of the Miziziibi, Alma waded through the same military formalities as on her previous visit to Fort Snelling.

"We're preparing the prisoner for transfer to St. Paul for tomorrow's trial." The major glowered at her from behind his desk. "Can't you wait and speak to him then?"

His sour expression did not touch her smile. "I must see him today."

He uttered a curse under his breath and scratched a few lines onto a small square of paper. "Give this to the guard. You found your way to my office again, I trust then you know your way to the round tower."

She hurried past the barracks and armory toward the old fort. Stewart had stayed in St. Paul to sort through all the documents and testimonies from White Earth. He would meet with Asku tomorrow before the trial, but Alma could not wait to deliver the good news.

The same boyish soldier stood guard inside the tower. This time, he was not asleep, but throwing his knife at a makeshift target painted onto a stack of crates. Nicks and scratches covered every corner of the crates, most far outside the bull's-eye. He beamed at her behind a flourish of soldierly bravado and led her up the stairs.

"I'll fetch a chair and bring it up," he said. "Remember, none of them funny Indian words, now."

The soldier's voice had alerted Asku and he stood waiting at the bars, expression guarded. "Azaadiins."

"I have wonderful news. Really, my husband should be the one to tell you." She dismissed the idea with a wave of her hand and closed the space between. The iron bars now seemed a mere formality. A few days' time and he'd be free. "Stewart will go over all the legal rigmarole with you tomorrow morning before the trial, but I couldn't wait. I couldn't bear that you should spend another night in fear for your life."

She scanned Asku's face for a flicker of curiosity or twitch of relief. Instead, he leaned back, the hairline creases around his eyes deepening. "I told you I did not want your husband's help."

"I know you're wary, but you needn't be. We just returned from White Earth. Minowe told us what happened with the timber allotment. We interviewed Zhawaeshk and that filthy gun merchant. Looked all through the agency's records—"

Asku's face darkened. "You went to Gaa-waabaabiganikaag?"

She glanced over her shoulder. The soldier clamored around downstairs, perhaps looking for a suitable chair. Still, she whispered. "I knew you wouldn't kill anyone. When you wouldn't talk, we traveled to White Earth to learn why."

He stepped back from the bars and clenched his hands. White sinew streaked his knuckles. "I told you to leave it alone, Azaadiins."

"Asku, you're my friend, Nisayenh. How could I not help you?"

"Damn your help!" He backhanded his chair with such force it flew across the cell and struck the iron bars. The whole cage rattled. "You force it on us. Insist you know best."

Alma shuffled backward. In all their years together at Stover, she'd never seen him lose his temper.

Footfalls bounded up the stairs. Flush-faced, the young soldier rushed into the room and puffed out his narrow chest. "What's all this yellin' about? You all right, ma'am?"

She swallowed her emotions and steadied her voice. "I'm fine. It's nothing."

The soldier strode to the thick bars of Asku's cell and banged against them with the butt of his throwing knife. "No yellin'. You hear me, savage? I don't know why, but this fine lady's seen fit to see ya. Try to be a gentleman. Gen-tal-man."

Asku's nostrils flared and his full lips flattened into a razor-sharp line.

Alma touched the soldier's forearm. "The outburst was my fault. Please, we're fine." He sheathed his knife but continued to leer in Asku's direction. She drew the boy's gaze back with a light squeeze to his arm and feigned a smile. "Please, I'll call if I need anything. You'll be just downstairs, right?"

Alma watched him peacock from the room, then turned back to Asku. Again the age of his face startled her—the deep furrows that cut across his forehead, the sunbaked skin and hollow eyes. "You haven't even heard the good news. My husband thinks we have enough evidence to provide sufficient doubt. Especially if you take the stand."

He drew his weathered hands down his face and shook his head. "Alma, I—"

"Don't worry about your testimony. My husband can coach you."

"You don't understand—"

"He's already prepared his line of questioning, you need only answer honestly and—"

"I'm guilty, Alma."

"Be sure to hit on a few key—what?" She recoiled from the bars. "What did you say?"

"I killed him." He spoke each word with matter-of-fact precision. No emotion. No contrition.

She had the strange sensation of being back at Stover, seated beside him in the classroom. Chalk dust filled the air. Their wrought-iron desk creaked. A cold draft stole through the thin windowpanes. Asku, as he was that first time she saw him—black hair brushing his boyish cheeks, dark eyes wide and curious—stood. *I killed him,* he said, straight-faced and serious, as if reading a phrase from the blackboard or reciting a line of text. *I'm guilty.*

The cry of a riverboat called Alma back to the present. She groped behind her, but the soldier boy had forgotten her chair. Her legs wavered. Why was Asku saying this?

"I shot Agent Andrews two times in the back."

"No, it had to be someone from the timber company."

"With a .38 Colt Lightning I bought this summer."

"Another Indian who lost his allotment."

"I waited behind the general store until I saw him walking down the road." Still that calm, detached voice. "I raised my gun and fired."

She flung her hands to her ears. "Stop."

"I stood above him and waited for his breath to stop." He looked her straight in the eye. "Then I dropped the gun, walked back into the woods, and waited for them to arrest me."

"Stop!" She let the weight of her body carry her to the floor, her knees banging hard against the wood. One hand steadied herself, the other snaked around her stomach.

"Minowe said the agent had changed his mind, was considering a new allotment."

"Agent Andrews was a crook and a coward. He never would have reallotted the timber lands. But that's not why I killed him." He crossed to the wall of his cell and stood there, facing away, his finger tracing the crumbling mortar between the stones. "I never wanted to come to Stover. But my father said we must, Minowe and I. Gichi-mookomaan ways were the ways of the future, he'd said. We would help our people survive, shepherd them into a new circle of time."

He'd never wanted to come? None of this made sense. "You worked so hard. Did so well."

"I worked hard to honor my father, my people."

All those years—first to raise his hand, last to quit the study room—it must mean more than honor. "But . . . but you were happy."

He spread a hand out over the rock, bracing himself it seemed, as if the weight of his body were too much to hold upright. "I don't know anymore."

"No!" She slammed her palm against the floor. "You were happy. I remember. Something happened to you at Brown. Everything was fine before you left."

"Is that what you want to hear? That they mistreated me there? That I didn't fit in?" He pushed off the wall and stalked the perimeter of his cell. The tremor of his steps reached her through the floor-boards. "It's true. There was no place for a red man in their world. I wasn't welcome in any of their social clubs or study groups. I was behind in class from the moment I arrived there."

"Nonsense."

"Those boys were learning Latin before I spoke a word of English. They didn't spend half their school day harvesting crops or sanding wood."

"You just needed time."

He pushed back his shirtsleeve and brandished his arm. "Time won't change the color of my skin!"

Alma flinched and pulled back from the bars.

He glared at her a moment, then hung his head and sighed. He looked like a weatherworn scarecrow whose straw stuffing had blown away with the wind. "At Brown I was too Indian to fit in. When I returned home, I was too like the white man."

Alma rose, ignoring the dirt smudged across her skirt. He followed her with eyes as dark and empty as the void between the stars. "You could have put your learning to use. Worked at the agency or taught at the day school."

"So my people could despise me even more?"

"You could have done anything. Been anyone you wanted to be."

Asku righted his chair and collapsed onto it. "Except be an Indian."

She crossed to a nearby window. It was yet afternoon, but the narrow opening strangled back the sun. Her thoughts clattered, one against the other, impossible to right or tame. "I think it best you don't take the stand. I'm sure Stewart will agree. Even without your testimony we can win your case."

"I don't want to win the case, Alma." The edge returned to his voice. "I'm guilty."

"Judge Baum might dismiss the case outright."

"No, go back home."

Her eyes clung to the sliver of pale-blue sky visible through the window. "At the very least we can show mitigating circumstances. Plead for a lesser sentence."

"I said I don't want your help!"

"I'll not let you die to prove some silly point."

His chair legs scraped against the floor. The cell bars shivered beneath his grasp. "I spent every day at Stover ashamed to be Indian and every day since ashamed I am not Indian enough. I killed Agent Andrews in the name of Anishinaabe justice. In the eyes of my people I am whole again—not Harry Muskrat, but Askuwheteau, son of Odinigun. I would rather die beloved by my people than live a ghost in their world."

Alma shook her head, as if doing so would dislodge his words from her ears. "That's suicide."

"It is the way I have chosen."

She still could not look at him. The blue sky bled into the gray stone walls through the prism of her tears. "You're going to fight these charges. Fight them and win."

He shook the bars so violently the bolts whined and bits of the stone ceiling struck the floor like hail. "It is right that I should die. I will hear the drums of my forefathers and dance with them in the sky. Don't rob me of that honor."

Footsteps pounded up the stairs. The lighter step of the boy watchman and another heavier set. She did not turn around when they entered the room. Did not turn around as they berated Asku for the ruckus and told him to prepare for transport. The cell door creaked open. Chains clanked. Locks snapped shut.

Again, the world seemed to wobble. How dare he ask her to let him die. After all she'd done to try to save him. After she'd already watched another loved one hang. Alma braced herself against the wall. The chill of the stone reached her through her gloves, traveling up her arms and down her spine until her whole body shivered.

"Azaadiins, please."

Even his voice, raspy with emotion, a voice as familiar as the churning Mississippi, could not compel her to turn. His shackles rattled down the stairs. It was a halting sound—the thud of a footstep, the clang of metal, a moment's pause, and then another thud—that harried her nerves. None of this made sense, his confession of murder, his will to die. Another stair. Another thud and clang. Why hadn't he told her sooner? Told her the truth from the beginning. Why had he let her believe they'd ever been happy?

CHAPTER 41

Minnesota, 1906

Alma's eyes climbed the red and white edifice of the Ryan Hotel, lighting on the fifth floor. Behind her, carriages and bicycles rattled. Automobiles honked. Streetcars whined along their tracks. Her bounding pulse had not slowed in the hour-long ride from Fort Snelling, nor had her mind quieted. How could she face Stewart? What would she tell him—that Asku was guilty? She hardly believed it herself.

Her feet echoed as she crossed the marble foyer. The gears of the elevator worked her nerves. Inside the room, Stewart was already preparing for dinner. "Hurry and change, darling," he said, slipping an arm into his freshly pressed dress shirt. "We don't want to miss our reservation."

She sat on the edge of the bed and watched him dress. He worked through his buttons and donned his waistcoat—white on white. Embellished satin upon starched cotton. His face, reflected in the vanity mirror, wore a cheerful expression she'd not seen since they crossed the Mississippi. A good meeting with Mr. Gates then. Agreement all around they could win the case. Save for one small detail: Asku wasn't innocent. Just thinking the words pained her. How could she utter them aloud?

Stewart picked up his bow tie. Also white, though black was in fashion now too. He whistled as he worked it round his collar and began to tie. She could see the deft movement of his hands in the mirror. Over, under, fold, around. "I thought you might like your blue chiffon," he said, and gestured toward the chaise. "I already laid it out for you."

She glanced over at the dress. The window above the chaise looked out over the skyline. Shadow had fallen and the sky colored over like a bruise. If only she'd passed over the morning paper that day, left its stories silenced between the pages, thrown it out with the breakfast scraps. She would never have returned to Stover and seen the injustice her childhood eyes could not. She would never have lost her fantasies of prosperity to the reality of life on the reservation.

Stewart's cufflinks snapped into place. Fabric rustled as he shrugged on his tailcoat.

Could she leave Asku for the gallows, let him die when she had the power to save him? In lieu of an answer, her father's voice came to her, warm, robust, humming with excitement: *We're their salvation.* He'd said those words the very first day the Indians arrived. How fervently she'd once believed them.

But then, for all their good intentions, they hadn't really saved them at all.

"Aren't you going to take off your duster and dress for dinner?"

She jogged her head and turned to her husband. How handsome he looked in his double-breasted jacket, the silk-faced collar shining in the lamplight. His hair was neatly combed, his cheeks freshly shaven, his hazel eyes expectant. She pulled off her coat and laid it beside her on the bed. As an afterthought, she removed her gloves and unpinned her hat too. Sweat clung to the palms of her hands. She wiped them over her skirt. "I have to tell you something."

"Yes, we can talk at dinner."

"No, here."

He hesitated, then sat beside her.

She searched the silence for the best way to begin. It offered nothing. She ran her hands over her dress for the second time, then hid them in folds of fabric when she noticed her reddened and haggard nail beds. "Why do you love me?"

His brow furrowed. "What?"

"When you first saw me at the picture show and afterward, during our courtship, what made you fall in love with me?"

He flattened his lips and sat back. "I guess it was many things. Your sweetness, your intelligence, your pensiveness—"

"My frailty?"

"I never saw you as frail. Melancholy perhaps. But with that comes grit. Having borne something terrible and survived. For that I loved you too."

"But you never asked after the circumstances."

He shrugged. "I figured you'd tell me when you were ready."

At last perhaps she was.

"I told Harry what we found at White Earth. He still refuses our help."

"What?" He started to chuckle, but the sound sputtered into a wheezing exhale. "You're serious. Why?"

"He told me, that is, he confessed that"—Alma swallowed—"he killed Agent Andrews."

Stewart blinked. "He's guilty? We did all this, came all this way, to help a murderer?"

Alma winced at the word. It still seemed impossible, her beloved Asku a killer.

"Why didn't he tell you this at the beginning? Before we wasted all that time at White Earth?" Stewart jerked to his feet and paced the length of the bedroom. The pendant light above swayed on its gilded chain, casting roving pools of light and shadow. "If he thinks I'm going to walk into that courtroom and convince the jury he's an innocent man—"

"That's not what he wants." She paused. The testimonies, the letters, the fraudulent documents they'd uncovered on the reservation—they could still use them to save Asku's life. She brought her fingers to her mouth, stopped, and let her hand fall to her lap. No. Asku had made his choice. Who were they to override it? "He wants to plead guilty. He's ready to die."

"As he should."

"Stewart!"

"Alma, he killed a man. Not to mention he embroiled us in his deceit, sent us out on this frivolous hunt to uncover evidence that didn't exist."

"He didn't send us. We went of our own accord, remember."

Stewart continued to pace. He tugged at the knot of his bow tie as if his collar were strangling him. "Mr. Gates is going to be furious. Judge Baum. The whole courtroom will be in an uproar."

"Let them be."

"How can you be so calm about this? We've made a disgrace of ourselves here. Inserted ourselves into the investigation. Aroused trouble on the reservation. All this for a murderer? Tell me at least that he's repentant."

"No."

Stewart balked. "No?"

"Sit down, dearest. Please."

She gestured to the bed, but he flopped down on the chaise, brushing aside her dress as if it were a rag.

"It's hard to explain." She fought the tremble in her voice. "Harry knew full well when he shot the agent he would die for it. He did it for honor."

"Honor?" His head fell back against the wall. "Honor? What does honor—"

"You saw the reservation. The corruption. The poverty." She looked down at her dust-stained skirt. She had to say the words, as much for her own ears as Stewart's. "It's more than that, though. It was the school—Stover—that was the start of it."

He stood and set again to pacing—around the bed between the vanity stool and lacquered table to the chaise and window and back. She imagined the thoughts working through his head. *You said Harry thrived at Stover. How could something that happened all those years ago lead a man to murder? I thought the schools were set up for the Indians' own good?*

Whatever his thoughts, he said nothing and Alma bore the silence. In time, the clap of patent-leather shoes atop the floor softened to a hum. "Tell me what this is about, Alma. All of it."

And so she did. She told him of the very first day she'd met Asku, how he clambered so bravely from the wagon. She told him of Minowe and the doll. Of Miss Wells and her ruler. Of their lessons and their games. She told him how they'd sneak out into the woods, dance their forbidden dances, sing their forbidden songs, speak in their foreign tongues.

". . . for me it was fun, an adventure." A tear trickled from her eye, cutting a path down her face for others to follow. She rifled through her handbag. When she remembered she'd given her silk hankie to Minowe, she wiped her face with her sleeve. "I didn't realize these rituals were a way to keep a piece of their original selves alive. Their struggle, their homesickness, the discrimination they faced—it was all around me and I did nothing about it."

Stewart sat next to her. "It's not your fault, Alma. You were just a girl."

"And Harry?"

He frowned, dragged a hand down his face, and sighed. "I'll speak to Mr. Gates tomorrow before the trial, convince him we must let Mr. Muskrat plead guilty."

"Thank you."

"I'm not saying I agree with any of this—the murder, staying silent about what we uncovered on the reservation—but if your friend is ready and willing to die for his crime, well, I suppose that's justice."

"There's something more I must tell you." She fished again through her purse. Her fingers clasped around the necklace. She'd held it so many times, worked over every inch, knew each plane and curve. How smooth the beads and quill felt. How cold. She pulled it out and handed it to Stewart. "A boy came to Stover when I was fourteen. They called him George, but his name was Tshikwā'set . . ."

CHAPTER 42

Wisconsin, 1891

The moments after the hanging were a blur. The sound of a knife sawing through rope. A thud. Alma shrieked and fell to the ground, tearing out her hair and balling her fists over her ears. She closed her eyes to rid them of sight—the jaundiced torchlight, the frayed rope unraveling as it swung from the tree.

Mr. Coleman picked her up and carried her home. The smell of pitch and smoke and horse sweat lingered in her nostrils. She could hear Mr. Simms and her father trailing behind.

"I can't believe . . ." her father muttered. "I never meant . . ."

Her mother sat waiting for them on Stover's veranda. Still in her nightclothes, with her hair lying over her shoulder in a frizzled braid, the woman's eyes blazed mad.

When Mr. Coleman set Alma down, her legs wobbled. Or was it the earth that wobbled, and she the only steady thing upon it? Even in the darkness, pity showed on Mr. Coleman's lined face. She could see contempt, too, a general distaste for the whole incident, but also kindness—something void in the other faces around her. He shook his head and prodded her toward her mother. The woman grabbed her arm, digging her fingers into Alma's skin, and forced her up the steps and into the house.

"What have you done, Alma? Every household in La Crosse will be talking about you tomorrow. You've shamed us—this family, your father and his work, yourself most certainly—all beyond repair." Hysteria edged the woman's voice. Her breath came ragged between swallowed sobs. "You selfish girl, did you ever stop to think how this would ruin us?"

The words sounded like the lines of a play, scripted and surreal. Her mind felt scrambled, her senses numb. Her mother threw her into her room and locked the door. Alma lay upon the wooden floor where she had landed, silent and unmoving. He couldn't be dead, her Tshikwā'set. It had been someone else they'd pulled from the forest. Tomorrow she'd sneak out and join him on the train.

A few minutes later, Mr. Simms entered with a hammer and nailed shut her window. Something about the sound—the initial loud whack, the cry of wood split by a rusty nail—struck open her consciousness. Tears came first, followed by crushing pain. She curled into a ball and wailed. She clawed at her clothes and banged her head against the floorboards. Dawn came and still she hurt. Her final hope—that it had all been but a dream—faded with the morning sun.

Two days she lay on the floor of her small room. Outside, life at Stover continued. A bugle sounded for morning drills. A whistle cry heralded meals. Synchronized footfalls marched to and from the classroom. Machinery brayed from the wood shop, and sewing machines hummed in the nearby parlor. The sounds stabbed through her temples. The light trespassing beneath the drawn curtains stung her eyes.

She wondered if the Indians knew of Tshikwā'set's death. Did they whisper about it at night in their dormitories? Were they angry, frightened, scared? She worried for Hįčoga. Did they know she'd helped Alma escape? Had they punished her too?

Her thoughts wound to Minowe. Why hadn't she come to her, slipped a note, a ribbon, any token of solidarity under the door for comfort? Surely she'd heard Alma's cries. Did their years of friendship mean nothing?

Later, after still no sign, Alma decided Minowe must blame her for what happened. They all did. How could they not? But for Alma, Tshikwā'set would still be alive.

On the third day, her mother unlocked the door and strode in. Her appearance was once again immaculate, but her face looked aged, as if the stress of the last few days had proven too much for her nightly regimen of creams to erase lines from her skin. Her blue eyes lit on Alma for a moment, then focused on the blank wall above. "Get up and dress for the train."

"Where are we going?"

"*You* are going back to Philadelphia. Aunt Tucia has agreed to take you in." Without deigning another glance in Alma's direction, she turned to leave.

Alma scrambled to her feet. "I won't go."

Her mother wheeled around, lips stretched thin across her haggard face. "Have you any idea what you've done? Not a decent family in all of La Crosse will receive my call. People snicker at your father when he goes into town. You've jeopardized the school, our livelihood, everything. This is how you repay our love?"

"Love? You never loved me."

"I gave up everything for you." She stormed toward the door, but Alma caught hold of her arm.

"Let me see my friends, please. Rose and Margaret, just one more time."

A cruel smile spread across the woman's face. "Why, don't you know? It was Margaret who told your father of your wicked plans in the first place."

All feeling left Alma's limbs. That was impossible; Minowe would never tell. "You're lying."

"Even she could see you and that boy didn't belong together." Her mother strode out and slammed the door behind her.

It wasn't true. It couldn't be. She sank down onto her bed and stared at her wrinkled, dust-covered dress. After three days of wear, the layers of stockings and petticoats beneath her skirt clung stickily to her legs.

It was a lie. Her mother would say anything now to hurt her. She remembered the way Minowe had held her hand that first night in the woods when no one else wanted Alma to tag along, how they'd passed notes and whispered secrets during class and study hour, how they'd huddled close atop the roof and told stories of the stars.

And yet besides Hičoga, Minowe was the only person who'd known of Alma's plans to elope.

Her mouth felt suddenly dry. She crossed to her vanity and

slurped down water from the washbowl. It tasted cold and stale and bitter with perfume.

No one else but Minowe had known. No one else could have told.

She splashed her face and let the water drip down her cheeks onto the collar of her dress. In the mirror, her face looked gaunt, her eyes a crosshatch of red, her lips pale and cracked.

Nindaangwe, her dearest friend, had betrayed her. Why? The water roiled in Alma's stomach, threatening to rise. She thought back to the night she'd first confessed her love for Tshikwā'set to her friends. Even then Minowe had disapproved. Did she really care so much about the color of their skins? Did she really think telling Alma's father would make it all go away?

Alma picked up the silver-handled brush beside the washbowl and threw it at the mirror. The glass cracked and splintered, distorting her reflection into that of a stranger, a monster, a Windigo, a ghost.

When Mr. Simms came to collect her for transport to the train station, Alma was too tired to resist. Nothing remained for her here anyway. The hallways of the great schoolhouse lay as empty as they had the first day she had skipped down them, waiting for the Indians to arrive. It was as if everything between that day and this one had been erased—the lessons she had learned, the friendships she had made, the love she had nurtured. She felt hollowed out, an empty shell that would soon weather to dust.

Her father watched her go from the doorway of his study. His beard was overgrown and the skin beneath his eyes blue and puffy. Several days of dirt and scuff marred his once-glossy boots. She met his stare, feeling her jaw tighten and fingers clench, even as her heart lurched. His glassy, reddened eyes were the first to look away.

She strode past him through the foyer to the front door. Her hand was on the doorknob when his voice stopped her. "Alma, I . . ." He cleared his throat. "I never intended for this to happen. Had you not taken things so far I . . ."

Behind her, the grandfather clock murmured through the seconds. The smell of roasting mutton and burnt coffee wafted from the kitchen. She even thought she heard the soft whisper of chalk against slate. Of course the schoolhouse was not empty as she'd imagined. Only she.

Her hand, still on the knob, twisted.

"Kitten, I'm—"

Without word or backward glance she opened the door and hurried to the landau. When at last she did look back, the school was only a red smudge through the tangle of trees.

Eventually the forest thinned and the road descended downward from the hills. Her heart pounded as the carriage reached the base of Grandfather's Bluff. A rope still hung from the box elder's branches, frayed at the bottom where noose and body had been cut free.

She sprang from the landau and rushed to the tree. Falling to her knees, she groped madly through the dirt and brittle grass. Not until her hand grazed the smooth beads of Tshikwā'set's necklace did she realize what she sought. She grabbed hold of the broken strand of quill and beads just as Mr. Simms pulled her from the ground and back to the carriage.

CHAPTER 43

Minnesota, 1906

Not until she'd finished her story did Alma dare look up. Stewart
stared at her with wide, flat eyes. Pallor had overtaken his cheeks and
his mouth hung open like a broken hinge.

The silence pared her all the way to her bone.

After a moment, Stewart's lips began to move, silently at first,
then with the accompaniment of words. "But you weren't . . . inti-
mate with him."

Tears dripped from her chin onto the collar of her dress. She
didn't bother to wipe them away. "We were."

He stood and turned away from her. Both hands hung at his sides,
one opening and closing, the other strangling the necklace.

"I'm so sorry I never told you. It happened long before we met. I
love you and didn't want you to think—"

His hand flew up and silenced her. "I need a moment. A moment
to make sense of all this." He stood like that, hand raised, fingers
splayed as his watch ticked away in his waistcoat pocket. Each second dragged longer than the one before.

"Please, my love, you have to understand, I never meant to hurt
you with any of this. When I read about Harry's trial in the paper . . ."
She thought back to Minowe's words. "Some part of me believed that
if I could save Askuwheteau, I'd be saving Tshikwā'set as well."

He cocked his head in her direction and stared at her like a
stranger. Then his red, vacant eyes clouded over with anger. "You
lied to me. All these years."

She flattened her hand over a sob.

"You fornicated with some Indian and then presented yourself to me unsullied."

"That was your doing," Alma cried. "You'd cast an image in your mind of who I was before you even met me. There was no room for who I really was."

"Our entire marriage has been a farce." He snapped the mended necklace and threw it to the floor. Black beads and porcupine quill rolled helter-skelter across the Oriental rug. He marched from the room, through the parlor, and tore his overcoat from the rack.

Alma hurried behind. "That's not true! I love you." Something cracked underfoot. She froze. Beneath her slipper lay a shattered porcupine quill.

A slamming door brought her head up. Stewart was gone.

Dawn broke gray and cold. From the hotel window, Alma watched the streetlamps flicker off. Newsboys staked out their corners and merchants unlocked their shops.

Stewart had not returned. Where and how he'd spent the night, Alma had no guess. With each passing hour, her chest squeezed tighter. Surely he would be back to dress for court. He hadn't his shoulder bag or even hat and gloves.

She fled the window and paced the room, wringing her hands until they tingled from loss of blood. He hated her. He must. How could he not after all she had done?

With each turn through the parlor, she checked the polished oak clock atop the side table. Asku's trial began at eleven. The hotel footman knocked with breakfast trays just after eight. The steaming coffee cooled, and the untouched toast grew stale. By nine, her entire viscera had wound itself into unending knots.

Whatever happened, she could not leave Asku alone. She unpinned the sagging remnants of yesterday's coiffure with an unsteady hand and undressed. Wrinkles lined her skirt where it had bunched beneath her as she slept, kneeling on the floor, head resting on the couch, waiting for Stewart to return.

She laid a fresh outfit across the bed and stared down at it. A chill prickled her naked skin. She dressed slowly and with care, one layer of fabric at a time, buttons aligned, seams straight. She restyled her hair and pinned atop it a wide-brimmed hat. The clock in the parlor struck ten. With each chime, her heart rocked.

Stewart was not coming back.

Her eyes were spent of tears, but her breast trembled with dry, silent sobs. She forced herself toward the door. Halfway there, she stopped and glanced at his hat and gloves nestled atop the hall stand. Her fingers brushed the soft fur felt and kid leather. The scent of his Bay Rum aftershave still lingered in the air. She breathed in deeply and held the air in her lungs until they burned. By the time she returned from the trial, the smell would likely be vanished, his trunks packed and gone. She took another breath, a parting glance, and departed for the courthouse.

CHAPTER 44

———»•◦•«———

Minnesota, 1906

Alma pushed her shoulders back and entered the courtroom. A smartly dressed man with a trim mustache lounged behind the prosecution's table. Across the aisle sat Mr. Gates, shuffling through a stack of papers. The chair beside him—Stewart's chair—was vacant. Her carriage sagged. The heavy mahogany door banged closed behind her and Mr. Gates turned around. Relief flashed across his face. He daubed his forehead with a hankie. Almost as quickly as it had come, his smile faded. He rose to his feet and craned his neck to see around her.

"Mrs. Mitchell," he said when she sat down behind him in the gallery's front row. "Is your husband not with you?"

Alma took a deep breath. "I came alone."

"But . . . er . . . he is coming?" Mr. Gates tugged at his collar. "It's quarter to eleven. I'm hardly prepared to introduce the evidence he found at White Ash myself."

"White Earth."

He looked at her blankly.

"The reservation." She made no attempt to dull the edge in her voice. "Gaa-waabaabiganikaag, if you prefer."

"Yes. Yes. Either way, what am I supposed to do with this?" He gestured to the jumble of documents strewn across the counsel table.

She glanced back at the door. Without Stewart, she'd have to fight for Asku herself. "Mr. Muskrat would like to change his plea to guilty."

"Guilty?" He grabbed a fist full of papers. "Then what's all *this* for?"

"We, that is, I thought it would help the case. I was wrong."

"Mr. Mitchell seemed mighty convinced yesterday when he was explaining it all."

"Mr. Muskrat is adamant."

"What a mess!" He mopped the sweat from his lined brow and shook his head. "If we don't submit this, we'll look like fools. Your friend will hang."

Alma gritted her teeth. "I'm well aware of the ramifications."

"Judge Baum's going to be furious."

"You can't ignore Mr. Muskrat's wishes."

"Clearly he's not in a right state of mind." Mr. Gates turned around and began shuffling again through the papers. "There's got to be something we can use in here."

Alma glared at the back of his head. He hadn't read one page of the brief Stewart had prepared for the court. He didn't care about this case, about Asku. All he'd seen when Stewart walked through his door was an opportunity to better his record.

Behind her, the courtroom door shuddered open. Both she and Mr. Gates swiveled around. Two men entered. The first was a portly man Alma did not recognize. He strutted down the aisle with the affected confidence of a mid-level bureaucrat. Agent Taylor walked beside him.

He flashed Alma a cocky grin and tipped his hat. "Mrs. Mitchell. Always a pleasure. This is Mr. Raton." He motioned to the larger man. "Head of the Indian Office here in St. Paul."

Alma nodded at the man but offered no pleasantries. She turned back to Agent Taylor. "White Earth's quite a distance hence. With all your agency attends to—intimidation, usury, illegal land transfers—I'm surprised you had time to come."

His smile held but his blue eyes darkened. "Just here to make sure justice is served." He followed Mr. Raton into the bench behind the prosecution.

She looked down at her knotted hands, then up to the courtroom's vaulted ceiling. Electric lights dangled down like globes on a gilded string. She hated these men—the lot of them—all profiteering at the Indians' expense. It wasn't just money, but lives—hers, Tshikwā'set's,

Minowe's, Asku's. Her blood turned cold at the thought of his name. Could she really let her friend die? Warm air rose from the brass floor registers spaced about the room, but Alma pulled the lapels of her coat tightly together.

Just before eleven, the bailiff entered through a side door at the front of the room. Twelve men—all of them white—sauntered behind. Alma scrutinized their faces as they seated themselves in the jury box. Their expressions were a checkerboard of curiosity and indifference, broken by the occasional puritanical scowl. What qualified these men to pass judgment on her friend? Without intervention, Mr. Gates would blunder through the trial, cheapening Asku's bravery with every step, robbing him of his self-determination. And these twelve men, their latent prejudice inflamed, would in turn rob him of his life.

The bailiff left the room and returned a few minutes later. Asku shuffled behind, the chains fettering his ankles scraping over the maple floor. Another set of shackles bound his wrists. His face was calm, but his hands clenched and unclenched as he walked. Alma bit down on her lip, her teeth unyielding even as she tasted blood. He wore the same gray trousers and dirty white shirt she had seen him in on both her visits to Fort Snelling. Why hadn't she the presence of mind to bring him a change of clothes? She remembered his fastidious attention to dress. Even the cheap wool uniforms at Stover, sent in crates from the Indian Affairs Bureau, he had tended and worn with impeccable care.

He stared forward as he crossed the courtroom, eyes fixed on some distant point, never veering toward Alma or anyone else seated in the whispering audience. But she wanted him to look at her; wanted to let him know she finally understood. A guard walked beside him, his meaty hand tight around Asku's arm, steering him toward the defendant's table. She expected the guard to remove the chains once Asku reached his chair, but he did not. If she reached out, the tips of her fingers would brush Asku's shoulder. Yet the gulf between them felt impossibly wide.

Before Asku could sit down, the judge entered the courtroom and everyone stood. Alma glanced once more at the door behind her. Her last spark of hope fled.

The judge lumbered to his bench. "Be seated, everyone."

His surly expression was just as Alma remembered from their first encounter, as if the rutted brow and compressed lips were etched permanently on his face. He glowered at the docket, then glanced in the defense's direction. "Where's our esteemed counsel from Philadelphia? Not lost on the reservation, I hope?"

Mr. Gates rose to his feet. "He did return, Your Honor, but I'm afraid . . . um . . . If I could just ask for a brief recess—"

"Recess? After ten days' continuance?" Judge Baum chuckled. "I think not. The trial will progress as scheduled."

Mr. Gates groped for his chair and sat down. Asku watched with a tight expression. Then his gaze flickered askance to Alma. The weight of it crushed her. Shoulders held wide and chin raised—he sat proud, assured, defiant, just like the color-plate images of warriors of old. But his eyes, deadened as they were, still resembled those of the little boy who'd leapt from the wagon, the childhood friend she'd dearly loved.

"I call the court to order in the case of the United States versus Harry Muskrat. Prosecution, you may—"

Asku stood, his chains clanking. "Your Honor, I would like—"

The judge rapped his gavel upon the desk. "This isn't a free-for-all, Mr. Muskrat. If you wish to address this court, you may do so from the witness stand." His pinched gaze shot to Mr. Gates. "Control your client, counselor, or I'll hold you both in contempt."

"But Your Honor." Alma was on her feet too, her hands throttled about her handbag. "The defense wishes to change—"

"Madam, you're not entitled to address this court."

Alma's pulse beat in her ear. She pushed through the bar toward the bench. Mr. Gates grabbed her arm, but she shrugged him off. "And the defendant?" She gestured wildly at Asku. "Is he not entitled? You silenced him before he even began."

"If you think I won't throw a lady out of my courtroom you're mistaken, Mrs. Mitchell."

She didn't care. What more did she have to lose? Too long she'd been silent. "This man has been denied a voice—his true voice—all his life. I won't let—"

"Bailiff!" the judge shouted.

Before the bailiff could move, the rear door burst open, swinging so wide it struck the wall behind it. The windows rattled in their frames and the dangling lamps swayed.

Stewart marched down the center aisle, still wearing yesterday's eveningwear. "I beg the court's forgiveness for my tardiness." He passed through the bar and stood beside her.

Judge Baum scowled, his narrow eyes measuring every inch of Stewart's appearance. "I don't know how they do things in Philadelphia, but in the great city of St. Paul, court convenes on time, and we reserve full evening dress for the dining hall and ballroom."

Her husband's lips spread into a boyish grin. "Good thing I opted not to wear my top hat."

The relief that had transformed Mr. Gates's face upon Stewart's arrival melted into wide-eyed horror at the pert remark. The bailiff chuckled into his fist.

Judge Baum flashed him a withering look, then glowered back at the defense. "Your wife is edging upon contempt, Mr. Mitchell."

Stewart turned to her. Stubble covered his tired face. His hazel eyes were bloodshot. He blinked slowly and breathed a ragged sigh. The adoration she'd seen a million times was gone from his gaze. Yet in its place was forgiveness. Acceptance. A love less perfect but more true. He squeezed her hand and she returned to her seat.

"Good," the judge said. "Now, if the interruptions will finally cease, the prosecution may deliver their opening statement."

Stewart threw his overcoat on the back of his chair, but did not sit. "Actually, Your Honor . . ." His voice broke off. He glanced down at the spread of documents they had compiled at White Earth. The interviews and land deeds. The tale of treachery, corruption, and greed. His jaw muscles tightened and he swallowed. He glanced at Asku and regarded for the first time the man who'd set their journey in motion. "Aaniin."

Hearing the *Anishinaabe* greeting, a smile fluttered at the corners of Alma's compressed lips.

Asku nodded, his expression guarded.

Judge Baum cleared his throat.

"The defense would like to withdraw its plea," Stewart said, his voice solemn and steady. "And enter instead a plea of guilty."

The judge's nostrils flared. "If this is a stunt to garner concessions from the prosecution—"

"It's not, Your Honor. We're not angling for a plea agreement." Stewart looked at Asku, who again nodded. "We accept the charges as they stand."

Relief washed over Alma, leaving a tender rawness in its wake. Her hands still trembled with anger. Everything had been taken from Asku. His life . . . his death was all he had left to give.

She listened for an aftershock of murmurs, but silence gutted the courtroom. Mr. Gates slumped down in his chair and hung his head. The prosecutor scratched a few notes onto his pad with a dull pencil.

Asku's face bore no emotion, but the knotted muscles in his back relaxed and he stood a bit taller.

"I see your trip to the reservation yielded no results." The judge spoke with a note of amusement.

Stewart's hands flexed. His chest rose with a deep inhale, but he said nothing.

"Very well. Bailiff, dismiss the jury." The twelve men scuttled from the room, and the judge continued. "Harry Muskrat, known in Indian as Ask-you-wheat-eo, the United States District Court of Minnesota accepts your guilty plea in the murder of Mr. Blair Andrews." His gavel struck the desk. "On to sentencing."

The prosecutor adjusted his spectacles and rose to his feet. "Considering the savage nature of the crime, the state requests a sentence of death by hanging."

Though she'd been expecting it, each word had teeth like a blade. "Who are you to call the murder savage?" she shouted at the prosecution. "You sit there with your tidy suit and—" A clap from the gavel, and Alma swallowed her words. Even seated, she felt dizzy with rage and wondered at Asku's unflinching composure.

"Does the defense wish to contest this?" Judge Baum asked.

Stewart's hand opened upon the desk, his fingers brushing the bottom edge of the documents scattered before him. He drank in three slow breaths and again looked to Asku. The Indian shook his head. "No, Your Honor."

"You have nothing for the court's consideration? So be it. Will the defendant please stand?"

Asku rose.

"Harry Musk—"

"I would like to say some words, Your Honor."

The judge pursed his lips. He had risen slightly from his chair, as if he intended to pound his gavel and scurry off to lunch with its echo still resounding. His eyes flickered to Alma and back. He sank back down and waved his hand. "Very well."

Asku straightened. Gone was the boy of Alma's remembrance, standing atop the bandstand, nervously clenching and unclenching his hands. Gone were his youthful visions of the future. Here was a man, worn yet proud.

"Nine years I attended Stover School for Indians and was educated in the ways of the white man. But all the education in the world could not change the color of my skin. I was not a white man and would never be treated as a white man. So I returned to my people. But even there I was an outcast for I no longer remembered the ways of the Indian. For years I lived a lonely life. A shadow life." He paused. Anger lit his eyes, but his voice remained steady. Alma hid behind the wide brim of her hat and pressed her fingers like floodgates over her eyes as he continued. "Agent Andrews was a despot and a crook. I shot him so that I might have a place among my people. I am again one of them. I shall be hanged, and my Indian brothers will bury me a warrior."

Muffled chatter erupted on the heels of his words. Mr. Raton shot to his feet, tugging down on his shiny silk waistcoat to keep the ends from furling over his round belly.

"Agent Andrews was no despot. He was upstanding in every—"

"Of that, sir, you are greatly mistaken."

Alma had never heard her husband's voice raised in such contempt. He too had quit his chair and stood brandishing his index finger at Mr. Raton. "I have evidence of usury, embezzlement, racketeering, corruption—"

The judge clamored for order. "The time for submitting evidence has passed, Mr. Mitchell."

Stewart straightened and righted his bow tie. "I am well aware of that, Your Honor. I have no intention of making a submittal to this court." He glowered over at Mr. Raton and Agent Taylor. "But I shall be releasing my findings to the Indian Affairs oversight committee in Washington and the local press."

"Enough!" The judge banged his gavel and silence resumed.

Throughout the fray, Asku had remained a statue, standing face forward, his dark eyes locked in a diffuse gaze.

"If I may, Your Honor," the prosecutor said. "The Indian's speech only highlights his barbaric nature."

"So it does . . ." Judge Baum smoothed a hand from mustache to chin, then turned to Asku. "Harry Muskrat, for the willful murder of Agent Blair Andrews, I sentence you to hang by the neck until you are dead." His gavel rattled the windows a final time. "This court is adjourned."

Alma sat breathless. Papers shuffled and the court's various attendees rose. She clutched the edge of the bench and stared at the maple-slatted floor, trying not to vomit.

Asku's voice came calm and somber. "Thank you, Mr. Mitchell." Then, to her, "Miigwech, Azaadiins."

She looked up and met the eyes of her friend. Something in them was renewed—not the hope and curiosity she had seen in them as a girl, but some of the spirit hitherto obscured.

She rose and grabbed his hand.

"Azaadiins?" Stewart said.

She smiled at her husband, though the expression was heavy to wear. "It's the Indian name Asku gave me. It means little aspen tree."

"Aspen tree?"

She gestured at her skin. "Their bark is white."

The bailiff scuttled over and grabbed Asku's arm. "Let's go, Mr. Muskrat."

Alma clasped his hand all the tighter, as if never to let go. Asku squeezed back, then gently pried his fingers from her grasp. "Not because of your fair skin," he said as the bailiff led him away. "The aspen is a strong tree. A resilient tree. The first to grow back after fire has scarred the earth. For this reason, I named you Azaadiins."

CHAPTER 45

Minnesota, 1906

From the train's window, the Mizi-ziibi looked like a ribbon of black satin, a shade darker than the rest of the night-bathed landscape, but equally as tranquil. For several hours they had rocked along, mirroring the great river's bend and sway; then the tracks veered east. Alma craned her neck and watched the smooth water vanish from sight. For a moment, her gaze lingered, searching the receding darkness for a final glimpse. Her breath made clouds across the window. She rubbed them away with the sleeve of her nightshirt and at last turned away.

Stewart lay beside her in their sleeper car, the rise and fall of his breath a gentle melody played in time with the hum of the train. She tried not to think of another train, one racing northward, carrying the body of her friend.

He had died with the same dignity with which he had lived; brave Asku, who as a boy was the first to leap down from the wagon into a new world. Before the execution, Alma had brought him fresh clothes laundered with crushed pine needles so that it might remind him of home. She stood beyond the bars of his cell, her entire body heavy, searching for the *Anishinaabemowin* word for goodbye. It did not come. Instead, she kissed him on the cheek, flashed her bravest smile, and left him to change.

Outside, brown grass and dried leaves crunched beneath her feet. A single line of chairs stood before the gallows. She sat down beside Stewart and squeezed his hand until her fingers went numb. It was quiet on the parade ground, even as Asku ascended the wooden steps to the platform. But in her mind, Alma heard drumming—hands thumping hollowed logs and upturned pots stolen from Mrs. Simms's kitchen. Stomping feet echoed the drumbeat. Frederick's voice cut in and then Minowe's clear soprano.

She glanced up at Asku. His dark eyes met hers for a final time and she knew he heard them, too, the drums, breaking through the silence.

More drums would sound tonight at White Earth during the *Midewiwin* funeral ceremony. The northward train carrying his body had probably already pulled into the Detroit Lakes station. Part of her longed to be there, to hear the Mide's chants guiding Asku to the Land of Souls, to keep vigil over his body beside Minowe and the others in the birch bark lodge and later at the grave. But that was not her world.

She lay down beside her husband. He turned toward her in his sleep and she welcomed his warm breath against her skin. Her arm wound around his head and she twirled her fingers through his soft sand-brown hair. For once, she felt entirely free to love him, to enjoy their happiness together without guilt's nagging prick.

Her eyelids drooped with the train's sway. The well-oiled gears and spinning wheels sang out a lullaby. In this bleary half sleep, a memory floated across her mind—she and Asku at the train depot in La Crosse before he had left for Brown.

"I hate goodbyes," she'd said after kissing him on the cheek. Tears sprang in her eyes and drained down her face.

He swept his thumb over her wet cheekbone. "The Anishinaabe have no word for goodbye."

"What do you say in parting?"

"You see life as a straight line. But for us, life is a circle. After something or someone enters our circle, they travel with us forever, influencing us even if they are not physically present. To us, there is no such thing as goodbye."

Once again water filled her eyes as Asku's voice became an echo in her thoughts. But unlike those tears shed at the La Crosse depot or beneath the torch-lit elder tree, these bore not the ache of misery but the salve of long-awaited peace.

She looked out the train window again. A ribbon of color rippled

Amanda Skenandore

across the black of the horizon. She smiled, remembering the *Anishi-naabe* believed that the sinuous colors were the spirits of the dead dancing through the sky. Tonight Askuwheteau danced with them, beside Tshikwā'set and Hįčoga, beside his brave and intrepid forebears whose great imprint on the earth could never be learned away.

AUTHOR'S NOTE

While *Between Earth and Sky* is cast with fictitious characters, the historical events underpinning the story are true. Beginning in the late 1870s, several off-reservation Indian boarding schools were established across the United States and, until the 1930s, operated in much the same manner as portrayed herein. Stover School for Indians is a fictional amalgamation of these schools, patterned after historical accounts. Other locations in the novel—La Crosse, White Earth, etc.—though sketched with an eye toward authenticity, are used fictitiously. The massacre at Wounded Knee, the Dawes and Nelson acts, the exploitation of Upper Midwest Tribes' land and timber rights are all part of recorded, though oft-forgotten, history.

The circumstances of Askuwheteau's life after leaving Stover were inspired, in part, by the real-life experiences of a Lakota man named Tasunka Ota. An attendee of the Carlisle Indian Industrial School in the 1880s, he shot U.S. Army Lieutenant Edward Casey in the aftermath of the Wounded Knee Massacre. During his trial, he cited his time at Carlisle and his desire to be reunified with his people as impetus for the killing. Ultimately, he was acquitted and returned home to the Rosebud Reservation. My hope in writing this story is to bring to light his struggle and those of the many Native American children whose lives were damaged or destroyed in the name of assimilation.

The curious reader may enjoy the following texts, many of which were instrumental in my research: *Away from Home: American Indian Boarding School Experiences,* edited by Margaret L. Archuleta,

Brenda J. Child, and K. Tsianina Lomawaima; *Education for Extinction: American Indians and the Boarding School Experience, 1875– 1928,* by David Wallace Adams; *My People the Sioux,* by Luther Standing Bear; *The Heathen School: A Story of Hope and Betrayal in the Age of the Early Republic,* by John Demos; *The Struggle for Self-Determination: History of Menominee Indians since 1854,* by David R. M. Beck; *Wisconsin Indian Literature: Anthology of Native Voices,* edited by Kathleen Tigerman; *Living Our Language: Ojibwe Tales and Oral Histories,* edited by Anton Treuer; *The Mishomis Book,* by Edward Benton-Banai; *The White Earth Tragedy: Ethnicity and Dispossession at a Minnesota Anishinaabe Reservation, 1889– 1920,* by Melissa L. Meyer; *Rez Life,* by David Treuer; and *In the Shadow of Wounded Knee: The Untold Final Chapter of the Indian Wars,* by Roger L. Di Silvestro.

Tragically, today many Native American languages face extinction, due in no small part to the boarding schools, day schools, and mission schools established at the turn of the last century. Some, however, like *Anishinaabemowin,* are enjoying a revitalization, thanks to the tribe's careful stewardship. In writing this novel, I made every effort to render the Native American languages accurately, employing the help of native speakers, dictionaries, ethnological surveys, recorded tales, and oral histories. All errors are my own, and for any such occurrences I sincerely apologize.

ACKNOWLEDGMENTS

Anishinaabe *Midewinin* tradition reminds us that humans are but a small part of the *ishpiming,* the greater universe. So too am I but one part of this story's transformation from flickering idea to published novel.

Many thanks to my agent, Michael Carr, for believing in both me and the story, and finding us a home at Kensington. To my editor, John Scognamiglio, whose wisdom and commitment helped *Between Earth and Sky* achieve its highest potential. To Kristine Mills for the book's beautiful cover, Paula Reedy, the production editor, Sheila Higgins, the copy editor, and the entire Kensington team. Your hard work is deeply appreciated.

Miigwech to Dennis Jones for aiding me with the Ojibwe translations and Randy Cornelius for his help with the Oneida. To Joe Bauer and Robert Itnyre for their woodshop expertise. To Jay Jorgensen, Alex Ip, and Gayle Nathan for advice pertaining to the trial.

To my early readers: Kasandra O'Malia, Kristin Spear, Colleen Morton Busch, John Jorgensen, Christina Salmon, and the Henderson Writers' Group. Special thanks to Heather Webb, an amazing mentor; Pam Harris, editor extraordinaire; and my faithful A-group, who not only read and reread, but who encouraged and believed: April Khaito, Alyssa Shrout, Angelina Hill, and Jenny Ballif.

Finally, to my ever-supportive, ever-loving family. My mother-in-law, Alice, who sparked my interest in this era of history and challenged me to see the world through eyes other than my own. And to my husband, Steven, the greatest man I know. Thank you.

BETWEEN EARTH AND SKY

Amanda Skenandore

ABOUT THIS GUIDE

The suggested questions are included to enhance
your group's reading of Amanda Skenandore's
Between Earth and Sky!

DISCUSSION QUESTIONS

1. When the story opens and Alma first meets the Indian children, she realizes they look nothing like the "strange and fearsome" drawings in her father's old color-plate books. In what ways do we continue to exoticize Native Americans and their cultures today?

2. Colonel Pratt, founder of the Carlisle Indian Industrial School, famously said, "Kill the Indian in him, and save the man." In what ways does Stover embody this principle?

3. When Alma first meets Asku in his prison cell, she defends her father's actions at Stover saying that he "meant well." Do you agree? Are his good intentions enough to exonerate him?

4. Consider Asku and Tshikwā'set's perceptions of Stover and the changing world at large. Tshikwā'set calls Asku "the white man's pet," while Asku maintains Tshikwā'set lives in the past. Who was right? In the end, did either perspective serve them?

5. Tshikwā'set describes his and Alma's worlds as being "like the sky and earth . . . They get very close, but never touch." To Alma, they share the same world. Who was right? How does this relate to the title of the book?

6. Several types of love are portrayed in the novel—familial love, the platonic love of friendship, as well as romantic love. Consider the impetuous, consuming love Alma felt for Tshikwā'set and the more staid love she felt for Stewart. Which, if either, was stronger? If Tshikwā'set had lived, would his and Alma's love have endured the racial hardships of the day?

7. Names play an important role in the story, mirroring the way the Indian children are forced to straddle two different cul-

tures. Was it difficult to keep track of characters' names? In the end, Asku reveals why he gave Alma the name Azaadiins. Do you think it a fitting name for her?

8. Alma begins the novel convinced that proving Asku innocent will be easy and reinforce her notion that Stover was an "imperfect means toward a perfect end." Why does she cling to this idyllic conception? How is her understanding altered through the course of the novel?

9. When Minowe first learns of Alma's love for Tshikwā'set, she calls Alma giiwanaadizi—*crazy*. Why is this her reaction? Did you foresee her larger motives as she later describes them to Alma, saying, "You stole everything! . . . I couldn't let you steal him, too." As girls, why did neither notice the other's affection for Tshikwā'set? Is their friendship healed in the end?

10. What did you think of Alma's father's reaction to her plans to marry Tshikwā'set? Did it surprise you?

11. Midway through the novel Alma thinks back to visiting her father's gravesite and wishes "she'd left the flower to decorate his grave." Do you think Alma fully forgave him for what happened to Tshikwā'set? Would you have forgiven him?

12. In 1891, a Lakota man named Tasunka Ota (Plenty Horses), who had spent several years at the Carlisle School, killed a U.S. Army Lieutenant in the wake of the Wounded Knee Massacre. During his trial he stated, "I shot the lieutenant so I might make a place for myself among my people." In the story, Asku's rationale closely mirrors that of Plenty Horses's. What led Asku to feel this way? Do you think his actions were justified?

13. Much of Native American history is compressed and omitted in the K–12 curriculum. Did you learn about the Indian boarding schools in any of your classes? What other topics, time periods, or perspectives do you feel are eschewed?

Connect with U(s)

Visit us online at
KensingtonBooks.com
to read more from your favorite authors, see books
by series, view reading group guides, and more.

for sneak peeks, chances to win books and prize packs,
and to share your thoughts with other readers.

facebook.com/kensingtonpublishing
twitter.com/kensingtonbooks

Tell us what you think!

To share your thoughts, submit a review,
or sign up for our eNewsletters, please visit:
KensingtonBooks.com/TellUs.